Mother Trouble

Eva Leppard

BLACK COCKIE PRESS

About The Author

Eva Leppard grew up in the 70s and 80s on a steady diet of BBC comedy and Douglas Adams books. Having spent most of her early years prowling through the bush with a pocketknife and a cat, she had plenty of time to start creating her own fantasy worlds. She still lives in the Australian bush, but now dreams of a penthouse in a big city with fewer chickens and more coffee shops.

1

Lauren rearranged her new shipment of smoky quartz in the shop's front window, carefully aligning the crystals in an attempt to catch the midwinter sun's morning rays. She had just stood back to admire the aesthetics and decide whether the prisms would now draw more customers inside when the entire world exploded around her.

When she lifted her head from the floor after everything had stopped swimming around in an unpleasantly drunken fashion, she saw that nothing was out of place.

The quartz was exactly where she had left it, stubbornly not catching the sunlight, the feathered dream catchers hanging from the ceiling were swaying gently in their usual manner, and the stream of incense floating up from the Green Man sculpture that sat on the shop's counter continued to drift in gentle wafts.

Maybe the world hadn't exploded after all.

Lauren pushed herself up onto her hands, then rose unsteadily to her feet, glancing around to see if anyone had noticed that she had just bodily hurled herself to the floor with little to no apparent provocation. The customers were carrying on as if nothing untoward had happened, but given the fact that The Tantric Om was the kind of shop that hosted classes such as 'Face Your Fears Through Crawling Therapy', 'Screaming Meditation', and 'Make Your Own Yoni Eggs; It's All About Placement!', falling to the floor while clutching your head wasn't that odd, and moaning a little was something that was encouraged rather than tolerated.

Taking deep breaths through her nose in an attempt to stave off the nausea flitting around in her stomach, Lauren fixed a tight smile to her face and took a seat behind the counter. Smoke from the incense floated into her nostrils, and her stomach gave a hearty lurch. Without thinking, she grabbed the incense, holder and all, and dropped it into the burbling water feature that also sat on the counter. The glowing incense sizzled dismally to itself for a moment then died.

Lauren frowned. That was … aggressively out of character.

She rubbed the bridge of her nose. Air. She needed air. Fresh air. Or as fresh as the air could be in the middle of Melbourne.

'Morty,' she called to the wispily bearded young man who sat in an armchair by the beaded curtain at the back of the shop's long main room. He was reading a copy of Meditation Nation and rolling a herbal cigarette.

'Morty, can you come here and watch things for a minute? I need to nip out.'

He slid the magazine back into the pile, jumped up eagerly and beamed. 'Of course. That's why I'm here. On the off chance that you'll need me.' He slid his tall thin body into the chair Lauren had just vacated and, frowning slightly, eyed the submerged incense holder. 'Everything okay?'

'Don't change the music,' Lauren said, gingerly lifting her handbag from the floor. Her head was beginning to pound, and she suspected that bending down would bring on another collapsing situation. 'Before you start, the Whale songs are staying on. The customers like it, and your band's demo tape doesn't vibe with the deep sense of connectedness and willingness to part with their money that I want from my customers.'

'You've become so mercenary,' he muttered, drying the Green Man on his hemp shirt. He scratched at the soaked residue with his fingernail. This was going to be an absolute bugger to get out. 'You've lost your hippy heart since you were given this place.'

'Bills, my love. Making the coin. That's what it's all about. I'm a boss babe business chick now. Or something.' She kissed him lightly on the cheek, his wispy beard tickling her lips. 'I'm not sure how long I'll be. I'll send you a message.'

'You said a minute,' he called after her retreating back as she pushed open the glass front door, the reproduction Celtic bells hung on the handle jangling.

As she waved without turning around, she reflected, not for the first time, how lucky she was to have an unemployed twenty-eight-year old in love with her.

The street was busy, of course. It was a main commercial road, and people flocked to it, milling around, window shopping and looking for just the right flavour of artisan hand raised coffee bean. Lauren noted that no one else looked as if they had just experienced a brain melding explosion, and this was the final confirmation she needed to understand that whatever had just happened had happened to her alone, and she had a sick, dawning realisation that she might have had what was usually described as a 'medical event'. Whipping out her phone, she searched, 'am I having a brain aneurysm'. Headache, check. Nausea, check. Drooping facial features. She looked at her reflection in the window of her shop, peering through narrowed eyes to try and make out her face in the glass. It didn't look particularly droopy; it looked like its usual blue haired, slightly rounded, increasingly care worn forty-five-year-old self, but maybe it was hard to make important judgements about your health when you were in the grips of a major episode. Vicious cycle and all that.

As she took in the last symptom on the list, 'hearing a loud pop', she realised that she absolutely had to get to a doctor as quickly as possible, but at that moment, the world exploding thing happened again, and this time when she dropped to the ground she didn't open her eyes for a long time.

2

The tall man with angular features and a dark swipe of black hair glanced around as he adjusted the device inside his ear. He hoped that it was small enough to be hidden, but also knew that the being he was about to meet would probably see it within about five seconds.

Egragore wanted to disaster proof as many areas as he could before things kicked off in the full knowledge of how spectacularly badly this might end up. Of course, he would have preferred it if it was his boss standing here instead of him, but that wasn't possible.

Apparently.

As the bitter wind cut into him, he pulled his favourite burgundy velvet smoking jacket tightly around himself. He wouldn't have chosen the In Between Places to meet either, truth be told, but his boss had quite specific instructions about how this should be done. Lull him into a false sense of security, pretend everything was okay, then bam, banishment.

He felt a drop in the air pressure and looked around again. Within a few metres of where he was standing everything disappeared into a murky, ghostly fog which he knew stretched out to infinity all around him. What irritated him even more was the fact that there was a perfectly lovely tropical biome just a slight dimensional shift up from where he was standing, but that wouldn't have worked according to his boss. Everything needed to be cold and bleak and atmospheric for this job.

He could be so bloody dramatic. Amazing boss, fabulous in all ways but just a little bit...dramatic.

So he had delegated.

Of course, he wanted to still be involved.

Hence the earpieces.

A resonant gong echoed in the air, and a being stood before him. A familiar being, but his appearance always caused Egragore to jump. The stacked heel boots made him a little less short than he was naturally and the sneer tended to remind those who saw him of a young Elvis. Momentarily, that is. The thought of 'Oh that guy reminds me of a young Elvis' was usually hijacked by the thought 'this is utterly terrifying and horrific and I think I'm about to die.'

The being glanced around, a flicker of surprise flashing across his eyes before the steely glint returned to them and he fixed his eyes on Egragore.

What?' he said. 'I was in the middle of something. Why isn't he here? I don't deal with underlings.'

'Oh Lucius, you bloody do,' snapped Egragore. 'You'll deal with anyone if you're bored enough. Don't try that tough guy routine with me, I've seen you with a deep moisturising mask on remember.'

'Yes well, you need to learn to knock before you walk into people's hotel rooms.'

'Where is Devin anyway', said Lucius, pushing his fringe out of his eyes. 'He should be here. I thought he'd want to see me.'

'I'm here on his account. He doesn't even know this is happening.'

'Oh rubbish. There's no way that you'd be here if it wasn't on his say so. I don't know why you even bother to try and lie, that's my job, remember? Prince of Lies and all that?'

There was a low whisper in Egragore's earpiece. 'What's going on? Don't let him distract you. Don't get lost in the impossible blueness of his eyes, just focus on the job at hand.'

Egragore ignored it.

'We have a problem,' he said.

'Good,' said Lucius. 'I like problems. They're kind of my jam.

Is it a bad problem? Does it involve people dying or misery or some such? That's my favourite.'

'You've been down on Earth again,' said Egragore, refusing to be sidetracked.

'Yes,' said Lucius. 'That's allowed. Do I need to show you the contract?'

Egragore tapped the folder that he clasped firmly in his hand. 'No need, I've got it right here. And funny you should mention that because legalities are what we're discussing today. You've been involving yourself in some unsanctioned behaviour.'

'Once again,' said Lucius with an odd little twist of his head, 'kind of my jam. If I wasn't doing unpredictable and unsanctioned things then what kind of Adversary would I be?'

'But this time,' continued Egragore, 'you're dealing with Imagos. And that's a problem.'

'I'm not dealing with them,' said Lucius, a glint in his eye, 'I'm killing them. Painfully, if possible.'

'You need to stop.'

'That's not going to happen. Imagos are rodent scum and deserve to die. Especially the misshaped ones. The ones with miniature heads and strange wings and ducks feet for legs. Those ones I really can't stand. I killed a baby the other day, a little girl. Blinked it right out of existence. It screamed for its mother before it went. They don't have souls either apparently so when they're done they're done. No Other-world for them.'

Egragore felt his chest tighten. The voice buzzed in his ear again. 'What's happening? What's he saying now? Is he wearing that denim jacket I bought him?'

Egragore pressed his finger against the earpiece to silence the voice.

'Imagos are created by humans, as you know,' said Egragore.

'Exactly, all the more reason to get rid of them.'

'No, exactly the opposite. You only have authority over

humans.' He opened up the folder and pointed to a clause with a string of Roman numerals next to it. 'See, here. You only have jurisdiction that He gives you, and 'human created beings that were not created at the outset' (designated section 52 delta hydro) do not fall into those parameters.'

Lucius shrugged. 'Don't care. That's a stupid rule. They're just vermin anyway. Why in Hades is he worried about me killing them? Let me talk to him. Is he around here somewhere? I can clear this up in two seconds.'

Egragore shut the folder tersely. 'I don't think that you understand the gravity of this. You need to stop killing Imagos. It's extremely serious. I'm not prepared to go into all the details, but I have clear and specific instruction to tell you to cease and desist immediately. This isn't just shits and giggles Lucius, this means something. There are flurries in the undertow.'

'Why would I care about that?' said Lucius. 'I like it when they scream. It's very entertaining.'

'Well in that case you leave me with no choice.'

There was a buzz in his ear again as the earpiece turned itself on.

'Right, I've got vision of you both now. Did you tell him that there are flurries in the undertow? That his actions are causing a flux in the trans dimensional continuum of alternative realities and if he keeps killing them it will cause a rip in the space time fabric of reality? Did you tell him that?'

'I mentioned the flurries,' muttered Egragore into his collar, not caring if Lucius heard him at this stage, 'but not the rest because I feel like that's something that he would quite enjoy and he'd just lean into the whole process even more. I'm trying not to mention it.'

'What's that?' said Lucius. 'Who are you talking to? Are you miked? Is he watching us?'

He stepped back and looked up into the air. 'Come and talk to me Devin. I miss you. Come and talk to me and we can discuss this. Together.'

Egragore raised his voice and opened up his folder to the 'break glass in case of emergency' section at the back. 'I will ask you one more time, will you stop killing the Imagos?'

Lucius ignored him. 'Devin,' he called. 'Devin please come and talk to me. I miss you.'

'In that case,' continued Egragore, 'By the power vested in me,' and as he read the next few lines, Lucius' face began to blanch.

Behind him, a small vortex formed in the air just above Lucius' head. It was just a transparent wobble at first, barely noticeable, but it grew quickly until it began to tousle his hair.

'You must be joking,' he said. 'Devin would never have agreed to this! There's no way I can spend thousands of years stuck in a…'

Before he could finish the sentence, the vortex throbbed, a flash darted out of it, and Lucius' body, impossibly elongated, disappearing into the air like wet spaghetti down a plug hole.

Egragore sighed deeply, smoothed back his hair, and headed back to the office for what he suspected would be a day of work that stretched into the evening.

<h1 style="text-align:center">3</h1>

Lauren woke in a startlingly bright room. A hospital, she assumed, what with the stark whiteness and the lights and the beds and all. As she swam back to consciousness she remembered being in the street. The pop. The brain aneurysm. Well, good. She was in the right place. She clearly needed urgent medical care.

As she laid, looking up at the white ceiling, the brightness began to seem odd to her though. Surely blinding patients wasn't best practice? The room was lit up like a football field in the middle of winter, a tessellated pattern of bulbs above her leaving shifting patterns on her retinas. To be fair though, she didn't work in the medical field, so what would she know. Maybe someone had got a grant, and there had been some new research. That kind of thing happened all the time. Someone did a study, and all of a sudden, people were eating a frog enzyme from the Amazon and growing back amputated limbs or some such. Maybe getting your retinas burnt out was all the rage now.

She pushed herself up onto one elbow and looked around. It wasn't just a bright room, it was stark. Jarringly so. Her bed was covered with a white sheet, but it was just a shade too crisp to be comfortable, and the walls that stretched off into the distance were just a touch too shiny to be pleasing to the eye.

If she was in a hospital, then it was definitely the public system.

Hers was not the only bed, of course. There were many more spaced out at appropriate intervals, and each had a trolley placed next to it covered with stainless steel instruments. There were no windows, nothing but trolleys and beds that could moonlight as ironing boards if the need arose.

It was very quiet. There was a low hum as if from an air conditioner, but apart from that, all she could hear was her own heart beating, which was a positive development, all things considered. She swung her legs over the side of the bed, noticing that they were bare. A white fabric brushed over her knees, and she realised that a cowl necked, long sleeved gown made from a comfortable knit type fabric hung loosely around her. Hospital gowns were fancy now, apparently.

And her headache was gone. She tilted her head from side to side, testing for, well, she wasn't sure what the aftermath of an aneurysm was, but she felt entirely clear headed and alert and decided to chalk that up to an efficient drug administration and good doctors.

They had to be spending the money somewhere, after all.

Standing on the white tiled floor, she flexed her legs and

tensed her body slightly. All normal, it would seem. Her hands smoothed down the gown she was wearing, and she wondered if Merino wool had a thread count; if so, this would be in its thousands. She would have preferred her own clothes, but a quick glance around told her there was no point looking for them; there were no cupboards or lockers in the room at all. So she sat back down, fully intending to wait patiently to be told her next move.

This patience lasted precisely half a minute, which, if her friends had been putting bets on it, was longer than they would have predicted by about twenty-three seconds.

Lauren stood, wandering around the beds. She had no idea how long she had been unconscious for; some inner compass told her it was longer than a day, and she began to berate herself for leaving Morty in charge. He didn't even know the code to the alarm, dammit. She had the vague suspicion that, finding himself unable to lock up for the night, he may have just bunkered down on the floor and waited, and while she would feel slightly bad about that, it would be the wisest move given the circumstances. Salt lamps and amazonite crystal grids were valuable merchandise, after all.

'Hello?' The echo of Lauren's voice cut off abruptly as if there wasn't enough oxygen in the room to sustain the sound, but as soon as the word was out of her mouth, there was a shimmering in the space around her, and a figure materialised.

'Goodo,' said the figure, looking down at a clipboard and ticking something. 'You're awake then.'

The figure was tallish, with a vaguely human form which seemed to lose focus and become amorphous as it progressed downwards, and instead of lower limbs and feet there was an indecipherable grey haze. Despite this, the figure had an almost ethereal glow about them that made Lauren feel as if everything as all right with the world, even if she was stuck in an over-lit sterile prison, wondering where her pants had gone. The figure wore a grey gown with a hood which partially covered its face, and gave off the vibe of 'matron' more emphatically than Lauren had ever felt a creature give off a vibe in her life.

The figure stared at her expectantly. She stared back for a moment before realising that the question may not have been rhetorical, and she might in fact be waiting for an answer.

'Yes?' said Lauren with apologetic uncertainty.

'Excellent.' The Matron clicked her tongue against her teeth. 'Come with me,' she said, and glided off. After a moment Lauren pattered after in her bare feet, eager not to lose track of what seemed to be her only lifeline.

'What should I call you?' Lauren asked. 'Can I call you Matron? You seem like a matron. You have that vibe. I'm going to call you Matron.'

'No need for that,' was the reply, and as they got to an indeterminate patch of white wall, the figure pressed one four fingered hand against it, revealing a door for Lauren to walk through.

'No need for …?'

'Names. There's no need for an exchange of names. We won't be seeing each other again. Dealing with your kind isn't part of my job. Everything else is, if today's schedule is anything to go by, but not you, apparently. You've been ear-marked for another jurisdiction entirely.'

Stepping through the door, they stood in a room that was precisely four thousand times more comfortable than the ward they had just left. An overstuffed armchair, a coffee table strewn with magazines, and a drinks machine filled the small space. The Matron gestured to the chair, told Lauren to, 'Wait here,' and dematerialised as determinedly as she had appeared.

Lauren took all of this fairly well, considering.

There was comfort in the fact that this wasn't her first brush with the weird and the otherworldly, even if she was trying her best to forget about what happened last year and how she had lost her best friend, Brigid.

<h1 style="text-align:center">4</h1>

Sybella didn't know exactly when the spectral lion had attached himself to her. Not precisely. Yesterday she'd had no idea of his existence and now he was here, and she wasn't sure what had happened in the intervening time, but something was certainly different.

All she knew was that she had gone to bed last night as her normal self, and now she was awake and things seemed to be … different. Not necessarily oddly so, but different.

Which was odd in itself.

After she had got out of bed, cleaned her teeth, dressed, and stared at herself in the mirror for so long that she had started to question the lines in her own face, Sybella began to have the barest glimmer that she might not be dealing with your usual, common or garden, linear day.

She had gone to sleep, she had woken up, and now things were…

Different.

It was as if she had forgotten something very, very important. As if the niggling thought in the back of her mind wasn't about something as banal as the fact she had left the stove on, or that her suede shoes had been out on the back porch all night in the rain. The niggling thought seemed to be about something truly monumental, but she couldn't for the life of her remember what it was.

As if having a huge, slightly judgemental, spectral lion foisted on you all of a sudden wasn't enough, part of her memories seemed to be missing.

She headed down the stairs to the kitchen, and behind her she could feel the lion drawing himself together, summoning all of the pieces of himself into one central focus, as if to call into being his ultimate, complete lion-ness.

'Is this going to happen all the time now?' she called over her shoulder. 'Am I always going to be aware of you, even when you're all shimmery and not even a real solid lion?'

She could hear the pad of his feet on the floorboards behind her now, the gentle tick of his claws.

Manifestation complete, she assumed.

'That's how it's always been in the past.' The rumble of his voice seemed to move directly from his chest into her brain. 'Thought forms haven't previously needed to be conventionally visible for humans to know they were there.'

'Isn't that a tautology? Surely 'conventionally visible' is literally just 'visible'? What would unconventionally visible mean?'

'Ah, you get defensive when you're nervous. That's a useful thing for me to know.'

Sybella decided that coffee would probably help.

He found a space to occupy in the kitchen. Or, more accurately, he made a space. The room had expanded slightly to accommodate him, a flaring out of the windows besides the dining table, the molecules expanding, so it seemed, to fit his enormous form.

'What's your name?' she asked him.

'Robellian Heraklonius Susan the minus sixth,' he said.

She stared at him. 'I'm obviously not going to call you that.'

'Of course. Calling me by my actual name would be ridiculous. What was I thinking?'

'I'll call you Leo,' she decided. 'That's good and lion-y. What are you doing here, anyway?'

'I am literally your thought form,' he said. 'You called me into this particular physical manifestation. You decided your life was dull and deliberately called me to you in order to, what was the expression? Oh, yes, that's right. 'Zhoosh' up your life. Your words, not mine. I'd never heard of the expression before your request came in, and, to be quite honest, I don't care for it.'

Sybella poured the boiling water into the freeze dried coffee in the bottom of her cup, and the smell that hit her nostrils was, as usual, the most sensory pleasure that she would have all day.

'I don't think I did do that though, did I?' she said. 'I don't remember it at least. I have been bored with my life, yes, but I don't remember summoning you. And even if I had, I wouldn't have expected you to just turn up out of the blue. I feel like I should have got some warning. I didn't make any request.'

He shrugged in the manner that Sybella was getting used to. No physical movement; she just knew it was happening.

'Your personal timeline is different to mine and of no interest to me. Your human timelines are different to every other dimension, now I come to think of it. You really are strange little outliers, aren't you? And yes of course you called me. You summoned me. At great personal expense, I might add. Maybe not consciously, but you did do it.'

Sybella had no good reply to this but also suspected that he didn't need one.

Leo continued. 'And there's a process, too. You can't just click your fingers and have us appear like that. We're not genies. Now that's a plumb job if ever there was one.'

'But when I looked it up,' Sybella protested, 'it said that summoning something like you means I'm creating a totally new thought form, projected from my own consciousness, and that you should only exist in my head. Didn't I make you completely...' She searched for the right words. 'Didn't I make you as a completely new creation?'

'You looked it up?'

His words hung ominously and judgmentally in the air, and

Sybella felt the same feeling in her chest that she used to get when she asked a question at school and the phrase 'there are no stupid questions, only stupid answers' was proven to be incorrect for the eight millionth time.

'Yes I looked it up and I did some reading about it but I didn't realise that I'd actually…done it. Properly, like.'

'You looked up how to summon a thought-form. You just pulled up a totally anonymous website, one that could be and probably was, written by an ignorant know nothing cretin, and then you just mindlessly carried out what it prescribed, did you?'

'Not just the internet,' she protested. 'My friend gave me pointers. And advice.'

'I just need…' He squeezed his eyes shut tightly for a moment and let out a huge sigh. 'I just need to clarify a few things even though I am almost certain of the absolute travesty that has occurred here. Did you use the Necronium of Clovoid?'

Sybella looked at the lion blankly.

'The Book of Deutonicum?'

Her cheeks began to redden.

'Look, I just need to come out and ask you bluntly. Are you even a warlock?'

She barked out a laugh. 'No, I just—'

'Yes?'

'I got some links from Wikipedia. And I'm not a warlock. I work in a real estate office.'

He sighed again. 'Remind me to warn you of the evils of the internet when I get a moment. This is precisely why we are dealing with the issues that we are dealing with at the moment on this planet. It is somewhat ironic that my being brought here is, it appears, through the exact same way that the Imagos are scraped into existence. Now that is irony, isn't it?'

She nodded, very keen to take back some of the ground that had led Leo to believe she was a compete and absolute idiot, even though she had no idea what she was agreeing with.

'Can I just ask though. Are you a thought form? A tulpa? Is that what I've made? Are you really a lion? Is this your...'

'Ultimate self,' he prompted.

'Okay then, ultimate self. What actually are you?'

'All right,' he said. 'Let me try to put this simply. There are a great variety of different thought forms. All are somehow brought about by the human mind, hence the name. They take years, I repeat, years of studying and meditation and soul work to create. I want to make that quite and demonstrably clear. It is a very, very skilled calling to create a tulpa. A proper tulpa. Do you understand?'

She nodded.

'I am a thought form of a kind, but I am an ancient and eternal soul who can be called down here to Earth on occasion to involve myself in very important business. I am, as I said, ancient and oftentimes revered.' The lies spilled effortlessly from his velvet mouth.

'So you're very powerful then?' Sybella asked.

'Frightfully.'

'And I've managed to call you to me?'

He eyed her grimly. 'There appears to have been a bit of a cock up along the way. I was led to understand that you were slightly more important than you appear to be. But I'm here now. Let's make the best of it.'

'Sorry,' she said. 'But I hardly feel it's my fault. I don't even know what's going on.'

'Right,' said the lion, drawing himself up and squaring his jaw. 'Let's get on with it then. I feel I should tell you...' He stopped and looked off into space.

'Yes?'

'I feel like I should tell you that we have stepped outside of time.'

'Oh.' Sybella bit her lip. 'Can I stop getting ready for work then?'

He sighed, and decided that he should be happy that he had managed to convince her that he was here totally by her behest, rather than a manipulation all of his own making.

Everything was going to pan out exactly as he and Lucius had intended.

5

It wasn't until Lauren began to vandalise the drinks machine that anybody remembered to pay attention to her, and, in hindsight, she thought there was probably a life lesson in that.

Not intentional vandalism, of course. She wasn't just willy-nilly attacking inanimate objects for the fun of it. It was just that she had, by her rough estimate, been without any form of food or drink for at least fifteen hours, and given that she had experienced some kind of life threatening medical event, she thought it was pretty poor form that no one had thought to supply her with sustenance. So she decided to take matters into her own hands.

It looked like a perfectly normal drinks machine, apart from the fact that there was no coin slot, which made no difference either way to Lauren because her handbag had disappeared somewhere between the shop and wherever the heck she was now. She ran her fingers around the side of the glass but could find no hole, gap, or place to pry it open. After she had rested her forehead against the cool glass for a while, gazing longingly at the fizzy drinks within, she decided the best way forward was the way of the anarchist and began to push the machine back and forth in the hope that something would dislodge. What then happened surprised Lauren as much as anyone, as the bulky machine gained so much momentum that it tipped over, entirely obliterating the glass coffee table that stood next to it and making such a noise in the small enclosed space that Lauren wrapped her arms around her head and waited for the ringing in her ears to stop.

Just as she thought that everything had come to rest, the last leg of the coffee table gave way under the weight of the machine that lay on top of it like an amorous and not very tactful water buffalo. There was a final puff of pulverised glass, and after a few almost melodic tinkles, everything was still.

She felt as if her head had suffered way more than was warranted today.

The grey, ethereal figure appeared again, seemingly out of thin air. She looked at Lauren, at the shattered remains of the room's sparse decor, and then back to Lauren again. 'Did you do that?'

Lauren shrugged in guilty embarrassment. 'Not on purpose.'

'Why did you do that?'

'I was thirsty.'

Matron performed a small movement that could have been anything from a gentle sigh to a full body dramatisation of 'Why am I stuck here dealing with such absolute cretinous bozos?', slightly adjusted her wimple and turned to face the wall.

'Come on then,' she said as the wall once again opened up to receive them. 'She's ready to speak to you now anyway.' Glancing back at the floor, she gave Lauren a withering look. 'I'm going to have to clean all of that up, you know.'

'I'm happy to do it,' Lauren said. 'If you can find me a broom and a dustpan or something I can … get rid of the worst of it, at least.'

'Don't be ridiculous. If you cut yourself, the paper work I'll be stuck with will drown the lot of us. Just don't touch anything and follow me.'

As Lauren followed her, the change in surroundings was sudden and utterly incongruous. The lights, the smells;

everything was different. They had stepped from a clinical set of rooms into something that looked like a Victorianaphile's wet dream.

The corridor that stretched out before them was lined with tall, wide bookcases. They were wooden, darkly panelled and crammed with the pleasant jumble of mismatched and eclectic books that were the mark of the true bibliophile. No time for picture perfect organisation here. Gone was any attempt at sticking to one method of stacking or neat horizontal piles, and as for colour coordination, the idea had never even been vaguely countenanced. These bookcases were organised along the lines of 'get them all in there and hang the consequences'. Hang the consequences, hang aesthetics, hang gravity. Just get them all in there by any means possible and call it good enough.

Lauren thought that it was glorious.

What looked like gaslights projected out of the walls in a manner that was both aesthetically pleasing and fitting to the tone that the corridor was managing to set — fitfully lit, with mysterious puddles of dark thrown just often enough to be moodily interesting, but not enough to cause you to actually trip on the carpet. Said carpet was thick and lush, the deep red colour filled out with green vine patterns that twisted through each other, kind of like a snakes and ladders board created by a very expensive interior designer. It could have looked dated and suffocating, but instead worked perfectly.

The sections of the wall that were visible through the wood panelling showed port wine velvet flocked wallpaper, and deeply set heavy doors that Lauren suspected were a very expensive, very endangered ebony.

'Is it 1890?' Lauren joked.

Matron turned her head and gave Lauren a withering look. 'Don't be ridiculous. Have you seen a time portal around here?' She tapped her teeth with her tongue in disapproval. 'I swear your kind doesn't think.'

She moved down the corridor; the smooth, even gliding was much creepier now they were out of the small room and in a space where Matron could really get some speed up. Lauren found herself trotting after her, her bare feet sinking deliciously into the carpet.

'Can I just ask—' Lauren called after the Matron's gliding back, but the figure gestured with one hand in a way that Lauren assumed was shushing her. 'I thought you said I wouldn't be seeing you again, anyway,' Lauren muttered. 'I'm supposed to be spending this evening with some friends for an important meeting, so I need to be getting back home soon.' But Matron either hadn't heard her or had decided just to ignore her. They continued their journey in silence.

As they progressed along the corridors, Lauren had time to settle into her surroundings and pay more attention to them. Her initial observations, that they were in a faux Victorian era library, remained with her, but the corridors they were winding through seemed to be becoming increasingly Escheresque. They twisted and turned, and with stairs now added into the mix and forks that sometimes involved five options, Lauren found herself wondering not only where she was in relation to their starting point, but also what form of reality the building itself was placed within.

And she was beginning to really, really hope that the spell her coven had worked the week before had nothing to do with any of this.

6

'What do you mean, stepped outside time?' Sybella asked. 'Is this some strange thought-form speak that I hadn't previously been aware of? Am I going to have to learn a whole new language now?'

Leo rolled his amber eyes. 'It would have been opportune for you to pay close attention to words before you involved yourself in all of this, can I just say, because it would have avoided some of the issues you are regretfully about to become aware of. But, in short, no. It's not a new expression. We have literally stepped outside time. I thought it may be a good idea to stop and take stock of what is happening here.'

Sybella glanced around nervously.

'We need to stop and ruminate on the fact,' he continued, 'that now I am speaking with you, I am increasingly aware of the fact that you have done most, if not all of this, by accident, and that's a bit of a worry to me if I'm being completely honest.'

Sybella grasped onto the part of this that she understood. 'Oh, no, I did want a lion to be my friend. That bit isn't made up.'

She scrabbled through a pile of papers that teetered precariously on the table in the middle of the kitchen. Pushing aside junk mail, receipts, menus and recipes printed from the internet, she pulled out a small piece of paper. 'See?' She held up the scrap on which could clearly be seen the sketch of a lion surrounded by symbols and archaic markings. 'I did draw a picture of you. When I was a little girl, I really wanted a lion as a friend. I imagined it so vividly. He followed me around and sat with me and kept me company at school when I was eating lunch on my own. I called him Jep. So I guess I just revisited that. I wanted something powerful in my life, something to protect me. And now I've done it properly. I think. Also, I was a little bit drunk when I drew it.'

His face darkened. 'So, what I'm hearing is that I, the most powerful of the Mages, The Great Robellian Heraklonius Susan the minus sixth of the Shadow Realms, have been brought to this plane of reality because some insignificant human got a bit drunk one night and got lucky with some conjuring. Is that what I'm hearing?'

'A lot drunk if we're really opening up and bonding with each other. Is that a problem? I feel like you're blaming me for something that isn't my fault. I just wanted a lion to hang out with. I can't help what happened. Maybe I'm very powerful. Did you ever consider that?'

'I very much doubt it,' the lion said grimly. 'And how this happened is something I fully intend to get to the bottom of once I get back to the office, trust me. I can't believe I'm actually here.' He stopped, wondering if he was laying it on a bit thick now.

'You have an office?'

The lion stood up, his body unfolding slowly as the space around him expanded in deference to his bulk. 'You ask questions about the strangest things,' he said. 'I tell you that time has been suspended, and you don't seem bothered, but you want to know about where I work.'

'I just want to stick to topics I have a chance of understanding. I have serious doubts about whether I'll be able to come to grips with the time issue.'

'It's very simple,' he said.

Sybella held up her hand. 'Before you start, does it mean that I don't have to go to work today. Because if you've suspended time, then I assume I've got the day off.'

He gestured towards the window with his massive velvet head. 'Have you looked outside yet this morning?'

'Not yet. It's dark.'

He didn't reply.

'Actually,' she looked at her watch. 'Shouldn't it be light by now?'

Sybella walked to the window and pulled the curtain aside. She peered out, cupping her hands around her eyes and resting them against the glass. There was a deep, deep darkness but also —

'Where's my yard?' she asked.

There was a pause.

'Where's the ground?' She turned to look at him, her hands on her hips. 'Did you do this?'

'It's quite hard to get you to focus on things, do you realise that?'

'I have been told that, yes.'

'And the best way to suspend time is to create a void. That's fairly simple entry level physics, which, of course, I thought you were aware of when you put in your request.'

'A request that I knew nothing about,' she said.

'We are just going to have to agree to disagree on that particular point.'

Sybella bit her lip nervously. She felt enormously out of her depth.

'I decided a good way to proceed would be to put everything on hold for a little while, for you to take stock and think about what you want from me, and then we can kick things off again once you have decided where and when you want to be. I mean,' he cleared his throat, 'you did summon me through all the appropriate channels, and I'm here now. Since it's all been given official approval, I don't see why we shouldn't have a little fun with it. And I haven't been down here on Earth for a while, and there's a few little admin things going on that I'd like to take care of. Since I'm here, and all. Be silly not to really.'

Sybella clapped her hands together. 'That sounds like a plan. Take me somewhere fun then.'

Time and space bent a little.

✵✵✵

'No,' Sybella said, looking out across the vast swathe of Pacific Ocean stretching majestically out in front of her. 'This is just a beach. This isn't a fun thing.'

'It's not just a beach, thank you very much. It's the greatest ocean on the planet, and there…' Here he pointed off at a small black speck in the distance. 'There is the first boatload of people ever to travel to the land that will be called Aotearoa. Or New Zealand as most of you insist on calling it these days. You are literally going to see the birth of a new human culture.'

'What makes you think I'd be interested in this?' she asked moodily.

'Let's try again then,' Leo said grimly.

❋❋❋

The sharp sun beat down on her face, and she shielded her eyes from the glare. Miles in the distance, a monolith stood, thousands of people swarming around its base.

'The pyramids,' he said. 'One of the most amazing building endeavours in your human history.'

'What am I expected to do here?' she asked.

'Just … witness it,' he said. 'Be part of history.'

'It's too hot to enjoy myself,' she said.

'In that case,' he said, grinning as much as it was possible for a lion to grin, 'how about this?' There was a slight shimmering in the air, and Sybella found herself plunged into a cool darkness.

'Where are you?' she said, her voice sounding muffled and claustrophobic. The was the sound of a match being struck, and a small flame burst into life next to her. She and the lion were warmly lit by the small light.

'How did you do that?' she asked him. 'You don't have an opposable thumb.'

Leo ignored her. 'Here you go,' he said. 'This is cooler, but still fun.'

She looked doubtfully at the huge stone slabs and pillars that loomed around them. 'Where are we now?'

'We're in the burial chamber of the Great Pyramid.'

'It's a bit bleak,' she said. 'I would have expected more gold.'

They stood in the glow of the light. Shadows jumped off the walls around them. 'We can go now,' she said.

'Just a minute,' said Leo. 'Let's just enjoy the ambience for a minute longer.'

'What ambience?' asked Sybella. 'I think I can smell rats.'

There was an uncomfortable few minutes of silence.

'Lovely, isn't it?' said the lion awkwardly. 'Just a few more...'

A sudden blast of air swept past them, blowing out the flame. Sybella stumbled a little, pushed off balance by its force, and her hands grabbed at the lion's thick, warm mane.

'What the hell was that?' she said into the dark. 'How is there wind in here?'

She felt Leo's body tense as the discombobulating feeling she was becoming accustomed to each time they travelled between time overtook her body again.

'I've got no idea,' he said soothingly. 'It's just a trifle. I'll have us out of here in no time. Not to worry.'

Sybella's head began to ache.

After she had rejected Mardi Gras, the fall of the Berlin Wall, and one of Andy Warhol's more dynamic Factory parties, the lion sat Sybella down for a heart to heart.

'The reason,' he said, 'why I am finding this so difficult is because you have given me no specifics. No guidance. I don't know you, you see, and while I have many gifts that your mind would find hard to understand, I can't just give you what you want with no guidance.'

Sybella rubbed the area between her eyes. 'I don't know what I want,' she said finally. 'That's the main problem in my life. I don't know what I want. Anyway, you might as well take me back home. This whole thing has been a massive waste of time, and I need to take some paracetamol before my friends come around tonight. Can you please turn time back on, or whatever it is that you do?'

He contemplated just eating here then and there, hang the

consequences.

'All right,' he said. 'We can go back. But as I said, I'm with you now. We may as well make the most of it.'

'The coven meets tonight,' she continued. 'It's the only vaguely interesting thing I've got going on in my life at the moment, so I probably should turn up. I think we have a ritual for the Cailleach tonight or something. Roxy sent an email about it.'

The lion had gone very still. 'What?' He swallowed deeply. 'What was that name you just said?'

'The Cailleach,' Sybella clarified. 'It's who our coven is dedicated to.'

'Shit,' Leo said. 'Shit.' And as they wended their way back to the appropriate time and space, Sybella could have sworn she heard him muttering something along the lines of 'interfering old busy body who knows too much,' but it could just have been the sounds of the Universe rushing through her consciousness.

7

Matron finally came to a halt in front of one of the heavy doors that looked, as far as Lauren could tell, identical to every other one they had passed.

She knocked on the door briskly and pushed it open without waiting for an answer. Gliding in, she stood to one side and impatiently gestured for Lauren to enter. The room was even darker than the corridors, and as she stepped inside, it took a moment to register that sitting at the huge desk that filled most of the room was her now second best friend, Brigid.

Brigid. The friend she hadn't spoken to for a year. The one who (and she hadn't had the chance to share this with her yet) had been demoted to second best friend in that intervening time.

Third best, if that bridesmaid invitation from Sharon came through.

Brigid. The one who had up and vanished without a word. And the one who had saddled her with the noose around her neck now known as her shop.

But here she was. Brigid. Looking more or less exactly the same as she had the last time they had seen each other.

'Hi,' Brigid said brightly, but Lauren could detect a slight sharpness in her voice. 'I like the blue hair.'

Lauren stared at her.

'How have you been?'

'How have I been?' Lauren glanced around the room as if she expected a TV crew to jump out and yell 'surprise!' at her. 'How have I been? What the hell happened to you?' Lauren advanced on the carved, velvet inlaid desk. A banker's lamp threw a wan yellow light across the jumbled piles of paper and books that were strewn across it. 'Where have you been? Why did you just leave all of a sudden? Just up and move to Ireland without telling me? Or anyone? Seriously, who does that?'

Brigid glanced nervously at the Matron, who gave her a small shrug and then left the room, pulling the door firmly shut behind her.

'I thought you'd been murdered for weeks! I got Morty to help me hold a seance to try and contact you, for fuck's sake?'

'Oh, that clears that up for me,' Brigid said. 'I'd been wondering what that was. I had a buzzing voice in my head for days. Thought I was developing tinnitus.'

'And then,' Lauren continued, 'I got a letter from a lawyer telling me that I own a shop! I rang the lawyer straight away, of course, and asked her if it had been left to me in your will. No, she said. From Kilkenny. In Ireland. She's in fucking Ireland, she said. She didn't say fucking she just said Ireland, and here's your shop, she goes. What the fuck was I supposed to do with a shop?'

'But it's your favourite shop. It's the Tantric Om. You've always spent half your paycheck there. I thought you owning it would just cut out the middle man.'

'I haven't submitted a tax return for twenty years, and all of a sudden, I'm a business owner? Do you have any idea of the stress that placed me under?'

'Okay.' Brigid took a deep breath and pressed her lips together. 'I can see that we have a lot to unpack here. First of all, I tried to clear up any misunderstanding with the emails. Didn't they clarify things?'

'Eventually,' Lauren snapped. 'Eventually I got some emails. I've decided to move to Ireland, the weather's shit, oh, and I got married to that guy who wears velvet pants more often than is socially acceptable. That's called clearing things up, is it? You up and left your entire life, and I had no idea what was going on.'

'You know things had been weird. There were some time distortions that got in the way of communication.'

'Time distortions such as the fact that I thought you were my best friend, a high school teacher, but you were a human embodiment of the ancient Goddess Brigid and also the co ruler of the universe. That kind of time distortion?'

'I don't know if it strictly falls into that category, but I do think that I was having a bit of a mid-life crisis,' said Brigid in an attempt at clarification.

'Why does this always have to be about you?' Lauren was trying to stop her voice from shaking.

'I can see that you're angry,' Brigid started.

'Don't start that,' Lauren said. 'Don't start with that kind of bullshit talk. It makes me think you've spent the last few months on a management course.'

Brigid spluttered a laugh. 'As if.'

'You're my best friend,' Lauren said. 'You just left. I'm not angry; I'm upset.'

'I couldn't tell you the truth,' Brigid said after a moment. 'Things were getting progressively weirder, and I didn't want to burden you with everything. And I was just trying to help. You loved shopping at the Tantric Om, so I thought you might like to, you know, own it. Give you something to do.'

'Something to do?'

For the first time, Brigid looked uncertain. 'Did I misjudge things?'

Lauren raised her eyebrows at her friend and decided she needed to sit down.

'Things haven't been going swimmingly for me over the past year, to be honest,' Brigid said, pushing her red hair, now streaked through with grey, out of her face. 'Ever since I discovered I'm not actually a mild mannered high school teacher, but I am, in fact, a physical manifestation of an ancient goddess come back to Earth for a bit of respite because I was over it all, things have been decidedly weird.'

'You've never been mild mannered,' Lauren said.

'Fuck off,' Brigid replied, and they smiled at each other warily.

'Are you back though?' Lauren asked. 'Properly?'

'That's tricky. There's still some flux. Flurries in the undertow from what I've been able to pick up. Every time an Imago is killed it causes flux, and if too many are murdered then there will reach a point of critical mass where it affects the trans dimensional continuum of alternate realities. There's talk of a hole being ripped in the fabric of space and time and I'm not sure what that is, but I'm almost entirely sure that it's a bad thing.'

Lauren stared at her. 'I have little to no idea of what you're talking about. Let's start with something easy. Where are we?'

'Ah, I know this one,' Brigid replied. 'The Upper Realms.'

'Excellent,' Lauren said. 'Good. Strong start. Last time I saw you, you were the accidental ruler of the Universe. I was there for that bit. And then I rang your parents, Pat and Frank. We Facetimed a bit, and they filled me in on the rest, to be totally honest.'

'But not from me. You didn't hear all of it from me,' Brigid said, finally understanding that what Lauren felt, at its most basic level, was left out.

'That's exactly right,' said Lauren. 'But not from you. I wanted to hear things from you. You were my best friend. I shouldn't have to hear things second-hand.'

They looked at each other for a moment.

'Anyway, Upper Realms. Fabulous. More information, please.'

'All right, we are currently in one of the offices of the major governing body that oversees all the goings on down on Earth and also in the Other World.'

'Right,' said Lauren said nodding sagely. 'Nope. What's the Other World?'

Brigid blew out a breath of air and thought for a moment. 'I'm not used to having to explain this. Let's see. The Other World is just … everything. It's the dimension that exists just above the Earth and includes the vast panoply of gods, lesser deities and supernatural beings that move between here and the planet. Oh, and in some of the other more evil dimensional areas, but there tends to be more lurking there than I'm completely comfortable with.'

'Lurking,' Lauren repeated.

'Some things like to lurk. It's their jam.'

'I feel like I'm getting very good with a fair degree of weirdness these days.'

'Good,' Brigid said, 'because things are probably going to get exponentially odder.'

'And just so I know, are you still the ancient Goddess Brigid?'

'Not really. I'm supposed to be living an entirely human life down on Earth and baking bread and possibly having some babies or puppies or some such but,' here she gestured about,' you can see how well that's panning out for me.'

'Yes,' Lauren said. 'But maybe you could tell me why I'm here.'

'How did you deal with getting brought up here?' Brigid asked.

'Not great,' Lauren said. 'I've become an anarchist, I think. I smashed a drinks machine.'

'That was only a matter of time.'

Lauren nodded philosophically.

'Anyway,' Brigid said in a businesslike manner. 'As I said, it turned out that rather than just Brigid Humboldt, I'm actually Brigid, Goddess of the Flame and the Well, Divine Mistress of Spring and New Growth, Font of all Inspiration and Creativity, and I popped down for some earthly incarnation as a break.'

'Inspiration and creativity?' choked Lauren. 'You can't even scrapbook without making a spreadsheet. I would have been a far more likely contender for goddess if that was the job spec.'

'I was having a break,' Brigid pointed out. 'It would hardly be a break if I was being all creative and inspirational, would it? Anyway, apparently, I was needed again because god forbid I get a lifetime to myself, and then it was decided that I should stay in Ireland and lay low for a while.'

'I didn't know you'd been in Ireland at all. Until the lawyer told me.'

'I'm fairly sure she wasn't supposed to tell you that,' Brigid said.

'Fortunate that she did, if you ask me.'

'It did all get a bit complicated, but I got married, so that was fun.'

'Yes, okay, I do want to get back to that point, but do you have anything that I wear? This is lovely, but it's still a hospital gown. And could we find shoes, perhaps?'

'Sorry about all that. You had to be quarantined. And your clothes had to be cleaned. Or burnt. Something. I don't entirely know how it works, but better minds than mine have told me that's the case.' She opened her hands and shrugged her shoulders. 'I just go with it. Actually…' She turned and scrabbled through some of the papers on her overflowing desk, frowning. 'I think there's a note about it here somewhere.' She looked for a few more moments before turning back to her friend, slightly crestfallen. 'I thought I had a memo about it. I haven't read it but —'

'Do you actually have any idea what's going on?' Lauren asked, a look of worry creeping across her face.

'Going on? Not specifically. I mean, I have a rough idea but specifics, no. I do need to talk to you about something important though, and I had to get you up here for that to happen.'

Brigid opened cupboards and draws searching for something. She pulled out a bag and stared at it.

'That's my bloody handbag,' said Lauren, taking it from her. 'I wondered where that had got to.'

A large wardrobe, the kind that Lauren had sat in as a child hoping to feel snow and fur coats on her face, stood against one of the walls, and Brigid threw open the door and leaned in, most of her body disappearing from view.

'I know there are some clothes in here,' Brigid said, her voice muffled by the thick cherry wood. 'I left some things in here when we had a Lughnasadh party a while back. Things got a bit wild, and I decided it would be better to hang my good stuff up. Ah, here we go.'

She backed out of the wardrobe, holding a long button-up yellow linen jacket. 'Here you go,' she said, passing it to Lauren. 'Just pop it over that. It will go quite well with the off white.'

Lauren put in on, deciding, wisely, not to get sidetracked with all the new questions that had sprung into her mind.

'Shoes?' she asked hopefully.

Brigid opened a draw and produced a pair of slippers with an open toe and a burst of merkin like fur on the tip.

'I do not want to know why you have those,' Lauren said, rejecting them on sight.

'Wise,' Brigid said. 'That whole evening was better off forgotten anyway.'

'You mentioned getting married,' Lauren said, after she had smoothed the jacket over the gown and decided that it could be worse. Not much worse, but worse. 'It was to Egragore I hope?'

'Yes, Egragore. Of course. He's the only man who doesn't give me the shits. We have this little cottage, you know. In Kilkenny. It's four hundred years old. Bits of it, anyway. Gorgeous. He's been working on this new species of rose that he's managed to kind of, trail around a trellis and up around the door. It's fantastic. He's surprisingly good at roses.'

'But he's not here?' prompted Lauren.

'No,' Brigid said simply, and that conversation topic was over.

'That jacket looks good,' Brigid said.

'Thanks. Could you please tell me why I'm here? It's great to catch up with you and everything, but I'm going to assume there's a good reason rather than a fun chat. I'd be pretty unimpressed if you'd caused all this fuss and, let's be honest, discomfort and embarrassment, just for a quick catch up.'

'Look at you all assertive.' Brigid beamed at her. 'Are you getting better at boundaries?'

'Yes, I am,' Lauren said brightly. 'Thanks for noticing. I've been working on it.'

'Good job,' Brigid said, 'I'm proud of you. But, yes, you're right, I do need your help.'

'Can we just put on the record that I'm still annoyed at you for disappearing, giving me a shop I didn't want, and hauling me up here. I also want it noted that your best friend status is still hanging in the balance.'

'Yes,' Brigid said, nodding firmly. 'Absolutely noted. I'm

happy to circle back to that later if you would like, but right now, as I said, I really need your help.'

'I could do with a new project. Go.'

'Right, so you are aware that there's a goddess called the Cailleach, yes?'

'I am familiar with her, yes. Actually, she's —'

'I thought so,' Brigid interrupted. 'To be quite blunt, she's in Australia, and she's overstayed her welcome, and we need someone to get her to go back home.'

'Wait, what?'

'I know. Annoying, right? Nothing worse than an ancient goddess who's gone rogue and outstayed her welcome. She's annoying everyone from what I've been told.'

'She's in Australia?'

'Yes,' Brigid said. 'That's what I said.'

'But that's incredible,' Lauren said breathlessly. 'She's who our coven is dedicated too. We're the Coven of the Cailleach's Cauldron. That's bizarre.'

'What a coincidence,' Brigid said drily.

'That's amazing,' Lauren continued, her gaze drifting off. 'So serendipitous.'

'It's really not,' Brigid said. 'You've got that name because you're on the land she's been living on for two hundred plus years. Practically every Wiccan group in that whole region has taken on her name, or it's in their charter, or they just end up invoking her name far more often than you'd find if it were just based on chance. She's been in the country since 1788, and she moved down to the Mornington Peninsula sometime in the 1830s, apparently.'

'Before land prices took off, I'm assuming.'

'Exactly. She's been making a nuisance of herself and needs to move on.'

'Making a nuisance of herself how?'

'I think it's the fact that she's just there, more than anything else. She came over on the First Fleet to support the Irish convicts, but as you can appreciate, there haven't been Irish convicts here for a while now, so now she's just lurking and influencing people. And...' Here Brigid's voice dropped to a whisper. 'It's not like Australia doesn't have its own spirits. It's become increasingly awkward for all of us, the fact that she's there. The original inhabitants have been perfectly nice about it, but their patience is running low now, and they've contacted us and asked if we could please get her to leave.'

Lauren stared at Brigid for a moment, searching her eyes to see if she was joking or not. 'Wait, you communicate with the ancestral spirits?'

'Oh, god no,' Brigid said. 'No, no. This is all taking place way over my head. They're the old ones. Like, seriously old. Even when I'm doing the whole 'Goddess Brigid' thing they're way out of my league. I've just been told to try and shift the Cailleach, that's all.'

Brigid turned and made a seat for herself on the cushion covered overstuffed sofa that sat to the left of the desk.

Lauren sat next to her, her friend's words playing through her head. 'So you have to convince her to leave.'

'I've been asked to, yes. Apparently the ancestral spirits contacted management here and asked us to take care of it.'

'Why couldn't they just do it themselves?'

Brigid shrugged. 'Below their pay grade. And it was allocated to me.'

'Why you?'

Brigid rolled her eyes. 'Because of some perceived bond Cailleach and I have, which just goes to show that management up here really doesn't have a hugely developed idea about what happens on Earth. I mean, I grew up in Australia in the 1980s, so how am I supposed to have some intuitive connection with a non-corporeal goddess crone of death or herbs or whatever?'

Lauren felt they were finally in an area she could contribute something too. 'Actually, she's more appropriately seen as the keeper of the cauldron of knowledge, and she speaks into our need for change and transformation.'

'See?' Brigid waved a hand in the air. 'This is why I need you. You're perfect for it. You've always been much more into this whole witchy coven type palaver than I have. You know the whole thing makes me feel awkward.'

'Yet you're an actual goddess.'

'Not a very competent one though.' Brigid looked at Lauren. 'I can rely on you to fix things?'

'Can you rely on me to convince an ancient goddess to abandon her antipodean playground? How the fuck do you expect me to do that?'

'Ah, well,' Brigid said, tucking her feet up under her. 'I've been thinking about that. You and your friends still have your coveny thing, right?'

'Yes,' Lauren said patiently.

'Great. So how about, and I'm just throwing ideas around here, you do a ritual ceremony and banish her.'

After a few moments, Lauren realised she was staring at Brigid in horror. She wanted to tell her friend that was the most spectacularly dangerous and foolhardy idea she had ever heard of. For all her background, Brigid knew absolutely nothing about the practice of witchcraft.

'Sure,' she said eventually. 'We can cobble something together.'

Brigid's brow furrowed and she gazed off into space for a moment, a look of intense concentration on her face.

'Are you okay?' Lauren asked.

'You said something important, and I completely skimmed over it, and I'm trying to remember what it was.'

'I've said quite a lot of important things so far,' I think,' Lauren said. 'Was it about the trauma that I'm still holding on to surrounding the fact that I thought you'd been murdered?'

'No.'

'Did you think of where to find me more appropriate shoes?'

'No, and those ones are fine.'

'Maybe it was something to do with me becoming an anarchist?'

'Yes.' Brigid clapped her hands together. 'A drinks fridge. You mentioned a drinks fridge. Do you think you could find it again? I'm desperate for a coke.'

8

Morty barely had time to find the first track on his demo tape before the bells on the front door jangled harshly, and a nondescript man entered the shop.

Nondescript usually means, of course, someone who rarely attracts notice and/or attention. So the fact that Morty's attention was piqued by the entrance of a random person would seem, at first, to be counter-intuitive.

One can't pay attention to every customer who walks into a shop, of course. What with all the filing and stocktaking and unpacking and rearranging and chatting that looking after a shop entails. Eyeballing every person who walks through the door is difficult, if not impossible, which is just as well because there is nothing worse than being swooped on by a shop assistant who asks if they can help you before you have even got your foot in the door.

However, Morty had just glanced up from the stereo when the door was pushed open, and it was the fact that he could distinguish precisely nothing about the person who was walking towards him that initially got his attention. It's hard to be seen as nondescript while wearing a charcoal three piece suit and winkle-pickers, but this man was managing it effortlessly.

Even afterwards, when he was trying to remember the details of what had happened for the police, he could give no more of a definite description than 'medium height' and 'no beard' although on reflection this was more of a general vibe than a reliable memory.

Of course he didn't know he was going to have to make a police statement as the man was walking towards him. He just knew he couldn't make out the person's face properly and had a moment of panic that Lauren had sent someone in to tell him to change the music back to binaural beats.

'Are you Cernunnos?'

The man had a flat, toneless voice, and Monty had to think for a moment to register what he'd said.

'Me? No, sorry. I'm Morty. I don't know who that is.'

The expression on the man's face didn't change. Maybe it couldn't, Morty thought fleetingly. The calm, impassive expression seemed immovable, yet the feeling of 'Oh shit' was coming from every pore on the man's face. Morty thought he could see a thin sheen of sweat break out on the man's brow, but this could have been a trick of the light.

'He is here.' The man's voice was more high pitched this time.

Morty shook his head. 'Nah mate. He's definitely not. Maybe you could—'

He felt the force throw his body backwards even before he started moving. Almost like the wall had become a magnet and had decided to suck him into it with a warm, dangerously impactful embrace. He lost all sense of balance, the floor moving out from under his feet, a feeling of panic and terror engulfing his body, just time for an indignant thought of 'what the fuck' before he was slammed into the wall.

The realisation that this man wasn't human at all, that it was something dreadful, wearing a metaphorical skin suit, came to him with sudden and complete clarity. The knowledge that the figure was very strange, very inhuman and very, very scared was crystal clear, and Morty realised he might actually be good in a crisis if this clarity of thought was what came to him as he was bodily being thrown against a wall by a non-human entity of some kind.

'I was told he is here. I've been ordered to make him stop.' The voice was a shriek now, and objects began to fly off the walls around them. Bowls of small rocks and crystals began to bubble as if they had been left on a hot plate too long. The multitudes of wind chimes, dream catchers and sun catchers that hung from the ceiling vibrated crazily, filling the room with a cacophony of sounds that only added to the ringing in Morty's ears.

The books Lauren had been lovingly arranging on new shelves for the last two weeks slid off as if they were on the deck of a ferociously rocking ship in the high seas, and from his position on the floor, Morty had the vague realisation that if any of them were damaged, Lauren was going to be mightily pissed off.

He lay slumped against the wall as the vibrating rumbling noise in the shop reached a crescendo. Just when he thought he couldn't bear it for another moment, it cut off abruptly, and the shop was deathly silent, except for the tinny jangle of one sphere of a finger cymbal that was just finishing its last chime as it rolled to a stop. As it too fell silent, the creature in front of Morty looked up sharply, an expression of abject terror on its face. Above him, a faint glow began to appear in the air, a certain thinness that distorted the ceiling, a feeling that a large hole was opening in the air that hung dankly above their heads.

It was the feeling of a hole rather than an actual hole. More of an absence of light, a deep thickening of the atmosphere that formed a dense, dark emptiness.

As this darkness solidified, the creature, who had now stumbled back several paces and was almost standing on top of

Morty (Morty had the sudden, irrational impulse to put his body in front of the creature, to protect it from whatever was coming) raised its hands in front of its face as a penetrating, hissing voice came out of the void.

'I gave you one fucking job. Do you know how much effort its taken me to be in three places at once? It's giving me vertigo and it's going to play hell with my worry lines.'

As these words faded, there was a smell of sulphur in the air, and Morty realised that the creature in front of him had started to steam a little. His clothes were emitting the vaguest little puffs of steam, and as Morty watched, these puffs became more voluminous, as if he were wearing a wet woollen blanket and had taken to sunbaking in January's heat. These steaming areas began to crackle, and shoots of lightning started to project from the creature's head, up towards the dark void that loomed, utterly menacingly, above them.

A high pitched screaming noise began to come from the creature, although Morty couldn't tell if it was a sound he was hearing in the real world or if he was just intuiting it as if it were happening on another plane entirely. Its body began to vibrate at an alarming rate, as if it were sitting on one of those frightfully expensive massaging posturepedic chairs, although the look on its face wasn't one of blissful relaxation, but rather utter terror. What with the screaming and the lightning and the steaming and the vibrating, Morty felt a tad overwhelmed and closed his eyes for a moment in the vague hope that it would all just stop and leave him in peace to listen to some ambient rainforest sounds, but just as he closed his eyes and decided it was probably high time that he really committed himself to some breath work, there was a muted, muffled pop, like a cracker going off inside a hyperbaric chamber, and the creature, the void, and the noise were gone, leaving behind the acrid smell of chemicals and a disastrously shattered shop.

9

Lauren struggled to find the alcove where the drinks fridge had been located, which was hardly surprising. After she and Brigid had been wandering around, directionless, for a good ten minutes, the obvious occurred to her. 'Hang on, shouldn't you be the one leading me? Aren't you at least vaguely aware of the layout here?'

Brigid shook her head. 'No, I told you. This isn't really my area. I'm here occasionally for a meeting or some such but even given that, it's all a bit vague. And when I was up here, you know, in charge of everything, the decor was very different. I'm not sure where all this has come from.' She gestured at a huge gilt mirror that reached from floor to ceiling and reflected the dark, dramatically woven metal chandelier that hung from the roof, just a little too close to their heads to be entirely comforting. 'This isn't my style at all.'

'I wonder who's in charge of the decorating. And, like … why? Seems an odd thing to be focused on in the administrative hub of the Universe.' She glanced questioningly at Brigid. 'This is what the Other World is, isn't it?'

'It's complicated,' Brigid said. 'I mean, I going to say yes, but if I was writing a thesis on it, there would be eight volumes of footnotes and appendices.'

'In that case, I don't want to know.'

'Anyway, I'm hoping I'll be heading back home soon.'

'Home home or Ireland home?'

'That depends,' Brigid said, and glanced down a quadruple forked corridor. 'This way maybe?'

'Let's veer to the left,' Lauren said. 'I tend to have more success in life when I veer to the left.'

After a few more minutes of misdirected meanderings, they found a small room. It contained two chairs in the Queen Anne style and a whatnot covered in a mindbogglingly extensive collection of dust catchers such as shells, curious little paper things, desperately unsettling figures of anatomically questionable dogs, and china dolls with pose-able limbs and long horse hair eyelashes. Sitting on a low filigree table between the chairs were two steaming cups of tea, in pale pink cups, ringed with gold.

'Do you think they're for us?' Lauren asked.

'They are now.'

'So, this home business,' Lauren said as they sipped what turned out to be perfectly made cups of Earl Grey tea. 'I feel like you're not entirely happy with what's going on, and we need to talk about it.'

Brigid sighed heavily. 'I know that being part goddess sounds awfully exotic and everything, but half the time, I feel like a dogsbody being told to do other people's business.'

'You've delegated some of that business to me, if that makes you feel any better,' Lauren said. 'And you've done it pretty effectively. Definitely a proposal I didn't feel I could say no to. So, well done on that account. Do you think there's any way that we could get a biscuit? I quite fancy a Butternut Snap.'

There was a sweeping sound in the air as if someone had briskly walked past them, and a small plate, one that clearly was part of the same tea set, appeared in front on them.

'How about a curry?' Lauren said loudly.

'Don't tease them,' Brigid said mildly. 'It will just cause confusion.'

Lauren took a biscuit and dunked it into her tea. 'You seem stressed.'

'I'm living in a freezing cold ancient house in the middle of a fucking bog. I have no friends and a shitty internet connection, and every now and then, I'll get summoned up here to do some bullshit random job, even though I am explicitly supposed to be living a life as a human at the moment. So I'm not totally human and not totally goddess, and I don't have any particular special powers at all, and I'm just as bored as I used to be before I knew any of this, except now I have to wear gumboots every time I leave the house.'

'Okay,' Lauren said, taking another biscuit. 'But at least you have Egragore, right? And he's super hot, so, yay you.'

'Husband, yeah that's right,' Brigid said. 'We got married. He's great, yes. I don't mind him at all. There's just the slight matter of…' Her voice trailed off.

'Yes,' Lauren prompted after a moment.

'I don't actually know where he is.'

Lauren glanced around, taking in the carpet, the bookcases and the velvet flocked wallpaper. 'What do you mean? Is he supposed to be here?'

'No, I mean, I don't know where he is in general. I got back home a few weeks ago, and he was gone. No note, no explanation. He just wasn't there.'

Lauren looked at her with a stricken expression on her face. 'Do you think he left you?'

'Of course he didn't bloody leave me. He adores me. As if he'd just leave me. I'm worried, is all.'

'Kind of like you did to me,' Lauren said without recrimination. 'Maybe it's an Other World thing, like yours was? Maybe he's been commandeered or something.'

'Either way,' Brigid said. 'I don't like it.'

Lauren looked around again. 'This is giving me the shits,' she said finally, draining the last of her tea and placing it none too delicately back on the table. 'We can't wander around this labyrinth indefinitely. Hello?' she shouted. 'Can we please speak to someone? We need some help here, thanks.'

They waited.

'Brigid, Goddess of the Flame and the Well, Divine Mistress of Spring and New Growth, Font of all Inspiration and Creativity would like some attention please,' Lauren said loudly.

'Oh, god, don't,' Brigid said, rolling her eyes. 'That sounds so pretentious. It's like putting your PhD on everything and calling yourself a doctor. Insufferable.'

Still nothing.

'Anyway, a title isn't very impressive around here. Everyone is something paranormal or super-normal or interesting. I'm not that special.'

'I'd say you were a bit special.'

'Maybe I'm a bit special.' She smiled at her friend. 'I missed you.'

'When I pushed over the drinks machine someone came and found me pretty sharpish,' Lauren said. 'Is there something around here that I could trash?'

Brigid looked around. 'Just the bookcases. And you're not going to throw books.'

For the first time, Lauren turned and studied the actual books themselves. They were a general mish-mash of colours, covers and textures, but as she looked closer, something occurred to her. She pulled one from the middle of the closest shelf, and it fell open in her hands. 'This book is blank,' she said.

'Maybe it's a notebook or a journal,' Brigid suggested, taking one from the shelf and flicking it open.

That one was blank too.

As they pulled more out, they discovered that all the books that lined the walls of the corridor were blank.

'But why?' Lauren asked. 'What's the point of hundreds of—'

'Thousands.'

'What's the point of thousands of blank books? Why go to all the trouble? Maybe they're journals. I love a journal. Blank notebooks are amazing for reflection and shadow work and stuff.' Lauren thought for a moment. 'I don't think these are meant to be journals though. I think they're just here to make whoever created it feel smart and look well read and intelligent. Like performative public reading.'

'Wait.' Brigid was staring fixedly into the gap made by some of the books that now lay in a heap on the floor. She squinted her eyes and drew closer to the hole, tilting her head, peering closely. 'Get down here,' she whispered, pulling her friend's hand abruptly so that Lauren jerked forwards and found her eyes on the level of the shelf.

Lauren too narrowed her eyes, looking through the gap. She felt herself draw an abrupt breath while at the same time her mouth fell open.

Instead of the dark black-wood back of the case, as one would have expected to see she could see straight through into a bright, cavernous room.

10

After he had picked himself up and dusted himself off, literally and metaphorically, Morty decided he was probably in shock and came to the logical conclusion that what he really needed was a stiff drink. Or a light cider at least. He also needed someone to talk to, someone who might believe, or at the very least listen without laughing, to what he had just gone through.

So he headed to the pub.

He wasn't typically a huge pub-goer, but a kind of ancestral memory stirred within him as he pushed open the door of The Cranky Emu, the offer of warmth, sustenance and mateship drawing him in.

Mateship wasn't something he usually had much truck with, but it had been an odd day, after all, and given that Lauren didn't seem to be anywhere around, his options were thin on the ground.

He had never been into this particular pub before. Sure, he had passed it, or at least the alley it was tucked away in, hundreds of time, but he had never taken a great deal of interest in it. It was slightly seedy, for one, a bit grimy, for another, and it wasn't, and this was the main factor, somewhere that Lauren frequented. Many of Morty's decisions were based around where Lauren was, where she was going to be, or whether, in her absence, there were going to be people who he could talk to her about, and since this pub didn't fit into any of those specifics, he had never bothered with it.

He made his way to the bar and perched on a stool. Tables and mismatched wooden chairs were scattered around the dark room, but the bar, at least, looked as if it might have been wiped down today, and when you have a deep need to speak to a stranger in a pub, your best bet is usually the bartender.

Seeing the open yet flushed face of the young man who had climbed somewhat unsteadily up onto the wobbly bar stool, the bartender stopped wiping down the surface at the far end of the counter and grimly steeled himself. This, he thought, was a man who wanted to talk. This was a man who wanted to share and, by god, talk about his feelings, and by the looks of it, he was going to be the one to bear the brunt of it.

He wasn't necessarily psychic in the technical sense of the word, but after two hundred years in the pub game, one develops a sense of these things.

'A cider, thanks, Mate,' Morty said, a little too eagerly. 'How's your day going ... chief?'

He heartily regretted this as soon as it was out of his mouth.

'Good, thanks. Yours?'

'Funny you should ask. You'll never guess what just happened to me.'

'Try me,' the man said. He might as well gird his loins and get ready for it.

Morty looked at the bartender. He was the kind of person Morty hoped he would become if, eventually, he grew up. Not exactly hewed out of a single piece of granite, but masonry tools had definitely been brought into play somewhere along the line. He wasn't oddly tall, probably just a little over six feet, but he was thick and solid, from muscle rather than fat, and he had the vibe of someone who took motorbikes apart and then rebuilt them in new and interesting ways in his spare time.

He looked very, very capable.

This man looked at the facial hair that bikies or ageing rock stars grew, and he laughed at it. He had had a better beard than them by the time he was twelve years old, and while the concept of beard jewellery was something that many people found laughable and mocked incessantly, they certainly never did it within his presence, or indeed withing several hundred miles of where he had ever been.

Morty decided to change tack. 'Have you seen anyone strange around here. Maybe in a suit? With, like, a face?'.

The bartender flicked his eyes around the room. No one in there, it could be said, was normal. It was 3.00 pm on a Wednesday, in a drinking establishment that had never become fashionable or lauded by the beautiful people in any way. This was not where people came to see or be seen. This was where people came to drink, to drown their sorrows, or to drown other people's sorrows. People largely came here to be on their own, and if not on their own, then with other people they didn't wish to be associated with in the real world. Meeting with a dealer, a hit-man or with a pimp were to be expected, and various private rooms led off the short corridor adjacent to the bathrooms for that very purpose. The bartender didn't necessarily endorse these dealings and certainly never involved himself in them in any way, but he did, as they say, have bigger fish to fry, and in an expression well known in the Upper Realms, 'mortal business is mortal business'.

Many, many strange things happened in The Cranky Emu, and they were just the things that most people could see. They didn't account for the other beings that, arguably, made up the bulk of his clientèle.

The bartender whose name was currently Connall, was the manager and owner of the establishment and had been for around two hundred years. This would be quite a big ask for a human, but given he was only moonlighting as one, this didn't cause as many problems as one would think. It was much easier to renew his alcohol serving certificate if he could apply in person, so to speak, and grease the palms of people who wanted to know a) why he looked so young, b) where his birth certificate was and, c) how he had been able to avoid going to jail for all the shady dealings he had apparently been involved in over the past few centuries.

The answer was a little bit of bribery but mainly charm and just a touch of Other World mental manipulation. A sexy barkeeper with the ability to slightly bend minds could get a lot done, it seemed.

Connall pulled Morty a beer and slid it in front of him. 'How'd you mean, strange?' he asked.

'Well,' started Morty, taking a doubtful sip of the drink that definitely wasn't cider. He looked at the bartender who raised an eyebrow at him.

'You need a beer, not a cider.'

Morty took another sip. 'I don't quite know how to say it.'

Connall was a man who had seen some shit. He had been around the block; he had not come down in the last shower and other appropriate aphorisms. And he could tell, just by picking up on the slightest hint of Morty's auric energy, that the issues that the young man was currently dealing with might be his specific skill base.

From down the bar, Morty noticed a faintly glowing diminutive man had slunk in through the door. He was strangely unclear, almost misty, and his downcast eyes seemed determined to ensure he appeared as a threat to no one. Two small, oddly misshapen wings protruded from his back, and he wore a kind of a sack with holes cut out at the back, designed, Morty thought, as a way to let his wings escape while still trying to cover the rest of his body.

He sidled up to the bar, every fibre of his being apologising for his very existence, and Connall quickly excused himself from Morty. He moved down to the other end of the bar, rightly deducing that if he didn't greet the man immediately then he might simply fade away into nothing. Running a halfway house for abandoned or otherwise forgotten spectres, waifs, elementals, and other conjured and/or lost preternatural creatures was a never ending job but one that he took very seriously. He never knew when he would be called on to jump into action, and he was constantly on the alert for that slight frisson in the air that indicated someone or something needed him.

'You right?' he asked kindly, addressing the figure, who seemed to be fading by the moment.

Morty glanced around, wondering if anyone else was seeing what he was seeing, but the few customers in the place were heavily into their drinks and weren't looking around hoping to catch random people's eyes.

'Are you Connall?' the man asked. His voice was faint, not as much soft as if it was coming from an enormous distance to reach his ears.

Connall nodded.

'I was told to find you,' he said.

The voice was fading, and Connall could see the heavy wooden door that served as an entrance to the pub through him. The ephemeral presence was becoming less visible by the second. 'I've come down from the country. I don't have any people now.'

Connall's stony visage became even more edifice like, and Morty saw him shake his head and rub the space between his eyes. 'Fucking monsters, the lot of them,' he spat.

The man in front of Connall blinked back tears and fought back a sob, and Morty could see that he was moments away from disappearing completely. Morty gripped the damp glass of his beer, and he wondered if he should call the police, or an ambulance, or a crystal healer or some such.

He didn't expect what happened next to happen. Connall leaned over the bar, spread out his arms, and offered an embrace to the almost invisible man. 'Bring it in,' he said. 'You need a hug.'

Now this was something Morty understood. He had been trying to persuade Lauren to let him teach a Cuddles for Universal Peace and Healing class in the shop for months, but she was worried people might catch something. As if in a roundabout vindication to Morty's pleas to Lauren, a beatific grin spread across the fading being's face as he opened his arms, and Connall engulfed him in a warm, tight embrace. As he watched on, Morty saw the man become, as if a switch had been flicked on, solid. More solid than he had been when he had entered the bar. If fact, if it hadn't been for the empty feed sack he was wearing and the wings that projected out of his back, he might be just a normal, ordinary patron of the bar.

Connall tightened his arms around the figure once more for good measure and then pulled back. 'You right now?' he asked, one eyebrow raised. The man nodded, smiling a childlike, open grin, and Connall took the cloth he had over his shoulder, took a glass off the counter, and began polishing with his full attention. 'Better head upstairs then,' he said. 'Someone will show you where to sleep.'

Morty drained the last of his beer, pleasantly realising that the taste was becoming less offensive the more he drank. Just an hour ago, he had been worried he was going mad, and now he realised that, even if he was, this disturbingly attractive bartender was firmly in the same boat with him. And he was just the kind of person Morty needed to be talking to today. He held up his empty glass and called down the bar. 'Another one of these, please.'

'Sorry about that, mate,' apologised Connall, 'Just had to help him out for a minute. Never ends, does it?' He rolled his eyes companionably, bringing Morty into the exclusive clique of people who were clearly very put upon and busy but nevertheless had their cross to bear. 'Personally, I'm not a big fan of hugging random strangers, but all they need is a bit of affection to get them geed up again. And once he finds his people, he'll get what he needs.'

'I feel as if this is a bit of a superfluous question given what just happened,' Morty said, 'but where do you stand on high strangeness, paranormal phenomenon and things of that ilk?'

'That, my friend,' said Connall, pulling himself a beer, 'is my particular skill base. What have you got for me?'

11

'And I'm hosting everyone tonight, so I should probably tidy things up a bit.'

Sybella ignored the irritated expression on the lion's face and started moving around the room, putting books and random pieces of paper onto other books, and moving piles of papers onto already overladen shelves. Rather than create a sense of order, this merely served to make a series of precarious, Escheresque systems of sculpture over every available surface. She rubbed at the space between her eyes. She had taken painkillers for her headache, but she had come to the conclusion that time travel didn't agree with her at all, and she wouldn't be bothering with it again.

'How could this have happened,' Leo muttered, seemingly to himself. 'How could I have missed this. She's going to be a problem, I just know it. She can be so intimidating when she wants to be. Those beady little eyes.' He shuddered involuntarily.

'Missed what?' Sybella asked as she carried five mugs filled with an unidentifiable dried brown substance to the already packed sink. 'Can you carry things? Because don't hold back if you get the urge to help me. I won't be offended.'

'So you're a member of the Cailleach's Cauldron,' he asked again, as if hoping for a different answer this time.

'Yeah,' she said. 'I told you that. Why? Have you heard of us?'

'I've heard of the Cailleach, anyway. And covens associated with her are a dime a dozen around here. I can't believe you haven't noticed.'

Sybella shrugged. 'I don't pay that much attention to other groups. I just like to muck around with my friends.'

'Mucking around,' Leo clarified. 'You see this all as mucking around, do you?'

'Mainly, yes. I mean, it's something to do, isn't it. Staves off the boredom for another day. The existential angst, I mean.'

'Out of interest, how many of your decisions are made as a band-aid measure to stop you from being bored or as a desperate attempt to have some fun and avoid the bleak hole that is your existence,' he asked.

'Most of them. Is there something wrong with that?'

'Do you have a life plan or any sort of direction to speak of?'

Sybella raised her eyebrows at Leo. 'Look, I know we haven't known each other for very long, but has anything I've done over the past few hours given you any reason to think that would be the case?'

He conceded the point.

'And just, while we are, you know, chatting about unrelated and insubstantial subjects here, does your coven ever do anything that has, you could say, lasting effects? Do you create rituals or spells or the like that actually, well, work?'

'What?' Sybella asked, turning to look at him, a dusting rag in her hand that seemed to be pushing dust around rather than actually removing it. 'Do you mean do our spells and rituals bring about any concrete, lasting change?'

'Yes,' he said. 'What kind of things do you try to conjure, for example?'

'Oh, I don't know. Just the usual. Fulfilment and health and general goddessy goodness, I suppose. And recently we asked for a good harvest for a small village in West Wales.' She frowned. 'Actually, now that I say that out loud—'

'Doesn't that strike you as odd?' Leo asked.

'It does. A bit.'

'Have you done anything tangible that has got results?' he asked. 'Something a bit easier to nail down than whether a man named Osian has a bumper crop of barley?'

Sybella blew out a breath slowly while she stared off into the distance for a few moments. 'We did work on getting Roxy a boyfriend a few months ago. That seemed to work out okay. But, mind you, if I were the Cailleach, I'd pay attention to Roxy when she asked for something too.'

There was a pause.

'And Roxy is…'

'Our high priestess.'

'Of course she is. And who else is in this coven of yours?'

'It's just me, Lauren, Lauren's friend Morty, Roxy and Demniac.'

'Demniac,' said the lion doubtfully.

'You're not in a position of criticise anyone's name, Robellian, my old mate. He's just a friend of Roxy's. Into chaos magic or some such, but I feel he thinks the rest of us are holding him back most of the time. He was the one who mentioned the whole 'summoning a thought form' thing to me, so you should be thankful, actually.'

'I should?'

'Yes, otherwise I wouldn't have summoned you, and you wouldn't have ended up here.'

'Yes, of course. This is the highlight of several lifetimes. I can't wait to meet him and thank him in person for enabling this entire wonderful adventure to occur.'

'But you're not an actual tulpa, in the way that I understand it, Didn't you say something about that? Even though I invented you in my head and then summoned you?'

Leo concentrated on maintaining his placid demeanour. Letting her think that his entire presence was due to her summoning prowess was an important part of his mission, despite how it made his teeth ache every time she mentioned it.

'None of you know what you're doing when it comes to thought forms, and that's why we're in our current predicament. I mean that on a global level, you understand, not you and I.'

Sybella looked at him blankly.

'What you humans think is creating a servitor, or a tulpa, or an Imago or whatever lexicon you choose, which is basically using your thoughts to create an imaginary friend in your head, doesn't do what you humans think it does.'

'It doesn't?'

'No. What your friend Deodum—'

'Demniac.'

'Quite. What your chaos magic loving friends suggested you do is what people have been doing for time immemorial. Now it's got a different name, and it's quirkily fashionable in certain groups, but creating a thought-form that resides in people's heads has been happening for hundreds, nay thousands of years. The only problem is that it's not just contained to people's heads.

'No,' said Sybella, with a look on her face of someone who was being asked to understand something very, very basic. 'Obviously. Because you're here.'

'I am. Good job. I am, in fact, here. And you have not only seen me, but you have adapted quite well to it. Actually, extremely well, now I come to think of it. You've coped with not only my manifestation, but also my whisking you off to various places for your entertainment. Which,' he added as an aside, 'you weren't very gracious about.'

'Sorry about that,' she said. 'Time travel isn't really my thing, apparently. That pyramid was dank and musty as all heck. Not a fan at all.'

'But the fact is, you dealt with it very well. Apart from the complaining and the migraine, I suppose. I wonder why?'

'I dunno,' she said, shrugging her shoulders. 'I guess that when you're confronted with two situations you have the choice to either collapse in a screaming heap or just firm your chin up and face whatever's coming at you.'

'Yet you're living a life of what many would call quiet desperation. You make absolutely no move to create anything interesting or stimulating in your own life, but you deal with it well when it is thrust upon you.'

Sybella shrugged. 'Whatever. But, yeah, we have weird things happen within the circle, so it's not as if I don't know that there is high strangeness out there. I just don't usually expect anything like that to happen to me. I'm an innocent bystander typically.' She laughed unconvincingly. 'I'm happy with the way things are.'

'However,' he said, casting his mind back a few minutes, 'I was trying to make a point about the immense folly and ineptitude of people who try to try to create Imagos.'

'Why do I feel as if I'm not going to come out of this well?'

'The problem,' he continued, ignoring her, 'is that you people, you human people, I mean, like to play around with things, and for the most part you have absolutely no idea what you are doing. You just don't understand the mess that you leave behind when you either summon or create entities. As you can see, I'm quite real, yes?'

She reached out a hand and tousled his rich golden mane. She wanted to rub her face in it, but knew that would be pushing her luck.

'So, your friend had this idea of creating a servitor, or a tulpa, or a thought form, or whatever you call it. You decided that you should create a friend who exists in your mind, but is a separate and real entity, yes?'

'That's what I was led to believe.'

'All right, every time someone creates a thought form, every time someone creates an imaginary friend and really focuses on it, it comes into existence.'

'In people's heads, you mean.'

'No, that's just it.' Leo's voice took on more emotion than she had heard him speak with before; a mix of anger and passion. 'Every time it happens, a real creature is created. A real being is brought to life, with the exact mission and appearance that their creator imagined. But when it is ill formed and ill considered, as it so often is, the creator either can't see them, don't realise they exist, or they panic so much when they realise what they have done that they shut down that side of their mind so they don't even acknowledge their creation anymore. So the thought form is cut off and utterly alone and abhorred, with no one to help them make meaning in their life.'

Sybella had raised her hand to her mouth, a look of horror on her face. 'But that's horrific,' she whispered.

'Yes, it is,' the lion said. 'And immensely irritating from my perspective, So every time someone who doesn't know what they are doing, every time that one of your lot decides that this would be a fun thing to play around with, they are bringing misery into existence.'

'So what happens to these poor creatures?'

'Oh, there a few avenues. They may try to find someone to help them. They try to find others who can help them make meaning of their existence. There is one Other World being who has made a veritable hobby of this, against all bounds of decorum and good sense. Others just wander around as ghosts or wraiths, trying to find places to exist. Always a subclass though. Anything created by humans is always going to be ill advised and substandard. The best they could ever hope for is to be a pitiful underclass, having to rely on others for everything. Leeches, if you like. Others, if they can find no fulfilment or love or meaning at all, just fade away. Then, from what I can tell, they are caught in the grey fog between two planes. For eternity.'

'That is the most awful thing I've ever heard,' Sybella whispered, her eyes dark in her blanched white face.

'It is. It's absolutely dreadful. The psychic toll on the rest of us is just awful. We can feel every scream of loss, every cry of despair. I mean, we can shut out most of it, but it's just an added hassle that we legitimate thought forms don't need, you know? These non-sanctioned thought forms add an extra stress to the rest of us. And sully our good name. '

'So this is about you, is it?' Sybella said stonily. 'A whole race of creatures have been created and abandoned, and you don't like it because they give you a headache?'

'There are many reasons why creating unsanctioned thought forms is a bad idea, and, yes, the emotional toll that it heaps on me is one of them. And further confirmation, I would think, of why people who don't know what they are doing shouldn't screw around with magic.'

Sybella cleared her throat. 'This feels like a slightly awkward thing to ask at this stage of the proceedings and coming on the back of that—'

'Yes?'

'But would you like to hang around and meet the coven tonight?'

12

Morty sank his committed and single-minded attention into his fourth beer. The bar was filling up now, the conversations taking place around him becoming a hubbub that cocooned him in a comforting fug. However, the more relaxed and settled his mind became, the more he realised that many of the patrons who had made their way to the tables and booths which edged the room looked a little odd.

Decidedly odd.

He wasn't one to judge though, he reminded himself. He was too evolved for that kind of linear, black and white thinking. He saw everyone as a glorious and worthy manifestation of the…

This beer wasn't bad though. Had beer always been this good? And the glass was something tangible, something he could hold, something that he could understand and that made sense to him. His new appreciation of the amber liquid did seem to make a lot more sense that the other inexplicable things that had been happening here today.

He wished Lauren were here. He loved her so much. He'd tell her how he felt about her if she were here right now. He loved her because she was amazing, not just because she was the only woman who had ever—

'You're quite sure a vortex opened up in your shop?' Connall made his way back to Morty. People kept needing his attention, which Morty felt was deeply unfair. He still hadn't finished debriefing about what had happened to him.

'It's not strictly speaking my shop; it's actually Lauren's, but in a general sense then, yes, that's what happened.'

'And you couldn't make out the creature's face? The one with the suit?'

Morty thought about this for a moment. 'It's not so much that I couldn't make it out, it's more that it was unmemorable. Just bland and unspecific. I mean, I could see the face, it was right there, I just...' His voice trailed off. 'I just couldn't see it, if that makes sense.'

Connall rubbed his hand across his forehead. 'No, it doesn't, but I understand what you're saying. I don't like the sound of this. I'm really very uncomfortable with what I'm hearing. They'd better not be after the Imagos again.' He frowned off into the distance, his brow furrowing even more deeply, which Morty though was a spatial impossibility.

'No, it's not that great,' Morty agreed. 'I really appreciate your sympathy. The shop's an absolute mess; I don't know how I'm going to get it back to a semblance of organisation before Lauren gets back from where ever it is she's gone. And that's a whole other issue. Where is she? We're supposed to be meeting tonight, and I don't see the point of even bothering to go along if she's not...'

A couple had stepped up to the bar next to where Morty was sitting. The man was extraordinarily tall, well over seven feet by Morty's boggle-eyed estimation, and with him was a short, enormously large woman, almost as wide as she was high. They greeted Connall with a familiar enthusiasm and seeing that he and Morty had been having a conversation turned to include Morty in their greeting. At this, his polite social smile froze rigid as he realised that only one eye stared at him from the woman's face. An absolutely beautiful eye, admittedly, one that shone clear and bright, with a depth of clarity and emotion that took Morty's breath away. But the fact that it was three times an eyes usual size, and placed directly in the middle of her forehead, meant that he was unable to stop a look of horror from racing across his face. The woman hastily rearranged her thick golden fringe, and Morty glanced away in embarrassment, his eyes moving to the tall man. His clothes bulged oddly, as if his body was having a hard time being confined in the fabric that encased it. Knots and ridges could be seen protruding in various places. Morty dropped his eyes back to his glass, not trusting his own ability to make small talk or to otherwise behave like a member of polite society. The couple exchanged a few merry words with Connall and then took their drinks over to a table, where a group of people greeted them with cheers and huge smiles.

Huge, cheerful, and for the most part, strangely formed smiles.

Morty, keeping his voice low, leaned forwards and spoke to Connall conspiratorially. 'I don't mean to be rude but...' He stopped, unsure as to how to go on.

'I was wondering what...' His words trailed off again as, out of the corner of his eye, he saw something floating through the air, something else heading over to the table, something that was...

He jerked his head back to Connall, reprimanding his own errant mind. His eyes clearly couldn't be trusted today.

'Yes?' Connall asked.

Morty couldn't speak.

'Do you have a question about my clientèle?'

'No, no.' Morty brought his attention back to his drink, trying to establish the conversation back onto less problematic territory. 'You do believe my story, right? You believe what I told you about the ... whatever it was?'

'Oh, yeah, yeah absolutely. You're lucky you didn't end up dead. No part of you wanted to explain it away as a trick of the light, or blame a bad kebab from the night before?'

'That would be a bit hard, wouldn't it? I mean, I was right there. I saw it all.'

'Yeah, nah, I know. I know that you did. But human beings

have a way of ignoring what's in front of their eyes. Most people will just cut something out of their field of perception if it interferes with what they already believe about the world.'

'Not me,' Morty said. 'I've done a lot of Kundalini and third eye work. I like to think I have a certain universal consciousness.'

'Most people,' Connall said with a half-smile, 'when seeing a levitating child sized being with T-Rex arms would immediately erase it from their, as you said, consciousness.'

Morty took a deep breath. 'Look, I feel like I've had a lot happen to me today, and I feel like a lot has been asked of me, in both a general and a specific sense, and while I don't, deep down, feel as if it's particularly fair I've been put in this situation, I am willing to try and get my head around it, but if you have any information that you think would help me understand what happened in the shop earlier, then I would appreciate that, if you don't mind, thank you very much.' He spoke these words in one breath and then downed the rest of his beer. 'Sorry to be so blunt. I'll have another one of these please.'

After a moment, Morty was gripped by the sudden and unshakeable certainty that Connall was having some kind of apoplectic fit. Wave after wave of what looked like pain crossed his face, and his hand was massaging his chest.

'Oh, god, mate,' Connall choked finally, as he wiped his eyes with what Morty judged to be a very hygienic bar cloth. 'Crikey, mate, look.' He rested both hands on the bar biting back a last bark of laughter. 'Look, I like you. I really do. You seem like a decent bloke, and you're willing to acknowledge what's right in front of your nose, which is a rare quality these days. But if you want to be part of this, then you're going to need to take the stick out of your arse, all right?'

Morty had no idea what he was talking about. 'What stick? Part of what?' He cast around in his brain, trying to find something familiar to hang the words on but failed miserably.

'You haven't had to deal with that much today, all right? Not really. Not in the scheme of things. Yes, you nearly got hit by a Tibetan singing bowl, and you've had an insight into a hidden world, and, sure, that's shaken you a bit. I get it. But you're still able to stand on your own two feet, and the way that you're knocking back those beers tells me you're doing okay. You'll be fine. You need to have more confidence in your own abilities. You need to back yourself more.'

'But I saw someone explode, Connall.' Morty's voice was high pitched, even to his own ears.

'Nah, it was vaporised. And it was just a mestomorph, if that helps at all.'

That didn't help in any way at all, and Morty told him so.

'Low level enforcers. Barely sentient. Easy to conjure and dominate, so that's why you'd see them called up for the kinds of dog's body work you saw today. Getting vaporised was probably the best thing that could happen to it. A quick and painless end.'

'I don't think so. You should have heard him scream.'

'All right, not painless then. But still, lucky escape.'

'I definitely need another drink,' Morty said weakly.

'Nah you're good,' Connall said. 'However…' He let the word hang in the air for a moment while he served more customers.

Morty stared fixedly down at the counter, strenuously avoiding eye contact with any of the other patrons. He needed to carefully curate what his brain could take on at the moment, he decided.

The counter was made of heavy, dark wood, etched with untold year's worth of scratches and nicks. He idly ran his fingers over some of them, the deep grooves catching the tips of his fingers, varnish from what looked like a recent attempt to bring some life to the bar pooled in little dry pools in the gaps. He picked at one of these gaps while he listened to the conversations taking place around him, conversations about normal, mundane things. Cash in hand jobs available, the latest sushi drama, footy, things he would chat about if he were sitting in a pub in the afternoon with his friends. All sounded totally normal. As long as he didn't look up.

'However,' Connall continued, 'the fact remains that someone was looking for…' He paused for a moment, 'For this Cernunnos character, and it doesn't sound like they were just delivering a Tupperware order. Do you have any idea why this Laura —'

"Lauren.'

'Lauren, then, would be attracting this kind of energy to her shop? Why did a mestomorph end up randomly looking for this character where you work? How are you two related to any of this?'

Morty shrugged.

'Are you aware of what kinds of paranormal dealings she usually has?'

'Paranormal?'

'Yes, does she dabble in Other World dealings as a matter of course? I understand that you may not think of these things as Other World specifically, so we can just say paranormal, if you prefer.'

Morty looked at him blankly.

'Come on, you're her friend and colleague. Does she have regular communication with paranormal beings? Dealings of high strangeness? Portals or the like?'

An idea suddenly came to Morty. 'Oh, well, she's a green witch. And we're all in a coven together. That's probably it.'

Connall smiled a tight, patronising smile. 'Every white girl in Melbourne has a witch phase. I doubt it's that.'

'I don't know,' he conceded. 'I'd say no then. She would have told me.'

'Would she?'

'Yeah, probably not.'

Connall sighed heavily, something that he seemed to do an

awful lot, Morty thought. Then again, he was used to people sighing heavily around him.

'I'm not going to have time to deal with this at the moment, and I know you're not going to want to hear this right now, but it does need to be dealt with. Mestomorphs don't just get sent out, and portals don't get opened up on this plane of reality for no good reason. It is something that is going to need to be dealt with, and I'm flat chat already. You're going to take care of it for me.'

Morty let out a small yelp. 'I can't. And you're not that busy, surely. Can't you hire someone else to, I don't know, wait tables and pull beers? Actually, I can do that! I can work here, and you can go and … deal with it. See, I don't even know what the dealing with involves! I'd be much better at the beer pulling, really.'

Morty's fevered attention was drawn to the steep staircase than ran from the far side of the bar up into the dark recesses of an unseen upper level. It was partly hidden behind the half wall that closed off the bar, and the stairs twisted up narrowly, each step sunken in the middle where countless feet had trodden the grey ironbark down until each was a sculpture, a testament to journeys taken and ages past.

Wordlessly, every person still remaining in the bar had piled up their empty glasses, scrunched up their paper napkins, finished their packets of chips and placed everything in the centre of their tables. They had tidied the detritus the best that they could and then, without speaking, by what seemed like a silent and yet tacit agreement, each of them stood and made their way upstairs. As they trailed past him, Morty couldn't help but look. Every one of the people, for they were without a doubt people, even though their forms and outward appearances were nothing like he had ever seen before, gave Connall a smile, or a wink, or a wave, and because Morty sat with him and had been the focus of his attention all afternoon, they included him in these greetings too. So, Morty found himself giving a small, one fingered wave to everyone who passed him; the woman with the figure of a young Sophia Lauren and a single long beak, pelican like, that made up the front of her face; the man who walked on legs that looked as if they belonged to a small giraffe, with vines and leaves that trailed from his head down his back; a girl who looked entirely normal to Morty, until she turned and he saw that a thick, prehensile tail extended from what he assumed were custom made jeans. All these and more passed them by and headed up the stairs.

Connall watched them go and then turned back to Morty. 'Yeah, pulling beers isn't what takes up my time. Do you want to hear about it?'

Morty knew, with every fibre of his being, that if he said yes, then he would become part of this new world he had been given an insight into. But he also knew that as the last person had smiled and headed up the stairs that the choice had been taken out of his hands.

He helped clear the tables while Connall talked.

13

Leo assured Sybella that he was infinitely capable of blending into the background and that there was little to no chance he would be seen or even sensed, no matter how, and here he cleared his throat, 'intuitive and powerful' her friends might be. She pointed out though, quite accurately, that his very being filled most of the room in a way she couldn't quite put her finger on, and even if he made himself ephemeral or spectral, there would still be a good chance that someone would end up sitting on him, and while he might be perfectly comfortable with it, she would find it creepy.

They decided that the garden might be an appropriate place for him to spend the evening.

He said he was keen to watch what kind of rituals they got up to, and she clarified that through the window would give him all the access he needed.

Yes, he had agreed grudgingly. Through the window.

Roxy arrived first, which, as high priestess, she considered to be her duty. Sybella had always suspected that it was primarily to bark at people about what they had done wrong, or how the furniture should be arranged, or to critique the snacks. Roxy was a fun mix between a wiccan and a school prefect.

Sure enough, as Roxy stepped through the front door a few minutes after 6.00 pm, she frowned and then sniffed suspiciously, thrusting a bottle of red wine into Sybella's hands at the same time. 'Why can't I smell dinner?' she asked.

Sybella tilted her head to one side, perplexed. 'I don't really know how to answer that question. Is it a trick?'

'Really? It's not that cryptic, surely. I'd have thought it was pretty basic. Doesn't bode well for the evening if you're already stumped.'

Sybella rolled her eyes and checked the bottle, a nice South Australian Cab Sav. She turned and headed down the hallway, assuming that Roxy would follow her. 'Why are you in a bad mood already?' she called over her shoulder. 'You don't usually get to this stage until you've had to talk to Demniac for a while.'

'It's been a long day. This mood has been brewing since eight this morning, trust me.'

Roxy found many of the people she encountered over the course of a normal day to be idiots.

'It's your fault for becoming an accountant,' Sybella said, placing the bottle on the clear kitchen table. 'But then again, you wouldn't get to spend so much time looking harried and put upon if you had a job you actually liked, and then what would you do with yourself. It would spoil your whole aesthetic.'

Roxy and Sybella had never been able to quite establish which one of them annoyed the other more, but impartial observers seemed to think that each had their moments, and in general, it was pretty evenly matched.

'Wait.' Sybella's hand was still on the bottle, and she looked off into space for a moment. 'Was there something I was supposed to be doing?'

'Oh, for god's sake, are you serious?'

A faint, niggling memory began to stir in the back of Sybella's consciousness.

'This is a new level of flakiness, even for you,' Roxy was saying. 'I knew I should have sent out a clarifying email.'

'But isn't there a sabbat ritual tonight?'

Roxy glared at her. 'Is today a sabbat, Sybella?'

No ... ooooo?' Sybella chanced, taking the cues from Roxy's unimpressed face. 'Not even a minor one? Okay no, it's absolutely not. Who would think such a thing. Amateurs.'

'No,' Roxy said. 'No, it is not. You're the one who wanted us to get together, have dinner and talk about how to summon a thought form. Remember? Demniac is very excited. He's going to give us a masterclass or something dreadful like that. On thought forms. Because, and I remember this quite clearly, you were interested.'

She placed a bag on the table and glanced around the kitchen/ living room area, a not unappreciative expression on her face. Sybella had hit her stride with the tidying up near the end of the day, assisted by helpful suggestions from Leo. The benches and tables were cleaned off and wiped down, and all of the dishes had been washed and put away. The last of the afternoon's sun glinted through the large windows above the sink and cast rainbow shards of colour from the mismatched crystal and wine glasses on an exposed pine shelf onto the floor, creating a multi-coloured waterfall on the lino.

'Not bad,' Roxy said. 'I like what you've done here. Flowers too. Good touch.'

Sybella frowned at the vase of sunflowers that sat in the middle of the table. It was true; it was a nice touch. She just had no idea where they'd come from. She glanced out the window, trying to catch a glimpse of the lion. He had his back to her, looking over the fence at a sheep who lived in the small garden next door who had evidently wandered over to see what was going on.

Very biblical, she thought.

'Are you seeing someone then?' Roxy asked abruptly.

'Okay, is this entire evening going to consist of you asking me questions completely out of context? Because I'm going to need to open this bottle before the others get here if that's the case.'

'No, I just wondered if you were seeing anyone because your eyes are doing this unusual twinkling thing, and you keep grinning. You look really happy. It's not like you at all. And,' Roxy gestured to the table, 'we have flowers.'

'I don't have to have a girlfriend to be happy,' Sybella protested.

'Although all the evidence over the past ten years would say otherwise, sure, we can go with that it you like.'

'But, no, I'm not seeing anyone. Not since Allison, and you know how that ended.'

Roxy shuddered involuntarily. 'How's that freezer spell going?'

Sybella went to her freezer and opened it, scrabbling at the back amongst the trays of ice blocks and banana she'd frozen in the vain hope she might become a smoothie person. 'Here it is,' she said, pulling out a ball of ice with a piece of paper frozen in its depths. 'Here she is.'

'She hasn't contacted you for a year now,' Roxy said sagely. 'I'd say its work is done and you can chuck it. And in future, try to resist your desire to date unbalanced and narcissistic women.'

Sybella shrugged. 'It works for a while. Hot makes up for a lot of sins.' She stroked the petals of the sunflowers that had appeared on the table. 'I don't think sunflowers are very romantic though. They seem so brusque and bony. I wouldn't fall in love with anyone who gave me sunflowers.'

'Choosy.' Roxy went to the sink and ran herself a glass of water. As she drank it, she looked out into the backyard, which was filled, as far as Sybella could see, with a huge lion involved in what looked like a very contentious conversation. 'That sheep is very interested in your yard,' Roxy said conversationally as she rinsed the glass and set it to dry in the tray. 'He needs a friend. The poor thing looks stressed.'

'I did forget about dinner, sorry,' Sybella admitted. 'And I forgot all about Demniac's masterclass thingy. For some reason, I had it in my head that it was a minor sabbat or some such today. I even had a shower for the occasion.' She gestured to the white cotton dress she was wearing. 'I'm feeling very vague today. I mean, oddly tidy, but vague.'

'Don't worry about it,' Roxy said, glancing over at her outfit, and Sybella knew that this magnanimity came from a deep desire to annoy Demniac more than from any genuine grace or forgiveness. 'We can just get pizzas or something. It's not that important. It's just nice for all of us to get together, you know? I haven't seen Lauren or Morty for weeks.'

'Ah, bless,' Sybella said.

Poor, put upon Morty.

There was a hard thudding on the door, and Roxy sighed. 'That'll be Demniac. I'll let him in.'

Sybella reached up and pulled down some wine glasses, then rustled through the fridge for some dip. She wasn't typically an inept hostess; the fact that she hadn't cooked a three course meal shouldn't reflect badly on her, she reasoned. And who volunteers to host a dinner party on a weeknight anyway? No one who knew her would expect such plans to actually eventuate. No, some hummus, corn chips and wine would have to do. They were here for high, spiritual reasons, and an unnatural focus on food would just stunt their growth.

And they could call for some Indian later.

She placed the just barely within the use by date tzatziki and some brie on the sink, and stifled a shriek as she saw the lion's huge face pressed up against the window.

'What are you doing?' she hissed, winding it open a touch. 'They'll be back in a second, and I don't want them to see me talking to you.'

'They won't see you talking to me. They'll see you talking to nothing.'

'Worse then. What's the matter?'

'I'm bored.'

She pursed her lips and put her hands on her hips. 'What am I supposed to do about that?'

'I think I should come in. I can transmogrify myself a bit and just kind of hover around. Behind the sofa, maybe. No one would know I was there. I'd get to listen to this Demniac character's wisdom, and I wouldn't be stuck in this yard with a sheep.'

'He's a perfectly nice sheep. His name is Nibbles.'

'He's a communist, apparently. I've no time for his ranting.'

Sybella glanced behind her, hearing voices drifting up the hallway. 'All right then. If you can shrink yourself down then come in. But I don't want to have to explain you to anyone, okay? Both Demniac and Roxy would be awfully annoyed and competitive if they discovered I have a real live thought form around. I find it hard to deal with their alpha-ness at the best of times, and typically I don't even have anything they're jealous or competitive about. I hate to think what would happen if they felt threatened by me.'

There was a shimmer in the air, and the lion disappeared from the window. She made a mental note not to shove the sofa too hard up against the wall if they decided to sit on the floor at some stage during the evening. Not being corporeal and all, she assumed he would be fine, but it was always prudent to err on the side of caution.

Demniac stepped into the room, already deep in conversation with Roxy. 'Actually, strictly speaking, an avoidance of the anthropomorphic ideas of religion is vastly preferable to a kind of convoluted and theoretically tenuous…'

Sybella had no idea how he had got to that stage already. He'd only been in the house for two minutes.

'Sybella,' Roxy said somewhat shrilly. 'Look, Demniac is here. Demniac, say hello to Sybella.'

'Yeah, we've met,' Sybella said. 'You know, about six years ago. And every month since. Why are you all nervous and babbly?'

'Just checking,' Roxy said and took the bottle from his hands. 'Another red. Fabulous. We're set for the evening.'

'As I was saying,' he continued, whereby both Sybella and Roxy quickly started an impassioned conversation about the weather. It was best to head him off at the pass as quickly as possible when he was in full flight. After all, he would have his turn talking at them later in the evening.

'Isn't anyone else here?' he asked, looking around suspiciously. He wasn't a suspicious person, as a matter of course, but for some reason his face indicated to the world that he was deeply suspicious about everything, everyone, all of their motives, and the world at large. He had a fussy little beard, which he had grown, Sybella was convinced, because he felt like it made him look ironically like an old timey magician.

All in all, he ended up looking like someone's pervy uncle, but no one had offered this feedback to him. He didn't take unsolicited advice very well.

'Morty and Lauren aren't here yet. I haven't spoken to them for a few days, but as far as I know, they're planning on being here,' said Sybella.

'That gives me time to get my PowerPoint ready,' he said, heading towards the living area.

'Don't move the sofa to find a power outlet,' Sybella called after him. 'A PowerPoint?' she hissed at Roxy. 'What the hell have we done to deserve this?'

'I promised him a chance at lecturing us last year, after that debacle with the orgy, remember? He was so disappointed that it didn't all pan out, so this was his consolation prize. He seemed excited about it.'

'To be fair, you never said anything about an orgy. It was his fault for misinterpreting 'group spiritual massage on the astral plane'.'

'I know, but he'd been so keen, poor love. I felt bad for him.'

'We all feel bad for Demniac. He relies on it.'

'Don't worry if you haven't brought your own pens for note-taking,' Demniac called from in front of the screens he was setting up. 'I've brought pens and notepads for each of you.'

Sybella deeply hoped that Morty and Lauren would arrive soon.

14

As they removed the books, a gargantuan white, shining chamber came into view. A wall, far in the almost indiscernible distance, curved around, as did the floor and the ceiling, and it looked like nothing so much as the inside of a huge unbroken egg. The white had a faint blue sheen to it, and recessed lights threw patches of illumination into the edges. It looked as different from the room they were currently sitting in as it was possible to be. It was as if someone took a designer from 1911 and one from 2100 and told them to collaborate on a visionary and exciting new project. Neither of them were able to agree, so they reached consensus by putting both things next to each other and splitting the difference.

A few extremely incongruous orange bollards blocked off a section just to the right of the gap they were peering through, and a series of what looked like operating tables. They were lined up, with stainless steel benches running along the side of them. A few piles of towels were scattered between them, and a huge movable spotlight on wheels sat in between, its power cord trailing off into the far distance.

Apart from that, the room was empty. Huge, empty, humming slightly, and inexplicably creepy.

'What is going on?' Brigid hissed.

'That reminds me of the area I was in when I first arrived,' shuddered Lauren.

She reclaimed her seat, looking around to see if there was a teapot so she could pour herself another cup. She couldn't see one, but noticing that Brigid hadn't finished hers, she decided that would do.

'What is going on?' Brigid said again, turning away from the bookcase. Her brow furrowed, and she bit her lip thoughtfully. 'I know that place.'

'This is cold,' Lauren said.

Brigid glanced over at her. 'That's my tea.'

'Do you want it?'

'Not now. It's cold.'

Lauren drank it.

There was a pause.

'I don't like the look of it in there,' Lauren said simply.

'Yes, it's a bit stark, isn't it. It looks like the kind of place where they do experiments on animals. I think...' Brigid tilted her head to one side as if clarifying a thought. 'I think it may be where the administrative hub of the Other World used to be.'

'Remind me of what makes up the Other World?' Lauren

asked. She finished the cold tea and returned the cup to the saucer.

'There's the Heavenly Realm, which is where you end up if you've been a vaguely decent person. It's where you'll find angels and the Chief Executive Officer, or God, whatever they're currently being called. The Shadow Lands are basically administration, where the assessors and reapers work. Lots of filing cabinets and meetings. And the Great Abyss is where … well, you know. Pretty bleak, really. Punishment and torment and algebra and the like. I mean, I ordered it shut down when I was in charge for a while, but who knows what's been done since then. A whole lot of re-branding probably. They really did need to re-look at the way things were being done. It was an absolute shemozzle.'

'So in there might have been the site of the main offices?'

'Possibly. It's got the same vibe.'

'I'm not going in there,' Lauren said simply.

'I'm not suggesting we do,' Brigid said. 'But I'm curious as to what's going on. Devin should have kept me in the loop.'

Lauren wasn't listening. 'I want to go home now.'

'Oh, really?' Brigid sounded crestfallen. 'I'm enjoying hanging out with you. I'll be bored when you go.'

'Come with me.' Lauren's voice rose in excitement, and she leaned forwards, her elbows on her knees. 'To Melbourne. You know, your proper home.'

'Yeah, I could, I guess,' Brigid replied. 'I could just pop down and catch up with everyone. See what's happening.' She looked around. 'Not strictly sure how to make popping home happen though.' She stood and peered down the corridor. 'I still don't know where everybody has gone. It's very quiet and weird here today.'

'This is bullshit. Matron!' yelled Lauren.

'Who?' Brigid glanced around, puzzled.

'That glidey being who brought me to you. She seems to have her finger on the pulse.'

Brigid nodded. 'Oh, her. You call her Matron, do you? That's funny. She'll hate that. And there'll be hell to pay for these books on the floor. I'm not taking the blame, just so you know.'

A familiar shimmering caused a wave of distortion in the air, and a figure appeared. She looked at Lauren with a pained expression. 'I'm not called Matron, you know.'

'Yet here you are. Things would have been easier if you had just told me your name at the outset.'

'I didn't realise we'd be interacting quite this much.' Her gaze came to rest on the books strewn all over the carpet. 'Really? Again? I've been sweeping up glass for the past hour.'

'Sorry about that,' Brigid said. 'Would you like some help?'

'Don't bother. I'll do it myself just like I have to do everything else around here given it's time for the Tournament'

Brigid's eyes grew wide. 'It's not, is it?'

Matron nodded.

'Already? Well, I'll be. That comes around quickly, doesn't it? No wonder everyone is off getting organised.'

'Exactly. And they haul you up here to get you to deal with Cally. I mean, of all the times.'

'I know, right?' They rolled their eyes at each other in faux exasperation.

'She knows about that?' Lauren looked back and forth between the two. 'The Cailleach business?'

'Of course I know.' The Matron busied herself slipping the books back onto the shelves. 'Why wouldn't I know?

'I thought it might be high level goddess business. Need to know, secretive business. Special stuff.'

'Yet here you are.'

If Lauren hadn't known better, she would have thought she saw a twinkle in Matron's eye.

'She said yes, by the way,' Brigid said. 'I asked her if she would help with the … situation, and she said she'd be happy to.'

'Steady on,' Lauren said. 'Happy is a strong word.'

Matron eyed Lauren again. She had never in her life felt so spectacularly judged.

'Do you have a plan?' asked the Matron.

'A plan? Not yet, clearly. I've just heard about it. I don't think it's unreasonable to not have a plan about how to psychologically manipulate an ancient crone goddess yet. I mean, I'll have to mull it over for a while. Give it a bit of a think.'

Matron finished pushing the empty books back on the shelves and blew out an exasperated puff of air. 'Don't let yourself get intimidated by the hype. She may be an ancient crone goddess, but her bark is worse than her bite. I remember when Brigid here was a baby and we —'

'All right, thank you,' interrupted Brigid sharply. 'Anyway, I was thinking of heading down to spend some time in Melbourne.'

'Excellent idea,' Matron said. 'Get yourself busy. I wouldn't mind some pasta and coffee myself, if I didn't have a million things to do up here.'

'Except I don't have any powers at the moment, so I can't get back.' Brigid looked at her expectantly. 'And neither does Lauren. Because we're human. Remember.'

Matron put her hands on her hips. 'No, I can't remember, to be honest. I can't keep up with whether you're a human or a goddess. You've been flip-flopping for over forty years now. It's giving me a headache. Can't you find a portal?'

'I have not been flip-flopping,' Brigid argued. 'I was quite decisively and convincingly a human for fortyish years until someone (and here she spoke into the air above their heads, and Lauren peered around looking for a camera of some sort but could see nothing) 'decided to ruin my sabbatical and make me do things.' She put her hands on her hips and glared at Matron. 'Twice.'

'Don't take that tone with me,' Matron protested. 'I told them not to.'

'Yes, yes, I know. I'm sorry,' Brigid said. 'But if you could just show me where the nearest portal is then we'll head down.'

Matron thought for a moment. 'Now you're testing me. They've been moving things around in preparation, of course. I think … I think there's one in the cleaning cupboard. A portal that is. It hasn't been used for ages. Actually…' She cast around under her robes and pulled out a carabiner with several devices on it that looked like a remote car unlocking device. 'We don't even use portals anymore. They were phased out. We have these. Dimenso-Zaps, they call them. Apparently, that went very well with the focus group, although it's a ridiculous name if you ask me.' She handed one to Lauren and one to Brigid.

'Why did they phase out portals?' Brigid asked as she turned the device over in her hand. 'I love them.'

'People kept finding them on Earth and walking into them. I blame that whole global Earth consciousness palaver that you're all obsessed with. There's a new interest in portals and other dimensions.' She glowered at Lauren. 'Isn't there?' she asked pointedly.

'Don't blame me,' Lauren said. 'I just sell books about it. It's not my fault people want to read them.'

'Anyway, when they phased out portals they made hundreds of these, but I think most have been lost or are down the back of couches somewhere. You might as well have one each. Save us having to listen out if you need to come up any time.'

Brigid sighed and took it from Matron, shoving it in her pocket. 'I don't want to be coming up and down; that's the point. And should you really be giving Lauren one? She's not official in any way, shape, or form.'

'Oh, it won't matter,' the Matron said. 'They'll all be wiped when the next person to win the Tournament is decided anyway, so she won't have it for that long.'

'What is this Tournament anyway? Asked Lauren.

'Just the way of deciding who rules all space and time for the next 3 thousand years,' replied Brigid.

'Oh, is that all. Lauren took the device and looked at it curiously. It was about the size of her thumb, curved, with one button on the front. There was a white symbol on the button that looked like a box with an up and down arrow in it. 'This looks like the button in a lift,' she said.

'That works,' Matron said. 'Now off you go.'

'Fabulous.' Brigid held out her hand to Lauren. 'Would you care to take a take a short trip with me?'

Lauren laughed and said that there was nothing she would rather do.

After all, she couldn't leave poor Morty alone. She hated to think what disasters he had already caused.

15

The room had been darkened for the occasion. Candles were lit, and incense was pouring out of the mouth of a green man cone burner. Sybella had grabbed some foliage from her garden to decorate the room, but the look of nature-based worship was somehow diminished by the fact that her big screen TV was hooked up to Demniac's laptop. The accessories and fripperies of the coven were usually hotly contested. Demniac strongly believed that his use of technology was an integral part of the chaos magicians experience, even though the apparent extent of his technological prowess was a PowerPoint with the fragment effect.

'We can't wait for them,' he said after Sybella had finished arranging a eucalyptus bough along back of the sofa, thinking this might prevent anyone moving it and creating lion issues that she didn't want to deal with. 'They'll just have to miss out. I've sent them each numerous messages, but they haven't replied, so it's their loss.'

'Maybe they finally hooked up and they're in a motel somewhere,' Roxy said.

'Ew, don't,' Sybella said, folding one leg under her as she perched on the end of the sofa with a glass of wine. 'First of all, gross. Second of all, he'd die if she said yes. You know he only loves her because she's unattainable.'

'Let's get on with it then,' Roxy said. 'Let's just get this over with.'

Demniac glowered at her.

'I mean, let's get started. Super keen.'

'Right,' he said briskly. 'Let's see what knowledge we're starting with. What prior understandings we have.' He handed out some sticky notes and pens. 'Obviously, this would work better if we had a quorum, but let's just do our best.'

Roxy rubbed her head. 'We're doing audience participation now, are we? That's a fun little extra.'

'You're not an audience, you're my students. And I want to get an idea of what we're starting with. If I say tulpa, or thought form, I want you to write down the first thing that comes into your head.'

'I bet you don't,' Sybella muttered. She could feel something moving behind the sofa. Something bulging, as if a large dog were trying to squeeze in behind it. She cast a sideways glance at Roxy sitting next to her, but she hadn't noticed and was already scrawling things on the yellow sticky notes she had been given. Deciding to humour Demniac, she wracked her brain to think of something useful to write, settling on, 'Creating a thought form isn't as hard as we've been led to believe. Also, tulpa isn't the correct word'. She needed to write on the back of the paper to fit it all on.

'Right.' Demniac took the notes from both of them and stuck them to the screen. 'As I said, this works better if we have more knowledge to draw on, but we'll have to make do.'

He stood back and read out loud the comments that Roxy and Sybella had written. 'My Little Pony,' he said shortly.

'Yes,' Roxy said. 'From what I've read on the internet, tulpas basically involve young adults with social anxiety making imaginary ponies to have sex with.'

Demniac's lips pressed together, but Roxy continued. 'They make up these imaginary friends, and then they think they've actually come to life, and I don't know how, but they have sex with them. I saw an actual My Little Pony sex doll advertised the other day. With holes and a nylon sheath over it and everything.'

'Fuck off,' Sybella said, aghast. 'That's a freaking kid's toy. That's not okay.'

'I know. I hate to kink shame, but … actually, no, I don't. That's rife for shaming. Maybe if these stunted adults left their bedroom occasionally and met — '

'Anyway,' Demniac said, finally unpursing his lips. 'If we could move on. Sybella, you've written…' He cast his eyes over her notes. 'Isn't as hard as we've been led to believe. And some other strong opinions.' He clapped his hands efficiently. 'I can see tonight's masterclass isn't coming a moment too soon. We're dealing with some deep misconceptions here.'

'Not according to Reddit,' Roxy muttered, and Sybella giggled.

'Actually,' started Demniac, which only made Sybella giggle more.

'Actually,' he plugged on regardless, 'the current idea of tulpas in popular culture is part of a far, far older Tibetan idea, and that is what we will be studying tonight. Yes, there has been a resurgence of interest of late, but it is a deeply mystical concept that was seen, within Buddhism, as one of the fruits of contemplative life. This new fad of conjuring up furries is a fad and a pale imitation of what they're supposed to be. And, obviously, not real.'

Sybella felt another stirring behind the sofa and pushed her elbows back in an attempt to stop the movements.

'Many of the so called tulpas,' Demniac said, starting the PowerPoint, 'that are created today are, to be honest, merely laughable delusions, and the incredible dedication, learning and trance state needed to hold the space necessary for bringing one to fruition is something that the new generation just doesn't have the capacity for.'

'Bullshit.' Sybella heard a rumble from behind her. 'This boy doesn't know what he's talking about. Ask him about other species of thought forms. I don't think he's working with all the information. Where did he learn this rubbish?'

Sybella leaned forwards, fixing Demniac with look. 'What about other categories of thought forms and summoned entities?' she asked. 'Is this just confined to tulpas and 'kids these days'? They must have existed in other cultures as well?'

'My particular sphere of interest has looked at the phenomenon from the perspective of eastern practitioners, but I would certainly say that the absolute steely quality of the contemplative mind needed to make any real material changes to the physical Universe can only be accessed by those undertaking deep, almost cellular meditative states.'

The lion spoke again. 'That's not true. Tell him he doesn't know what he's talking about. You drew a picture after looking it up online for ten minutes, for goodness' sake. And I'd be willing to bet that the closest you've ever got to a cellular meditative state has something to do with that glass of wine in your hand. It's far more common than he thinks. Why has he set himself up as the teacher? Does he have some deep wisdom that he's hiding?'

'Are you sure it's that hard to do?' she asked Demniac, quite politely she thought. 'Because as far as I understand it—'

'As far as you understand it?' he said, pointing to her note that he had now affixed to the back of a dining chair. 'What, this? This is your understanding, is it? I am a chaos magician and—'

'Careful, tiger,' Roxy said. 'You don't need to be quite so defensive just because someone else knows something about your particular obsession.'

'I'm just asking,' Sybella continued, 'because I'm wondering whether Buddhists have the monopoly on this. A friend of mine has told me that creating thought forms from consciousness is pretty widespread.'

'It most certainly is not.'

'I think you'll find that it is. My friend—'

'Rubbish.'

'Demniac, why are you taking this so personally? She's just asking genuine questions. Why is it so odd that other people might know about this too?'

'This is my thing,' Demniac said. 'I've been researching this for weeks.'

A choking cough came from behind the sofa.

'My friend—'

Demniac held his had up in a peacemaking gesture. 'Look, I know. I'm sorry. I had a specific idea of how this class was going to run, and you two are not sticking to the script. Which friend are you talking about?'

Sybella thought for a moment. 'Leo, his name is. I met him through ... Lauren. He works in the shop. He's created one of these thought forms that you are talking about, but it's not called a tulpa. That's only the Tibetan ones.'

'Have you seen it?'

Sybella decided to jump right in and hang the consequences. 'Yes, I have.'

Demniac looked thunderstruck.

'Tell him it's cultural appropriation,' a growl came from behind her. 'That'll throw him.'

'And since they are Tibetan, wouldn't trying to manifest a tulpa be cultural appropriation? Shouldn't you look to other … species of thought forms?'

Demniac's facade of authority and control began to crumble. He had placed his lecture notes on the table and was rubbing his hands together anxiously. 'I hadn't thought of that,' he muttered. 'But you say you've seen this? You've met a sentient thought form? With its own consciousness.'

'I have,' she said. 'Honestly. He's quite opinionated.'

'That's incredible.' Demniac's eyes had become wide with something like excitement. 'Could I meet him? Could you introduce us?'

From behind the sofa, she heard Leo begin to make a comment, when suddenly the door to her bedroom swung open and out stepped Lauren, followed by Brigid. Given that her bedroom had no other doors apart from the one they had just walked through, Sybella's focus was immediately taken up by the question of where the hell they had come from and what on earth Lauren was wearing, and Leo's question was lost in the noise.

16

By the time the bar area was clean, and Connall had finished talking, it was a deep dark outside, and the lights had been turned on. The bare bulbs that protruded from the wall sconces threw out dull, muted light, and the shadows that drew around the men as they sat by the fire seemed companionable, adding to the feeling of homeliness that had settled around the room.

Upstairs, the noises of scuffling, footsteps and the bangs of activity had gradually died down as people had laid down their swags, their sleeping bags and arranged their many and varied anatomies in the most comfortable ways they could, and now all was quiet.

Morty stared into the fire. His eyes seemed to rest comfortably there, relaxed, while his mind raced.

'So,' Connall said after a moment. A log burned through and fell, sending sparks from the embers beneath it. 'That's the story. I've never told anyone the whole thing before. You either know this information or you don't, in general. But after your run in with the mestomorph today, you seem to have become involved with Other World business, wouldn't you say?'

Morty nodded. 'These beings...' he started.

'People,' Connall prompted. 'They think of themselves as people. But they are also called Imagos.'

'These people, then. These people are ... real. They exist. And they live amongst us, but we are completely unaware of it?' Morty was glad his beer buzz had worn off hours ago. He was finding it hard enough to make sense of things as it was.

'Do you need the cliff notes version again?'

'I think so, yes.'

'Scientific explanation or basics?'

'Basics. You lost me with the technical stuff. Give me an overview then I'll ask focused questions.'

Connall smiled and held his glass up to the fire, watching the flames through the liquid. 'To humans they are, by and large, invisible, and to Other World beings they are an embarrassment. They are created out of people's ideas and dreams and for the most part aren't psychically attached to their creators, so they have no one. No support system, no one to depend on. They try and attract attention, like the child of a neglectful parent, but their creator writes them off as a bad dream or a delusion, not able to imagine that they themselves have created it. If they catch a glimpse of them out of the corner of their eye, they will think it's a trick of the light or their imagination.

'But I can see them,' Morty protested. 'I saw them all around me today.'

Connall nodded. 'That's true. You did. Some people can see. Some rare people who have had certain experiences—'

Morty nodded sagely. 'That would probably be the Arcturian healing chamber transmission I received last year.'

'It most definitely wouldn't be that. That kind of thing is a load of absolute gobshite. It's more likely to be left over resonance from your run in with the mestomorph. You know that there are other things out there, so now you see them.'

Morty looked perplexed.

'There's no reason why Imagos can't be seen. They aren't strictly blood and bone like you, but they also aren't ephemeral or spectral. People have just enough awareness of them not to run into them in the street. You'd veer around them not knowing why you've randomly stepped into the gutter.'

'Are they still being created?'

'Yes, all the time. Some aren't strong enough to manifest completely, and they just fade away. Others follow their creator around hoping for love and attention. Most eventually leave to find other Imagos. The majority die off.'

'Die off?'

'Nothing to live for. And they're not officially sanctioned beings, so there's no afterlife for them. Unless a being was created by the big guy, then you're on your own. It's bullshit.'

'Why are they disliked? Because they're...' Morty tried to find the right words. 'Slightly unusual looking?'

'Not really,' Connall said. 'There are plenty of more ridiculous looking beings that have their place in the grand scheme of things. No, it's because they're created by humans who have no clue what they're doing. You're not evolved enough to bring new beings into existence. Because of that, they're seen as little more than vermin, an irritant. Some particularly nasty Other World beings make sport of killing them. Just like your lot would too, I suspect, if they were more widely known.'

Morty frowned. 'Your lot? Does that mean you're not human?'

Connall smiled. 'Let's just say that I've been around for a long time. So long that I've had a chance to really decide what I wanted to do and work on it. I realised that these poor creatures needed a champion, someone to advocate for them, so I stepped in. And also there's the less selfless but more pressing matter of the fact that the murder of Imagos is causing a dangerous instability.'

'Where?'

'There are flurries in the undertow.'

'That sounds quite fun.'

'Decidedly not fun. It's quite bad, all things considered.'

'All right,' said Morty. 'But you're not one of them? An...'

'Imago? No, I'm not.'

'I have so many questions.'

Connall yawned. 'I can imagine. But I have to do the night shift tonight, so I can't stay here much longer.'

'Can I...' Morty paused, wondering how to pose this question. 'I mean, I'd like to...' He took a deep breath. 'I want to know more about this, and I want to help. Do you need someone to help you? To work here? With you? Because if what you've told me is true, then there's a whole world I didn't know about, and I need to be part of it.'

Connall stood to unlock the heavy door, the cold night air sweeping into the warm open bar area. 'Look, mate, I do appreciate that, but I've been doing this on my own for a long time.'

'Even more reason for you to get someone else involved,' Morty said as he stepped outside.

'How about you come back tomorrow then. Sleep on it and see what you think in the light of day?'

Connall looked after the young man as he stepped quickly

down the dark street. He didn't need to use his powers of foresight to know that he would return tomorrow.

17

'Oh, shit,' Lauren said, laughing nervously. 'I thought this was your house, but I wasn't totally sure. Lucky, hey. Sorry I'm late.'

Everyone in the room had paused, seemingly in the middle of a vigorous conversation

'How did you get into my bedroom?' Sybella asked, quite politely she thought.

'Um.' Lauren glanced behind her, looking back into the room. 'Window? Yes, definitely window. You shouldn't leave it open. Dangerous. Stalkers. Are we getting Indian for dinner? I bet Brigid would love some. What have you been eating anyway, Brigid? Potatoes, I bet. She's just got back from Ireland. Jet-lagged. Dip?'

During the minute between she and Brigid materialising in the room, and her realisation that she was going to have nothing like a good explanation for how she had got there, she had decided that dash and bravado was going to have to do.

It seemed to be working.

Roxy stood and offered them the sofa, Demniac grabbed some wine glasses, and Sybella put the hummus and flatbread within their reach.

'How are you, Brigid?' Roxy asked tightly. 'Nice to see you're not dead. Back for good or just a holiday?'

'Just a holiday,' Lauren said, not trusting Brigid to speak for the moment. She was looking slightly goggle-eyed at her surroundings. 'I think you've met Sybella but not Demniac. Demniac, this is my friend Brigid. She's been away, but she's dropped in for a while. She's staying with me.'

'Oh, no,' Brigid said, seemingly coming to her senses. 'No, no, I'll stay at my place. Thanks, though.'

'Is your place still there?' Lauren asked.

'Yes, of course. Why wouldn't it be?'

'Because you moved,' Roxy said. 'Quite quickly, if I remember correctly. You just left, with no explanation or, you know, bags. Right? Out of the blue. Lauren was very upset. We had a seance.'

'Yes,' Brigid said, her smile fixed. 'I did leave quite quickly, but it wasn't exactly my choice, and I never sold it, so I don't see why it wouldn't still be there.'

'Goodness.' Roxy smiled in a frighteningly unnerving manner. 'It was a rush, wasn't it.'

'It was a tricky and delicate situation,' Brigid said tightly. 'Things crept up on me, and they were slightly beyond my control. I couldn't just make a phone call, could I?'

'You couldn't?' Lauren asked. 'You couldn't contact me in any way at all? I thought you'd gone to Ireland, not 1760.'

'Oh, for god's sake, don't you start.' Brigid put her hands on her hips and glared at Lauren. 'I thought we'd sorted this out? I did send you an email, and I also bought you a fucking shop, and you got to have a fun seance in the bargain.'

'Um, actually,' Demniac said, happy to be able to have something to offer to the conversation. 'It wasn't that fun. I think there's still something residual in my apartment, as a matter of fact.'

'I am not taking the blame for that,' Brigid snapped.

'While we're on the topic, we need to talk about the shop,' Lauren said. 'I have some feelings about it that we need to get out in the open.'

'We are not 'on' the topic,' Brigid said. 'But obviously we still have some issues to thrash out surrounding this. Maybe they could wait until we aren't guests in someone's home?'

'Are you two dating?' Demniac asked.

'No, not at all,' Brigid snapped. 'I'm married. To someone else. We just need to clear some things up.'

'You've timed this well,' Demniac continued. 'We're not having a full ceremony tonight.'

'This is your coven, is it,' Brigid said. 'Cute.'

There was an awkward silence in the room.

'We're just talking about tulpas, and Sybella said your friend Leo is a bit of an expert, and I was hoping I could have a chance to meet him.'

'You find the coven cute, do you?' said Roxy whose eyes were fixed pointedly on Brigid.

'She's jet-lagged,' Lauren snapped. 'I told you that. She only got back today. Give her a break. And who's Leo?'

'Remember Leo?' Sybella's eyes bored into Lauren in a non-negotiable way. 'I met them in your shop. You introduced us. It's a pretty important thing to remember.'

'Er, no,' Lauren said. 'But I meet a lot of people and... oh, hang on. Yes, yep. Absolutely. I remember totally. Leo. Fabulous. Love him. Big fan.'

'I'd love to meet him sometime,' Demniac said. 'I'm fairly well versed in the whole tulpa phenomenon, but from what Sybella has been saying, there may be an entire area that I've been ignorant of, and I'd love to speak to someone who knows about it.'

'Yep, sure, whatever,' Lauren said. She was about done with the day. It had been one of twists and turns and migraines and reunions, and she decided that she was ready to wrap things up. 'Where's Morty?'

'We thought he'd be with you.'

'No, I haven't seen him. I left him in charge of the shop.'

'That was brave,' Roxy offered. 'He's probably still there, waiting for you to tell him to close.'

'Look, given that Brigid definitely needs to go to bed and my shop might be in ruins, we might have to call it a night.'

Demniac was looking off into space. 'I think it's probably for the best all things considered. If this is true, and there really is an entire realm of this phenomenon that I'm unaware of, I need to do some deep study before I continue imparting information about it to others. I'd say I need a day or two before I'm fully versed in it. As I said, I'd love to meet with your friend, but I'll also have a read around and—'

Another rumble came from behind the sofa. More annoyance. 'I'll talk to him if it means he will start to take things seriously and not dance around with concepts he doesn't understand.'

'I think Leo would be happy to meet with you,' Sybella said.

'Great. Well, this has been, er, fun, but I think it's best we wrap it up now and reconvene at a later time.' He was packing up his laptop and carefully filing the sticky notes.

'I'm not leaving,' Roxy said, making herself comfortable at the table. 'All this discussion has made me even hungrier, and I'm not going anywhere until I get my Baingan bharta.'

Brigid laughed, apparently not at all bothered by Roxy's abrasive manner. 'I'm starving too. Lauren's right. That jet-lag's an absolute bugger. Anyway, who wants to hear all about the roses that my extremely handsome husband planted for me?'

<h1 style="text-align:center">18</h1>

Brigid still had her house key, which Lauren thought was strange, but admittedly not the strangest thing that had happened that day. She pushed open the door and automatically reached for the light switch.

'Huh,' Brigid said as the lights flared on in the hallway. 'That's surprising.'

'Why is your electricity still on?' Lauren asked.

Brigid shrugged, throwing her keys on the table near the front door. 'To be honest, I don't even ask about the things that happen to me anymore. I just duck and weave when the occasion arises and hope I'll find a sofa to lay on every now and then.' She glanced into doorways as she walked towards her lounge room, seemingly happy with what she was seeing.

'Why isn't this place dusty?' Lauren asked, running her fingers along the clean mantelpiece. 'It looks like you've had a cleaner coming in?'

Brigid frowned. 'Actually, yeah, that might be it. I don't think I ever cancelled him. It's been getting cleaned every fortnight I guess.'

'But didn't—'

'Money direct deposited and he has a key. I guess he just liked the fact I didn't leave passive aggressive notes about what I wanted done. I hope he's been feeding the fish.'

She bent down and peered into the glass, the slight glow highlighting the rocks and perspex branch that stretched across the bottom of the pebbles. 'Ah. Apparently not.'

'Delightful.'

Brigid grabbed a cloth from the kitchen and draped it respectfully over the tank. She put her hands on her hips and looked around. 'I must say, it's quite nice to be home.'

'Where is your cat?' asked Lauren.

'She went to live in the country,' replied Brigid.

'Oh my god,' said Lauren, her hand raising involuntarily to her throat. 'The poor little love.'

'No, she really did. She went up to Mum and Dad's. That's not a euphemism.'

'Thank god for that,' said Lauren. 'I missed you.'

Brigid smiled at her. 'I missed you too.'

'But I made Sharon my best friend in the interim.'

'What? Sharon from the corner shop?'

'Yes, she makes a good curried egg sandwich. And she was around to listen.' Lauren looked around the room. 'Is this all as you left it?'

'Pretty much. I think so. I mean, I didn't know the day that I left would be the day that I actually left, if you know what I mean. Want a cuppa?'

There was fresh milk in the fridge.

Cup in hand, Brigid picked up a white furry throw that was draped over the sofa and frowned at it. 'This isn't mine,' she said.

'It's in your house.'

She glanced around the room, frowning. 'That's not my picture either.'

Lauren looked at the print of Van Gogh 'Sunflowers'.

'You hate Van Gogh.'

'I do. Unmitigated tripe, his stuff is. Rubbish. I'd never put that on my wall.'

'Well, it's there. Look at it. It's positively looming at you.'

'I could paint better than that.'

'You could.'

'What's going on?'

'Dammit,' Brigid sighed, laying back on her chair and closing her eyes. 'All I wanted was a nice bit of time here at home, maybe hang out with you, maybe try going back to the gym or something, passing on the fact that it would be great if you could convince the ancient Goddess Cailleach to rack off back to where she came from, and now it looks as if I have to deal with people breaking into my house and leaving things lying around. Do I sound to you like I can deal with that kind of ridiculousness?'

'Yes, but surely having someone come into your house and bringing random decorative items is better than someone coming in and stealing your DVD player?'

'Does it have to be one or the other?'

'Apparently.'

Lauren reached out and picked up a paperweight from the table beside her. 'This is new too, isn't it?'

Brigid took it from her and peered into its depths. 'There's a beetle in here. Yuck. Whoever is leaving me stuff needs to get a more finely nuanced understanding of my taste; otherwise, I'd prefer they started nicking stuff.'

She laid it gently back on the table and ran her fingers through her hair. Pulling the strands in front of her eyes she sighed. 'Look, my hair's not as red as it used to be either.'

'We're getting old.'

'No, it's not as red as it is when I'm in the Other World. It's just a further reminder that I'm not my full self when I'm down here. It's fucking annoying, if you ask me. When Devin and I arranged that I would spend a lifetime on Earth, he really didn't make it clear I'd be a half person.'

Lauren coughed on her drink. 'Half a person?'

'I was supposed to be a proper, impressive person here too, yet even my hair won't stay fiery. Devin said—'

'Sorry, who's Devin?'

'The one in charge. The CEO. God, if you like. But as I said, they're moving away from traditional nomenclature—'

'God's name is Devin.'

'Yes.'

'Huh. I always thought God was like, a rough amorphous thing, a quality, if you will. An ephemeral presence. Not an old white guy with a beard.'

'He's not an ephemeral presence, that's true, but think 'hot young guy' and you're on the right track. He used to be old, but I think he's ageing in reverse. He had a really stressful time last year, but things seem to be smoothing out a bit.'

'God is hot?'

'So hot.'

'And you know him?'

'We hang. Have hung, at least. Most of us, you know, higher deities spend time together when we get the chance. It's kind of a whole lose pantheon if you want to be precise, but you need someone to oversee everything, don't you? I'm one of... well, hundreds really. It's a flexible management structure.'

'It's weird that we've never had this conversation before,' Lauren said. 'I feel like it would have come up by now.'

'Most of this is news to me too. Devin and I agreed to wipe my memory completely and have me born on Earth. I needed a break.'

'You really couldn't think of any other way to relax, but becoming a human? You couldn't have tried yoga or taken CBD? Humans are the most uptight things in the Universe, surely? Or you could have been a cat. They give zero fucks.'

Brigid shrugged. 'I dunno. Seemed like a good idea at the time, and Devin knows better than to argue with me when I've got my mind set on something.'

'Do you regret it?'

The sound of a noisy clock ticking reverberated through the room.

'No, not at all. I don't think so, anyway.'

'But at least you know that you're special and important now, right?'

'I am. I'm very special and important. That's why my house is increasingly full of budget warehouse post-impressionist prints.'

They both jumped as Lauren's phone trilled from within the depths of her bag. She started digging through the detritus that filled it, thrusting a glitter notebook, a limp stuffed bunny and a tin of barley sugar towards Brigid, before victoriously pulling the phone out and pressing answer before 'Slice of Heaven' could finish its second refrain.

'Morty, hi, love, how did the day go? What's happening? Are you okay? You weren't at Sybella's house. Please tell me you're not still at the shop?'

There was a pause, and Lauren listened carefully, her eyes bulging out a little in her head, and as far as Brigid could tell, her breath stopping entirely.

'Trashed? Who....' She listened intently for a moment and then began to gesticulate wildly with her hands. 'No, of course it's not your fault. I'm not saying that it is. I just... yes, yes. Okay. Okay. I'll see you in the morning. Try to sleep okay?'

Feeling uncomfortable at overhearing what seemed to be a fairly emotional and fraught conversation, Brigid stood and wandered around her lounge room. Things looked mainly as they had when she had left it so quickly a year ago, but now that she was paying attention, there were some subtle differences. Extra pieces of decor had been added, and she couldn't be entirely sure, but she had the strong suspicion that the carpet was a different colour.

'Somehow, my shop got trashed today,' Lauren said, finishing up her conversation. 'Something strange happened, and now Morty is raving about imaginary friends and serial killers, and I'm really worried that my insurance might not cover it if he's ended up with PTSD from being damaged by a break in when I left him in charge. I should have known it was a bad idea, but nooooo, it couldn't wait, could it?'

Brigid stood up. 'Right, we clearly need to sleep on it. Do you want to stay here for the night?'

Lauren pulled the furry throw around her and decided that the sofa would make the perfect bed, and that everything else could wait till tomorrow.

19

They surveyed the wreckage.

Morty vowed that he wasn't going to be the first one to speak. He was absolutely not going to be the first one to speak. He knew once he started, he would begin to babble, and that would make it sound like this was all his fault. It wasn't his fault at all, and the more he talked about it, the less he would believe that.

'It's not my fault,' he said.

'Theoretically, I know,' Lauren said. 'I do, I promise. I'm just finding it a bit hard to take this all on board right now.' She was looking up at the ceiling, which caved ominously. 'Is that structural, do you think? Or can I paint over it?'

'There was a vortex. And a guy in a suit. Without a face. Well, he did have a face. It was a mestomorph, apparently, but I didn't know that until after the fact. A mesomorph with a face in a suit with a vortex—'

'Morty, stop.' Lauren held up her hand. 'Even you couldn't make this much of an absolute cock-up on your own. Stop babbling because you're making me annoyed at you whereas I should be focusing on whatever the hell happened here.'

'They were looking for someone called Cernunnos, and when I said they weren't here they—'

'They were looking for the horned god of the forest?'

'That doesn't sound right, now you say it like that. Is that who Cernunnos is?'

'You need to brush up on your Celtic mythology. So, the question is, why were they looking for him here, and why do they, whoever they are, want him?'

'They got liquidated when they couldn't find him, so I'm assuming it's not a good reason.'

Lauren began to pick up tubes of activated charcoal henna toothpaste that were scattered around the floor. 'I'll need to get the insurance people on to this anyway. Did you call the police?'

'I wasn't sure whether you would have wanted me to or not but yes.' He took the tubes from Lauren and placed them in a basket on the front counter.

'Do you think you have PTSD?' she asked, peering at him closely. 'Are you traumatised?'

'I wouldn't think so. I had a pretty good debrief after it.'

'Really?' Lauren looked surprised. 'That's great. Good on you.' She sat on a stool and looked around. 'Look, I might continually complain about this place and feel like it's a noose around my neck, but I'd rather not have it destroyed. I wonder if this has anything to do with Brigid. She's back by the way. Sorry, I forgot to tell you. Everything's happening at once. She's a goddess now.'

'What, and actual goddess? Which one?'

'Brigid, obviously.'

'Of course,' said Morty. 'Silly question I guess. Does she have any powers?'

'I don't think so.'

'Pity. She could have helped tidy up all this mess. You're going to be doing some high level goddessy stuff, are you?'

Lauren nodded with a touch of pride. 'You might be involved too, now I come to think of it. Coven business, I suspect.'

'That's quite a coincidence because I had some extreme high strangeness happen to me last night, and I'd love to talk to you about it. I just need to make sure I'm not getting in over my head.'

'I know about the odd thing that happened to you yesterday. I'm standing in the middle of it. Literally, I'm standing on a crushed dragon egg snow globe in a drift of tiger's eye gem chips.'

Morty shook his head. 'No, there's something else. Unrelated. Although maybe it's not. It's a bit odd that everything's happening at once. But no, it's a special thing. For me. I want to show you something.'

'You want to show me something?'

He nodded.

'As long as you understand this isn't the time to be trying to get into my pants again.'

'No, I'm not this time, I promise. Unless you'd...'

She shook her head.

'Okay fine, sorry. But I need you to come with me to a pub because there's another very odd thing happening, and I'd love your perspective on it. Plus, I've made a new friend.'

'Fine, sure, I've been telling you to find some new friends for ages, so I'm happy to support you in this. And I could do with a drink. But later, we need to try to get this place organised first.'

After several hours of work, they had barely made a dent in the mess, and Lauren decided to leave the door open on their way out. With any luck, someone would come and steal everything and save her some effort.

***

It was early evening by the time they made it to the pub, and Morty knocked on the heavy wooden door as Lauren pulled her coat more firmly around her and gazed into the alleyway. It was an old area; there was a plaque on the building opposite that said the street had been the site of an uprising of some two hundred years earlier. A group of Irish convicts had decided they'd had enough of being oppressed, thank you very much, and had taken off into the bush, knocking their overseer on the head on the way out.

The plaque was not a memorial to the tragically departed overseer, but to the convicts who had fled and become bushrangers, terrorising the outskirts of the settlement for the next twenty years.

Lauren took a moment to be proud of the fact she lived in a country where bosses being murdered by poverty stricken criminals was celebrated rather than reviled.

She realised that Morty was still banging on the door.

'No ones there,' she said helpfully.

Morty cupped his hands around the grey glass on a window that was set into the sandstone and peered in. There was nothing moving in the dark depths of the pub.

'No, there is,' he protested, knocking his fist against the door again. It's full of people. At least it was last night.'

'Of course it was full of people last night. It's a bloody pub. Is

102

your new friend the owner? They probably needed a break after meeting you yesterday.'

'You don't understand,' Morty said, his eyes beginning to look manic. 'This is a big thing. I'm becoming part of something really important. And this guy he was … he was amazing. There must be someone here. It's the only place that's safe for them.'

'Are you sure you're all right?' She reached out her hand and felt his forehead. 'Maybe you are traumatised. I've got a crystal grid that can analyse trauma back at—'

He pushed her hand away, irritated. 'I'm not traumatised, okay? Stop patronising me. This is important.'

Morty's heart was pounding, and he couldn't quite put into words the terrible, dawning realisation that this might have all been an elaborate prank, that there were no Imagos that needed his help, that there was no incredibly handsome, bearded man who...

'Hi, there,' Connall said, coming up behind them. 'I don't think you can diagnose trauma by taking someone's temperature, but to be fair, I'm not a doctor.'

Morty felt his heart fall back into something akin to its natural spot. 'Connall! I was just knocking.'

'I know,' Connall said. 'I could hear you from out on the road.'

'I wanted to introduce you to Lauren.'

'The famous Lauren, already?' Connall said. 'Isn't it a bit early to introduce me to your people? We've only just met, after all.'

Lauren barked out a delighted laugh. The man in front of her was the singularly most handsome man she had ever seen. He looked like Jason Momoa's rugged older brother, with a side of ZZ Top thrown in for good measure. She held out her hand.

'I see that my reputation precedes me,' she said, regretting it utterly and completely the moment the words were out of her mouth.

He gave her a wide grin, his eyes laughing.

'How's your shop?' he asked.

'Cactus,' she said.

'That's no good.' He twisted a large tarnished metal key in the brass lock and pushed open the door. 'That's really rough. There's nothing like having your own business to really wrench your heart out of your chest.'

'You own this, do you?' Lauren asked. 'I mean, it's your pub?'

They stepped into the cool room, and he locked the door behind them. Morty walked to the bar and took a seat on one of the stools.

'Its been mine for two hundred years,' he said.

'You mean, in your family,' she clarified.

'If you like.'

'I've only had The Tantric Om since last year, so it's not really comparable to what you feel here, I'd imagine.'

'It's making her very mercenary,' Morty shared. 'She used to be a total anti-consumerist hippy, but now she has an accountant and uses spreadsheets and everything.'

'I don't think we're here to discuss me though, are we?' Lauren snapped.

'Yes, on that point, why are you here?' Connall asked. 'Does Lauren know … what's been happening?'

'The evil infused portal in my shop, you mean?' she asked.

'Among other things, but yes,' Connall replied.

'I'm not surprised. Ever since I bought those knock off Ouija boards, I've been waiting for something to happen.'

'Nah,' Connall said, crouching down to light the fire that took up a significant proportion of the wall next to the bar. Its deep recess was banked with stone, and Lauren wondered how many drunken dock workers had tumbled into it over the years. 'I don't think that's it. Mestomorphs aren't ones to be interested in Ouija boards. The only entities that get involved in Ouija board shenanigans are between jobs or are having a mid-existence crisis.

Mestomorphs are gainfully employed.'

'All right,' Lauren said. 'So, do you know what's going on?'

'Someone wants Cernunnos for nefarious reasons, and I've decided to keep my head down and ignore it; that's what's going on.'

'Great, thanks, right.' She turned to Morty. 'Why are we here then?'

Morty looked rattled. 'There's a lot of other things going on, and I want you to know about them. And Connall could tell you.'

'Have you told her about my guests?' He waved his hand vaguely towards the ceiling.

'No, of course not. I didn't know if you'd want me to.'

'I'd much rather hear more about these mestomorphs than whatever English backpackers you've got upstairs. Weird paranormal stuff is my jam,' Lauren said.

'That makes things easier,' Connall said. 'Luckily. Don't make me regret bringing you into this.'

Morty gave him a cheerful thumbs up. He just felt happy to be included, as a matter of course.

'So, Lauren.' Connall pulled her a beer without asking, which she heartily approved of. 'It's your jam, is it? So you're fully comfortable with the whole gamut of paranormal and high strangeness events?'

'Very,' she said. 'My best friend is a physical manifestation of an ancient Celtic goddess, after all.' She laughed to make it quite clear that she could possibly have been joking if things got awkward.

'Really?' He placed the beer in front of her, his face interested. 'Which one? Ceridwen? The Cailleach?'

She stared at him through narrowed eyes. 'Are you making fun of me?'

'What?' He glanced back and forth between her and Morty. 'Weren't you being serious?'

'Um, yes, I was. Were you?'

'Yes.'

They stared at each other.

'Brigid.'

'Really? Brigid, Goddess of the flame and the well, etc etc?'

'Yes, that one.'

Connall let out a befuddled snort. 'She's over here now, is she?'

'Yes, in a manner of speaking. I mean, she's mainly here.'

'In Melbourne?'

'Yes. And a bit of Ireland and the Upper Realms a bit lately, but I got her to come down here.'

'You know about the Upper Realms?'

Lauren nodded proudly. 'I know a lot about the Other World actually.'

'Bugger me. And another old country goddess.' He chucked in amusement. 'Fancy that.'

Before Lauren could ask for further clarification around all this, there was an almighty smash, and the window next to her exploded, and all she had time to do was to think 'another bloody explosion', before she was thrown to the floor.

20

Lauren had just enough time to see a brown bottle hit the floor in a torrent of broken glass before a flash temporarily blinded her, and then everything was a blur of shouts and yelling and rapidly spreading heat. Connall seemed to be everywhere at once, pulling her behind the bar and away from the flames, ripping an extinguisher from the wall and shoving it into Morty's hands, and running up the stairs, yelling to unseen people that they needed to get out; there was a fire. She cast around, desperately trying to find something she could attack the flames with, but the fire extinguisher seemed to be the single nod to any health and safety measures. Morty had pointed it at the fire, but the crudely made

Molotov cocktail had done its job, and the spray from the nozzle was no match for the licks of flame that had run along all the ignition points spread by the exploding petrol, and had begun leaping onto the exposed, dry, old wood that made up the very bones of the aged building. She retreated to the door, coughing as the billowing smoke filled the room. It had happened so quickly; Lauren had always imagined she would have time, in an emergency such as this, to be heroic, to drag people to safety or to smother the flames before they grew too great, but she was reduced to staggering backwards, hand to mouth, hoping that Connall was exiting via some unseen upstairs exit.

She heard the thud of footsteps descend the stairs and instinctively moved towards Connall as he appeared. Something about his sheer size, his beard, and the authority he commanded by virtue of some undefined quality drew her to him. He stepped out of the smoke, like a Viking warrior striding across the grounds of a plundered monastery, but what he was holding in his hard was a baby, rather than a hefty and murderous weapon, and rather than a flaming field, he was stumbling over discarded chairs.

There was a flash, brighter than the fire, and for a moment the image of Connall with a raised arm and a stream of silver flooding from his hand burnt onto Lauren's eyes. Water, or at least a liquid, cascaded between them and then there was a barrage of noise on the stairs, feet running into the room, and then a rush of people, or at least approximations of people swept past him and out through the door which had been cornered off from the fire. It now burned quietly but still fiercely behind what looked like a plexiglass shield. The flaying heat no longer barraged her face, and she realised that she could breathe again.

'What the hell is that?' she screamed through the rushing noise of what felt like hundreds of bodies.

'Just a trick.' Connall's voice came from behind her. 'The fire will notice that it's an illusion in a moment, but we'll have time to get everyone out. Those who can fly have made it out of the upstairs window, but Morty's making sure it's all clear up there.'

She finally saw Morty emerge. 'That's the last of them,' he wheezed, and she briefly hoped he'd remembered his asthma puffer.

To the side, Lauren could see the clear shield beginning to melt like a glacier in Greenland, and the crackle of the fire became audible again. Whatever trick had convinced the fire that burning down this particular heritage building tonight was a bad idea had obviously worn off, and the room filled with heat once again. Connall shepherded her out of the door, holding her by the hand, and she breathed in with relief as the cool night air hit her face. In the distance, she could hear the warble of emergency vehicles.

In deference to many years of habit, Connall pulled the door shut after him as he stepped down the sandstone step and clapped his hands to get the attention of the people milling around. 'Right, the most important thing we can do right now is stay together,' he said, his deep voice almost tinny in the cold night air. 'I know you don't like to be out in the open, but there's no immediate danger as far as I know. If you give me a few minutes, I'll come up with a plan.'

'Connall,' Morty said, catching his eye. He gestured to the trickle of people who were disappearing into the night. Connall dropped Lauren's hand and shouldered his way through the group. 'This is a bad idea,' he said. 'We don't know whether it's safe.'

Lauren pulled Morty aside and whispered into his ear. 'Why wouldn't it be safe?'

'An Other World being, we think, has been picking off lone Imagos one by one. Killing them. It hasn't happened for a few weeks, and Connall thought it might have stopped, but this is too risky. Being out here is too risky.'

'You seem to know a lot about it,' Lauren grumbled, trying to hide the pang of jealously she felt at how quickly the two men had formed a connection. Morty was her adoring annoyance. She didn't want him to become smitten with anyone else.

'He hasn't had many people to share this burden with,' Morty said.

'I'm sure you're more than happy to share his burden,' she snapped.

'We can't be out here.' An old, grey faced man with impossibly long fingers and dark oval eyes was speaking to Connall, and as his words hissed in the air, the murmuring crowd fell silent. 'We can't stand here while we wait for you to decide where we can go. All of us together like this? We'll attract attention. From humans, too. They can ignore a few of us, but fifty, sixty of us together? We're safer making our own way tonight.'

Connall reached out a hand to grab his arm, but the man shook him off.

'Please,' Connall said. 'We need to stay together.'

The old man spoke patiently yet firmly. 'We're not children. We appreciate all that you do for us, but we are free. We have agency and are able to handle our own destiny. For now.'

As he turned and left, a small but steady stream of Imagos trailed after him as he headed off into the darkness.

'Fuck,' Connall spat. 'This is ludicrous. What are they thinking?'

'Is it really not safe for them?' Lauren asked in a hushed voice, wrapping her arm around one of the smaller Imagos who had started to shiver. 'It's Melbourne. It's a safe place.'

'Nowhere is safe for Imagos,' Morty said.

Lauren put her hand on Connall's arm. 'Where are you going to take them?' He was pacing back and forth, watching the flames glowing from inside the pub. The group had moved back as the heat intensified.

'I'll have to make a few calls,' he said, his eyes continuing to skim the Imagos, checking to see who was still there. 'It'll need to be one of my people. We can't just go to a bloody motel.'

The fire engines had now reached them. Cutting their sirens, they crawled carefully down the narrow street, the flashing lights eerily illuminating the surrounding buildings. The firefighters jumped out, and Connall rapidly shouted the details of what had happened. As they leapt into action, Lauren noticed the strangest thing. It wasn't that the firefighters ignored the Imagos as such; there's a certain carriage of body taken on when ignoring someone, a kind of studied nonchalance that's impossible to fake. But there was none of that. Instead, they seemed to have no concept that the Imagos where there. Except...

In all the purposeful running and dragging of hoses and frightfully competent firefighter business, they were managing not to run into the Imagos. Despite the fact there were fifty bodies milling about in the narrow street, the firefighters who Lauren were convinced couldn't see them, were also not running into them. It reminded her of her long ago school experiments with magnets, the way that two positives repelled each other. Every time someone got near an Imago, they skimmed away from them as if a powerful force were acting on them, a curious little dance that left Lauren with more questions than answers.

The Imagos had drawn back into a tight cluster, some holding each other, more looking around nervously, and Lauren realised what she had to do.

'They can come to my house,' she said, calling out to Connall. 'They can stay at my house. For now. Well, a while. Until we come up with a better plan.'

And with that 'we' Lauren's destiny was well and truly decided.

21

The Imagos thought they were safe. Not happy of course, but safe like dust under the floorboards; hidden and forgotten. The ultimate safety. And the man seemed to understand us.

He seemed to care.

But then came the heat.

Imagos poured out like mice from a burning barn, their forms stuttering under the weight of attention. The hugeness of the sky, the sharpness of the air. They didn't belong in the open, so they scattered. They should have stayed together; it was what the man was telling us to do, but they didn't listen.

Some ran, some floated, some simply stopped moving completely, hoping stillness might count as invisibility.

But it didn't.

The alleyway seemed safe; quiet and dark. A dead end yes, but was that a bad thing? Something solid at their backs felt safe. Contained and secure. And when they saw her at the entrance, they thought help had arrived. A woman, with a smile on her face and her hand outstretched.

'Good evening,' she said, and her voice was soft like a lullaby from a storybook that never finished. The kind our creators used to hum, before they grew up and forgot us. But one look into her eyes and we know that she wasn't here to help. She was no safety.

The child didn't know this though. He stepped forward when she smiled. Of course he did. He had been made for stories and magic, for a mother, for the soft-lit glow of an outstretched hand.

The other Imagos tried to stop him but by then it was too late; the dust was already shimmering, glowing. The little one reached for its tendrils with a chubby hand. He smiled, his face alight with joy and wonder, even as it covered him.

They felt his stillness immediately. Not peace, not silence, just an eternal stillness that echoed backwards through us.

The second was gone just as quickly.

One tried to run, its only recourse. It wasn't made to fight, It was made to listen, to comfort, to whisper secrets into the ear of a lonely teenager. But It too was stilled, its own voice freezing in its head as the light caught it too.

It was so beautiful.

But it was wrong.

The eyes, the only things that could move, looked at the others. It thought they saw it; it hoped they did. They were together in that moment, at least.

And then they were not.

The pull was almost from inside. The stream, the current that they had always drifted along shuddered. The thing that linked them all shuddered. the Imagos felt it pulse.

The woman who was no woman watched. Could she see the stream? She seemed to feel it. Felt something. She didn't know them, knew nothing about Imagos.

Not really.

Then their magic, their very being, unravelled from the husks and was drawn into her outstretched hand like it were worth something, a glowing orb that lit her face momentarily before she stored it away. Like it had value. A glimmer of stolen life.

And then the Imagos were gone. No one would find them. There was nothing to remember.

22

Sybella sounded relieved the next day when Demniac rang and asked if he could meet Leo. 'Yes, please,' she said. He could hear the crunching sounds of something being eaten at a rapid pace. Chips, he decided.

'Please meet him. He needs a hobby. He keeps lurking around the house, and it's getting on my nerves. He needs more attention than I've got the energy for, so it would be good for him. I feel like I haven't slept in weeks and I've managed to hurt my ankle, somehow. Come and babysit.'

Demniac heard a rumbling sound on the other end of the phone, and Sybella covered the mouthpiece. As he waited for her to speak again, he paced. There was a smooth causeway cut into the carpet in the hallway of Demniac's flat. It was depressed, the feet that had paced along it hour upon hour, day over day, had tramped what was once a fairly uninspiring hexagonal pattern into a shapeless blur, but this wasn't the kind of thing that he put much mind to.

Decor wasn't his area.

He had other things to think about.

The corridor was dark, as were the three other rooms that ran off it. Not the moodily lit deliberate dark of interior designers whose work appears in publications as superbly pretentious as Casa Sublime, but the kind of dark created by someone who has the absolutely inability to buy the right wattage of light bulbs on a fairly regular basis.

He heard Sybella's voice appear on the other end of the phone again. 'Sorry,' she said pointedly. 'He doesn't need attention, and he doesn't need a hobby in any way at all, but yes, he would like to meet you because my company isn't the scintillating delight of the circles he usually runs in. He's heard you're a chaos magician, so now he's very interested, for some reason.'

He heard her voice move away again. 'Who do you usually hang around with, anyway?' There was another pause, and Demniac thought he saw something dark dart away, just out of his line of vision. He ignored it and focused on her voice. 'Oh, actually, to be fair, that does sound more interesting than me. You probably do need a wider social circle. Do you want us to come to you? Or meet somewhere else?'

'Maybe a park?' Demniac said, glancing around nervously. He

seemed to be developing a tic, and glancing around nervously had become as natural to him as breathing. 'I've been getting some bad vibes around here.'

He had never seen his flat as a place of pleasant repose, rather one of utilitarian function, but just lately, the place had become somewhere to dash in, use the toilet, then move out sharpish, paying as little attention to the accusatorily dying pot plants and shadowed corners as possible.

'What did you do?' Sybella asked. 'Summon something you shouldn't have summoned?'

'Ah,' he said, and he realised it wasn't just his glance that had become permanently nervous. His voice seemed to be following suit. 'Not summoned, exactly,' he said. 'I've been trying some new things and—'

'That's chaos magic, my friend. That's what you've signed up for. You want to franken-spell your own tradition—'

'There's no tradition. That's the whole—'

'You want to franken-spell your own tradition then you have to be prepared if your system of magic goes and starts to do its own thing. Ever since you decided you didn't need to call in the corners anymore, Roxy has been worried.'

This was a conversation they had had many times before.

'Do you even smudge anymore?'

Demniac hung up on her.

✳✳✳

They met in a park disastrously named 'The Rager's Hangout'. The local council had completed it a year earlier after receiving a grant intended to try and find something for unspecified 'youths' to do on the weekends. Instead of a room with beanbags and charging ports that their focus groups had explicitly told them they wanted, they decided that a Fit-U-Fun X-treme customised playground would be just the thing to entice teens to spend their valuable gaming time outside.

Obviously it was never used. Occasionally, late on a Saturday night, hooded figures could be seen spending time ironically swirling around on the Spin-Fin-I.T, and then disappear with the dawn, leaving some cans, the occasional bong, and graffiti to the effect that Allison is a Bridge Troll and Anarchy is Truth. This also meant that none of the middle-class parents would let their little ones within a bull's roar of it, day or night, so Sybella and Demniac could safely spend as much time as they wanted here without danger of being questioned.

They huddled together under a small open sided shelter. The low dark clouds had begun to drip smudges of rain, which didn't seem to affect Leo at all, which was just as well as there was no room for him anyway, and a breeze had begun to pick up. Sybella pulled her coat tightly around her and wondered, not for the first time, what it would feel like to run her face in Leo's mane. She liked to think there was a kind of giant spectral lion in existence that would permit strange women to run their faces in their fur, but she was completely sure that Leo wasn't the one.

'So,' she started after a moment, realising that Demniac was busy kicking bits of loose concrete around (the tender to the park had gone to the lowest bid, and so the whole thing was rapidly sliding into the water table) and refusing to make eye contact with Leo who, Sybella had guessed, scared the willies out of him. 'You wanted to meet a real thought form.' She gestured to Leo, 'this is it.'

'I am one of many but undoubtedly the greatest,' Leo rumbled. 'I am one of the higher orders. I understand you are interested in me and my kind, boy. And it was under your tutelage that the girl summoned me in the first place, although I think you should have guided her with a firmer hand.'

'She wasn't under my tutelage exactly,' he protested. 'I just suggested that—'

'It makes no difference,' Leo said. 'I hear you are a chaos

magician, and I wish to enlist your help in solving a grave problem that has been unleashed on the world. You humans have been poking around in spheres that do not concern you, and now we all must pay the price.'

'Crikey,' Sybella said, laughing awkwardly. 'I feel like this escalated quickly. You haven't mentioned this to me.'

'I have,' he said. 'You just haven't been listening. You've been napping an inordinate amount as far as I can tell.'

'It's self care,' she protested. 'It's important.'

'Self care from what?' he said. 'You haven't been to a job since I met you.'

'I was looking for a reason to quit anyway.' She shrugged. 'You're more interesting.'

'You've quit another job?' Demniac said.

'We must all pay the price,' Leo said again, a little louder this time.

Sybella and Demniac paid attention.

'The human race has developed the ridiculous propensity for creating entities out of nothing.' Leo directed this to Demniac.

'Right,' he said uncertainly.

'Not this high level meditative work that you are so well versed in. I mean ordinary, everyday people, bringing their imaginary friends to life.'

'Right. Could we just get back to the bit where you said—'

'Of course, the Upper Realms have tried out some ideas, played around with some ways to make them more acceptable, but none of it is working. They have no position, no status. They just don't belong.'

'Couldn't someone give them some status then?' Sybella suggested.

'What do you mean?'

'Couldn't they be given an official status? Have one handed to them? Isn't that how status works? It's not a real thing, after all.'

'Something made entirely by humans be given official status? Don't be ridiculous. Devin would never agree to that. Devin is well aware than I am the only, the most...' Leo's voice was tinged with anger. 'You can't just hand things out like that. Not when I was created especially for...' He stopped.

'Can't you do something about it?' Sybella continued, pushing the issue.

'Me? No, of course not. I don't even like to be this close to the whole situation, to be honest. The point is that I want people to stop doing this. We actually. We want people to stop doing this. It's creating too many problems, and we upstairs have enough to deal with trying to corral species and principalities who have a rightful place in the —'

'Vast panoply,' Sybella suggested.

'That's right, vast panoply of existence, without new things being called into existence willy-nilly. It's not proper, you know. It wasn't part of the Grand Plan. I'm sure that Devin really isn't too happy about it. He knows its important to me, too and I'm fairly special to him, all things considered. That's why I'm here, asking you to stop, please.'

'Me?' Demniac asked uncertainly. 'You're asking me?'

'Yes.'

'To do what?'

'To stop people creating Imagos.'

'You want me to stop people from creating Imagos.'

Demniac looked at Sybella for help, but she shrugged her shoulders.

'How?' he asked simply.

'Surely that's up to you? I was hoping that I'd just tell you to take care of it and you'd take care of it.'

Demniac's eyes were now darting around uncertainly, like a small fish trying to escape from a wine glass.

'I don't really know that much about it,' he admitted. That's what I was trying to tell you.'

'But you're a powerful chaos magician, right?'

'I dabble.'

'But you're a chaos magician, yes? You have apprentices under you? The next generation of people who are going through this process. They are the ones that you can speak to. They are the ones who you can have an influence on.'

Sybella interrupted. 'But you know so much,' she said. 'You do all those Power Points, and you say things like,' she pulled a piece of paper out of her jacket, 'the development of an ambivalent ally by way of manipulation of molecules via counter cultural preconception class indicators.'

'You wrote that down?'

She slid it back into her pocket, her face reddening. 'I like the sound of the things you say sometimes.'

The lion emitted an energy that is known in every known and unknown civilisation as one of extreme irritation. 'I fear I may have been misinformed,' he said, pursing his lips inasmuch as a giant spectral lion is able to purse his lips. 'I was of the understanding you have more, shall we say, clout.'

Demniac shrugged impotently. 'Sorry. I don't really know what I'm doing. I just—'

'Yes?'

'I read some blogs.'

There was a pause.

'I suppose I could try and find out who is doing it and, you know... talk them out of it,' he said. 'Just politely suggest that they, you know, go out and get a real-life friend or something. Meet some girls. Go to the pub or join a society of some sort.'

'Things are in hand,' Leo said ominously. 'Things are in hand to bring all of this to a close, but it would be better off that those things not already in motion were stopped. It would make things easier in the long run and quite honesty cut down my workload, which I, for one, am a big fan of. However, from what I can tell, you're my best bet. I think it would be best if I came and stayed with you.'

'But,' Sybella said. 'What about me? Aren't you here for me?'

Leo looked at her as if he had forgotten her existence. 'Yes, in a manner of speaking.'

'But I summoned you. Aren't you here just for me?'

'Let's just say it was a convenient confluence of events. This job popped up, and it was decided that I could maybe kill two carts before the horse with one stone or whatever the expression is.'

Sybella's eyes filled with tears. 'So you won't be staying with me anymore?'

He looked to Demniac and back again. 'I really need to get on with this. It's important.'

'Okay, fine,' she said and plunged her hands into her pockets. 'I guess I'll see you both around then.'

They were already in deep conversation by the time her figure had left the park.

23

While inviting approximately fifty people that she knew only tangentially to stay in her house wasn't the worst idea that Lauren had ever had, it was certainly in the top five of her most dubious ones. She decided to lodge it between 'getting a tattoo from a stranger with a new inking kit at a party when she was fifteen' and 'using coconut oil to get a really good tan consistently between 1991-1999'.

For a few hours, she had basked in the glow of approval and appreciation from Connall, but there were just so many of them. The house was bulging at the seams, and another issue was how quickly Connall and Brigid had taken to each other. Within half an hour of being introduced, they had played the 'working out which friends they had in common' game, all of whom seemed to be gods or well known Other World figures, and for the most part, the discussions occurred well above Lauren's head.

'Is she going to deal with the Cailleach then?' Connall asked on the second night of the sleepover as he poured Brigid a class of Cabernet Sauvignon. 'Or are you going to do it? Because someone has to, and I've got my hands full trying to keep this lot under control, and I doubt she will even talk to me.'

'Who won't?' Brigid took a sip of her wine.

'The Cailleach. She knows I'm here, surely, and she's chosen not to even drop in for a beer. I'm surprised she's still about.'

'Oh, she's still here all right. Pissing off the original inhabitants no end. And she won't be told. That's why I've enlisted Lauren.'

'Why can't you do it?' Connall asked looking at her suspiciously. 'Aren't you and her talking?'

Brigid shook her head. 'Don't want to discuss it. Anyway, point is, Lauren has been tied up with her for years without anyone knowing about it.'

'Oh, yes, I've heard about that. The coven, right?'

'How have you heard about this?' Brigid asked, exasperated. 'How has literally everyone else heard about things I have no idea of? I'm supposed to have my finger on the pulse.'

'No, you took your finger off the pulse when you allowed yourself to be reborn as a human. We've all been doing the heavy lifting on your behalf. You decided on this life.'

'Yeah, I know, I know. But you're not in a position to talk. You're babysitting Imagos.'

'True,' he said, unpacking the dishwasher.

'You've got something killing your lot, do you then?' she asked, he taking the dishes from his hand and arranged them on the shelves.

'Something like that. Still haven't got to the bottom of exactly what's going on.'

'Remember the days when we used to have our finger on all the pulses? The collective pulse? There wasn't anything that happened, above or below, that we didn't know about.'

'That move to monotheism was a dubious one all around.'

Lauren decided she'd had enough of being sidelined in her own home. 'Can someone please give me an idea of what I'm supposed to be doing?'

'My idea,' Brigid said, 'would be to get your coven together, summon the Cailleach, and ask her to leave. Connall?'

He looked up from the bread he was now making. 'Yep, sounds good. A good start, anyway.'

Lauren seemed uncertain. 'It might be a bit more complicated than that though. Surely? If it's that easy then why hasn't anyone done it sooner?'

'Because no one knew it was a problem. It wasn't until there were complaints that anyone even remembered she was here. Most people seemed to have forgotten about her existence completely until she started annoying the Old Ones.

'Funny, given how important she used to be, right?' Connall said.

'I know,' Brigid agreed. 'Times have changed.'

'There's a lot I haven't been aware of considering, that I own a metaphysics shop,' Lauren said. 'An ancient goddess inhabiting this land and a city that's apparently teeming with Other World figures? What else is going on that I don't know about?'

'Your best friend was a literal goddess, and you didn't notice,' Connall pointed out.

'Oh, come on, go easy,' Brigid interrupted. 'I didn't even know myself at the time. It's hardly her fault.'

There was another knock on the door, and Connall went to answer it this time. Dirty Annie slipped in, smiled at everyone in the room, and headed through the house to the back rooms that were now covered in mattresses.

'I think you need a cat flap,' Brigid said. 'Or you're going to be answering doors as a full-time job.'

'I could get a whole bunch of keys cut,' Connall offered. 'That might be an easier option.'

Lauren bit her lip thoughtfully. 'Look, I'm absolutely willing to have to them all stay here for the time being, given, you know, the trauma and the homelessness murdery stuff and all, but I don't know if fifty people having keys and coming and going is going to work. It doesn't feel very safe.'

'I'm open to other suggestions,' Connall said. 'And if this doesn't feel good for you, then I'm happy to try other options.'

'Ooooh, I have an idea,' Lauren said suddenly, her face brightening. 'I've just thought of the perfect thing. You know that place up in... where was it? The Other World, Brigid? That big open white place we saw through the bookcase. Couldn't we put everyone up there?'

'Dimensionally shift fifty Imagos?' Brigid clarified. 'You think it's possible to dimensionally shift Imagos and put them in an abandoned, gutted office warehouse type place?'

'Wouldn't that work?' Lauren said. 'No one would even notice. There was hardly anyone one around up there. It felt totally abandoned. And they would be safe there, wouldn't they?'

Brigid frowned. 'My first thought was that it's a ridiculous idea, but actually, maybe it's not too bad. I can't think of any reason why it wouldn't work in theory, except I'm not sure how we could get them all up there.'

Connall cleared his throat. 'First of all, if my reckoning is correct, that space isn't going to be empty for much longer.' He brushed aside their questions and continued. 'And I need to point something else out to you,' he said. 'Because they weren't officially created by any of the officially mandated creators they have no statutory rights. They're stateless and person-less. Even heaven doesn't want them.'

Maeve crawled out of the bedroom, raised herself up unsteadily and toddled over to Brigid who picked her up. She looked, for all intents and purposes, like a human two year old, except for the fact she had the body of a caterpillar and a human head. She rested her head against Brigid's chest and made a purring noise. Lauren reached over and stroked her blond hair.

'They're seen as the lowest of the low,' Connall said quietly. 'That's why they're being hunted, and that's why I've pledged my life to protect them.'

'We'll see about that,' said Brigid said, squaring up her jaw. 'This must be because the Upper Realms don't know about it. Sure, I've had my run-ins with them, but they are good, loving people up there. They wouldn't stand for this.' She reached around Maeve and pulled her phone out of her pocket. She frowned as she scrolled through her contact list before raising the phone to her ear. 'I'm sorting it,' she said. 'Hang on. I'm calling Devin.'

'You're calling God?' Lauren hissed.

'Damn,' Brigid said as there was no reply. 'He must be in a meeting.'

'You have God's phone number?'

'Yeah, of course. It would be weird not to have it.'

'I suppose you and he are friends on social media too?'

'Of course. He's hilarious on social. Quality stuff. Really gives the fundamentalists a hard time. Lots of vegan memes, too, surprisingly.'

'I wouldn't bother,' Connall said. 'He knows. Everyone knows. This isn't new. Just because you're hearing about it for the first time doesn't mean it's new. I'm happy to take care of this, and you take care of the Cailleach business.'

'Are you sure you don't need help?'

'I've got it under control,' Connall said as an earth shattering shriek came from the back room, and there was a thump and a shatter, followed by wild laughter. 'But thanks for asking.'

'You want me to stay in my own lane?' Brigid clarified again 'Despite the fact you've commandeered my best friend's house, bits, from the sound of it, are falling off said house and potentially causing her a huge amount of stress.'

'No, no, it's fine,' Lauren interrupted. 'I've been planning on renovating for a while, so this is just the vigorous incentive that I've needed.'

'I don't think he's a good influence on you,' said Brigid.

'And I'm right here,' he said.

'Oookay,' Lauren said. 'As fun as all this is, and as much as I adore listening to you two bicker, I think I'll just grab my things and go and stay at Brigid's tonight. You seem to have everything under control here, and I must say I have no idea how a paranormal being can clog a toilet, but if what I just saw in my bathroom is anything to go by it's possible, so I'm nipping off for the night to somewhere with a functional bathroom, and if you could sort that out before I come back tomorrow I'd be really grateful.' She gave Connall what she hoped was a flirty grin, took Brigid's arm and steered her out of the house.

'I don't know why you're so rude to him,' Lauren said after they'd been driving for a while.

'And I don't know why you're so smitten with him. He's not interested in you.'

'I dunno. I'm getting a vibe.'

'The vibe is him trying to charm you because he has filled your house with impossible beings, and now bits of it are falling off.'

'Bits of my house, or bits of the Imagos?'

'Probably both.'

'Anyway, I think I'm in with a chance,' Lauren plunged on.

'No, he's definitely not interested. Morty is more his type.'

'That's unfortunate because Morty is into me, so Connall will have to console himself in my comforting bosom.'

'God, I'm glad I'm married.'

'Speaking of that,' Lauren said as they pulled up outside Brigid's house. 'Any word from the lovely Egragore?'

Brigid shrugged, the standard answer that she had taken to using whenever she was asked about him.

'I'm assuming an assignment or something. It's like you're in the bloody army or the CIA or something. Just getting deployed in the dead of night with nary a hows-your father. It's not on, if you ask me.'

'I've learned to stop worrying about the things in my life I have absolutely no control over,' Brigid said, stepping in through her front door.

'And which things specifically would they be?' Lauren asked.

'Last time I checked, everything, and if you ask me...' But her voice was cut off by the fact that at the precise moment, they both saw that the entirety of Brigid's hall way seemed to have been transformed into a rich and fertile crop of what Brigid reliably informed Lauren, in an oddly composed voice, was emmer wheat.

24

The golden crop, which seemed to be glowing from within, rippled slightly as if being caressed by an unseen breeze. The full heads of ancient grain nodded heavily, greeting the two bemused women who stood in the doorway. It spread down through the hallway and into the living area, filling all the available floor space and emitting the smell of a cereal factory in full production mode. Lauren cautiously put her foot forwards and moved some of the long strands aside and, yes, a red brown soil filled the rooms.

'Your floor now consists of what looks to me like a slightly loamy soil.'

'I'd been meaning to tear up the carpet anyway. Saved me the effort. Probably a good thing.'

Lauren reached out and plucked a sheath. It was warm, as if basking in the rays of an ancient sun. 'Wheat,' she said. 'Actual wheat. I mean, it's not an optical illusion or a light trick or anything. It's real.'

'Emmer,' Brigid said. 'Irish, circa 3000BCE I think I mentioned that. But, yes, it's real.'

'You don't seem surprised?'

'I wouldn't say that' Brigid said, peering over the crop at the sofa which could be seen peeking out of the crop a few metres away. 'I'm not 'not' surprised; let's put it that way. I wish she'd left a path or something, though. I can't even get to the kitchen to make a coffee.'

Lauren glanced behind them at the apparent normality of the open door and the path behind them. 'Should we go back to my house? We could just pretend this never happened and hope it goes away? I could make rice paper rolls, and we could paint our nails.'

'Go back to a house that's been trashed by otherworldly creatures or go to my house that's been filled with wheat by an ancient goddess who's forgotten how to communicate with people. Tough choice.'

'So you do know what's going on then?'

'Come on,' Brigid said, parting the crop and stepping tentatively forward. 'Just walk where I walk so we don't crush too much. I don't want to piss her off. She's so fucking temperamental it's like being in a co-dependent relationship where the other person keeps changing the rules and yelling at you when you don't know what's going on.'

They made their way forward, stepping carefully, the stalks seeming to lean towards them, caressing their legs as they waded through the flood of grains. There was a rustling whisper in the air as if the stalks were speaking, trying to share some kind of a cryptic message. They could see that Brigid's bedroom was equally full, but for some reason, the kitchen was clear, and that's where they set up camp.

'Does this have anything to do with all the mysterious changes that have been going on in here?' Lauren asked once the jug was boiling. She pointed to the clock on the wall, which was no longer the simple clock that had been hanging on there for years, but was now a silver plate with various cutlery pieces and steak knives sticking out of the circumference at angles that would have made the inventors of torture methods during the Spanish inquisition breathe heavily and mop their brows. 'That's new, isn't it? That's just suddenly appeared. You wouldn't buy that, would you?'

'I certainly would not,' Brigid said. 'I suspect she's been trying to get my attention, and when it didn't work, she decided to get really obvious.'

'Replacing your decor with interior design items that go against everything you stand for and believe in was too subtle, so 'she' has filled your house with wheat?'

'Emmer,' Brigid said. 'But, yes, I think that's basically it. Biscuit?'

'I feel like I've been doing really well with you back in my life and all, but I'm getting that headache I get just before I get a migraine, and I suspect it's your fault. Can you just tell me what's going on?'

Brigid wrested two chairs from around the dining table and dragged them into the kitchen, gouging up a huge divot of dirt in which a plump worm burbled around.

'You already know as much as I do, I think. It's what we've been talking about, the Cailleach. I told you I needed you to try and communicate with her through your little coven, but it seems she's cut out the middleman and come straight to me. It looks like we not only have her attention, but now she wants to annoy me about it.'

'I wish you wouldn't say 'little' coven. It's so dismissive.'

'I'm sorry, but I didn't see that much decent, wiccan work, did I? I saw people bickering about Power Points and tulpas or whatever, and what I was really hoping for was a decent circle casting and communicating with an ancient deity. That would have avoided my house turning into the next site for a really elaborate, ornate crop circle situation.'

The two women looked at each other. 'I'm not quite sure why you're annoyed at me, but it seems misplaced somehow,' Lauren said finally.

'Yeah, you could be right. I was just hoping that I wouldn't have to be the one dealing with her. I wanted you guys to just sweep in, convince her to move, and then we could have this whole thing over with. I didn't want to get too involved.'

'But why? Why do you think I would have a better chance of convincing her than you? What on earth do I and the coven have that you don't?'

'It's not that you have a better chance, as such, it's just that I don't want to open myself up to the inevitable politics and guilt and passive aggressiveness that will inevitably come at me if I put myself in the position of having to ask the Cailleach for a favour.'

'But why? I'm still not clear why there are political ramifications? Are there some statutes or edicts about involving yourself in the affairs of other goddesses that I don't know about? Does it need to go through some kind of a council? Because I'm definitely not qualified for that kind of thing.'

Brigid sighed heavily, opening a packet of sugar free organic biscuits that she would never have purchased and taking a tentative bite. 'Sugar free. Do you think this is about my weight? Because I have no problem with being heavy, and it's just like her to make a passive aggressive dig by planting healthy shit like this in my cupboard.' She checked the ingredients. 'Gluten free. That's a bit ironic, isn't it? I didn't think gluten free would be something she'd be buying into given all of that fucking wheat out there.'

'Brigid,' Lauren said warningly.

'All right,' Brigid said. 'She's my mother. She's my very judgemental and annoying mother, and now she knows I want something from her, I'm never going to hear the end of it.'

There was a long pause. The sound of the wheat rustling despite the absence of wind had taken on an ominous tone to Lauren's ears, and various horror movies featuring small black eyed murderous children creeping out of fields filled her mind.

'How does this tie in with all the decor changes?'

'Subtle suggestions as to how I should be living my life, I'm assuming. She doesn't like my choices, so she makes tweaks in the direction that she thinks I should be heading in.'

Lauren looked doubtfully at the clock. 'That's a subtle tweak?'

'She thinks she's funny sometimes.'

'Let me get this clear. Your mother wanted to get your attention, so she passive aggressively changed the decor of your house so that you'd pay attention to her?'

'I think so, yes.'

'That doesn't sound very likely.'

'Not very likely? Have you ever had a mother?'

'No, my mother was a bush band groupie. She didn't spend that much time mothering. She spent most of her time trying to learn how to play the lagerphone to impress some guy called Perion.'

'You're lucky. This kind of mother spends a lot of time assuming you know what's she's thinking and feeling and getting the shits on when you can't infer exactly what she wants. Hence...' She gestured outside the kitchen. 'Hence the emmer. I'm assuming she thinks this is too unsubtle for even me to notice. She's a fertility deity, and ancient grains is her special interest.'

'Hang on,' Lauren said. 'I know your mother. Pat. Your mother's Pat. I love her. She feeds me lentil dumplings and makes me crystal necklaces. Older lady, white hair.'

'All right. I'm going to explain this as clearly as I can, but I'm going to need you to stick with me, okay?'

Lauren nodded tentatively.

'I was born as Brigid and raised by Pat and Frank, yes?'

'Yes, that's right.'

'And I'm your best friend, and I get up to all sorts of crazy high jinks.'

'Actually, that's more me than you, but let's go with that for argument's sake.'

'So Pat is my human mother, and the Cailleach is my mother from the point of view of the vast pantheon of deities that hover in an otherworldly sense just above the reality as we know it. And she's much less fun and way more judgemental about all of my life choices.'

'Huh. I would have thought having an almost omniscient and eternal point of view and perspective on the Universe would make someone more accepting, not less,' Lauren said.

'Yes, you'd think so, wouldn't you.' Brigid gazed at the wheat for a while. It rustled back at her.

'This headache doesn't seem to be going away,' Lauren said, eating one of the dreadful biscuits with a grimace.

'But you get the general gist of what I'm talking about?'

'I think so. The Cailleach is someone you've had a long standing, nay thousands of years long, relationship with, and she has some kind of authority over you.'

'Not in any official governing sense, but in a very deep and profound way, in the sense that someone who knows you very well and can push your buttons with the slightest—'

'Change of decor.'

'Quite.'

'And you wanted me to take up this overstaying her welcome in Australia issue with her, but she seems to have bypassed our coven and come straight to you.'

'Yes, apparently. I'm surprised she caught wind of it, to be honest. She pretty much keeps to herself these days. The last I heard from her, she sent me a strongly worded missal about how my skin would freckle to buggery in the Australian sun, and that was the last I heard of her. She placed her hands on her hips and surveyed the room, frowning. 'Mum,' she said loudly. 'Mum, are you there?'

Nothing.

"Cailleach, then? Are you there?'

Still nothing, but the wheat continued to rustle.

'I don't think she's here,' Lauren said in hushed tones.

'Oh, she probably bloody is, but clearly, I'm doing something incorrectly, and she won't talk to me until I work out what I'm supposed to be doing.'

'I can see why you decided to be a human, if that's the mothering you were used to for the past hundred—'

'Thousands, actually,'

'Of years. I can see why you'd want to try something different. Pat's a much nicer mother. PAT'S A MUCH BETTER MOTHER THAN YOU,' Lauren projected into the room, feeling angry and protective on her friend's behalf.

'Can we not,' Brigid said. 'She's obviously got a bee in her bonnet as it is, and having her disliking to you isn't going to help. We're going to need to assemble the coven.'

'You know we're not very good, right? You know that she probably won't pay attention to us?'

'In a country where everyone has forgotten about her, and the

Irish convicts she once nourished and nurtured have now turned into true blue Aussies whose only connection with the Irish ancestry is putting green food dye in their Guinness on St Patrick's day? There's a group of people who get together and leave her offerings and bits of honey cake and the like. Oh, trust me, she knows about you.'

25

'I've only got a few minutes so let's make this quick,' said Roxy tersely. 'Your friend Brigid is demanding that I convene my coven, is she?'

The coffee shop they were in sat conveniently next to the Tantric Om, where Connall and Morty were cleaning up. They had offered to do it, and Lauren was not one to turn down the offer of manual assistance.

'That's a bit harsh,' Lauren said, caught off guard. 'She's not demanding anything. There's an issue that needs to be addressed with the Cailleach, and I think we can help.'

'We're not a service for hire, you know. We don't just go around fixing up other people's problems. This Brigid character can't just make demands.'

Lauren reflected that talking to Roxy was becoming a full contact sport requiring body armour and comprehensive health insurance. 'Hang on are you jealous?'

Roxy made a noise into her croissant that confirmed to Lauren that yes, she was actually quite jealous, thanks for asking.

'Of course I'm not bloody jealous. What a stupid idea.'

There was a pause.

'Why would I be jealous, just assuming for a moment that your ridiculous idea is right? Do you have any reasons for this stupid claim?'

'I feel that this might be an appropriate juncture to tell you something.'

Roxy took another bite of her croissant. 'You are just full of news and surprises these days, aren't you.'

'Brigid is quite special.'

'Is she.'

'And I don't want this to effect how you feel about her. Well actually I'd like it to make you bond with her but now I'm thinking that starting this conversation was a dreadful idea.'

Roxy looked at her watch. 'I've got things to do, you know.'

'Brigid is an actual goddess. A bona fide one. She lives between a few worlds and is immortal or something, but at the moment she's a human.'

Roxy sat back and crossed her arms.

'And you think that would affect how I feel about her? Why?'

'Possibly because she's a real goddess, and we're just ordinary people playing around with all this stuff on the off chance that it works? Because we have always suspected that this is true, but we didn't have any hard evidence until lately.'

'I don't have a desperate need for the validation of 'hard evidence', as you put it,' Roxy said. 'I'm not as flighty and needy as you are. I've always known that this is the reality. You're just used to buying into the whole materialistic scientific paradigm and don't follow your own truth.'

'So, we're just saying exactly what comes into our head today are we? That sounds character building and fun.'

'Your friend clearly doesn't hold us in very high esteem, so I can't imagine why she would need us.'

'Is this because of the cute comment?'

Roxy drank her coffee and glowered.

'She was jet-lagged, okay? I told you that.'

'We're not just playing around here, okay? We really do things. We make an actual impact on the world.'

'I know,' Lauren protested. 'I do know, okay? We've had lots of examples of that. We've manifested lots of things.'

'We have,' Roxy confirmed.

'Can you remind me of some?'

'That time Demniac needed a new job and we got him an interview.'

'Yeah, we did do that. He definitely got an interview. He didn't quite crack the job though.' Lauren played with the froth on the top of her cappuccino.

'That's because he totally rooted up the interview. We can only do so much; we're not complete miracle workers. We can't fix deep and ingrained personality failures.'

'It's just that…' Lauren chose her words carefully. 'You know how we're called 'the Cailleach's Cauldron'.'

'Yes.'

'Where did that come from?'

'From my deep and abiding interest in Celtic mythology.'

'Yes, fair. But has it ever struck you as odd that so many people here are set on calling things a derivation of the Cailleach?'

Roxy shrugged. 'Not really. Lots of us have European ancestry. It's in our genes.'

'Yes, I know that your DNA genetic testing results were quite conclusive regarding a small village in County Cork, but…' Lauren realised she was going to have to lay her cards on the table a bit more explicitly. 'Are you ready for some weirdness?'

'Always.'

'And can you try not to be a total bitch to me when I tell you because I'm going out on a limb here.'

'I'll do my best.'

'The reason why we're called the Cailleach's cauldron, and the reason why every second pub around here is called The Hag's Arms or The Crone's Rest, and the reason our entire Lammas ritual revolves around wheat production is because this entire area is occupied by an ancient Celtic goddess who has been an interloper here for 230 years, and it's the consensus of everyone involved that it's time she goes home.'

'All right,' Roxy said, quite reasonably.

'Also, she's Brigid's mother.'

'Of course she is.'

'And we need to summon her because she needs to be asked to leave, nicely, and for some inexplicable reason, it's been decided we're the best ones to do it.'

'Well, we are pretty good.'

'I feel like we're spectacularly unqualified, but I like your confidence.'

'I will say though,' Roxy said, that my knowledge of Celtic gods and goddesses, in particular, lead me to think that they can't be summoned. If they want to talk, they'll just turn up.'

'It's someone's mother, remember. She wants to feel needed. They had a falling out a while ago, and she's pretty pissed off at Brigid. Maybe there's the position of daughter up for grabs, if you're interested.' Lauren laughed to show that she was joking, but Roxy's face remained impassive. 'Anyway, she needs a big fuss and some pleading, and I imagine some baking of honey cake or mead or some such and maybe gnashing of teeth, I don't know.'

'That's more biblical. You need to stick to one pantheon if this is going to work. And don't tell Demniac or Sybella what we're doing, for fuck's sake, or they'll come up with some ritual they found on Wikipedia. No, this has to be taken seriously, and I'm the only one up for the job.'

Lauren could tell that the wheels were turning in Roxy's brain, and that this was, finally, something she could really get her teeth into. She tapped her sharply manicured nails on the edge of the plate in front of her and looked off into the distance. 'So this Brigid really needs us, does she?'

'You know, you could just call her Brigid, you know.'

'All right, I'm up for it. Give me a few minutes to make a phone call and cancel somethings and then we can get into it. I appreciate you telling me all this Lauren, I really do.'

Lauren didn't think she had ever heard Roxy speak so genuinely to her before, but that moment Morty burst into the cafe babbling something about a vengeful evil from another dimension.

26

It looked as if the boys had done a good job of restoring the shop to some kind of rudimentary order, but Lauren didn't get to enjoy the ambience because the six foot tall pacing bearded man who was vigorously rubbing his forehead and sweating slightly quickly occupied all of her attention.

As soon as she was inside, Morty locked the door and grabbed her hand urgently. 'We have a situation,' he said.'

'A bigger situation than the one we already have?'

'I think so,' Connall said. 'I'm not sure, I just...' He pressed his fingers to his forehead and closed his eyes for a moment. 'Things are not great.'

'Didn't we already know that?'

'More not great than we thought. I'm trying to piece together all the bits here, but there's an extra... layer, if you like, that I should probably tell you about.'

'On top of the layer that includes the fact that you're an Other World being trying to protect non-officially sanctioned creatures from some kind of misguided avenging serial killer?'

'Yes.'

'And that being the layer on top of the layer that includes that fact that my best friend is a goddess who needs me to convince her mother, who is also a goddess, but apparently quite crotchety, to leave Australia and go back where she came from?'

'Yes, it's another layer on top of all that. And I'd managed to completely forget about that particular bit, so thanks for adding to my stress levels.'

'What is with all you Celtic deities and Australia?' Morty asked Connall. 'Why the fuck are you all here anyway? What's wrong with your ancestral lands?'

Connall held out both his hands. 'UK weather/Aussie weather.' He waved them about in what Lauren assumed was supposed to be scales motion. 'It's not that complicated.'

'Wait,' Lauren said, realising what Morty had just said. 'What do you mean 'you deities'. What's going on? What am I not understanding?'

'Let me try to explain,' interrupted Morty. 'It was Connall they wanted when they came to your shop.'

'But they didn't ask for Connall. They asked for…' She looked to Morty for clarification.

'Cernunnos.'

'Yes, that's who they asked for.'

'And there's this.'

Morty pointed to a mark on the wall that had been previously hidden by a half torn Tree of Life wall hanging.

There was a straight line, intersected by three curved parallel lines that hung below it like fishhooks. Under this was a series of different sized half-moon shapes, some filled in black and some left as merely outlines. An oval scrawl surrounded the whole thing, drifting off at the edge as if its creator had been interrupted at the final stroke.

'Technically, if you want to be exact, it's my name,' Connall said. 'It's the traditional, ancient symbol of my name, given to me at the get go.'

'What's the get go?'

'I think you call it the Big Bang.'

'This is an archaic, mystical representation of Connall?' Lauren asked, squinting. 'I'm sorry, but I just can't see it.'

'Obviously not. Do you really think they came up with 'Connall' as one of the original labels at the creation of the Universe? Of course it's not Connall,' he said. 'It's my other name.'

'I suppose that makes sense,' she said. 'If you're, like, thousands of years old, or whatever. I suppose you've needed to change as you've gone through time, or whatever. Can't have Pilonious or whoever running a pub in the 21st century, can we now?' She giggled.

'You may as well tell her,' Morty said. 'She's just going to keep making jokes if you don't put her out of her misery.'

'All right,' Connall said, sitting down on one of the ottomans that made up the 'chillax' area of the shop, as Morty insisted on calling it. 'How can I explain this in a way that makes sense?'

'It's okay.' Morty laid a reassuring hand on Connall's massive arm and smiled at him.

'What, you're his emotional support animal now, are you?' Lauren asked.

'Keep in mind, the reason why I'm including you in all of this is because you've been a genuine help to me and the Imagos, and also because you're a friend of Morty's,' Connall said. 'So if you could try not to be so rude to him all the time I think that would progress our friendship by leaps and bounds.'

'But that's just our vibe' she said. 'That's our vibe. We joke. It's our relationship. Don't try and mansplain our relationship.'

Morty nodded. 'It is. Don't worry, it's fine. Just go on.'

'What would you say if I told you I'm actually an ancient Celtic deity too?'

'Um, I don't know. It depends on whether you're going to tell me that or not. Morty,' she said, turning her head. 'Morty, do you feel like Connall is about to tell me he's an ancient Celtic deity?'

'It's not quite the same though,' Morty continued on with the explanation, 'because Connall always knows who he is. He never had his memory wiped, and he never had an agreement with Devin about a sabbatical.'

'So not similar at all then?' Lauren smiled tightly. She was beginning to heartily regret becoming involved in this conversation in the first place.

'What do you know about Cernunnos?' Connall asked. 'He always had a role of kind of a green man wild thing but mainly known for bringing predators and prey together so they could live in peace. Sometimes known as the Horned God. Or I think lately they've been saying 'Lord of the Wild Things', but that's a new one, and I'm not keen on it.'

'Oh, him, yes, of course,' Lauren said. 'The Horned God.' She gestured over to a corner of the shop. 'Huge fan. He's a great little money spinner at the moment. I've got a bunch of books and about four different incense towers with his face on them. Also, there's an oracle deck kicking around here somewhere, although that reminds me, I need to order some more of them.'

Connall sighed.

'I told you she's become mercenary,' Morty hissed.

'People have always been into the whole Celtic pantheon, and over the last year, there's been a real uptick in interest in him. See?' Lauren went over to the cork-board that hung above the 'random acts of kindness moon cloth exchange' shelf and pointed to a poster that looked as if it had been drawn by hand. 'Finding Cernunnos: the Horned God Deep Inside Your Shadow Self.'

'Yeah, I saw that.' Connall said. 'I think that might be part of what's gotten me into trouble.'

'What do you mean?'

'All this Cernunnos stuff. It's really limited my ability to fly under the radar.'

'What? How?'

'Because it's me.'

'Sorry?'

'That's what I meant by a lot of Celtic deities being here,' Morty said excitedly. 'Three! Who would have thought it?'

'So you're this Cernunnos dude, are you?' Lauren stared at Connall.

'Sort of. It's a kind of archetype, to be honest, but if we're breaking it down to the lowest common denominator, then yes.'

'No wonder the original spirits of Australia are pissed off,' Lauren said darkly.

'Actually, they're not that fussed,' Connall said. 'We're pretty low stakes here, to be honest, and I've kept to myself. It's just the Cailleach that's giving them the shits at the moment, and that's more on principle because she keeps fucking with the weather and influencing people to use all their water to grow wheat and rice.' He glanced at Morty. 'Because I can't think of any other reason that supposedly rational people would try and grow such thirsty crops on a desert continent, can you?'

'Cernunnos, then?'

'Close enough, yes.'

'On a sabbatical, then, like Brigid? Needed a little break, did you? God, they really need to start giving far more vigorous job interviews up there in the...' She paused.

'Upper Realms,' Connall clarified.

'The Upper Realms. They need to have better job interviews in the Upper Realms or at least start introducing some really rigorous Myers-Briggs type tests because, as far as I can tell, you're all spectacularly unqualified. You just up and leave whenever you want.'

'I feel like you might not quite understand the pressure,' Connall said tightly.

'Aren't gods kind of necessary, though?' Lauren sounded indignant, as if she had been dealt a personal affront. 'Should you just be nicking off, leaving these gaping holes in reality all the time?'

'Eh.' Connall shrugged. 'It doesn't have as much effect as you'd think, to be honest. We're more like figureheads these days.'

'Like the king,' Morty said helpfully.

'Yeah, kind of. Anyway, my situation is different from Brigid's, and that's where we run into trouble. You see, I'm not here in any formally sanctioned sense. I'm here because Devin and I had a falling out, and I needed to make myself scarce. And, well, people from the old country were heading to Australia at the time, so I decided to join in. Make a new life for myself and blend in like any other convict starting fresh.'

'Is it that easy to hide from Devin, then?'

'I did have a trick or two up my sleeve. Remember, I am a god in my own right. But also I think he was probably turning a blind eye as long as I was keeping to myself because of the incident. We both needed to pretend the other didn't exist for a while. I think he was technically supposed to smite me, which is why I did a runner and why I think he was happy not to know where I was. No need for a follow up if I couldn't be found, and he was technically supposed to banish me or annihilate me or at least render me powerless, so it was easier all around to forget I existed.'

'Solid management technique.'

'I thought so.'

'So you're hiding because why? How does one piss off the ultimate and omnipotent leader of the known Universe?'

'There were quite a few things, if I'm being honest, but the main one was, if I remember correctly, was that I didn't want to wait till the next Tournament for my chance at the leadership, so I got drunk and tried to stage a coup.'

There was an aggressive banging on the door, and through

the glass, they could see Roxy glaring at them and vigorously gesturing at her watch.

'Shit, I forgot we had plans. With all this supernatural paranormal stuff going on at the moment, is there a chance that any of you have the ability to do something useful and clone me? Because I need to be in more than one place more often than not at the moment.'

'It's possible,' Connall said. 'But you wouldn't like it.'

'I've never actually asked whether there's magic wound up in all this, have I? I mean, I assume it's magic. That's always been my explanatory fall back.'

'Magic? Nothing so ephemeral, I'm afraid. No, it's all science. Primarily basic clinical transmogrification and non-consensual atomic manipulation. It's only called magic by people who never passed particle level physics. Or that weren't, you know, part of the creation team at the beginning of time and space, but that gives me a headache to think about. Your human brains would probably literally explode.'

'And we've just cleaned up,' Morty said helpfully.

'Okay, I'll be calling it magic then,' Lauren said.

Roxy banged again, and this time Lauren heard a thump that sounded suspiciously like a kick. She pointed to the lines on the wall that she had been able to rub away somewhat. 'What was the issue with this?'

'It's my name in the ancient language of the Upper Realms. I'd tell you, but human mouths can't say it properly, and it will sound somewhat embarrassingly biological. It's the Mestomorphs way of showing me they know I'm here. Because this place is full of Horned God stuff, they must have put two and two together and got five. So now I've been found.'

'But isn't that a really improbable coincidence? And then Morty just walked randomly into your pub?'

'First of all, I hate to sound like one of your affirmation cards, but there are far fewer coincidence than you'd think. And also, I suspect the Mestomorphs must have deduced that I live in the neighbourhood, and you've probably got a whiff of goddessness about you, given you've been close to Brigid for so long. They got a hit here, saw all this stuff, and quite reasonably concluded it was me who lived here. It makes sense.'

'And my shop suffered for it.'

'And so they left this symbol to let me know they would be back.'

'But why did the mesomorph get killed? And by who?'

'That would just be conjecture. A low-level minion looking for me before the big boys get into it. I've heard whispers that Devin has outsourced security, and maybe they went back through the books to clear up any unfinished business. And I have a strong suspicion I might be that unfinished business. What I am fairly certain about is that they haven't finished with me, and they will be back.'

27

'It's definitely going to need to be out in the bush. Somewhere deserted.' Brigid was emphatic about this particular element of summoning ritual when they met up to get things into a semblance of order.

'Why? I've cleansed my apartment specially. And I've rearranged things.' Roxy narrowed her eyes suspiciously. 'You're not expecting us to get naked are you? Because the last time we did that I nearly died of exposure. And I'm pretty sure that kind of thing is mired in Gardnerian misogyny.'

'God, no, everyone needs to keep their clothes on, or when my mum does arrive, she'll comment on how big peoples various arses have grown over the winter. This just needs to be in the bush.'

'Why?' Roxy's suspicion remained high.

'This isn't just your usual invocation. We're trying to get the attention of a real, eternally powerful goddess, and I just think that the true majesty of nature would be a better setting. Near water too. She's a big fan of water. She made Loch Ness.'

Roxy suspected that Brigid was making fun of her.

'And it's not even an invocation, precisely, is it?' she continued. 'Because none of you are offering to get possessed. You want the Cailleach to literally manifest in front of you.'

'No, you want the Cailleach to literally manifest. Don't forget that this is all on your behest.'

'You're not exactly running screaming, are you?'

'While we're on the topic, I didn't think you were going to have any part in it,' Roxy snapped. 'I thought you wanted to have a lot of distance from the whole process.'

'Yes, I do. I want nothing to do with it. But that doesn't mean I can't be kind of a consultant and pass on some pertinent advice. I am a goddess, after all.'

'Nice flex,' Morty said, nodding appreciatively. Roxy glared at him, but he just grinned back at her.

'Is there anything else we need to know?' Lauren asked, trying to move the process on.

'No, I think that's it. In the bush. Maybe a billabong nearby. Or the beach. The ultimate power and majesty of the ocean would be a really good idea now I think of it. Let's go with a beach. Unless you're worried about water spirits because they can be absolute buggers if they think you're trying to do some serious magic.'

'No, I know just the place,' said Roxy. She had an idea in her head of how this might go down, and while she didn't want to admit it, she was beginning to get excited.

And after many more arguments about whether there was going to be a Drawing Down the Moon ceremony, The Coven of the Cailleach found themselves on a beach on the night of the full moon in Virgo, with a carload full of candles and an air of great determination, a PDF of the Lesser Keys of Solomon and a slightly miffed Demniac who was disappointed because Leo had refused to take part in the ceremony.

✳✳✳

Roxy strode purposefully around the sand, placing candles at what appeared to be meticulously pinpointed intervals, occasionally peering off towards the moonlit horizon, and doing some quick, scattered motions with her hands. Demniac paced besides her, watching closely and imitating her when she wasn't looking.

He was very excited about the possibility of a real, live conjuring. All the entities he'd come into contact so far in his magical career seemed to think him an idiot, so he was enthusiastic about drawing in someone who might finally recognise his own self-identified magical prowess.

Sybella stood on the sidelines, away from the others watching. She had been very quiet and had driven herself down to the peninsula, protesting that she needed quiet time away from their babbling to compose herself.

She had a lot to think about.

Morty and Lauren leaned back on the sand, looking up at the millions of twinkling pinpoints of light.

'This is the first time we've been alone for ages,' Lauren said.

'Yes, I was just thinking that. Things have taken quite the turn of late.' Morty turned his head and smiled at her. 'Life suddenly got exciting.'

'Exciting or, you know, terrifying. I look at my life these days and don't even recognise what's going on. Do you still have a crush on me?'

He thought for a moment. 'I do still love you, I suppose. I probably always will because you're amazing. But I've got other

145

things to think about now. I think you were something for me to do when my life didn't have any other purpose.'

'Thank you very fucking much.'

'That wasn't meant to sound rude, sorry. But do you know what I mean?'

'Yeah, I suppose so. Will you still do things for me though? I need someone to hang on my every word and anticipate my needs.'

'Probably not.'

'Dammit.'

'You could get a puppy?' Morty suggested.

'So are you and Connall together now? Brigid seems to think you might be.' Lauren turned her head to look at Morty, but he didn't make eye contact.

'Does it matter?'

'Not specifically, but I'm curious.'

'We prefer not to put labels on it, but things are progressing.' She couldn't see in the darkness, but Lauren suspected that Morty was smiling.

'I don't blame you. He's fucking hot. I was hoping I'd stand a chance with him, but I feel like he only has eyes for you.'

'What can I say. I've got a certain something.'

The stars continued to shine above them.

'What's that thing that they say. Without darkness, the stars cannot shine,' said Morty.

'By 'they' do you mean that Affirmations for Dummies book I've had to reduce to $2.99 to get anyone to buy it?'

He humoured her with a smile. 'I mean, I know things are hard at the moment; we don't know what's going on, we've been sucked into events that don't concern us, and everything is in flux. But I think we'll come out of this with so much more than we started.'

'You'll come out with a hot boyfriend. I'm still not sure what's in all this for me,' she said.

'I dunno. Just watch Chuckles over there, and you'll come out of this being able to teach a summoning 101 class at your shop.'

They laughed companionably as Roxy finally stood in the middle of a rough shape constructed out of seaweed and candles and what looked like seagull bones. She raised her hands. 'We are ready. It can begin.'

'Shit, here we go. Things are kicking off.' Lauren stood and reaching out a hand helped Morty to his feet. 'Let's do it.'

'Do you think it will work?' he asked.

'I don't think the actual ritual has that much to do with it, from what Brigid has said. I mean, in a technical sense. I think it's a question of the Cailleach being impressed enough to deign us with her presence. I'm pretty sure no one has the power to 'make' a deity do anything, and if you think that you do, then you're in for a world of trouble.'

Morty dusted off his pants. 'Okay, it's go time.'

Lauren hugged him.

Roxy's arms were still extended above her head, and she stood within the circle. 'We shall begin,' she called regally. 'Stop slouching, you two. Project your etheric bodies out into the Universe. Hold your heads up! Feel numinous.'

They stood taller, glancing at each other. 'Feel numinous,' Morty hissed, and Lauren giggled, stepping into the circle that had been scraped into the sand.

'Oh, come on, guys.' Demniac sighed with exasperation and shook his head. 'You've just buggered up the inscriptions. Jesus, just stay there and don't move, and I'll write them again.' He took a stick and, glancing down, Lauren saw that there were words scrawled into the sand around the outside of the circle. Demniac bustled them into positions where they couldn't do any more damage and recreated the inscriptions.

'Fixed?' Roxy asked.

Demniac took a last critical glance at the large circle, the words scratched into the sand, the candles and the urns of incense that drifted their heady contents into the night air and gave Roxy a thumbs up before taking his place within the boundaries.

'Will you be joining us?' Roxy called to Sybella, who remained standing, arms crossed, on the water's edge. Her eyes were closed, and her face lifted as if tasting the breeze that blew in from the ocean.

There was a moment's pause. 'We need you,' Roxy added, and with that, Sybella turned and walked up the beach toward them.

Five souls, one circle. Time seemed to stand still. The only sound that could be heard was the eternal wash of the water gently lapping against the sand. A single owl hooted in the eucalyptus. Eternity held its breath.

'Great Goddess Cailleach.' Roxy's thin high voice broke the air. 'Great Goddess Cailleach, Goddess of the Cold and Wind, Venerated Veiled one and the Queen of Winter, Dark Mother, Creator of counties and reaper of harvests, we come here tonight to call on your majesty and beg of your presence.'

Besides her, Demniac repeated the words; he clearly had them memorised.

'Are we supposed to say them too?' Lauren hissed.

'No,' Roxy whispered back to her. 'Just stand there and try to draw in the presence. Concentrate on drawing her in.'

'Great Cailleach,' Roxy continued. 'Oh, exalted one, Great Ancient Grandmother, hear us now as we call to you and lay prostrate before you.'

There was a pause.

'Lay prostrate,' Roxy hissed.

They lay on the sand.

'Why are you still standing up,' Lauren asked, her voice

muffled by the grains.

'One of us has to keep things moving,' Roxy said.

'Sybella, why are you still standing up then?'

'I'm allergic to sand.'

'Oh, Mother Cailleach, great hag and progenitor of eons, hear our plea and bring your presence to the circle.'

Above her, Lauren could see Roxy moving about and wafting incense, making gestures in the air and doing curious little stepping motions around them.

'Maybe say she's fabulous, and we need her for advice or something?' Morty called. 'Brigid says she needs to be wanted.'

'Ssshhhh,' Roxy hissed.

'Has anyone told her that the precise ritual isn't necessary. We're not actually capturing her or forcing her to do anything. We're trying to convince a sulky old mother who feels snubbed by her people that she should come and talk to us. Has anyone mentioned that?' asked Morty.

'Many times,' Lauren said.

Roxy had come to a halt. There was no movement except for the water gently patting against the shore. Lauren rested her head on her arms and closed her eyes. It was an oddly relaxing situation.

A low whistling started up, somewhere in the air above the circle. It seemed to rise and fall on the air, drifting in and out, first with absolute clarity and then disappearing. At its loudest, it seemed to vibrate within Lauren, its tone matching some hidden place deep within her. Out on the water, some unseen bird heard the sound and matched it itself, its slightly higher call echoing until the ground itself seemed to vibrate with the sounds.

Lauren could feel herself drifting off. She seemed to be floating above her body, a strange but not unwelcome sensation. She could feel the breeze on her face, even though she knew that her physical self was still face down in the sand, and she could taste the salt of the water in her mouth as her etheric body begun to gently turn so that her body was facing the swollen moon, its pale light somehow warming her face. She could feel the slight pull of the glistening cord that joined her physical body with whatever she was now, but it wasn't unpleasant, just a memory. A reminder of who she was. But now other options stretched out before her; now there were other possibilities, and she wanted to—

A warm, wet tongue licked her ear.

28

There was an unpleasant whoosh as Lauren was sucked, disoriented, back into her body.

The warm wet sensation was joined by heavy breathing as heaving air covered the side of her face. She threw her arm up instinctively and cried out in alarm, feeling liquid trickle into the curve of her ear.

There was an excited bark and then, absurdly, a man's voice calling out over the sand towards them.

'Persephone! Persephone, come here. Come here, girl. Oh, my goodness, I'm so sorry. Are you all right? Why are you all lying there on the ground? Has there been a gas leak?'

Lauren stood up, somewhat woozily, and found herself using the large golden retriever that was now sitting amicably by her side, tail sweeping widely, to steady herself.

The man bustled into their midst, his shuffling feet spraying sand in all directions, and Persephone ran around in excited circles, obviously a big fan of the way that this night walk had turned out. What was left of the outline of the circle was destroyed completely. The dog's flailing tail snuffed the remaining candles, dispensing the artfully arranged seaweed in all directions, and all that was left were six people and a dog on a beach in the middle of the night.

'Is everyone all right? Do you need help?' The man pulled a misshaped beret from his head and rolled it around in his hands, a look of worry on his round face.

'We were fine. We were in the middle of something actually, so if you could just leave us in peace, we could continue,' said Roxy.

The man looked around, sensing that something was afoot. His eyes lit on the scattered candles, the urns and the rocks placed at significant intervals, and the look of worry on his face compounded to the power of twenty. 'Oh, I'm sorry. Are you hippies?'

'No we're wiccans,' snapped Roxy.

'I'm not,' Demniac protested. 'Neither is Lauren.'

'Or me,' Morty said.

Sybella had wandered off somewhere.

'I hope you're not stirring up the water spirits or, god forbid, the JanJans. They just calmed down after that kerfuffle last year, and I don't have the time or energy to talk them through their personal crisis yet again. They become discontented when you create flux, you see, and then they want to live here on the land, and they play havoc with the poor wombats who just don't understand why a water spirit wants to hide in the burrows they spent time and energy digging rather than in the water where they're supposed to be. They're tricksters at heart, and they spend time trying to find some poor backpacker to play silly buggers with and chip away trying to get at pieces of their brain. Some people don't energetically protect themselves properly, you see, and trust me when I tell you they can sniff those kinds of people out a mile away. I'm still catching up on my crosswords because of all the time I wasted trying to get them back into the water and sorting out their existential crises. So if what you're doing has any chance of getting their attention or upsetting them, then I really wish you'd find another beach to do whatever it is you're doing on this one because I, for one, am not as young as I used to be, and I just don't have the energy anymore.'

They all stared at him. Persephone's tail continued to sweep the ground. She had no idea exactly what was going on, but she was loving it.

'I'm sorry?' Roxy said.

'I hope you're not going to annoy the JanJans, is all.'

'We have no plans to.'

'That doesn't mean it's still not going to happen, in my experience.' He crossed his arms firmly.

Roxy opened her mouth as if to speak and then thought better of it. She took her hands from her hips and crossed her arms. Realising this didn't work for her either, she put her hands on her hips again.

Lauren looked around. Clouds were beginning to cover the moon, and whatever liminal vibe had been hanging over the area in which they sat had now been well and truly dispersed.

The man fixed Persephone's leash firmly to her collar and brought her to her feet. 'All right then, I'll leave you alone. But I would appreciate you taking this somewhere else in future, if it's all the same to you. Actions have repercussions, you know. Youth don't seem to understand that these days. You don't think, you know. You never think. And then the rest of us have to pick up the pieces.'

Lauren glanced around. Morty was staring down at the ground, kicking the sand awkwardly. Demniac was looking to Roxy for a sign of what to do next, and Sybella was standing at the water's edge, still staring intently out to sea.

He looked at her for a moment. 'Watch that one,' he said suddenly. 'She's opened too far.' He turned and shuffled away.

They glanced at each other, feeling as if they had just been told off by the principal for doing something not particularly naughty, but slightly against rules they hadn't known existed.

'What should we do now?' Lauren asked.

Roxy sighed and looked around. 'I don't think we should keep going. I doubt I can draw up that energy again. Did you feel it, though? I really think we were doing something here.'

Lauren nodded. 'Yes, I felt something. Like I was disassociating from my body. Something was certainly going on.'

Morty nodded excitedly. 'Yes, I had that too! Like space and time and eternity were all one, and I was just a microcosm of a microcosm in —'

'Well, it's fucked now,' Roxy said grudgingly. 'We might as well pack up and head home. What a balls up this has turned out to be.'

She and Demniac started picking up the detritus of the ritual, and Lauren walked over to Morty.

'Should you be the one to tell Brigid this didn't work?' he asked. 'I feel like she had a lot riding on this. She'll be disappointed.'

'Remember though, I'm the one who was asked to make this happen. Maybe I shouldn't have outsourced it to Roxy.'

'Sybella, can you come over here and help please? You're as useless as tits on a bull tonight, and its been a big enough waste of time as it is.' Roxy has reached the stage when all she wanted was a hot water-bottle and her bed.

'There's something in my head,' she called out.

'Yeah, okay,' Demniac replied. 'Can you move these rocks for me?'

'No, really,' she said as she glided up the beach towards them.

The voices calling from the water had begun as a small, almost imperceptible noise. A faint calling, like a dove cooing from far off over the horizon somewhere. As they had begun to get closer to the beach, the noise crystallised into a murmur of voices that was definitely coming from outside her head, as opposed to inside, as had been happening worryingly often of late.

She could pinpoint exactly when it had happened too. To the exact moment. It was when she had felt the burst of fetid air blast through her in the pyramid that Leo had taken her too. The fragmentation. The feeling that bits of her weren't where they were supposed to be, that they were rearranged, that new things had been added, and that some were missing completely. And after a while, while the coven were busy levitating and patting strange dogs, the JanJans spoke to her.

'There was something in my head. Or someone. I've just spent an instructive hour learning a few things from the water spirits. They've removed the interloper from my head, but that's not going to fix the issue, I'm afraid.'

'What, while we were doing the ritual?' said Morty.

'Yes. I think we might have a problem. Morty, you know how your Connall has an issue with something attacking his Imagos?'

'How do you know about that?'

'I know everything now. Well, maybe not everything specifically but a fair amount. The water spirits told me things. And Lauren can't keep a secret.'

'It's true, I can't.'

'The serial killer is a disembodied chaos spirit that takes over people's bodies and uses them for its own wiles. And I'm sorry to say that it's been using me.'

'What?' asked Lauren abruptly.

'I think that I've been the Imago serial killer. It's gone now. The water spirits removed it. Whatever they are, they have a soft spot for the Imagos, and they aren't a big fan of the chaos spirit or willy-nilly killing in general.'

'That's pretty awkward,' Lauren said breaking the silence. 'You were doing it? You're a killer?'

'Well, yes, but it wasn't my fault. They told me something entered me when I was inside the Great Pyramid. Something was in there with us. Something contained. Something banished and trapped on purpose, but for what, the spirits didn't know. They're better at general vibes rather than specifics. But it entered me and made me do things.'

They were all staring at her, horrified.

'What was it?' Roxy asked. Her eyes lit up with bright fascination.

'A chaos agent,' said Sybella simply. 'Something that causes misery and suffering. Its body is still trapped in the pyramid, but its soul was able to enter me. I didn't know about it until just now.'

'Wait, when were you in the Great Pyramid? And why?' Roxy was staring at Sybella intently.

'Leo took me there,' Sybella said, looking at Demniac pointedly.

'Jesus,' Demniac croaked.

'I know.' Sybella shrugged. 'I mean, I feel bad, obviously.'

'So you've been the one destroying Connall's Imagos?' Morty's pale face looked horrified. 'That's pretty awkward.'

'Look, didn't I just say I feel bad about it? I'm going to need some time to process this, and I've only done it once, the murdering, as far as I can tell. On the night of the fire. Oh, shit.' She bit her lip.

'What?' asked Morty.

'I caused the fire too.' Her eyes drifted off as she became lost in thoughts. 'It was terrible. He forced the part of me that was me deep inside myself and took control. I could feel the anger, the creeping evil crawling all over the surface of my mind like bugs, but if the essential 'me' stayed deep within myself then I would stay safe. I can't remember the details of what he was doing with my body exactly, I just know that it felt like I was having a night terror without any clear linear story-line, just hiding from the anger and the love of misery.'

'But this is monstrous. Horrific,' spat Morty.

'It was,' said Sybella, wiping tears from her eyes. 'I don't know how I'm going to heal from it.'

'You're the one we've been fighting against.' Morty would not be placated. 'I can barely look at you!'

'Just settle down, man,' Demniac said. 'It wasn't her, really though, was it? It was something using her body. She was just a vessel. A meat suit. A mindless—'

'Yes, okay, thanks.' Sybella cut him off.

Roxy cut in. 'What Demniac is trying, fairly ineptly, to say, is that 'she' didn't do it. Any more than a car is to blame if it mows down a pedestrian. She wasn't in control of herself.'

The coven stood and stared at each other.

'Better out than in, though, right?' Lauren offered and quickly wished she hadn't.

'The fact is,' Sybella said, 'that unfortunately, something was inside me, but now it's gone. That's a good thing, right?'

'Why didn't that lion thing know about this? He looks pretty bloody omnipotent. Why couldn't he tell that thing was inside you?' Morty clearly wanted answers, and he wanted them now.

'Hang on,' Demniac said. 'I think I've heard about these things. Yeah, I have, I've read about them. A chaos spirit. Ancient. Really, really ancient. A succubus, essentially. It feeds on misery and destruction. There have been reports throughout history of these arseholes bringing about some seriously bad shit throughout human history.'

'Are you sure this isn't just a myth that people started up to try and make excuses about the depravity that humans are responsible for? The devil made me do it and all that?' suggested Morty.

'Nah, this is older than the devil. This goes way back before any of your Abrahamic shenanigans. No, this is some really ancient, destructive shit.' He stopped speaking and looked at Sybella with a newfound respect. 'And you were a vessel for it.'

She shivered a little and hugged herself.

'I wonder why though…' he started but broke off.

'No, what?'

'I wonder why it would bother with you? And Imagos? Seems small beer for a protozoan spirit of chaos and destruction. Why would it be so set on unleashing fury and anger? It felt very personal. Occupying some nobody from Melbourne and killing weird things that don't even matter is a strange choice.'

'Excuse me?' Morty said.

'Come on, you know what I mean.'

Morty had to grudgingly admit that, yes, he did.

'I guess we'll never know now,' Sybella said. 'It's gone.'

'Well, it's somewhere.'

They all looked up into the night sky and instinctively drew together. 'It could be finding someone else right now,' Lauren whispered.

'I don't think we have the energy to get into that though,' Roxy said, the first of them to pull herself together. 'We need to get back home. The actual point of the evening, as hijacked as it's been by Sybella, was an absolute washout, if you remember.'

As they began to carry things back to the cars, and as Demniac began his usual 'shit where are my keys' moves, there was a call from the bush beyond the beach as Persephone's owner reappeared.

'Excuse me, but there's a lady here who wants me to tell you, and you must understand that I'm quoting her here, that she's fucking freezing her tits off, and if you want to talk to her, you'd best get moving because she's rapidly getting sick of the pack of you.'

<h1 style="text-align:center">29</h1>

Lauren had never had a fixed idea in her mind of what a divine hag and a weather deity should look like. Even at a pinch, the best she could have come up with was probably something with Medusa-ish hair. But within that fairly non-specific framework of not knowing, she was absolutely certain she hadn't expected a small, round woman with a face that looked like a dried apple, wearing a floral house-dress covered by a blue and red striped apron and a crochet green cardigan, her short body topped by a pink knitted beanie from which escaped wispy strands of grey hair. Leaning on a stick that looked as if it had been attached to a gum-tree a matter of hours ago, she looked like someone's adorable if slightly befuddled and musty smelling great-grandmother.

'Well, I'm here now.' The voice that came out of the impossibly wrinkled face demonstrated very clearly that her lungs might not be as old as the rest of her. 'Here I am,' she bellowed across the beach at them, leaning on the arm of the man as he brought her unsteadily forwards. 'Why the hell did you need to do it here, for fuck's sake? It's miles from home, and I've been walking for hours. My feet are killing me. I'm no good on the sand. I don't know how you didn't know that. This had better be good.'

They all stared at her.

She released the man's arm and reached up, giving him a quick peck on the cheek with her papery lips. 'Thank you, lovey, I can take it from here.'

'Are you sure you'll be okay?' he asked, concerned flitting across his face. He eyed the coven as if he did not, in any way, trust them to have this old woman's best interests at heart.

She patted his hand, beaming at him. 'I can look after myself.'

'Um, are you the Cailleach?' Roxy asked somewhat nervously.

'Yes, yes.' The old woman brushed her question away with a flick of her hand. 'Who else would I be? Who else would be stupid enough to be wandering around out here at one in the morning? Who else would do this for you, given the state of my knees? No one else would, let me tell you that right now. No one else would be there for you like I am. Or are you so incompetent that you were just calling any random being that happened to be flitting around? Are you that stupid? I can see that you've pissed off the water spirits, too, so you're really covering yourself in glory tonight, aren't you, girlie?'

The man let out bark of laughter, causing Persephone to come to his feet, sit and look up at him anxiously.

'You can look after yourself, can't you?' He grinned delightedly at the Cailleach. 'I haven't heard hide nor hair of you for years.'

'Yes, well,' she said. 'It seems as if I'm needed again. No rest for the wicked, is there?'

The man laughed again, absolutely delighted with this turn of events. Persephone stared at him as if she were a seizure dog alerting him to an imminent episode. She hadn't seen him this animated in years.

'You're back,' he chortled. 'Just wait till I tell Mavis. She'll be that tickled.' He glanced at the young people that still stood, bemused, around them. They had unconsciously formed a circle as she came across the sand, and now they seemed to be mirroring the ritual that they had so recently abandoned. 'I'll leave you to it, then. Feel free to come around for a cuppa if you're free. It'd be grand to catch up and chat about the old days.'

'Lovely.' She smiled at him again. 'Off you pop, now. I have business to attend to.'

Persephone sniffed then licked the old woman's feet, and the man and his dog headed back into the night.

'Well, I,' Roxy said, uncertainly. She simply didn't know where to go at this stage. 'Thank you for … coming.'

There was some uncomfortable clearing of throats and glancing around for a few moments until Demniac broke the silence. 'We are greatly honoured to find you within our presence, and we bow before you. Um... What would you have us do, O Great One?'

The Cailleach turned her laser focused, gimlet eyes on him. 'That's better,' she said approvingly. 'I like this one. Which one are you?'

'Demniac,' he said.

'Yes, of course, Demniac. Well, I've obviously been misinformed because from what I can tell, you're the only one around here with a sensible head on their shoulders.'

She held out her arm to him, and he took it. He could feel energy thrumming through her like an electric shock, but it rapidly dispersed, and he had the impression that he was simply holding the arm of a little old lady.

'You can call me Granny,' she said to him, patting his hand that held the crook of her arm.

Roxy stepped forwards, 'Well, Granny...'

'Not you,' she snapped. 'I'm the Cailleach to the rest of you.'

'Will we be going to your car now?' she said sweetly to Demniac, who began to lead her to the vehicles.

'Are we leaving?' Sybella called.

'Not you,' she said, swinging around with more agility that her appearance would belie. 'Not you though. I don't want to be in a vehicle with you. You're not right.'

'No, it's gone,' Sybella snapped back at her. 'The... thing, it's gone, and I'm fine now, thank you very much.'

'So you say.' The Cailleach frowned and looked up into the air for a moment. 'That's as may be, but I want to be well away from you for a while. You still have the stink of it on you. You need to go and wash. Didn't they tell you that?' She looked pointedly at the black ocean.

'What, in there?'

'Best place for a cleansing.'

'There's no way I'm going in there. It's the middle of the night, and it's freezing.'

'Suit yourself. But I'm not going to be anywhere near you until you do. And the fact that you didn't even know that this was going on until tonight means that you probably need to start taking advice from your betters.'

Lauren, Morty and Roxy looked apologetically at Sybella as they followed Demniac and his new best friend to the car park. They could hear Sybella muttering something about having bought her own car and not even wanting to ride with an old woman who smelled like moth balls anyway.

Roxy pulled Demniac aside before they all squeezed in the back seat together. 'So, you know something about this chaos agent, do you?'

He nodded. 'I've read about it. Proper books, not just the internet.'

'It's powerful, is it?'

He nodded again. 'Deeply old and deeply powerful. I've read that it's evil, but I feel like that's just our values being put onto non-human entities. It transfers its energy to whoever it possesses, as we saw with Sybella, but the concept of evil is relative, after all. Sure, I've heard it described as malevolent and depraved, but who are we to judge other's realities and thrust our patriarchal, capitalist interpretations on—'

She held her hand up to stop him. He had told her everything she needed to know.

30

'What do you mean, she's staying at Demniac's place?' Brigid said when she arrived at Lauren's house at precisely 9.00 am the next morning, searching for her mother. 'I've made up her room. I bought hand towels and tiny shell shaped soaps, for god's sake. I made it nice. She's supposed to be staying with me.'

'Well, you were pretty unspecific about that bit, to be fair,' Lauren said, yawning hugely and tying her hot pink flannelette dressing gown firmly around her waist. 'You didn't specifically say you wanted her to stay with you. You conspicuously didn't say you wanted her to stay with you, as I remember it. Non-invitation by omission.'

'She's my mother!'

'Exactly the reason why I assumed you'd want to avoid her.'

Frowning, Brigid blew the air out of her mouth and followed Lauren into the kitchen, where the jug was boiling. 'Did she ask about me then? Is she coming to see me or talk to me or ... anything?'

'Look, the whole thing was pretty haphazard, and we were all really tired. She just started talking like it was assumed she was staying with him, and so it happened. He had to swing by the twenty-four hour Kmart to buy an air mattress to put in his lounge room for him to sleep on, but it wasn't actually discussed as such.'

'But his place is a hovel. It's practically possessed. No, I think it's literally possessed. And doesn't he have that lion staying with him?'

'Yeah, well that's the funny bit. Within a few minutes of being there, the whole place felt lighter. As if it was filling with good energy. And that's not necessarily something I would expect, because your mum isn't, forgive me for this, full of love and light. I was under the impression that she was mean to everyone based on the two hour car ride that I endured. But when we left there at 3.00 am, she was sweeping the hallway and trying to get Demniac to nip out to the cemetery to 'acquire' some flowers for the vanity in the bathroom. And the lion was nowhere to be seen. Demniac thinks he might have returned to wherever he came from.'

'Yeah, actually, it's just me she's hard on. People generally love her. She brings a nurturing quality to the whole 'liminal crone' thing. She's a real fan favourite.'

'I can see that now you come to mention it.'

'If she loves you, she really, really loves you.'

'She loves Demniac.'

Brigid shrugged. 'That will probably be good for him. He needs to be taken under someone's wing.'

'Oh, and she hates Sybella already.'

'Why?'

'Apparently, she got possessed by a chaos agent thing while visiting the Great Pyramid five thousand years ago and has been killing Connall's Imagos. She didn't know until it left though.'

'Huh,' Brigid said eventually. 'I was not expecting that.'

'Neither was Sybella.'

'How is she?'

'When I spoke to her this morning, she seemed to be getting a cold because of a midnight skinny dip, or some-such thing. But she was okay. Roxy's staying with her. She's resilient. You know Sybella.'

'Not really. I mean, I'm surprised she was being possessed by a discarnate trans-dimensional entity, obviously, because she wasn't acting like a crazed killer, but I don't know her.'

'Should we tell Connall? Surely that means the main danger to the Imagos has passed.' Brigid suddenly realised that the house was conspicuously quiet. She glanced around. 'Where is he, anyway? What's going on? Where is everyone?'

'Oh, I've moved them in next door for the duration. The owners are running a retreat centre in Bali for a few months, and I offered to water their houseplants, so I gave Connall the key and moved the whole lot of them in there. I needed my house back.'

'You put them into someone else's house? Isn't that pretty unethical?' Brigid seemed aghast. 'They're squatters.'

'My taking on board the grey areas of decision making has come on leaps and bounds over the last few weeks,' Lauren said drily. 'I would avoid asking my opinion about the vast majority of things at the moment.'

'You didn't put anyone in my house when I was away, did you?'

'No, of course not. I couldn't get in. You didn't leave me a bloody key, did you? You're right, though. We'd better get Connall up to speed.'

A rough doorway had been cut through the grey wooden back fence between the two properties some time in the past, so Lauren didn't feel any pressing need to get dressed before they popped next door. Coffees in hand, Brigid and Lauren slid through the gap into what Lauren had always seen as the serenity of next door.

The yard was bigger than Lauren's, which had been subdivided during the heady property bubble of the 90s, and now both her house and the flat behind her existed on just enough lawn each to convincingly die and look stark and bleak every January.

Next door, however, the grass stretched back expansively. Aged, gnarled apricot trees dotted the grass, and just beyond a red brick wall that seemed to be attached to nothing was the remnants of an incinerator, a concrete block built square that

Australian fathers from time immemorial used to burn every piece of rubbish from their shed, creating a comforting, if not extremely toxic smoky fug, that hung above the roofs of the suburb at around 10.00 am every Sunday like clockwork. Until they were banned in the 1980s and granddads everywhere had to find alternate disposal methods for their soft plastics.

An empty veggie garden sat just outside the back door, the netting hanging forlornly until next spring, and through the glass window that made up the back wall of the house, Lauren could see figures moving backwards and forwards, leaning over the large wooden table that stood in the room, and carrying piles of papers and books. While they watched, Morty wandered in, still in his dressing gown, also holding a coffee mug. He walked over to Connall, who was sitting head down at the table and placed the cup in front of him. He wrapped his arms around Connall's neck and rested his chin on the top of the big man's head. Connall raised his hand and absentmindedly touched Morty's cheek as he kept reading what was on the table in front of him.

'Ah, shit,' Lauren said.

'Whoops,' Brigid said.

'Bugger it.'

'To be fair, he never really was interested,' Brigid said. 'He only had eyes for Morty from the get-go.'

'Oh, no, not him,' Lauren dismissed. 'Far too much work. It's Morty. He was my back up if I hadn't found anyone by the time I was forty-five.'

'Lucky escape for him then really, isn't it?'

'Speaking of which,' Lauren said. 'Is there any news on Egragore?'

'Egragore?'

'Your husband. Your actual husband.'

'Yes, I know who Egragore is, I just don't understand the

segue.'

'Possible husbands.'

'Ah. Perfect. And no, and I don't want to talk about it, thank you very much.'

At that moment, the back door opened, and Pearly Jean, a small boy with owl eyes and wings poked his head out. 'Hello, you two,' he called cheerfully. 'I suppose you've heard that our own genocidal maniac is currently a disembodied entity prowling around the country trying to find a new body to inhabit in order to continue to unleash untold destruction on our kind?'

'I knew it wasn't in Sybella anymore,' Lauren said. 'I hadn't extrapolated the rest of that, but it does make sense.'

'Great, well, in that case Connall said could you please get inside undercover where you're not, and I quote, 'two great big stupid sitting ducks standing in the middle of a yard like literal targets, for mercy's sake, what the fuck do they think they're doing, the bloody idiots?'' Realising that Connall was gesturing vigorously to them, they hurried inside.

The usually pristine sun-room looked like a war office. Piles of photocopied pages sat on every available surface, along with empty coffee mugs and plates holding unappetisingly dried morsels. Titles such as 'Trans-dimensional Ally-ship: Time to Bond', 'Cellular meditation for your inner soul healing', and 'The Ancient Messages of Fillair the Spectacular', were scattered over the rattan chairs.

'Jesus Christ,' Lauren said. 'You've only been in here for twelve hours. How the hell have you made this much mess already?'

'Where did these come from?' Brigid asked, leafing through one book and seeing 'Of Occult Philosophy Of Magical Ceremonies: The Fourth Book'.

'I printed them off last night,' Connall said grimly.

'This morning, rather,' Morty said. 'As soon as I got home, I told him about the whole trans-dimensional entity situation and, well, things kind of kicked off straight away.'

Various Imagos were coming and going, moving through the plastic fly curtain, a lingering remnant of the 70s, that separated the sun-room from the kitchen. Lauren recognised many of them, and they gave her a friendly smile or a wave, but their faces seemed pinched, worried.

'So Morty told you then? About our situation?' Connall asked.

No one answered.

'Are you angry at Sybella?'

'No.' Connall's monosyllabic answer hung in the air.

'Did you hear about The Cailleach then? How we managed to get her after all?'

Brigid nudged Lauren softly. 'I think they're a bit preoccupied,' she whispered.

Surely enough, Morty, Black Annie and Connall were oblivious to the questions. They were working through the papers methodically, highlighters in hands, sticky labels piled up between them. They were speed reading, flicking through the pages, underlining, looking backwards and forwards every few seconds and then discussing with each other, cross-referencing and turning the papers around so the rest of them could examine pertinent points and ideas of interest.

Ariadne pushed through the fly strip screen and beckoned to them. 'Come into the kitchen,' she said, the fins that ran down her back changing colours with each breath she took. 'I can explain what's going on to you if you like. They need to work.'

Gunter was standing at the stove, a grand fry up breakfast well underway. The kitchen was large and homely, with a table in the middle of the room which Harry and his wife had eaten around for fifty years, first alone, then with their children, and now with their grandchildren when said grandchildren had time away from their frightfully expensive boarding schools in Sydney. The family were aggressively more socially mobile each generation, and Lauren had suspected for a while that the blood line would probably be petering out soon. She had met the grand-kids. They were pretty ordinary.

'It looks like you're making yourselves at home too,' Lauren said nervously, looking around at the piles of dishes and plates that lined the usually pristine surfaces. 'You are being careful, aren't you? They will notice if anything is out of place when they get back.'

'I'm sure you checked that they were going to be careful before you gave them the key?' Brigid said sweetly.

'Of course we are,' Guntar said, turning around and using all three arms to serve Brigid, Lauren and Ariadne hefty plates full of bacon, eggs toast and tomato. 'It's just so lovely to have a place to call our own, a place that's ours. And I finally get to cook! I've never been able to cook. Never had a chance to. My father gave me the desire when he created me, but… You know how that all goes. And here we don't have to hide, you know? Even at the pub, we had to be quiet if we were upstairs during the day, and if we weren't there, then we just kind of roamed around, you know.'

'Until the killing started,' Ariadne said solemnly.

'That's right,' Guntar agreed. 'Until the killing started.'

'And do we think that's all stopped now then?' asked Lauren.

Ariadne snorted and Guntar rolled his eye. 'Hardly,' he said. 'That's what all that business in there is. They need to try and discover where the chaos agent might turn up. Didn't you notice all the ancient occult texts on the table?'

'Well, yes, although they didn't look that ancient. They're still warm from the printer.'

'Connall had to download them from the internet. He doesn't have the 1544 dodo leather bound version of the Necronium of

Bleratski just lying around, you know.'

'What it means, though,' Ariadne interrupted, 'is that now a disembodied spirit is flitting around the place, trying to find someone else to occupy. Connall doesn't understand why it's so fixated on us, or even what its true nature is, so that's why they're looking into it.'

'Why was it in Sybella, though?' asked Lauren.

'That's what they don't understand. The thought form took her to the pyramid where the spirit entered her, but we don't know why. We don't know what's going on. Connall will sort it, though. He always knows what to do.' Her eyes drifted towards to door, and Lauren saw in them a look that could almost be called adoration.

'Brigid,' Connall called. 'Can you come here for a minute?'

'Can I bring my breakfast?' she asked through a mouthful of bacon.

She took his huge sigh as a yes.

'I need your help. You and I have an advantage here. We are, after all, Other-world beings, despite our preoccupation with slumming it down here with the humans. If we put our minds to this, using our trace memories, we have to be able to come up with something. There must be a clue in here somewhere about what's going. About why a chaos agent is obsessed with Imagos and also where it's going to go next.'

'Yeah, all right,' Brigid said, pushing the papers aside to make room for her plate. 'Tell me what you already know.'

'Right.' Connall clicked his fingers, and Morty lifted up a pile of papers to his left, opening it to a premarked spot. 'So what do you know about chaos agents? Do you have any real world experience with them?'

'Not as such. Not real world as such. I don't have all those memories. And even if I did, I wouldn't necessarily know about trans-dimensional chaos agents, or whatever they are. If you want to jam about hearths and herbs and, I dunno, sheep, then I'm your girl. This whole trans-dimensional agent of chaos sounds like something out of a Lovecraft novel.'

Connall sighed. Again. 'I'm finding you immensely disappointing. The first genuinely expansive mind that I've come across in one hundred years, and you've got yourself all confined and boxed up. You're technically unlimited, you know.'

Brigid tapped her head with annoyance 'Not with this head, okay?' I'm better looking when I'm proper Brigid too, but you don't see me whining about it, do you?'

'You do say you wish your boobs were perkier,' Lauren offered helpfully.

'That's more of a 'me in my 20s thing' rather than a goddess thing, though,' Brigid answered.

'Right,' Morty said, deciding he needed to steer the conversation in a vaguely useful direction. 'Here's what we need. We need to understand who this chaos agent is exactly. We can't do anything about it until we have a better idea what we're dealing with. What do we know so far? Connall, go.'

'Traditionally, chaos agents are disembodied entities that prowl, figuratively, around the world, looking to create mayhem and distress. At all of the main hot-spots of human depravity throughout history, you can be guaranteed to find one or less often two of these in the mix. They possess a human and either mastermind the hate and distress, or they're in the thick of it, killing and maiming. The one who suggested that Jews were poisoning well during the Black Death, for instance, was a chaos agent. The voice on the radio during the Rwandan genocide was a chaos agent.'

'Are they ever in the bodies of world leaders?' Lauren asked, her face darkening up with a sick dismay.

'Not usually,' Connall said. 'Humans are depraved and

fucked up on their own, don't forget. Chaos agents are just the seasoning on top, really ramping things up now and then.'

'If they enjoy causing problems with people, why are they destroying Imagos?' Morty asked.

'That's what I don't understand,' Connall said, rubbing his head. 'That's what's stumping me. Why bother with them? They're nothing. Well, nothing, broadly speaking. Obviously, you're not nothing,' he said, reaching his hands out and taking Ariadne's.

'Do you think Sybella would talk to us about it?' he asked Lauren. 'She might have some memories that could help us.'

'Yeah, maybe,' Lauren said. 'I'll give her a quick call and see.'

'How about Devin?' Connall asked Brigid. 'Has he got back to you yet?'

'No' Brigid said somewhat awkwardly. 'His number's dead now.'

Morty giggled. 'Oh, shit, has God wrong numbered you?'

'No,' Brigid said indignantly. 'He hasn't wrong numbered me. It used to work. He's changed it.'

'That's a bit awkward, isn't it?'

'There's no one else I can talk to these days either. I'm out of the loop.'

Connall looked up from Brigid and rested his chin on his hand, frowning slightly. 'After we deal with all this, can you please remind me to get onto the issue of how you're being treated by the Upper Realms? Because it's sub-standard.'

'I'm not a huge amount of help then,' she finished.

'No, don't say that' Lauren said, patting her hand. 'You're very helpful.'

Connall grimaced doubtfully. 'Not with this though.'

'You know,' Lauren said, 'you haven't said much about what you're doing here. You're Cernunnos, you say, but what's the story? You're being very secretive.'

'I don't think I am,' Connall said.

'He's told me everything,' Morty offered.

'I know you're from the Other World,' said Lauren. 'You're not a mortal, you're another Celtic god who is apparently obsessed with hanging around, uninvited, in Australia. You've been here for two hundred years doing who knows what.'

'Pulling beers,' he interrupted. 'It's kept me surprisingly busy.'

'You've been here for two hundred years, and Imagos have only been around for, what, forty or so? So why have you been stuck here for all that time? What have you been doing?'

'This isn't the pressing issue of the day, you know. Is Sybella on her way?'

'Yes,' Lauren said. 'She's coming over, but she says she doesn't remember anything, but she's keen to be involved. She feels fairly guilty, all things considered.'

'We don't blame her,' Guntar said.

'I do,' Ariadne replied.

'Me too,' a voice called from the kitchen.

'Clearly, we've going to need to discuss this further,' Connall said grimy.

There was a flurry of noise and activity from the front of the house, and a banging noise could be heard and the hurry of feet. There were a few moments of quiet as they all strained their ears to hear what was going on before Dirty Annie appeared in the doorway.

'Connall, there's an old woman and a surly looking man here who say they want to talk to you about the fabric of space and time.'

31

Brigid left immediately through the back door. She did not feel emotionally equipped to see her mother, especially with a mouth full of bacon. She wasn't ready for pointed questions such as 'What's happening with your hair?' 'Where's your husband?' and 'So, is this living as a human thing panning out as you hoped because you're chunky and single by the looks of it, so if that was what you were going for then, well done, mission accomplished, I told you this was going to be a terrible idea.'

Mothers can be tricky at the best of times, and these were not the best of times.

She slipped in the back door of Lauren's house and stood there for a moment, listening to the silence around her. In her heart, she knew she should go back to say hello. Bite the bullet, as it were.

Having a mother disapprove of your life path was one thing.

Having your mother disapprove of your life path when she was a goddess who literally throws boulders at problems to solve them and reforms land masses as a parlour act was another thing entirely.

She contemplated for a moment ringing Pat for a pep talk, but decided not to involve her. Adoption could be tricky, even at this age.

She wandered into Lauren's lounge room, idly picking up pieces of clothing and coffee mugs as she went, trying to decide whether she should head home, or hang around so she could be close to the action if anything happened.

A man sat on the sofa.

He was a man, certainly, but also not quite. His skin glowed just a little. Not enough to be certain, just enough to make you think, hang on, is he glowing? But then narrow your eyes and decide it was just a trick of the light.

He was handsome. Very handsome, if you like that thin, haughty, self-possessed thing and didn't mind crushed velvet pants and a worrying preoccupation with satin shirts.

Brigid didn't mind this look at all. That's why she had married him.

The man stood. 'Hello, gorgeous,' he said and took a step towards her. 'You look amazing. I missed you.' He smiled, and Brigid's heart skipped a beat.

'I know things have been tricky lately, Egragore,' she said, 'and that we have been driven apart by circumstances, and you probably walked out on me for a very good reason, although I'm yet to hear what it is, but I don't think there's a justifiable reason for you to have grown a goatee.'

He grinned widely. 'I've missed you,' he said again.

Tears came to her eyes and, finally, she and Egragore embraced.

'Where were you?' she whispered into his neck. 'Where did you go? I came home to the cottage, and you were gone. Things have been really confusing since then. And my mother is next door, and I'm not mentally prepared for the disapproval.'

'I know,' he said soothingly. 'I know, I've been in the Other World on reconnaissance, and I've been watching what's going on. It's a bit of a dog's breakfast, I'm afraid, and mistakes have been made. Lots of mistakes.'

'By me?'

'No, not by you. By Devin, mainly. You would not believe the cock ups.'

'Devin?' Brigid pulled back and stared at Egragore. 'Devin has made mistakes?' Her voice was full of horror. 'But he's,' her voice dropped to a whisper. 'But he's the Chief Engineering Officer. He's the current God. God isn't supposed to make mistakes.'

'Oh, dear,' Egragore said. 'You really have been in this human body too long, haven't you? The more power you supposedly have, the greater the opportunity for cock ups, I'm afraid. Hence...' he gestured around. 'Hence everything. He's coming to the end of his tenure too, and that's always a difficult time, strategically.'

'Fuck me,' she said. 'This reminds me of when we first met when you were all in control, and I was totally clueless.'

'Yes, it does a bit, doesn't it.' He grinned.

'I hate it.'

'I'll get you up to speed with what I know so far, but there are things afoot that even we don't know about. There's flux in the trans-dimensional continuum of alternate realities, and what's going on there is anyone's guess, but it's definitely picking up speed and getting worse. I'm just doing my best and hanging on for dear life when things get tricky.'

'Right.' Brigid steeled her jaw. She didn't like the feeling of helplessness that had overcome her for a moment. 'The first thing I need to know is why did you just up and leave me without a word?'

He looked puzzled for a moment. 'It wasn't quite without a word though, was it,' he protested. 'I left a note.'

'No, you didn't.'

'I most certainly did,' he said indignantly. 'Do you honestly think I'd just up and leave you without letting you know? What sort of husband do you think I am?'

'Of late, a pretty shit one, to be honest.'

'I left a note. I left it on your desk.'

'Which desk?'

'The one in your office. In front of your computer.'

'But I never go in there. I don't use my office. It's where you keep the ironing board.'

'Not normally, of course, I know that, but I assumed you'd go in there to send me an email when you discovered I hadn't come home, and you'd see it. I assumed you'd send me an email to my work address given I'd told you I was at work.'

Brigid stared at him. 'But I never go in there.'

'I assumed that you would.'

'You're a very strange person, do you know that?'

'I missed you,' he repeated hopefully.

'Really?'

'Well, yes, theoretically. But I've also been extremely busy, so it's not as if I was crying myself to sleep every night.'

When she had fallen in love with Egragore, a reaper who assessed whether souls were good enough to go to the Upper Realms, her initial misgivings had nothing to do with the fact that he was an otherworldly being. His being in administration was the real issue.

'Out of interest, what did the note say?' she asked.

'Gone to work,' he said.

'Yeah, I still would have been pissed off at you even if I'd found it,' she confirmed. 'What have you been so busy with?'

'Come on,' he said, taking her hand. 'We need to go up. I've been working like a mad man trying to get things under control, but you can help me now.'

'I was up there,' she said. 'I didn't see you?'

'Up where?' he asked.

'In the Upper Realms. I got taken up there shortly after you disappeared. One moment I was drinking coffee and being mad at you, and the next moment I was in my old office being asked to convince Lauren to tell my mother to go back to Ireland.'

'Pat needs to go back to Ireland?'

'No, my other mother. The Cailleach.'

'Where is she?'

'She's been in Victoria for two hundred years.'

Egragore peered off into the distance for a moment. 'Okay, I didn't know about that. This all makes sense though. I can connect this up with what's been happening.'

'About The Cailleach?'

He dismissed the idea with a flick of his fingers. 'No, but I don't really care; it's not my area. I mean about you being taken upstairs and asked to do a job. And about people getting all up in the Cailleach's business. Who asked you to do this?'

'I'm not really sure,' Brigid said. 'I was just put in a room and, well, it was all a bit surreal, to be honest.'

'Lauren was up there too?'

'Yes.'

'Fucking hell. This is worse than I thought. They really are just casting about involving everyone who looks sideways at them, aren't they?'

'Egragore, what's going on?'

He looked at her grimly. 'This is on a need-to-know basis, you understand.'

She nodded. 'Clearly. And I need to know everything.'

'Of course, that goes without saying.'

'Mum's next door,' she said. 'Cailleach Mum. Apparently, she's been living here for hundreds of years, and now the indigenous spirits are sick of her, so she needs to go. And Lauren's coven has always paid homage to her, so they decided to get them to ask her to leave.'

'The ancient spirits want her to leave?'

'Apparently.'

'First I've heard of it.'

'How much dealing do you have with them?'

'Not much directly. They're way above my pay grade. Only Devin deals with them directly, and they're old even to him. But I can't imagine they'd be that worried about an old woman who lives in a hut in the bush. That seems pretty insignificant to me.'

'Well, that's what I was told. We were told.'

'I wonder...' Egragore said thoughtfully.

'What?'

He took her hand. 'Come on,' he said. 'Let's walk. We need to talk, and I like to talk and walk.'

'Remember that's what we did when we first met?' Brigid reminisced. 'We used to talk and walk. I usually didn't believe a word you said, but it was fun.'

They left the house, and Brigid deliberately led Egragore in the direction that led away from the house next door. She didn't want the Cailleach rushing out and accosting her.

She turned her head to look at him as they walked companionably down the street. 'I'm going to need you to get rid of that goatee,' she said. 'What were you thinking?'

'I just thought I'd try it. Don't you think it gives me a certain something?'

'That it does,' she agreed grimly. 'So what's been going on?'

'Basically, the long and the short of it,' he said, 'is that some of the jobs in the Upper Realms have been outsourced. It was decided by the administrative wing that they needed to put them out to tender, and so bids were taken, and they were outsourced.'

'What was outsourced, exactly?'

'Various areas. Budgets have blown out since that whole issue last year, and it was decided that things needed be taken in hand. So, Devin tried to work something out and take tenders and everything, but there was an enormous cock up and incompetent businesses were put in charge.'

'What happened?' asked Brigid aghast. 'Oh, god, please tell me you weren't in charge of the tenders.'

'Don't be ridiculous, of course not. I was called up to try and bring things back into some kind of order. The Shadow Lands, our administrative wing, has been languishing since I left, and so I've been trying to get things sorted. It's an absolute balls up. You wouldn't believe the mess. And some very dodgy tenders were given out, and they made some bad decisions.'

'Wait.' Brigid narrowed her eyes and thought for a moment. 'Did any of those bad decisions have anything to do with these

Imago things that are floating around the place here? Literally, in some instances.'

'Imagos are a sore point at the moment. They've become part of the power play between arguing factions. Devin's knows they're important, given they are tied in with the flurries in the undertow issue, from what we can tell. For some reason they seem linked and not in a good way. But he was trying to placate some of the old school principalities who seem to have taken quite a set against them. You know how some have very traditional ideas about what makes an officially sanctioned being, and all that.'

'Do I want to know what that means?' she asked.

He tried a charming smile, but she wasn't having it.

'Does this have anything to do with the fact that the entire admin wing of the Upper Realms looks like an operating theatre?' She was beginning to have some very worrying suspicions.

'It only looks a bit like an operating theatre,' he said. 'And it's only in a small area of a place that's been quarantined, anyway. The company that was outsourced to decided to get everyone to work from home to save on costs, and the office space was all reallocated. So there's no one working from there anymore. Except for—'

'Egragore,' she warned.

'Yes, okay, so there were some attempts to find out how… Look this is going to sound bad but I promise you there was a reason behind it. We tried just a few procedures to see how their death affected the flux. Hence the operating theatre.'

She looked at him in horror. 'That's the worst thing I've ever heard.' Brigid's face had blanched white, and her hand covered her mouth.

'I was all done very humanely and only to sick or dying ones. But you need to understand, this is a huge issue. The whole fabric of time and space is in peril. It was all pretty messy, but Devin's making moves to put everything to rights now.'

'They didn't … make it.'

'This is the worst thing I've ever heard. I can't believe Devin has let everything fall to pieces to this extent. What the fuck's been going on?'

'Oh, it's not his fault,' Egragore urged. 'These things happened out of his sight.'

'He's God,' she said between gritted teeth. 'There's not meant to be anything that's out of his sight. It's part of the whole omnipotent thing.'

There was silence for a moment.

'I hope no one is annoyed at Devin,' she offered.

'Annoyed? Gosh, no. No one's annoyed at Devin. Everyone loves him. There's no way this is his fault, as such. He's brought in new management strategies, and he's emphasising self-care and asking for help when you need it, so he should be lauded for that, if anything. Good on him for reaching out for support, really. We've all seen what happens when one person wants to absolutely control everything. Not good for anyone at all. Except…'

They had reached a park, a kind of mini botanical garden that sat at the centre of the suburb, and they walked to a wrought iron chair that sat under an iron statue of a man who had killed rather a lot of indigenous people, but oddly the plaque talked about the land that he had 'discovered' rather than the fact that it had been stolen off the people he'd had murdered.

'Except?' she prompted him.

He crossed one velvet panted leg at the knee and brushed dust off his lapel. 'Except,' he said, 'the organisations that won the tenders weren't best suited to the job.'

'Not best suited? Why did they get the jobs then?'

'They were the cheapest.'

'Fabulous.'

'Yes, quite. So they seem, from what I can tell, to be making a dog's breakfast of the jobs that were allocated to them.'

'What kind of jobs were allocated?'

He was looking off into the distance. 'Can you hear that?' he asked.

'No. What kind of jobs were allocated?'

'Well.' He cleared his throat. 'One was the Monitoring and OverSee of Recently Created Life Forms, as I've already explained.'

'Right,' she said uncertainly.

'Another was the Appropriate Conduct and Assessment of the Celtic Pantheon currently Stationed on Earth.'

'Okay,' she said, clarity beginning to come to her.

'Are you sure you can't hear that?' he said again, standing up and looking around them, eyes piercing their surroundings. 'A really high-pitched whistling noise.' He looked above them, eyes cupped as he looked up into the vivid blue of the morning sky. 'I'm sure there's—'

'So, how much of the absolute balls up going on right now has to do with this new allocating of responsibilities?

'Well, employing a chaos agent was clearly a bit of a cock up.'

'Clearly. Let me list the high strangeness that I'm aware of at the moment, and you tell me what's been caused by an administrative cock up.'

'Sure,' Egragore said. 'Go.'

Brigid counted things off on her fingers. 'The Cernunnos, aka Connall, is here running a pub looking after Imagos.'

Egragore nodded. 'Right, I did not know that. He's been keeping very quiet, hasn't he.'

'Surely he doesn't believe everyone's just forgotten about the fuss he caused back in the day?'

'Hardly,' Egragore said. 'No one's forgotten about that. Your mother will smack him into next week if she catches him. However, I don't think that's directly my issue at this particular moment. But stand by. That could change. The Imagos issue I am aware of, obviously.'

'Right,' Brigid said. 'There's also this thought form lion thing that's been inexplicably hanging around. Sybella summoned him. I feel like he's dodgy.'

'Also did not know about that.'

'And the Cailleach appearing last night because we summoned her, although she's been around for a while rearranging my house and trying to annoy me.'

'Are you sure she was trying to annoy you? Maybe she was trying to be helpful.'

'You don't have a mother, so you don't understand. So how many of these things are you aware of?'

'Right.' He ticked things off his fingers in turn. 'I know about the chaos agent. I'm aware of it, and I'm not happy. I gave it its letters of termination, and things got messy, but we've managed to exile him to a pyramid for the time being where he's well and truly trapped, so I can tick that off my list. The Ancient Egyptians were absolute masters at magic and conjuring and the like. They'll keep him well and truly locked down until I get a chance to —'

'That is so very much not ticked off your list.'

'Pardon?' he said patiently.

'Yeah, the lion took Sybella to Ancient Egypt and then she got possessed and brought it back, and then she killed some Imagos, and then the water spirits chucked it out of her, but now it's running wild again.'

'Did not know that' he said tightly.

'That's the short version,' she said helpfully.

'Yes, I assumed that.'

'The JanJans are involved now, are they?' He was looking

increasingly pale.

She nodded.

'And your friend was possessed.'

'Yes, that was a bit of a cock up, wasn't it?' If that was anything to do with you, then I suggest you pay for her therapy to deal with it.'

'It wasn't strictly anything to do with me, but I could probably find some discretionary cash somewhere. Are you sure you can't hear something?'

Brigid tilted her head to one side and narrowed her eyes. 'I do think I can hear something. Like, a kind of zooming sound?'

It sounded like the noise a motorbike made as it came towards you from a great distance. The sound got more and more intense and then there was a pop, as if air was suddenly being sucked out of the world's biggest balloon, and there in front of them stood a man. He was tall, dark and handsome, with tight black curly hair and the look on his face of someone who was having a very, very bad day.

'Devin,' Brigid said, delighted. 'How are you? Love the new goatee. Is that a fashion up there at the moment? Are you all doing a 90s retro thing or something? Big fan.'

Devin stepped forward and hugged her automatically, but his eyes darted around, coming to rest on Egragore.

'Things seem to be kicking off upstairs,' he said. 'I think it's started.'

'What, already?' Egragore seemed alarmed. 'But we're not ready. We haven't even finished practising.'

'I know, but it's too late for that. They've got the teams together, and it's starting.'

'Dammit,' spat Egragore, his brow beading with sweat. 'Okay,' he said to Brigid. 'Now we really do need you. It's time for the Tournament.'

'Already?' Brigid said.

'That seems to be the general consensus, yes,' said Egragore grimly. 'But it's scheduled for every three thousand years, so it's hardly come out of the blue, and I, for one, don't know how hard it is to put it in your damn calendar and get yearly reminders, but apparently that's just beyond everyone.'

'Can we use your office? Devin asked Egragore. 'Mine seems to have been terraformed out of existence.'

Egragore sighed and grasped Brigid's hand. This day was, he knew, going to be far more trouble than it was worth.

32

For all her tiny wrinkly old lady-ness, the Cailleach could dominate a room like no one Lauren had ever seen. She took every stereotype people have about very old women, wrung it out with her bare hands, spat on it, probably wrapped it in one of the plastic bags she kept in another plastic bag under her sink, and then buried it at the bottom of a very, very deep hole that she had dug in the early hours of the morning with a wooden spoon she had whittled herself, especially for the occasion.

She had marched through the house, stopping to smile at every Imago she passed, patting cheeks, tousling heads, and picking up the smallest ones, much to Demniac's chagrin.

'You'll hurt your back,' he protested as he paced after her.

'Oh, leave me be, boy,' she snapped. 'You worry too much. The day that I can't pick up a little one is the day that they put me in a box.' The fact that most of the small people she was picking up were not children didn't seem to bother anyone involved. When The Cailleach smiled her light onto you, then you accepted it with joy.

She stomped through to the back room where Connall and Morty had remained looking through documents and sat herself next to them, staring, waiting for them to speak to her. One could not ignore the Cailleach for long, at least one could not ignore the

Cailleach and stay in control of their senses.

'So,' she said. 'Here we are.'

'Hi, Cally,' Connall said finally looking up and flinching a little, as if he expected an imminent slap.

'What?' Lauren said.

'What?' Morty said.

'I'm sorry,' Demniac said.

Ariadne and Guntar giggled. They had learned, as a matter of course, not to make assumptions about anything in life and were usually just thrilled to be along for the ride.

'Hey there, lovey,' she said. 'What are you calling yourself these days?'

'Connall,' he replied.

She grunted 'It'll do.'

'So, what have you got yourself tied up in this time?' she asked. 'Looking after them that can't look after themselves?'

He laughed. 'Like you can talk.'

'That's true,' she said, pulling a chair to herself and propping both legs up on it. 'My knees are giving me gyp,' she explained to Demniac. 'Nothing that I don't know how to deal with.'

'I might pop into the chemist tomorrow and get you some anti-inflammatories,' he said.

She ignored him.

She noticed Morty, finally, who was gazing at her with a mixture of curiosity and reverence.

'You were there last night, weren't you boy?' she said to him.

He nodded.

'Did you have any idea what was going on?'

He nodded, but what came out of his mouth were the words, 'No, not really.'

'Seems like people are messing in things they've got no business in. Is this your friend?' This was to Connall, who raised one heavy eyebrow at her.

'Friend?'

'You know what I mean.'

Connall smiled and nodded, and Morty flushed.

'Thought so. Looks your type. Things seem like a right mess at the moment.'

'Again,' said Connall.

She laughed, a rich chortle that turned into a coughing fit. Demniac rushed to grab her a glass of water. She patted his hand as he gave it to her.

'Have you heard what's been going on up there?' she asked.

'Not really. There have been whispers.'

'I didn't know where you ended up,' she said.

'I didn't know where you ended up,' he echoed.

'They needed me for a while down here,' she said, 'but it's been quiet for a time now. They've forgotten their roots.'

'Irish convicts?' he asked

She nodded.

'That's been over for a while now,' he said.

'I've been keeping an eye on other things. There's always someone needs to be looked out for. These 'Australians' don't think they have a class system, but that's bullshit.'

Connall sighed. 'It's always bullshit.' He turned the paper to face her. 'So you know what's been going on?'

'I've heard nothing,' she said. 'I've been looking after orphaned wallabies, checking pouches on the highway for the past forty years. They keep me busy.'

'Same, really. I'm keeping busy with that lot.' he thumbed in the direction of the other room.

'I know.' She smiled and pulled Maeve onto her lap. 'They're blessed little creations, aren't they.'

Connall shrugged. 'Humans are more trouble than they're worth.'

'Don't have to convince me.'

He tapped the paper. 'Do you know anything about this? About what's trying to destroy them.'

She pushed the paper away, ignoring it. 'I've heard whispers. In the trees. There's things going on in the Upper Realms at the moment. Shenanigans.'

He sighed again. 'Which is why we're down here, right.'

She chortled. 'Right. That lot couldn't organise a root in a brothel. I'm not surprised they're cocking it up. It's the time of the Tournament,' she continued.

'Again?' he said, narrowing his eyes. 'Already? Seems like just yesterday.' Maeve slid off Cally's lap and crawled off to attend to other business.

'Three thousand years,' she said. 'Three thousand years since the last one.'

'Time flies,' he said conversationally.

'It's all a construct anyway.'

'It is.'

'Your idea, I believe?' he said to her, still pushing pages around the table.

'Yes, one of my many regrets. Seemed like a good idea at the time.' She shrugged, her bony shoulders moving under her green cardigan, and they lapsed into silence.

'So,' Lauren said nervously, taking advantage of the lull. 'I'm glad we found you.'

'You found me, did you?' She rounded her gimlet gaze on her.

'Well,' Lauren said, feeling the weight of ages rest on her soul. 'We've found each other, maybe?'

'All right.'

'And there's something that we need to talk to you about.'

'Where's my daughter?' the Cailleach said, sliding her feet from the chair and craning her neck around. 'Did she nick off when she heard me coming?'

The look of nervousness on Lauren's face deepened even

further, if that was possible. 'She's around … somewhere. There's something I need to talk to you about.'

'Is there indeed?'

'Oh, Cally,' Connall reprimanded. 'Stop teasing. You're terrifying her.'

She laughed a wheezing laugh again. 'All right, dearie, you wanted to talk to me about going back to the Old Country?'

'Oh, yes,' Lauren said, deflating with relief and anticipation. 'Yes, that's it.'

'Who sent you?'

'Well, Brigid asked me if I should —'

'Brigid asked you to?'

Lauren paused awkwardly. 'Someone asked her to ask me to ask you —'

'That sounds like an utter balls up too, to my ears. Was it an Upper Realms thing?'

Lauren waggled her head noncommittally. 'Well, from what I can tell, Brigid was taken up to the Upper Realms again, and then I was taken up there too, and —'

'What?' The crone's voice rang out, bearing none of the crackle that Lauren had previously heard.

'Um, well, I said that Brigid was taken up and —'

'Right.' The Cailleach pushed herself to her feet, using Demniac's readily available arm as a prop, and planted her feet determinedly on the ground. 'What do you know about this?' she shot towards Connall.

'Me?' he said, eyes wide. 'This has got nothing to do with me at all. I've been keeping my head down and keeping well out of Other World affairs, just like you have. I've got no idea what's been going on.'

'But you knew that Brigid, my daughter, decided to be born here as a human, didn't you?'

'Yes, of course,' Connall said. 'That's common knowledge.'

'And that then she was called on to take on her goddess form again, against her will?'

'I kind of knew that, but the stories have changed a bit. There has been gossip.'

'Well, she was. And then she came back to Earth, went and lived in Ireland, bless her, although she doesn't know that I know any of that, and now I'm hearing she's been taken up again? Involved in Upper Realms business without her say so?'

'I seem to remember, Connall said casually, 'that you were pretty pissed off when she decided to become a human. Wasn't there a 'never darken my doorstep again' production that went on?'

'I thought you had no idea what was going on?' she said drily.

'I hear things.' He ducked his head back down to his papers.

'Yes, I was pissed off when she decided to give it up and live as a human, but as it turns out...' She waved a hand in the air. 'I've been doing it for a while now, and it's not so bad. And that's not the point, anyway. The point is, she made a decision about what she wanted to do, and those bastards have got no right to play fast and loose with her free will. I might be able to judge her and make her feel bad, but I'll be absolutely buggered if I'll stand by and let anyone else do it.'

'She was a bit upset with all the stuff that you did with her house. You know, the clock and the, the wheat.' Lauren didn't really know how else to describe it.

The Cailleach laughed. 'Oh, I was just having some fun. Life's been dull for me lately. I can't go back home, so I'm stuck here where nobody wants me. All my convicts have moved on five generations, and now they have two storied brick monstrosities in Taylors Lakes, and the only thing they know about their roots is putting green food dye in their beers on Saint Patrick's Day. I just wanted to remind her that I was around.'

'By turning the majority of her house into a field of wheat?'

'I've been talking to marsupials for decades. I may have lost some of my social decorum.'

Lauren, who suspected that the ancient crone's social decorum had been tenuous at best, decided to leave it.

'Why can't you go home?' Connall asked.

'You know what it's like when a new person takes over. They don't like the old brass around telling them what to do. They made it quite clear that my time was up. When I had an opinion about it, they made sure I was left stuck down here indefinitely.'

'Really?' Connall said in surprise. 'They banned you from the Upper Realms? That's rude.'

'I thought so.'

'You didn't get to be the Cailleach anymore?' Morty asked, looking confused.

'Don't try to understand.' She patted his hand. 'Demarcation in our pantheon is notoriously tricky. I'm always the Cailleach, but I was also in charge for a while at one point. What do they call it now? Chief Engineering Officer or some such. God or goddess was good enough when I was up there. Anyway, what was I saying? Why am I standing up?'

'You seemed annoyed about something,' Demniac offered.

'Oh, that's right. They've been messing with Brigid, and I'm not having that. Connall,' she said. 'Did you hear that somethings been murdering the Imagos?'

'What?' He looked aghast.

She nodded. 'It's true. I don't know all the details. The JanJan get a whisper of things from time to time and tell me.'

'You're friends with the JanJan, hey? That's old magic.'

'But,' Lauren said, confused. 'The reason I was asked to talk to you was to tell you to leave, tell you to go because the indigenous spirits are sick of you being around.'

'Sick of me?' The Cailleach nodded peacefully. 'That's possible.

I can be annoying.'

Lauren looked doubtful. 'Well, that's what I was told, anyway.'

'Sounds like someone's up to some mischief making,' Connall said, peering at the Cailleach carefully. 'These stories aren't adding up.'

She caressed the top of her walking stick thoughtfully. 'Shenanigans,' she mused. 'Always the shenanigans. I thought things were getting more settled in the Upper Realms.' She tilted her head to one side and looked at Connall. 'At least they were last time I was up there. What's been happening? Forgotten the little people, I'd say.'

Morty looked at her quizzically. 'Little people?'

Connall laughed. 'Us. We're the little people, cosmically speaking. Shall we head up and sort it out?'

The Cailleach looked at him with a raised brow. 'I thought you were done with all of that. After the last time, I thought you wanted nothing to do with it all.'

He looked around the room. 'I've been scraping a living around here for too long. It's time I become a player again.'

'You've had your privileges revoked though, haven't you?' she said.

'Yeah, true. You too though.'

'Ah, yes,' she said. 'But there have been complaints about me, haven't there. I'm thinking that I'll be needed upstairs for a discussion about my behaviour. Especially if I don't do what this girlie has asked me.' She winked at Lauren. 'I've been terribly badly behaved. Probably need a good talking to upstairs, don't I?'

Morty and Demniac looked thoroughly confused, while Connall shook his head and continued to laugh to himself. 'You've manufactured this whole thing haven't you, Cally?'

She grinned at him, clearly delighted. 'You lot want to come along too?'

Morty shrugged. 'I don't know what you're talking about, but all right. Let's do it.'

The Cailleach chucked gleefully 'That's my boy. Now let's see what you're made of. She reached out one hand to Connall, who took her gnarled brown fingers in his, his hand dwarfing hers. Connall took Morty's hand, who stretched out his hand to Demniac, who took Lauren's, who in turn took the Cailleach's. Her hand was dry and papery, like autumn leaves, but Lauren could feel a fierce energy thrumming through it. Connall smiled and closed his eyes and breathed in deeply through his nose. Lauren could feel the Cailleach looking at her closely. 'Close your eyes and press the Dimenso-Zap,' she said. 'As long as we're all connected it will take us all up.'

'How did you know that I—' Lauren started, but she quickly realised that the Cailleach knew far far more than she was letting on. She pulled the device out of her pocket and slipped it into the hand that held the Cailleach's. There was a moment of disorientation, of dizziness, and before she knew it, the room had disappeared.

33

The small group stood, hands still linked, in the vast cavernous room that Lauren and Brigid had seen through the bookcase. At least, Lauren assumed it was the same room. There couldn't be two such improbably big rooms, could there? Unless the whole McMansion fad of the nouveau riche had escalated to 'put an infinite number of aircraft hangers together, make them bleak, and make them soulless, then sell them to footballers and their wives who have money for the first time', which was a possibility, now she thought about it.

The space stretched off into the distance, so far that Lauren imagined she could see the curve of the horizon. The room rose overhead, the colours blending so she couldn't even see where it finished, and she couldn't completely discount the glimmer of suspicion that she could see small clouds floating up there, just at the limit of her sight. The space felt so large that she wondered if it might have its own microclimate.

At least a thunderstorm would break up the monotony a bit.

She felt tiny. Exposed. Insignificant. And more than a little bit scared.

They dropped hands. At least, most of them did. Morty and Connall continued to grasp each other as they stepped back and looked around. 'Where are we?' Morty asked, awestruck. 'What is this place?'

'It's just the Upper Realms,' Connall said. 'At least part of it. Things have changed since last time I was here, though,' he said, his brow furrowed. 'This used to be all offices. Chunky curves and modular seats. A veritable hive of activity. It won an award for 'Fewest Right Angles in a Workplace'.'

'How long ago was that?' Morty asked.

'A couple of thousand years. I just haven't felt the need to go back. I've been busy.'

'Why?' said Lauren suspiciously, sensing something was not being disclosed.

'No reason,' he said airily. 'Time's just got away from me.'

'It's a bit bleak,' Morty said. 'I would have expected something more...' His words trailed off.

'More what?' Lauren asked.

'I dunno, with more panache? More zhoosh? Just not this.' He gestured around. 'I mean there isn't even a pot plant. Or, you know. A ceiling.'

'This isn't all of it though,' Lauren said eagerly. 'It's not all this vast. There's a whole Victorian thing going on through there.' She pointed to a nearby wall. Improbably, they seemed to have landed, if landed was the right word, near to where she and Brigid had originally peered through. Lauren also noticed that any signs of an operating theatre had gone.

'I don't like it,' the Cailleach said, grasping her stick firmly and shuffling forwards. 'I don't like what they've done with the place at all. What is this supposed to be? Is this what passes for homely these days?. I expected more of the new boy, I really did. You wouldn't have seen this kind of lack of hospitality when I was running things full-time. Makes me realise I should have been keeping a closer tab on things.'

Connall was standing back, craning his head and looking around and frowning. 'Yeah, it's lost a certain something, hasn't it? I wonder if there have been funding cuts.'

'It's bullshit, that's what it is? They're all clueless.' The Cailleach was heading off away from them.

'Where are you going?' Demniac asked, hurrying after her. 'You need to slow down.'

Her stick tapped on the stark floor, the sharp sound echoing throughout the vast chamber. She was heading for the wall where Lauren could see the small hole that she and Brigid had peered through.

'I'll be buggered if I'll stay in here like some kind of hired help. I need to find somewhere where I can take the weight off my feet. This is going to play gyp with my knees,' she yelled to no one in particular.

'Oh, hang on,' Lauren said. 'I know where you can go.' She followed after the Cailleach, who was in turn still being followed by a worried looking Demniac. 'There are some chairs through here, I think, although I'm not sure how to get in.'

The Cailleach reached the wall and stooped, peering at it intently for a moment. She placed one hand on the smooth surface, and a gentle vibration ran through her as if she was petting some huge, sleeping giant. The floor also seemed to be undulating, moving to some soundless beat, and Lauren nervously lifted her feet up one by one as if she didn't trust what she was standing on.

'Are you in there?' the Cailleach called sharply. She rapped her staff on the wall aggressively, the sound huge in the open space. 'I know you're in there. If I don't sit down soon, I won't be responsible for what happens next. I don't want to say do you know who I am, but I will if necessary.'

Immediately, the soft thrumming kicked up a notch, and a patch of wall in front of them shimmered and disappeared. 'Better,' the Cailleach said. 'Good decision.' She stomped forward, leaving Lauren and Demniac in her wake. The old woman planted her feet firmly on the carpet that Lauren immediately recognised as the luxurious weave she had been so impressed by, and she turned back towards them. 'Are you coming?'

'Where are we going?' Lauren asked uncertainly, glancing back to Connall. 'Shouldn't we stay together?'

'They can come with me if they want,' she snapped, 'but I have better things to do than wait to be invited in. Are you coming?' she repeated.

'I'm going to look for Devin,' Connall said to the old woman's stubborn back. 'I'd have thought you'd want to be there for that.'

The Cailleach ignored him.

'Will … will we get in trouble?' Lauren asked, following her. 'Are we allowed to just wander around?'

'Didn't you say you were here before?'

'Yes, but—'

'But what?'

'But I was with Brigid then. She's kind of … well, she's important. I know I'm allowed to just wander around when I'm with her.'

'Allowed?' barked the crone, her sharp voice blanketed by the wall hangings and bookcases. 'Allowed? Haven't you ever heard the phrase ask for forgiveness not permission? I swear to all things dank and briny, this current generation has no idea about feminism. You need permission to actually exist.' She stomped away from them, and Demniac darted after her, clearly deciding to place all his bets on this particular horse. Lauren could hear her complaining as they moved down the hallway, and she strongly suspected it was about her. She glanced behind her again, then peeked her head through the newly formed doorway, balanced between following what could potentially be a maniacal trespasser and going back to the safety of Connall. Before she could decide, the Cailleach swung around again and bellowed down the hallway, 'So you felt safe with my daughter but not with me? Well, would it make you feel better if I told you that up until this new guy took over, I was in charge around here? And I'm still the honorary figurehead?'

'Here?' Demniac said. 'By here, you mean—'

'The hub of the entire known Universe,' she snapped.

Lauren decided that it was good enough for her, thank you very much, and followed them.

After several minutes of stomping (the Cailleach), following (Demniac) and scampering nervously (Lauren) the old woman stopped and looked around.

'Right,' she said.

'Right,' said Demniac.

'Right,' agreed Lauren.

'I don't really know where I'm going,' the old woman admitted.

'Is it usually this quiet up here?' Demniac asked. 'Your house full of Imagos is busier than this,' he said to Lauren.

'It was like this when I was here too,' Lauren said. 'I just assumed that quiet and peaced out was the way it's supposed to be. You know, everyone meditating or praying or doing good deeds or the like.'

'You've obviously never worked in a big organisation. It's usually an absolute shit show of competing interests and pointless noise.'

'Oh,' Lauren said, surprised. 'Well, it was dead like this last time I was here, too. I wonder what's going on?'

'Hmm.' The old woman tapped her chin and looked around, frowning. 'That might be it. Ah, yes, that's it!' She grinned, looking pleased.

'I know how you feel though,' Lauren said. 'I had to kick over a drinks dispenser and break a table before anyone would pay attention to me.'

The Cailleach looked at her with something approaching approval for the first time. 'Did you indeed? I like that. Good job.'

'Would you like me to push over this bookcase?' Lauren asked eagerly.

The Cailleach waggled her staff noncommittally. 'While I like your enthusiasm, let's hold off on that for a bit.' She patted Lauren's face with her paper-like brown hand.

'There has to be someone around here. Especially given that it's nearly the Tournament. Or Game Day, some call it. Game Day is huge, you know. I've never seen one that wasn't absolutely frantic in the lead up. Oh, the fussing around and the passive aggression and the suspicions. It will absolutely warm your heart. If you like that sort of thing.'

Lauren wasn't sure whether she liked that sort of thing, but she was so pleased to be in what she assumed were the old woman's good graces that she made her eyes shine and she grinned excitedly. 'I'm in.'

Demniac nodded seriously. 'So am I.'

'Let's not make too much of a mess at the moment,' she said. 'I won't find where they've left it.' She ran her fingers over the spines of the books in the bookcase. The old woman's hand lighted on one, and she pulled it out, grinning, but after opening it her face fell. 'Fuck,' she said.

She ran her hands over another row of books, this time with

her fingers creeping around over the tops of them, but again she came away unsatisfied. 'I'm missing something,' the Cailleach mused, seemingly to herself. 'I know that I must be missing something.'

She held her hands up in the air and planted one foot behind her as if, Lauren thought nervously, she was about to start a particularly vigorous mime or, worse still, an interpretive dance routine. Her hands faced the wall, palms up, and she moved them around smoothly as if she were moving an invisible ball in her hand.

'Are you doing energy work?' Lauren asked eagerly. It reminded her of one of the exercises they did in the 'Heal Dolphin Trauma with Past Life Chakra Memory Recovery'.

The old woman didn't answer. Her eyes were closed, her brow was furrowed, and a dull humming seemed to be coming from the air around her. Her hands continued to move back and forth, and now she was rocking slowly on her feet. She moved like this for what seemed to Lauren like minutes but may have been only a few seconds. Lauren glanced behind them nervously. 'Can I help? she prompted. 'What are you doing?'

'I'm looking for the bloody key.'

Lauren bit her lip. 'Which key?' she whispered to Demniac. 'Do you know which key she's talking about?'

Demniac nodded seriously. This seemed to be his main form of communication now. 'I would say that it's a metaphysical key. It's kind of a soul's journey. She's reaching deep into her goddess-self to manifest the soul knowledge, the intuition, if you like, that the wisdom that her fore-mothers have been able to —'

There was a rough pop, as if all the air was being sucked out of a room that was in a dimension just beyond the one that they were standing in. Something slid into existence' at about eye level, appearing bit by bit like toothpaste squeezing its way out of a tube. Once it was fully visible, it shook itself a little bit, and then seemed to realise it was a solid, heavy thing that probably should pay lip service at least to gravity, and it fell gently into the Cailleach's now outstretched hand. She grasped it victoriously. 'I knew you'd be here somewhere.'

She glowered at Lauren. Only slightly, but it was definitely a glower. 'Did you make a mess of the books as well when you were up here last time? Did you throw them around and all?'

'Yes, but it was Brigid's idea.'

'You lost the spare key. It was in one of those fake books that you hide things in, but I think you knocked it from its hiding place. I had to convince it to uncloak.'

'Convince it? You're speaking of it like it's alive.'

The Cailleach held they key up to Lauren's face and waved it around a bit as if to make her point. 'Do you have any idea just how much stuff you don't know?'

'No.'

'That's right.'

'Spare key for what?' Demniac asked.

The Cailleach made a snorting sound of irritation. 'I'm just about jack of all these questions, to be honest with you both. The sooner we get in there, the sooner I can make you someone else's responsibility.'

Lauren and Demniac glanced at each other, seemingly daring the other to ask the same question again.

'But ... for what?' Lauren said, rising to the occasion.

The Cailleach looked around her again, her eyes seeking out a particular spot on the bookcase. 'No, I forgot the tea set,' she said. She bustled over to the table that held the pink tea set that was still there from where Brigid and Lauren had drunk it earlier. She looked into the empty cups. 'Did you drink all of this? She asked accusatorily.

'Um, yes,' Lauren replied, at this stage utterly unsurprised that she was being reprimanded for drinking tea.

'If this doesn't work then it's your fault that we're totally fucked. I hope you understand that.'

The old woman moved the teapot, the coaster and the cups around slightly, stood back and surveyed them through narrowed eyes, then did some further tweaking. 'There we go,' she said, turning and winking at her companions. 'It's showtime.'

She stepped back to the bookcase, moved several books apart, thrust the key forward and turned it with what seemed to be a curiously loud click. At that moment, the entire Victoriana decor experience winked out of existence.

34

'Who lifted the security level?' These were the first words out of Connall's mouth as he strode towards the tall man with dark curly hair, who glanced up at his approach. The look on his face, which had been one of simple overburdened stress, now changed to slightly annoyed overburdened stress. 'Who lifted it and made it so difficult for me to get here? Without telling anyone?'

Connall approached Devin, Egragore and Brigid, who were clustered around a standing desk in the middle of a corridor.

'Well, to be fair,' Devin said, 'telling everyone we were cloaking and upping the security would have been a stupid. Kind of negated the whole security thing, if you ask me. And how did you get in here? Any interlopers are supposed to be stuck in the Waiting Room.'

'I'm hardly an interloper. You could have told relevant people. Those who needed to know.'

'A group that wouldn't have included you,' Devin snapped. 'With respect, you haven't been a relevant person around here for quite some time. You're barely a blip these days, are you?'

'Still?' Connall said, glaring at Devin. 'Still, really? Still?'

'Yes, still,' Devin said pointedly. 'Because once someone has proved to me that they can't be trusted, then it's pretty bloody conclusive, wouldn't you say? And anyway, I'd have thought you would be expressing a bit more gratitude to me, as a matter of fact, rather than coming up here ranting and raving about what I'm doing wrong.'

'I'm not saying you're doing things wrong,' Connall started, but Devin cut him off.

'Coming in here telling me what I'm doing wrong rather than being grateful that I didn't smite you once and for all.'

'Oh, please, you were never going to smite me, and we both know it. You're not a smiter. Never have been.'

'Is that what you think?'

'It's what I know.'

The men glared at each other, almost close enough to touch.

Dropping Brigid's hand, Egragore moved between them. 'Now, now gentlemen, let's not bicker. You know what things get like when you two bicker. We can't afford another Atlantis cock up again, can we? Isn't it nice to see each other after all this time? It is, right? Remember the good times? The old days? When you were young and everything was new and the world was your oyster, metaphorically speaking? Fun times, remember?'

The men continued to stare at each other.

At that moment, a door in the wall burst open, and the Cailleach, followed by a harassed looking Demniac, Lauren, and a cheerful looking Morty, stomped in. 'Thank you very much for letting me in,' she barked at them. 'I've been wasting time sweet talking a stroppy key. Why are you standing in the middle of a corridor? Don't you have work to do?'

She noticed that everyone was glaring at each other. 'Oh, again? You two just can't leave each other alone, can you?'

'Our offices have disappeared,' Egragore snapped. 'The terraforming has started. We've left the Waiting Room there to confuse anyone uninvited who made it that far.'

'I'm not uninvited though. Someone needs to talk to me about my behaviour. I've been misbehaving, you know,' the Cailleach said gravely.

Egragore narrowed his eyes at her. 'You're a canny old thing, aren't you?'

Realising that finally someone had arrived who might tell him what was going on, Morty bent down to the old woman's ear. 'Who is that?'

Glancing into his face, the old woman reached up a hand and patted the young man's cheek. 'Don't you worry. They have a history. Can't live with each other, can't live without each other. But when they're together, bits of the planet tend to break off, so it's better for all concerned if we throw some water on this for now.'

Her voice rang out through the expansive space. 'Right, you two, step back. Stop showing off to each other. Hug it out and admit you missed each other.'

Devin and Connall continued to glare at each other.

She put her hand on Egragore's shoulder and squeezed it firmly. 'You're pissing into the wind if you think you can control those two. I take it you're my son-in-law?'

'Er.' Egragore looked uncharacteristically flustered. 'Er, yes, sorry about not inviting you to the wedding, but we weren't sure where you—'

'Oh, I don't care. I was at the others, so it doesn't matter.' She pushed him gently aside as she hobbled up to Devin and Connall, who now looked like two cats who wanted to be talked out of their fight but were too proud to be the first to slink away.

'What others?' Egragore said to Brigid, who pointedly

ignored him.

'Can we just assume that you're pleased to see each other, that everything that happened in the past stays in the past, and that we can move on? Because you're both going to need your wits about you to deal with what's coming, and the entire Universe knows that you two are better with each other than against each other.'

'What does she mean with each other,' Morty said anxiously to no one in particular.

The two men ignored the woman's words.

Reaching up, she smacked Connall on the back of his head with an open palm. 'Apologise to Devin for trying to take over his job when it wasn't your turn.'

Connall dropped his eyes and scuffed a shoe on the ground, lips remaining belligerently closed.

'Connall,' she barked sharply.

'Only if he—' She smacked him again, and he hurriedly spat out, 'I'm sorry for trying to take over your job.'

'When it wasn't your turn,' the Cailleach prompted.

'When it wasn't my turn.'

'You lost fair and square,' Devin started, but the Cailleach had already rounded on him. 'Right, and you need to apologise to Connall for rubbing it in his face when you won and also for exiling him and holding over his head the fact that you were going to smite him if he didn't do whatever you wanted for the next two thousand years.'

'That's not quite—' Devin protested.

She lifted her open palm towards him, and he quickly blurted out an apology.

'Righto,' she said. 'What else do we need to get off our chests? I won't have any ill feelings around here now that I'm back.'

'What do you mean, back?' Devin asked.

She gestured around. 'This. What you've been playing at. This place needs someone who knows what they're doing.'

Devin and Connall glanced each other warily.

'I know what I'm doing,' Devin said.

She shook her head in contempt. 'Outsourcing? Giving out jobs to the lowest bidders? Getting mestomorphs to be your security? What the hell were you thinking?'

'I didn't do that,' Devin protested. 'It was other —'

She raised her hand slightly, and he flinched. 'When you're the one in charge of the entire Other World, you need to know every single thing that's happening. You should know that. That's how it used to be, and I well know that you're aware of it.'

'We do thing differently these days,' Devin said. 'There are new management methods that —'

'You do things that are an absolute shit show, and you couldn't manage your arse out of a paper bag, that's what's different these days,' she yelled at him.

Devin, Connall and Egragore had all dropped their eyes to the floor, and there was a lot of uncomfortable shuffling of feet.

Brigid thought briefly that for someone who had been stuck in a cabin with wallabies for decades her mother seemed to have a firm finger on the pulse of what had been going on.

Glancing around, Brigid realised the space they were standing in had changed. There seemed to be rows of seats appearing in the distance, stacks of bleachers that reached up to a nose-bleeding height. Chairs had also begun to stretch around them, making a large semi-circle around where they were standing.

Devin saw Brigid looking around and realised what was happening. 'Right, we need to get sorted. Everyone will be arriving soon. Let's go somewhere more private to talk.'

'Good idea.' The Cailleach beckoned over to Demniac who was standing with Lauren. 'Give me your arm, dearie. I'll need all my strength for what's coming.' She waved her hand in the air, beckoning the small group to follow her.

'What do you mean. Why will you need your strength?' Connall asked suspiciously.

'Oh, support,' the Cailleach said. 'Or something. You never know what could happen.'

'You're not going to put your name forwards, are you?' he continued, pressing the issue. 'Not at your age?'

'My age?' she scoffed. 'We're all immortal entities, you bloody idiot. Or as close to immortal as makes no odds.'

'All right, with your knees then,' Morty said, offering his opinion even though he had no idea what they were talking about.

The Cailleach gripped his arm more firmly. 'My knees are my own affair. Come on, let's go.'

'I'll lead the way,' Devin said somewhat petulantly. 'I am still in charge, after all.'

'Of course you are,' she said, patting his hand.

He led the small ground through the hall, the echoing sounds of their feet now lessening the more the room filled. There was now a jumbo-tron, and it looked suspiciously as if there was some kind of a scaffolding going up on the ceiling although whoever or whatever was doing the work was nowhere to be seen.

'You go ahead,' the Cailleach said, dropping Demniac's arm as she seemed to remember something. 'I'll catch you up. I just have to have a word with my daughter.'

Brigid sighed and her shoulders sagged. She knew that this moment had been coming, and the sooner they got it over with the better. She pasted a bright smile on her face and turned around as the rest of the group continued away from them. But before Lauren could leave she grabbed her arm. There was no way she was going to have this conversation with her mother without backup.

35

'Hi, Mum,' Brigid said brightly as if they had just run into each other in the supermarket. 'Good to see you.' She leaned down and placed a kiss on the wrinkled brown cheek.

'Hello there, dear,' her mother said. 'You're looking healthy. Very robust.'

They looked at each other. Brigid maintained her bright and airy smile. Her face started to hurt.

'This is a bit of a turn up, isn't it, love?'

'Which bit in particular?' Brigid asked.

'You know that something's up, I assume.'

Brigid's smile faltered. 'Once again, more specific please.'

'Things up here are a mess. Lucky I'm back, really.'

'Yee-ess,' she said uncertainly. 'They are a mess, by the looks of it. But are you back, though? As such? I thought you were only here because you were annoying the JanJan. You're all up in their business, and they want you to go home.'

'Oh, rubbish. Those spirits don't have a problem with me at all. I just needed permission to come up again. Fixing myself to you lot was all I needed. You know I'm seen as an interfering old biddy, and they didn't want me around. But this utter shit show needs to be taken well in hand.'

'Yes, that bit's true, but if we can just circle back to the other bit. Are you sure the indigenous spirits don't have a problem with you? Aren't you a symbol of ... colonisation and oppression?'

'Me personally? Nah. And they know that I don't have any power on their land at all, really. Only what they've let me have. I've just been enjoying the weather for a few hundred years. If they had wanted me to go, they would have told me to my face.'

'And you would have gone?'

The Cailleach cackled. 'I'm assuming you've never had any dealings with the Old Ones?'

'Not as such, no.'

'Trust me, if they politely request something then you fucking do it. Yesterday, if possible.'

'Okay, let me get this clear. You couldn't get up here without our help, so you manufactured a situation?'

'Yes. Exactly. Good job. I planned this so I could have an excuse to be here. Now. At this particular juncture. I was quite happy in my hut tending to the wombats. But with you and Connall down there too, I've been reminded of all this. It never really leaves your blood, you know. And the ineptitude with which this place is being run—'

'This place?'

'The whole Universe. It needs to be taken in hand. New management techniques, my arse. Just an excuse for Devin to nick off for a massage and let other people do all the work, if you ask me. He was always way more interested in his own pleasure than actual work.'

'It's called self-care now, and it's quite a big deal.'

'It's bullshit, that's what it is.'

'I can't believe it's that time again,' Brigid said, sighing.

'Comes around quickly.'

'People keep alluding to this,' Lauren said, 'but everyone is talking in code.'

'Not code,' the Cally said. 'We Other World beings just forget how small your human minds are, sometimes.'

'Perfect, thanks,' Lauren said. 'Brigid, can you explain?'

'It's complicated,' Brigid said, thinking for a moment.

'But also really not that complicated,' offered Cally. 'That's the point.'

Brigid nodded. 'True. You see, when the Universe was

started, or rebooted, really, but that's a whole other issue, the first, well, we call it a CEO now (here Cally made a disgusted choking noise), but we all know it's God, decided that having one person hold the job forever was a poor way of going about things. She being omnipotent and all seeing and all knowing etc, etc, etc looked off into the future annals and decided that being in charge for billions of years, or eternity, or whichever came first, was a pretty rubbish idea.'

'Rumour has it,' the Cally said, 'that she saw a couple of particular events that she didn't want to get her fingerprints on, so to speak, and decided to change things up. A couple of lesser deities who had taken to hanging around with her on a Friday night put forward a new plan.'

'Rather than carrying out the extensive and comprehensive background checks and interview panels that you'd expect would be carried out on someone who was supposed to hold such high office,' Brigid said, taking over, 'they decided, after a few bevvies in the higher dimension, that the best way to decide who would be in charge of the bits of reality called the 'known Universe', would be a demonstration of the ruler's ability to communicate with those who would be carrying out all the day to day minutia of general leadership activities.'

'This is all hearsay, you understand,' the Cailleach clarified. 'We weren't there for it. Could never keep up with their drinking, to be honest. Terrible stuff they used to down. I remember—'

'Charades,' interrupted Brigid, keen to get the story finished. 'Well, any sort of party game would have done, I suppose, but it was decided that charades is always a laugh to watch.'

'Not as fun to watch as Pin the Genitals on the Asgaroth Mega-lobster, but they decided that it wasn't befitting the dignity of the leader of the Universe.'

'Dignity,' Brigid grinned, motioning air quotes with her

fingers, and they both had a little giggle.

'And anyone who wanted to throw their hat into the ring, so to speak, would get a chance to complete,' Cally finished.

'You're joking,' Lauren said. 'I hope you're joking.'

Brigid shrugged. 'It works.'

'Does it, though?' Lauren replied.

'Precisely why,' Cally said, tapping on Brigid's arm with a wizened brown finger, 'I hope I can count on you to be a member of my team.'

'What?' Brigid said, in something akin to horror. 'No. Absolutely not. I mean, I don't know. I don't even know who's going for it. And how do you know I'm not going to try out?'

The Cailleach gave her a withering look. 'You're not a leader. Everyone knows you're not a leader. You made that abundantly clear when you stepped down from your goddess duties.'

'Temporarily! I temporarily stepped down. I needed a break.'

'More of that self-care palaver?'

'It's a deep inner knowing about what's best for one's own soul,' Brigid snapped.

'It's self indulgent bullshit, that's what it is. Tells a lot about a person.' Cally looked to Lauren for support, but she refused to make eye contact.

'It tells you that being a goddess is fucking exhausting, and sometimes, you need a break,' Brigid snapped.

'You don't see me just stepping down when the going gets tough,' the Cally said.

'You've been living in a hut in the bush for an indeterminate number of years, talking to ring tailed possums, for pity's sake.' Brigid's voice was now high pitched to a point that only dogs could hear, and Lauren felt that she should take notes of this masterclass of how to really get under your daughter's skin.

The Cailleach dismissed this line of reasoning with a flick of her fingers. 'Can I rely on your support on my team, though?

You know me better than anyone. For my sins.'

Brigid sighed. 'I suppose so. The only other person I'd feel obliged to help would be Egragore, and he won't be putting his name forward.'

'Are you sure? He looks like a climber to me. Never trusted a velour pant.'

'He better bloody well not be,' Brigid said. 'Not without discussing it with me first.'

'So are we sorted?' The Cailleach peered closely at her daughter, her eyes like diamond cutters. 'No more issues to discuss?'

'I suppose so,' Brigid said, crossing her arms. 'Can you get rid of that wheat in my lounge room? I might need to sell the house soon, and it's going to attract rats, if it hasn't already.'

The Cailleach cackled. 'That's already gone. But you have to admit it was funny, wasn't it?'

'I feel like your sense of humour may have lost some of its nuance with all that solitary living,' Brigid said drily.

'It was pretty funny, though,' Lauren agreed. 'In an absurdist, utterly random and with absolutely no punch line kind of way.'

'Come on then,' the Cailleach said, 'let's get this over with, and then I can get back to sorting things. Those Imagos need some help clearly, and I'd quite like to keep the universe in a whole and functioning state if it can possibly be managed. I'd quite like to create them their own dimension. That should take me a few weeks. The we can—'

'You haven't got the job yet,' Brigid said, although she felt herself warming to the idea. 'Don't start making plans.'

'I've got my girl with me, though,' the Cailleach said, reaching out her hand and stroking Brigid's face. 'It's in the bag.'

36

'Can someone please explain what is going on?' Morty said when the door had closed behind them on the small empty room that Egragore had secured. It seemed to be relatively quiet, and there were no moving walls or levitating bleachers to distract them in here, at least for the time being.

'We need a strategy,' Connall said, ignoring him. 'Do you have a list of competitors?'

Egragore waved a notebook at him. 'I have some rough notes, but it's not definitive yet. You know it's whoever turns up on the day.'

Devin slumped against the wall and put his head in his hands. 'I don't have the strength for this again.'

'You don't have to do anything,' Egragore said, opening up his voluminous binder. 'You're not allowed to compete.' He handed Connall some whiteboard markers.

'I do have to do something,' Devin said. 'I have to adjudicate.'

'I said,' Morty continued, 'can anyone explain what's going on?'

Connall, who was using the markers to scrawl notes on the wall, turned to Morty. 'Its the tri-millennial charades Tournament to decide the ruler of the known Universe.'

'Oh, is that all?' Demniac said drily.

'Wait,' Morty said. 'That's not how the ruler of the Universe is decided.' It was a statement rather than a question.

Connall nodded. 'It is.'

'It's not.'

'You okay, champ?' Connall asked, a look of concern flitting across his face.

'That sounds a bit bloody unprofessional.' Morty would have been delighted to know that at this exact moment, he and Lauren were involved in the same conversation.

'Unprofessional?' Egragore said, glancing up and looking at him closely. 'How else do you suggest we do it then?'

'Well, a vote. Democratically.'

'You want the whole Universe to vote?' Demniac asked.

'Well…'

'You know it's infinite, right? All the polling booths would literally never close. By the time we had even a vague general idea about the winner, it would be time for the next election.' Egragore had taken to flicking back through his papers as he spoke.

'But there must be a better idea than charades, for goodness' sake. That's just absurd.'

'It makes sense, if you think about it,' Connall said. 'It means you can communicate and that you have a team around you. And that you can work under pressure and that you have a keen understanding of the absurd because fuck me, you'll need it if you get the gig. And it's better than some other party games I could mention.'

Egragore stifled a grin.

'So who do you perform for?' Demniac asked.

'You perform for the whole stadium, but the people guessing are your people, the ones who'll be working for you here if you become the ruler. Or just people who know you well. It's a vote of confidence, really.'

Demniac nodded, a thoughtful look on his face. 'That's not so stupid, actually.'

'What do you mean not so stupid? It's patently, completely, ridiculous! It's the most stupid thing I've ever heard,' Morty exclaimed.

'I feel as if you don't know that much about how things are run on any kind of macro level,' Connall said drily.

'Democracy,' Morty stammered. 'The best and the brightest

being chosen by their peers.'

Connall shrugged. 'Which is exactly what we're doing.'

'Are you going to throw your hat into the ring again?' Egragore asked.

'I may as well,' Connall said, as if the idea had just popped into his head. 'While I'm here.'

'Be silly not to,' Egragore agreed.

'Exactly. Rude not to, really.'

'Precisely.'

'Are you interested?' Connall raised one eyebrow at Egragore with an air of forced nonchalance.

'God, no. No, absolutely not. Brigid is pissed off enough that I've come back to work for a few weeks to get things organised. There's no way she'd want me to do this. No, definitely not on my radar in any way, shape or form. Right.' Egragore began to scrawl names on the wall.

1- Connall

2- The Atrearta of Quarn.

'Shit, not them again,' Connall said, pointing to the name. 'They're useless at it. They made an absolute balls up of it last time. It was so awkward I had to nip out for a quiet moment. It was a fucking embarrassment.'

'Yes,' Egragore agreed, 'but from what I've heard they've been doing a lot of personal development courses over the past few hundred years, so it will probably be good for their confidence. We can workshop it for them afterwards, give some constructive feedback.'

Connall shuddered.

'That reminds me,' Devin said. 'Percy wants to stand, too. He mentioned it to me the other day when we were on that massage retreat. Bless.'

'Aw, bless,' Egragore and Connall echoed. 'Has she got a team, or doesn't she understand that's part of it?'

'I think she just wants to be included, so let's see if we can swing something there, okay?'

Morty was looking backwards and forwards between the three men like it was a particularly confusing game of tennis that involved too many balls and possibly several kind of prehistoric aquatic creatures unknown to science. 'You agree that this is absurd, right,' he said, looking to Demniac.

'Oh, yes, absolutely,' Demniac said, nodding vigorously. 'This is all completely ridiculous.'

'Good, thank you, yes.' He glared at Egragore, Devin and Connall, feeling a rare solidarity with Demniac.

'It's just that...' Demniac said, his eyes travelling to the increasingly defaced wall.

'It's just that what?' Morty peered at him suspiciously.

'It's just that, is it so absurd?'

'Of course it is! It's patently ridiculous!'

'But if, objectively, there does need to be a ruler of the Universe, which I think we can all agree there has to be, then this is as good a way as any. In the absence of any actual good, sensible or sustainable methods.' Demniac seemed to be working through the argument out loud.

'But not this!' Morty couldn't quite put into words why he felt such a low level dread at the thought of this, but he felt that it was deeply and unfathomably wrong on a visceral level.

'The problem,' Devin said, turning from the wall, 'is that you're being shown how the sausage is made, so to speak, and it's giving you an existential crisis. I get it, honestly.'

'I don't have time for an existential crisis though,' Morty said. 'I'm in a lovely new relationship, and I'm in a parallel dimension thingy for the first time, and I'd quite like to enjoy it.'

'Are you enjoying it now?' Egragore asked.

'Not at all. I'm very confused, and I can feel a headache coming on.'

'That would be your crisis,' Devin continued. 'You're seeing how things are really run. As I said, how the sausage is being made.'

'Well, I don't like it.'

'Of course you don't like it. And so you're unable to make any clear judgements about it. You want there to be a ruler of everything, a god if you will, but you don't want to do the hard work of understanding how that all comes about. Or, worse, actually taking part in the decision process. But here you are.' Devin waved his hand around the drab little room. 'Right in the middle of everything. Renaissance Europe, to use an analogy from your planet. And if you were able to be objective, you would realise that charades is as good a way as any. Because none of us really know what's going on, and there is far more just making it up as we go along and hoping for the best than the vast majority of the population of the Universe could handle.'

'And you're God, are you? You're God, saying that.'

Devin nodded.

Morty decided he needed a little sit down, so Egragore found him an extremely uncomfortable chair from outside in the corridor. Connall fetched him a glass of water, and he sipped it quietly with his eyes closed for a while.

'So,' Demniac said. 'Is this official list needed in order for the Tournament to begin?'

'No, not at all,' Egragore said. 'It's pretty casual. We won't know who's up for contention until everyone is in the auditorium.'

Morty made a small high-pitched sound, but they ignored him.

'But I like to have a vague idea what I'm up against re organisation,' continued Egragore. 'Lay of the land, so to speak. It's good to know what kind of show we're going to get.'

'A show? It's seen as a show, is it?' Demniac seemed increasingly delighted the more he learned.

'Yes,' Connall said. 'We may as well all enjoy ourselves, hadn't we?'

'Here's what happens,' Egragore said. 'Every candidate comes with their team. They submit their name at the sign up. That's it. Then we play charades, and whoever has success in the shortest amount of time is the winner.'

'Can anyone do it?' Demniac asked.

'Yes, absolutely. Anyone who wants to can have a go,' Devin said. 'I didn't have a huge amount of experience when I put my hand up for it. It's open to everyone. Totally democratic.'

'Well, theoretically anyone,' Egragore said.

'Yes, theoretically, true,' Connall agreed.

'Everyone who matters, anyway,' Devin said, refilling Morty's glass.

'What do you mean, everyone who matters?' Morty seemed to have composed himself somewhat.

'For example, had you ever heard about this?' Devin asked him.

'No, of course not. You know I haven't.'

'Exactly,' Devin said. 'The vast majority of the Universe has no idea that the Other World even exists. They don't even know how the government works on their own planet. Or that they even have a government. Most beings are happily clueless. So they definitely don't know all the very important high-level stuff that goes on up here. Even if they did, they wouldn't know how to get up here. It's exclusive.'

'Not as egalitarian as you would have everyone believe then?' Morty said.

'It is utterly egalitarian and democratic,' Devin said. 'Just within certain guidelines. With constraints.'

'You couldn't have it completely open slather,' Connall said with a shudder. 'That would be dreadful. Imagine.'

Egragore shook his head in distaste. 'But,' he said, getting back to the main focus, 'theoretically anyone can compete. You just have to know about it and be able to get to the Tournament. But once that's sorted, then you're golden.'

There was the sound of voices in the corridor, laughter and loud exclamations coming closer. There was a thump on the door, and it burst open, the Cailleach, Brigid and Lauren entering like they were arriving at a cocktail party that was in full swing.

'There you all are,' Cally said, beaming at the three men. 'Why are you hiding in here? There's all sorts of exciting things happening out there. What are you doing?'

'Have you all sorted yourselves out then?' Connall asked. 'Everyone happy?'

'Of course,' Brigid said. 'We were always fine. It's just our thing.'

The Cailleach looked around. 'Where's my boy?' she asked.

'Do we have a list of who the viable contenders are so far?' Brigid asked, moving over to Egragore and placing her arm around his waist. 'Everything is certainly on the move out there.'

'This is what we know so far,' Egragore replied, gesturing to the wall.

'The Atrearta of Quarn,' the Cailleach read. 'Percy. Ah, bless. And Connall! That's nice, deary. Going to try and do it responsibly this time, are you? Very mature.'

'Can we not discuss that please,' Connall said tightly. 'We've all moved on, and clearly everything is fine now, and Devin and I are absolutely fine now. See?' He waved at Devin who gave him a half smile.

'I think 'fine' is an overstatement,' Devin said, 'but you just arrived here and started talking and, quite frankly, there's enough other things to worry about today than your piss poor historical behaviour.'

'Oh, let's definitely discuss this,' Lauren said eagerly. 'What happened? I sense a very juicy story.'

'Devin became CEO of the Universe in a bit of an upset, didn't you, love,' the Cailleach, who was clearly very happy to tell the story, said. 'And given this was three thousand years ago, Connall was younger and a bit headstrong, and he didn't like the idea that someone that he's always seen as an equal and a best friend and, yes, they had always been a bit competitive, was suddenly so much above him in the pecking order. So he got a bit stroppy, didn't you, love?' The old woman looked over to Connall, who refused to make eye contact.

'I wasn't my best self,' he said. 'I spent some time making bad choices, but to be fair, bad choices were made all round, and —'

'Especially after he made you his right-hand man and all of that,' the Cailleach said, seemingly feeling there were still some unexamined feelings that needed to be tapped. 'He made you his close adviser, gave you power and what did you do?'

'I know all that, but I didn't like being subservient to him,' Connall said. 'It was a long time ago, and I've done a lot of work on myself since then, and it's all about forgiveness, after all, isn't it?'

'Ye-ees,' Devin said, his head cocked to one side, his dark eyes peering closely at Connall. 'I feel as if there has to be some, you know, apology and reparations made in order for there to be forgiveness, though.'

Connall looked at him stonily.

'And because there was definitely none of that at the time, and because you literally tried to enlist forces against me and tried to take over the Upper Realms and usurp me from power, basically because you were jealous, I had to, you know.' Devin made a flicking motion with his fingers. 'Exile him to Earth. Send him down in a fiery blaze of anger and resentment. Make a spectacle of him. I needed to make it clear that no one can just go around willy-nilly trying to take over from me. I can't have unrighteousness.'

'Oh, get your hand off it,' Connall snapped. 'It's got nothing to do with unrighteousness. You always hated the fact that I'm better looking than you. Resplendent, I think was the word widely used.'

'Wait,' Lauren said, glancing back and forth between them. 'This reminds me of something.'

'Yes,' Morty agreed, 'me too. It couldn't be though, could it?'

'Um,' Lauren said, 'this feels a bit awkward to ask, but … are you Lucifer?'

Connall, Devin and the Cailleach burst into gales of laughter. 'What do you mean, am I Lucifer?' Connall asked when he had composted himself somewhat. 'What have I ever possibly done that would make you think that?'

She had to admit she hadn't seen him do anything apart from being unfailingly giving, polite and an absolute gentleman. 'It just sounds awfully like the story in the Bible about the fall of Satan, that's all.'

'Oh, that's right. I'd forgotten all about that book,' Devin said as a look of understanding crossed his face. 'But yes, now you come to mention it, I seem to remember that story was loosely based on our falling out. The majority of the main talking points were monumentally wrong, of course, because I'm pretty sure there were some agendas happening when it was written. Never read it myself.'

'I have,' Egragore said. 'Some good sexy poetry. Brigid and I quite like it.' He winked at Brigid, who blushed a little.

'The whole idea of evil beings trying to manufacture the downfall of humankind is totally true and on the money,' Connall offered, 'but it's got nothing to do with me.'

At this statement, Lauren noticed Egragore glance quickly at Devin, who frowned at him and then rolled his eyes, but the exchange was so rapid she wondered if she had imagined it.

'I'm not going to go and turn evil just because Devin rightfully got the shits with me for being a dick, am I?' Connall continued. 'Talk about things escalating quickly. No, that Bible thing that you humans put so much emphasis on has some snippets of truth, but on the whole, it's completely and wilfully misunderstood the entire history and motivation behind the Other World and what we do.'

'That's obvious,' Morty said. 'It barely mentions charades at all, from what I can remember.'

The Cailleach seemed to remember something. 'Where's my boy?' she said again. 'Didn't he come here with you?'

'He was here,' Morty said looking around. 'He was here earlier.'

'He can't be wandering around up here unsupervised,' Devin said. 'Everything is in flux today. There's no knowing what he'll find.'

'Or what will find him,' Connall muttered.

'It's very safe, thank you,' Devin snapped. 'There will be no 'finding'. Nothing is going to 'find' him.'

'That's what was said last time,' Connall continued. 'We never did find the Contrararidon again, did we? No idea where he ended up.'

'No, we did find him,' Egragore clarified. 'He was in a pocket universe. We can't get him out, but he's safe, and apparently, he's enjoying life surrounded by an infinite amount of magic mushrooms.'

'That would make time pass by, I'd imagine,' Lauren said.

'Yes, well, when you're an eternal being trapped in a discrete pocket universe with no way of escape, then you need to take your fun where you can find it,' Connall agreed.

'I hope that's not where Demniac is,' Devin said. 'I mean, a pocket universe. He's a mortal. That could get very messy. And

I'm not entirely sure that getting sucked into another dimension isn't possible at the moment.'

'What do you mean?' said the Cailleach.

'The flux. The flurries. The instability. There have been reports of humans disappearing. It causing even more instability.'

'We need to find him,' the Cailleach snapped. 'He's on my team.'

Devin nodded slightly to Egragore, who added the extra name to the wall.

'I could be on your team,' Lauren said helpfully.

'No, you'd be useless. I need my boy.'

'Oh, Mum,' Brigid said. 'Let Lauren play. It's not nice to exclude people, and what harm can it do?'

'It's bad form having dead wood. You want to bring your A team to play; otherwise, what would we look like? It's all about the performance, after all.'

'Um,' Morty said, turning to Connall nervously. 'I'm not the only one on your team, am I? Because I don't know how good I'll be at this, and I don't want you to lose because of me.'

'Oh, you want to be on my team do you?' Connall said.

Seeing Morty's face fall he continued hurriedly. 'I mean, of course. Great. You'll be absolutely amazing and helpful and, no, you will be, but it will be good to have some other helpers, those who have known me longer.'

'Like who?' Morty asked. 'People from Earth? Or here?'

'Actually,' Lauren interrupted, 'speaking of which, can you just get anyone to come up here to help out? How does that work?'

'Generally, yes', Devin said. 'Typical Other World rules don't apply during the Tournament. We lower all the security levels, and contenders can summon anyone they want up here for a short time.'

'I dunno,' the Cailleach said. 'From what I can see, you've just got people walking around here willy-nilly as it is. I feel that you're pretty lax at the best of times.'

'And this definitely isn't the best of times,' Egragore agreed.

'Anyway,' Devin said pointedly, 'contenders can call up whoever they want. Just for this specific time period. Normal rules don't apply. Because,' he said, glaring at the Cailleach, 'usually we only allow officially sanctioned parties into the Other World.'

There was low rumbling noise as the floor beneath them moved slightly, and Egragore glanced up. 'Ah,' he said. 'That will be the last of the terraforming. The area should be finished now if we'd like to go in and grab our seats. We aim for an infinity of seating in here, but given the infinite number of people who usually want to watch, it's usually a toss up between which infinity gives out first.'

'Pardon?' Morty and Lauren said at the same time.

Egragore spun around with a flourish. 'Let's find you a seat,' he said, his velvet suit flicking up slightly as he moved. 'It's show time.'

37

Demniac had slipped out of the room just after hearing that, in theory, anyone could stand for the position of leader of the known Universe. He stood in the corridor, hearing grinding and scraping noises coming from all around him, weighing up his next move.

He was on his own, in what was apparently the absolute hub of power in the known Universe.

Even if it didn't look like a hub of power.

Or sound like it.

Or behave like hub of power in any way that he would have thought probable until a few days ago.

He slid his hand into his jeans and pulled out a small box that had recently been full of matches. He pushed the compartment open with his thumb and it slid out. With the sound that static clothing makes when it comes out of the drier and you have to peel sheets off each other, the air shimmered for a moment, and there was a feeling of unfolding, and then the lion stood next to him.

'Well, that was singularly unpleasant,' the lion rumbled. 'A matchbox. Really. That was the best you could do, was it?'

'I'm not responsible for the fact that you wanted to hide from the Cailleach. I've never seen anything as big as you duck and cover so quickly. You positively went to ground.'

'She's not my favourite person, that's all. I'd rather avoid any interaction if it's all right with you. She knows far too much. A matchbox was a ridiculous selection, though.'

'You said you needed something subtle and under the radar to transport you in,' Demniac said. 'It fitted the bill perfectly.'

'You didn't have any kind of mother of pearl inlaid trinket box laying around? Don't look at me like that. You've got an actual human skull on your alter. I feel like a basic jade trinket box wouldn't be that much to ask.'

'A skull is very much different to a box, I think. And it's not real, of course, it's not. What makes you think it's real?'

'It keeps screaming at me.'

Demniac stared at Leo in horror. 'Are you serious?'

'There's a lot of untoward stuff happening in your flat, most of which you caused accidentally. You really do need to pay more attention to what you're doing.'

'I thought it was fake,' Demniac said to himself. 'Roxy told me it was fake.'

'That was your first problem, then. Trusting that woman. There's something deeply unsettling about her, and I thought that even before I knew that she dealt in illegal human remains.'

'She doesn't deal them as such, she just knew I needed something for my conjuring, and I assumed she'd source me a fake one and — '

The lion shook his massive head as if to break off Demniac's words. 'Still. I feel as if I've been brought fairly low on my little sojourn down to Earth, what with the matchboxes and the screaming skulls and no one down knowing who I am. It's done nothing for my self-esteem.'

'How do you even know about self-esteem? I wouldn't have thought that eternal or ethereal beings, or whatever you are, would have any truck with that kind of thing.'

'Just because I'm several pantheons above you on the spiritual evolution scale doesn't mean I don't have some room to grow. And getting folded into a matchbox and shoved into your seriously in need of a wash jeans isn't doing a lot for me. Anyway.' He pulled himself up to his full height and shook his mane. It gloriously and goldenly cascaded around his body. 'Let's get down to business.'

'I'm still not clear why I had to smuggle you in a matchbox anyway. You hedged around that quite a bit, you know.'

'I didn't have to hide,' Leo said haughtily. 'There was no hiding. I just didn't know how to get into this particular part. The Other World is expansive, you know, and exists on many different dimensions, all with their different rules and some with entirely different physics, which make organising Christmas parties a bit of a issue, from what I've heard. Much easier to hitch a lift with you. I knew you were going to be taken up, so I planned in advance.'

'You knew? What, are you psychic?'

'I can see a slight hint of the already decided future, nothing more. Barely useful, usually, except in this case. Once, I managed to deflect a chair that Moses threw at Thoth, which stopped an inter-dimensional war, so that was convenient. And

I get the odd telepathic blip from particularly powerful Old Ones from time to time, but that's more evolutionary than anything else.'

'Right, well, I've brought you here,' Demniac said. 'And I'd rather not leave Cally for too long, and if I have to choose sides, then she would come out on top.'

'I think she can probably look after herself, although your care for her well-being is extremely touching.'

'She reminds me of my Nanna,' Demniac said.

'I'm sorry. That must be awful for you,' the lion said, aghast.

Demniac laughed. 'No, no, its all right. I loved her. Sure, she smelled funny, and she lived exclusively in extra large cardigans and crocs and only ate instant mashed potatoes and kangaroo patties and swore like a trooper, but she made me feel the most loved that I've ever felt. And the Cailleach reminds me of her so much. So I...' His voice trailed off. 'So I guess I just want to be around her and make sure she's safe.'

The lion snorted. 'Her making sure you're safe is more likely, but yes, lovely story. Very heartwarming. But you can head off now if you like. I have business to attend to, and you probably want to watch what's going to happen.'

'Yes, a game. A Tournament.'

'Not 'a' tournament. 'The' Tournament. The big one. The ultimate of the ultimate. The absolute pinnacle of all Tournaments that have ever been conceptualised to ever occur in the—'

'You've gotten very wordy since you've been up here. Have you noticed that?'

'Yes, it must be something about the air of power. It makes me positively giddy.'

'Wait,' Demniac said. 'You're not thinking of competing, are you?'

'I'm not allowed to,' he said, and Demniac noticed that the

lion refused to make eye contact with him.

'The only ones who aren't allowed. Bit of a sore point amongst us conjured beings. We're kind of a grey area when it comes to our existence, and even though we are fully recognised and sanctioned, we're still thought to be a bit flighty and insubstantial to take on really big jobs.'

'Jobs like the leader of the Universe?'

'Quite.'

Demniac thought for a moment. 'So you do have some similarities with the Imagos then?'

'What? No.' The lion seemed taken aback. 'No, not really at all. I am a thought form, but I'm not created by humans. Sybella in no way created me. I have existed from the beginning. I just have certain properties that mean that I, like the other old school thought forms, can be summoned if and when you humans manage to get your spells or potions right.'

'That sounds a bit haphazard,' Demniac said.

'Yes, well,' the lion said, gruffly. 'It was supposed to be far more enmeshed in lore and procedure and technicality. Yes, once upon a time, only the great ones could call us into existence on the plane of your planet. Once upon a time, we were only called by great sages and magicians and thinkers. Your Jesus had me around for a while, you know.'

'Really?'

'Oh, absolutely. Where do you think all those pictures of him with lions came from? They never get my mane quite right these days, which irritates me no end. Historical accuracy isn't what it was. Then again, they tend to make Jesus white too, which is a bigger issue in the scheme of things, I suppose. He was a good magician, that boy. Yes, top notch. Too serious though. Didn't know how to have fun. Now, Buddha, he was an absolute riot. I remember once—'

There was a rumble under their feet, and the ground tilted.

Only slightly, but the ground tilting at all is always something that gives you pause for thought. Demniac put out his hand and steadied himself against the wall.

'Okay, yes.' The lion shook himself. 'We should probably get on with business. This place is going to be absolutely crawling with beings soon. I feel as if they could be a bit better organised. There should be ushers, at least.' He sniffed the air. 'Yes, I think this is the way. I can smell it.'

'I thought you had other business to attend to,' Demniac said.

'I said I had business. Not 'other' business.'

They headed off, Leo leading the way and filling up the entire corridor. Demniac knew the lion could take on any size he wanted but suspected he was trying to take on an imposing and awe-inspiring presence.

It was working.

'Can I just point us back to what we were talking about a minute ago,' Demniac said. 'Not the Jesus bit but about the Imagos. I don't mean to be offensive but—'

He felt the lion bristle slightly. 'I am un-offendable,' he rumbled. 'I am too majestic and glorious to be offended by anything that a human might say.'

'Oh, good because—'

'Although I can be pissed off. You could definitely piss me off.'

'Ah.'

'But go on anyway. I'm curious now.'

'What is the difference between you guys, the thought forms, and the Imagos that Connall has been looking after. Like, what precisely is the difference?'

The lion stopped in his tracks and swung his head around to stare at Demniac. 'I beg your pardon.'

'If it's not a rude question.'

'It's a stupid question, is what it is.'

'All right. Yes. Maybe. But I'd still like to know the answer, though, because there seems to be a bit of overlap. In my limited understanding,' he finished quickly.

'For pity's sake, I just explained it; what's not to get?' The lion sighed. 'Again then, the Great Ones were created at the beginning of everything, right.'

'Yes.'

'By actual gods. Thought forms manifested by the desires and deep motivations of gods and higher beings and the like. Yes?'

Demniac nodded his head.

'Who deal with really big concepts and serious issues, all right?'

'Yes.'

'And when these great ones and magicians and the like needed help and advice on really big issues, they created them.'

'Yes, got it.'

'So, I don't want to brag, but we're pretty impressive and wise, and we've got some history behind us.'

'Wait, you were saying 'them' and now it's 'us.' Demniac was confused.

'I'm a special case. I'm the greatest of the great.'

'Who created you then?'

'We have some history around us. That's all you need to know.'

'Are you going to answer my question?'

'No. The main takeaway is that Imagos and great ones are different, and I don't want you to go around telling people that they are the same. Its disconcerting and infuriating which is a mix that I'm really not comfortable with.' Leo kept padding down the corridor.

'But how is that different?' asked Demniac.

'Oh, come on, boy, use your brain. These Imagos are created accidentally by fifteen year old boys who want a girlfriend. Or thirty year old's trying to deal with their daddy issues. Which is why we get there poor blighted half-formed creatures who have no real purpose and were never meant to be in existence in the first place.'

'Yes, I do see your point, but you have to admit that when it comes right down to it, there are some similarities in how you're created. You see the confusion.'

'No, I don't. Not at all.'

'All right. You're very stubborn; did you know that?'

Leo ignored him.

'Do you have any sympathy for them at least?'

'Sympathy? Yes, in a way. But it doesn't make them right, and it doesn't make them worthy. I'm not a monster. I understand it's difficult for them. But they aren't part of creation, and that's not my fault.'

'Slightly awkward that the one who summoned you to Earth is also the one who got possessed by the chaos agent who went around killing them, isn't it?'

'That's not what actually happened, you know.'

'Coincidental too. Here's you, not liking Imagos, and you're the one who took her to Egypt and got her possessed. Sounds suspicious.'

He felt the lion tense. It made the hair on his arms stand up, and he questioned how far he wanted to take this.

'It was just...'

'Yes?' Demniac said questioningly.

'Just one of those things.'

'Is everyone going to accept that? That it's a coincidence?'

'The Universe is a very complex place,' the lion rumbled. 'There is far more going on than even my mind can grasp.'

'Still,' Demniac continued, 'if I were you, I'd keep a bit quiet about not liking the Imagos. Looks suspicious, as I said.'

'This is bigger than all of us now. What Devin wants is neither here nor there. He has made some decision, promised some promises, and what he has set in motion will keep moving. Imagos are a scourge,' Leo said. 'They are a scourge, but no one wants to come out and say it or do anything about it. If it was more than a coincidence, which it isn't, I wouldn't be surprised if I was given accolades for what happened.'

'If it wasn't a coincidence,' Demniac said.

'Which it was,' the lion finished.

They lapsed into an uneasy silence.

They had come to the end of the halls, and ahead they could hear a dull roar as if thousands of earth moving machines were rumbling, waiting for their work orders. It was a huge sound, but muffled as if coming to Demniac's ears through layers of bubble wrap.

'Probably through there then,' the lion said.

There was another burst of noise from the room beyond.

'Why exactly are you going along, though?' Demniac asked, realising that he still didn't know. 'If you can't compete.'

'It's become a chance to see and be seen. There will be important beings there, and I want to take my place amongst them. Represent. Since we all exist on different planes and different times of history and different dimensions, it can be hard to get together and catch up, so most of us Other World beings do try to make a point of being here, if we can.'

'I hope that chaos agent doesn't make its way up here too,' Demniac said casually. 'That would add some complexity.'

Leo laughed. 'What a production that would be.'

'I was only joking,' said Demniac.

'Lucky that you don't know what you're talking about.'

Demniac headed towards the noises that were growing in intensity and as he got to the entrance of the auditorium he looked back towards the lion, who had gradually dropped behind him. 'Are you coming?' he asked.

'You go ahead,' said Leo. 'I'll come in my own time. Don't tell anyone I'm here, alright?'

Demniac shrugged and disappeared into the noise.

38

Things were different in here now. The expansive white space that Brigid had remembered as being offices and where the Cailleach had once run a particularly debauched wine bar was no longer a room in the way that the word could be used in any commonly accepted vernacular. It had grown even larger in the space of a few hours, an expanse that now reached higher than the sky and longer than the horizon, yet there was still a perceptible roof and walls an immeasurably long way off. Lauren didn't understand the physics of it all; her head spun as Devin led them through the wide door that now had the words OMNIA ISTA LICET inexplicably engraved along the top in a curlicue of gold leaf.

'Is that Latin?' she asked, bemused.

'Adds a certain gravitas,' Devin replied. 'The Romans knew what was up, didn't they. They really meant business. Do you like what we've done with it? He asked, turning to the Cailleach and Brigid as their necks craned up. 'I've been putting a lot of thought into this over the last few hundred years. Got a Pan-Dimensional Event Planner to organise the decor and everything.'

'Who's doing the food?' the Cailleach asked. 'Never mind the decor. No one ever gives a hoot about that. The food is the big question.'

'I'm not worrying about the food this time. It ends up being an absolute waste anyway. Most of it ends up binned. No one cares about that except you, Cally.'

She stared at him with narrowed eyes. 'Yes, they bloody well do. They do care about the food. You'll have a mutiny in here if you don't give them something to eat. What were you thinking,

Devin?'

'Was there any food last time, at my do? I don't remember there being any.'

'Of course you don't remember. You were being sick in a bucket with nerves until ten minutes before you stepped out into the arena. To start with,' and she began ticking things off on her fingers. 'There were barbecue pineapple meatballs on sticks, crab Rangoon crescent cups, individual bacon jalapeno cheese balls and then some of those little pomegranate bites, you know, the cheesy ones with the coriander garnish.' She smacked her lips together as if remembering the delights. 'And that was just on arrival.'

Devin stared at her, mouth agape. 'This happened three thousand years ago. How do you remember that?'

'She's like a Labrador,' Brigid said, putting her arm around Devin's shoulder and steering him away from her mother before she could launch into a description of the next course. 'She's very food motivated.'

'It looks lovely, anyway,' Brigid said in a conciliatory tone. 'You clearly worked very hard on everything.'

Far in the distance, they could see the flocked wallpaper and underfoot was a repeat of the thick carpet they had recently seen in the hallways.

'We got William Morris to consult with the party planner too,' Devin continued, still keen to share his achievement. 'Pulled him out of the Shadow Lands, and he was quite happy to consult with me. Said it was a nice break.'

Rows of high-backed velvet seats stretched out to the horizon, an uncountable number on a scale that Lauren had never seen before. 'How many are there?' she asked, aghast.

'An infinity. I told you that. We accept all comers, so we need to be hospitable, after all.'

'But wouldn't those at the back not be able to see?'

There was a stage of sorts, a large circular area around which the seating was arranged, stretching outwards in a fan pattern.

'We have jumbo-trons every light year or so. It all works out. And if you're that keen to get a good view, you need to get here earlier, to be frank. I can't do everything myself. As for the comfort of the audience, we try to get the mix right, but there's always going to someone who doesn't think the hydrogen mix is going to keep them alive for the duration. A lot of our cohort don't breathe at all, of course, so that makes things easier, but the ones who come from other regions make things tricky.'

'Just out of interest, which ones don't breathe at all?' Morty asked, drawing close to Devin, Lauren and Brigid. The Cailleach was wandering around poking things with her stick, with a sense of interest rather than aggression, and Connall has sat himself on a chaise lounge and was gazing off into space, seemingly lost in thought, with Egragore squatting next to him, speaking into his ear.

'The dead ones,' Devin said simply. 'Obviously, one of my main portfolios is those who have made it into, well, what you call heaven and what we call the Upper Realms. Someone must have told you about that, surely?'

Morty looked at him blankly.

'So, this is as close to your idea of heaven as we get. I'm God. There are probably some angels around here, somewhere, if you'd like to meet one. I'm sorry. I thought you knew.'

'She did,' Brigid said, pointing to Lauren. 'I already told her.'

'Yeah, I knew.'

'Thanks for passing on what I would have thought was a fairly important piece of information.'

'Sorry,' Devin said. 'I really did assume that someone would have told you.'

'So, let me get this straight. You're the one in the Bible, then?'

'Allegedly. But a lot got lost in translation. Literally and figuratively. And I'm also … all the other gods that are worshipped on Earth, so it's a bit of a mess, really, but we all just muddle along. Anyway, we invite the good ones to come and watch. The ones down below won't get a chance to come up, obviously. We don't want evil ones coming up and getting ideas, do we!'

He laughed lightly, but Lauren noticed a hint of nervousness in the way his voice lilted. 'Surely they wouldn't be able to stand for contention though?'

'Actually,' Devin said, glancing over at Egragore for support, 'that's a bit of a grey area. Because we try, for the most part, to stick to moral relativism, so the whole idea of 'good' and 'bad' is something we've been encouraged to avoid in the past. I've had a bit of a push to redo things. I've made some heartfelt, and I think convincing, speeches about the fact that burning babies to death to appease, well, me, is pretty poor form. I mean, I am what they talk about when they talk about God, so what I say should go, right? But, technically, there's nothing stopping a being with a totally different moral compass from standing. Or no moral compass at all. But we've done our best to stop that happening. A bit of quarantining, as it were. Hey, Egragore,' he called. 'We did a bit of quarantining, didn't we?'

'Sorry?' Egragore said, walking over to them. 'Who's getting quarantined?'

'The only being we thought might cause a real problem today. The chaos agent, right? I've locked him safely away in ancient Egypt. Well, we did. Three thousand years ago. Time is relative and all that. That's one of the reasons I had to steal Egragore away from you,' Devin said to Brigid. 'Needed such a big job in safe hands. Couldn't outsource that one.'

Egragore's eyes shifted nervously, and he glanced about the area as if searching for an unnamed person who he could ask to do this particular bit of explaining. 'About that, Devin' he said.

'We need to talk.'

'What do you mean?'

Lauren could see the muscles in Devin's chiselled jaw twitching.

From amongst the seating, where the Cailleach has plopped herself down, came her strong voice. 'Everyone's arriving,' she barked. 'You need to get greeting, Devin. Start making people feel welcome.'

Lauren could see that a mass of shapes had begun to populate the seats as far as she could see, but there hadn't been an arrival in any sense of the word that she understood it. First the seats were empty, and then there was a shimmer, like the sun on a road on a particularly viciously hot day, and then forms solidified bit by bit, and then seats were full. She waved as she saw Demniac walking towards them.

'What's been happening,' she asked conversationally. 'Impressive hey? Did you get lost?'

'Just exploring,' he said.

'Probably best to stay in the one spot,' Lauren advised him.

Devin's eyes darted nervously, clearly torn between doing his duty and wanting to know the ominous news that he feared that Egragore was about to tell him.

'What do you mean?' Devin repeated, beads of sweat breaking out on his brow. 'Tell me, now. This is my responsibility, you know. This is all down to me. It can't end in disaster now, not after I've worked so hard on ... this.' He gestured to the decor, the artfully placed potted ferns, and the stuffed birds in glass domes. 'This is my legacy. All of this.'

'Wait.' A look of puzzlement crossed Lauren's face. 'Isn't guiding the Universe and making good decisions and being the Ultimate Ruler of Everything your legacy?'

'Well, yes, that too,' he said uncertainly. 'But mainly this, to be honest. You know what people are like. They only remember what's right in front of them.'

'The Atrearta of Quarn is here.' The Cailleach seemed to be settled into giving a running commentary now. She had taken Demniac's hand in hers and held it tightly. 'You'll need to have a good old chat to them Devin. You know they'll dissolve if they don't get some external validation.'

She saw Lauren's worried eyes and winked at her. 'Literally dissolve. They will. I've seen it. They go the pieces under pressure. Last time we needed to halt the proceedings while a clean-up was done. People kept slipping over in the mess.'

'God, Mum,' Brigid said, sounding exasperated. 'You're not being very helpful. You can see poor Devin is having a moment.' Devin's dark skin had paled to ashen, and he was urgently talking to Egragore.

The Cailleach cackled. 'All right, come on then. Brigid, you and I will do the greetings. We can get everyone settled in, and you go off Devin and sort yourself out. You're so handsome, and this is your moment. You need to compose yourself.'

She stood up and raised her head, smiling at a large, amorphous creature that was burbling towards the seats at the front. 'Attie! How have you been, dearie? You're looking well. How have the self-empowerment workshops been going? You remember my girl Brigid? And this is Demniac. He's my new favourite.'

There was a rough noise, like an unruly group of ally cats vomiting, and the Cailleach cocked her head forwards to catch what was being said. She burst out with a laugh and nodded her head. 'I know, she has, hasn't she? I've decided that it must be a gluten intolerance because...'

With the Cailleach granting him release, Devin grabbed Egragore's arm and pulled him into one of a series of rooms that were designed to give competitors a space to compose themselves, think and basically step out of the judgemental and watchful gaze of billions, or an infinity, of eyes, whichever came first.

Brigid glared at her mother. 'Would you stop making people feel relaxed by putting me down please?'

The Cailleach rolled her eyes and patted Attie on what she assumed was its back. 'So sensitive, this generation. Can't take a joke. Anyway, you get yourself settled into wherever you think you'll fit and also somewhere you won't make a mess. These velvet seats are a bugger to clean, so avoid them. I don't know what he was thinking.'

Noticing that a bevy of dog-shaped creatures from Epsilon Sagittarii were trying to take some of the choicer seats at the front that had been reserved for dignitaries or those that Egragore wanted to keep a tight eye on, she stomped over to get it sorted.

Lauren stood next to Brigid and put her hand on her friend's arm. 'I have to admit,' she said, 'I'm finding all of this a bit overwhelming.'

Brigid sighed. 'It can be frantic here at the best of times, and this isn't the best of times. I feel as if there are some critical areas that haven't been given the oversight that they needed. It's probably because Egragore came down to live with me rather than staying here and looking after Devin.'

'I hope you don't think this is your fault?' Lauren said. 'You can't take the blame for the mess that's happening.'

'I know. No, really, I do know. But it's also not as if I didn't know what could potentially happen, and it's not as if we haven't had fair warning. I've been around long enough to know that things that can go wrong, do, go wrong, and clearly, Devin has been hung out to dry when in comes to the leadership assistance he needed.'

'All you can now do is your best,' Lauren said philosophically. 'And I'm here to help you.'

'Mum looks like she's getting things under control,' Brigid said as she watched the old woman direct, order and generally begin to corral every being that manifested itself into the stadium. She grabbed Morty and Connall and some others who had wandered into her sphere of influence. Chairs were being moved, faux streetlamps were being dragged out of sight lines, and several tiger skin rugs were being rolled up and hauled out of the way. It was the first time they'd seen someone genuinely take charge of the situation for several days.

'She is pretty impressive, you have to admit,' Lauren said after a moment.

'Yeah, she is. She's pretty good value when it all comes down to it. She's just a lot of pressure as a mother.'

'There could be worse mothers though,' Lauren said.

'Yes, that's true, I guess,' Brigid conceded.

Lauren giggled. 'Some mothers eat their babies when they don't like them, for example.'

'I'm pretty sure that's hamsters, Lauren. Not necessarily comparable.'

Brigid wrapped her arms around Lauren and hugged her. 'I'm glad you're here. Both because I need your company and because, well, this is a big deal thing. Humans don't usually get invited up here.'

'Yes, I wanted to ask you about that,' Lauren said. 'I'm a bit confused about the … I don't even know how to describe it. Who actually is up here?'

'You know that many species exist in the other dimensions that make up the Earth planes. And because of wormhole travel, we can open it up to all of space and time. It's quite convenient, really.'

'You'd hope so, given it's the Ultimate Ruler of Everything. You'd think that everyone would like a chance to take part.'

'Yes and no,' Brigid said. 'I mean, yes, in theory, but people are busy and getting on with their own lives. Often just knowing that someone is in charge, or even just knowing that someone is planning on being in charge, is enough to keep people happy and going about their business. A lot of being in charge is just about crowd control when it comes right down to it. It takes a fairly unique kind of being to want to do it.'

'Which, at the moment, is going swimmingly thanks to your mum and the boys,' Lauren said, nodding towards the hive of activity and goodwill that had broken out amongst the crowd. Someone had come along with their own fairground popcorn machine, and the smell of doughnuts cooking inexplicably drifted to her nose. Someone else had fashioned some drums out of an elephant's leg umbrella holder, and the carnival air was starting to permeate the whole area.

Morty rushed up to them, breathless, eyes shining. 'Have you heard? Cally has worked out a registration system with spot prizes, and the winner gets to have their own pocket universe! Make sure you get a ticket!' He rushed back to be given his next set of orders.

'He's calling her Cally now. That won't end well.'

They looked towards where Cally was patting the boy on the cheek, and Brigid shrugged. 'I don't know. She's happiest when she's in the middle of things.'

'Mum,' Brigid called over the hubbub. 'How long until you think things will be able to kick off?'

The old woman looked over to them and waggled her hand noncommittally. 'Things are settling down now. Once everyone has their snacks and Connall has connected up the jumbo-tron, we should be good to go.'

'Are you going to get all the competitors into a huddle for a pep talk?'

The Cailleach frowned and put her hands on her hips. 'That's really Devin's job. That's figurehead kind of stuff, that is, not real work.' Just then, she saw a group of burly, what looked like cavemen dragging what seemed to be a fully equipped pizza oven towards them and was gone.

Brigid looked towards the door that Egragore and Devin had disappeared into. 'Should I go and check how they're going? Hurry them along a bit.'

'How long can it take to tell Devin that an untold horror has been unleashed onto the world and may very well try to take control of the Universe?' Lauren said. 'See, took me five seconds. Done.'

'Oh, god, all right.' Brigid pulled Lauren along with her for emotional support and slipped through the door, which led through a small corridor that led the small room that served as dressing rooms and offices. She tapped on the door and peaked around to see Devin breathing into a paper bag and Egragore crouching next to him, counting down from ten.

'How's everything going?' she asked, overly brightly. 'All good? Happy? Sorted?'

Devin's frantic eyes were bright above the paper bag, and Egragore leapt to his feet and strode towards the women. 'Not happy, not sorted,' he said. 'Do you have any Valium?'

'Gods don't take Valium,' Brigid said.

'It might be a good time to start.'

'I'm going to find some,' said Devin, and headed out the door.

'You told him about the chaos agent then?'

'Yes. He's not taking it well.'

'Why is it such a big deal?' Lauren asked. 'In that room out there, and in here, actually, are some of the most important and powerful gods in the Earth's history. I mean, I saw Tezcatlipoca out there a minute ago eating popcorn. Surely they can take on this chaos character if things kick off.'

Egragore took Brigid's arm and pulled her out into narrow the corridor. Lauren followed and noticed that the hum in the arena was all pervasive now, the chattering of millions of voices a dull roar.

'It's not that easy,' he said, glancing around as if expecting an all-pervasive evil to jump out from behind a coat stand and say boo. 'It's not like it's just going to come in here in a scary clown costume and start to smite people. That would be easy. This is why we had it safely ensconced in ancient Egypt, or so we thought. Out of the way and not a problem at all.'

'Why ancient Egypt?

'Oh, they're the absolute pinnacle of magic and curses, that lot. The chaos agent would just be another ancient horror. Not special at all. It wouldn't find anyone to give up their power to its evil plans there because evil spirits and cursed possessions are a dime a dozen.'

'What do you mean?'

'It's most powerful when someone willingly gives in to it. Thinks they can handle being possessed by it, so they offer themselves up, and Bob's your uncle, their soul is a shrivelled black husk, and their meat suit is doing terrible things.'

Lauren looked aghast. 'But Sybella didn't willingly give in, and her soul didn't end up being a husk. Did it?'

'I think that had something to do with the JanJans.' Egragore nodded towards Brigid. 'The Old Ones in Australia are far older and more powerful than the magic of the rest of the world. They exist in another realm completely, above ours, and they rarely pay heed to Other World business. They think it's newfangled shenanigans, and, to be honest, I think they see us as a bit embarrassing and immature. But occasionally, their attention gets piqued by something happening here. I think that's why Sybella was left unharmed.'

'Why, did they like her especially, or something?'

'No, they just don't like bullies.'

'Which is also why they don't care if your mum is here or in Ireland, I take it?'

'Yes, they don't care at all,' Egragore continued, 'at least from what I can tell. They're quite happy that she checks pouches on the highway and bottle feeds the orphans. No, she just manufactured that as a way to get up here. I should have seen that earlier, clever old thing. She could have just asked, though. Devin isn't nearly as threatened and scared of challenge and other people's opinions as he used to be. I've managed to talk him down a lot of late.'

'Are you scared this chaos agent is going to take over someone, get them to compete as themselves, and then take over as the Ultimate Ruler of Everything?' Lauren asked. 'Because that would be awkward.'

'Yes,' Egragore said. 'Which is why having it released from Egypt is a bit of an issue.'

'I don't think it should be allowed to take over under false pretences,' Lauren said.

'And I don't think ethical leadership is something it's particularly interested in,' Brigid replied drily.

'But is there a law?' she said, almost frantically. 'Surely there are rules or laws to stop this kind of thing?'

A dishevelled Devin stepped through the doorway. He had changed into an outfit that made him look like he should be poking sticks at lions in a circus. He brushed his hand down the red tailcoat, burnished with gold trim, and adjusted his cravat. The paper bag was still clutched in his hand, but he squashed it into a ball and tossed it into a potted fern as he walked towards them. 'It was on the list,' he said, his chin now lifted and his voice regaining some of its strength. 'Enacting a statute to formalise exactly who can and cannot stand and the circumstances around it was on the list of things to do, but three thousand years goes by far more quickly that you'd think, and as I think I mentioned, I had this do to organise, so there's the last five hundred years accounted for. No, at the last minute, when we saw it was raising its profile again, targeting Imagos, causing no end of trouble, so we decided that sending it to Egypt a few thousand years ago would do the job nicely. We didn't realise that the bloody lion thought form would free it, did we? That wasn't part of the plan.'

At that moment, the door that connected the corridor to the auditorium burst open, and the noise, the sound of an infinity of beings all hyped up on fizzy orange cordial and popcorn and ready to see the show they had been anticipating for millennia, that had been kept at bay by what Lauren suspected was tempered steel encircled them.

'Right, there you all are,' Morty said. We've got a situation.'

Lauren peered at him from between narrowed eyes. 'You look different,' she said after a moment. 'You feel different. What's going on with you?'

'Nothing,' he said, brushing off her words. 'I'm just busy.'

'Yes, we know,' Egragore said. 'We're coming and ready to start.'

'That's not it,' he said. 'That lion's here, and he thinks he deserves priority seating. Said he knows people or some such. Where should I seat him? Cally's up in arms and doesn't want to let him in at all.'

❋❋❋

Roxy (but-not-Roxy) knew what they were looking for, but with the immensity and the wending of corridors and the general hubbub that was to be expected on the day of the Tournament they were finding it hard going. While technically not out of place- everyone in all of time and space seemed to be popping up today, they preferred to keep on the low down.

Important plans were afoot. Drama and theatre and pizzazz were calling.

Roxy knew that the switch board was located in a cupboard, but they were surprised when they happened upon a door that was labelled 'Earth's Heating System- Authorised Access Only.'

This was going to be almost embarrassingly easy, they thought as they slipped inside the unlocked door.

39

Sybella flitted around her apartment, trailing her fingers idly over surfaces, tracing the grain in the wood of the bench, finding herself transfixed by the eddies of dust that danced in the beams of sunlight slanting through the windows. She had been experiencing a series of Very Strange Days, and she felt that she had almost settled into it as a kind of normality as if it was just the way that life was now. And the voices in her head were still whispering messages to her, very quietly, but unmistakably. There was a knock on the door, more of a scrape really, like someone was rapping on it with a stick.

The mote of dust she had been tracking for the last few moments disappeared as she blinked, and she realised she had been in a kind of a limbo since last night, waiting for someone to let her know what she was supposed to do next.

And this was it.

Clustered around her doorstep were group of misshaped, oddly formed beings. But this wasn't what Sybella found herself focusing on. The sunlight was dimmer than it should be. Not in the way that the sun becomes dim because a cloud has covered it or because of its particular seasonal position on the sky. It was high in the sky, just past overhead, there were no clouds near it, and it was definitely and absolutely much dimmer than it should have been. She had been in intimate communication with it for her entire life, not in any odd way, just in the way that a human living on a planet relies utterly and completely on a ball of gas and plasma for every facet of its existence. As such, she was certain she knew how the sun should look.

'What's wrong with the sun?' she said, peering up into the sky and ignoring the group of Imagos who stood on, next to, and below her front doorstep. 'Does it have a filter on it or something?'

The Imagos, who had all been prepared to justify their own existences, explain their presence, and possibly spend some time explaining the geography of some of the more unique ones amongst their faces, were unprepared for this.

Jack the Fish glanced up. 'A filter?' he said uncertainly. 'Like, on a photo?'

Sybella was covering her eyes with her hand now and glancing from the sun to the darkening street.

'I can look right at it,' she said. 'See?' She gestured, encouraging the Imagos to look up at it.

They looked at each other uncertainly. They had formulated action plans for a variety of things they thought might happen while on this front doorstep, but being asked to stare directly at the sun by a woman wearing a bunny onesie hadn't been part of any of them.

'I shouldn't be able to look at it. It should have burned a hole right through my retinas by now.' She frowned and glanced around, pursing her lips and putting her hands on her hips like an annoyed kindergarten teacher.

'Did you have anything to do with this?' she asked them pointedly.

Gunter glanced at Pearlie Lil, and Frankie gave a little nod as if to say, 'We've got a live one here, just plug on, and I'll cover if things get hairy.'

'We need your help,' Gunter said.

'The JanJans didn't say anything about the sun fading away. I knew someone was going to come and visit me, but I didn't hear anything about the sun. This worries me, to be honest. You don't look worried though.'

Comfrey Tim's three eyes widened, and he stepped back, making way for Frankie to step forwards.

'We need your help.'

She looked at them properly for the first time now. Their faces were pale in the dimming sunlight. 'Does this mean you forgive me?'

'Forgive is a strong word. We're pretty sure that you're not going to suck out our life force now, so we're willing to chat to you,' Gunter said.

Sybella nodded and considered this. 'Sounds reasonable. And you know I'm sorry, right?'

'We know it wasn't your fault, but we do have a bit a trauma surrounding you, so just go easy on us.'

'Oh, wait. Trinity Hourglass thinks it was your fault.'

There was a murmur amongst the crowd, and fingers were pointed to an Imago standing at the back. 'Yes, she thinks you were probably complicit in some way, but she's willing to put up with you and give you the benefit of doubt for the time being, seeing as we've been told you can help us.'

'Speaking of helping us,' Sybella said, dropping the hand that was covering here eyes as she realised that the sunlight was so dim now that she didn't need to shield herself. 'What do you need?'

'We need to get to the Other World,' Frankie said. 'And you can help us.'

Sybella smiled at him. 'Yes.'

'You can get us there?'

'No, I don't know what that is.'

'You don't know what the Other World is?'

'No.' She glanced around nervously. 'Should I?'

Trinity Hourglass sighed and started to head down the path. 'I told you this would be useless.'

'I'm pretty sure that you do,' Gunter said.

'Do what?' Sybella asked patiently.

'Know what the Other World is.'

'I feel as if you could infer it if you put your mind to it,' Trinity said wryly from the footpath.

'And I feel like you and I need to work through some issues,' Sybella snapped.

Frankie, who seemed to be the leader, or at least the one who was most invested in getting the situation sorted out rather than have it devolve into petty squabbling, held up his hand. 'You know all these non-human entities you've been dealing with lately? The lion and the old woman and your friend Brigid's alter ego and everything?'

'Yes.'

'It's where they all come from. Or go to. It's … it's the world that exists in a liminal space above this one. Where the rules and the laws of physics and science and often the basics of good sense are a bit different from what you're used to.'

'The JanJans haven't mentioned it,' Sybella said.

'No, they wouldn't,' Guntar explained. 'They're above all that. They're in a different sphere entirely.'

'They're the ones I mainly talk to.'

'Really?' The Imagos at the front of the group looked impressed.

'And this Other World is where you guys are from?'

'No, not us, we're different. We're just from here. But I don't want to get bogged down in this kind of thing. The basics are that we need to get up there because we think—'

'We've been told, that is—'

'That Connall might be in trouble. Or that everyone might be in trouble. And that you can take us there. To help.'

'How would I get us all up there? I've got no idea where it is or how to get there, so how am I supposed to know?'

'Dammit,' Frankie said. 'I was hoping you would have a bit more clarity surrounding this, but let's not all freak out yet. I'll come up with a plan.'

'He's the ideas man,' Dirty Annie said.

Their surroundings had been plunged into a kind of twilight now, the sun easily able to be viewed with the naked eye, and people were coming out of their houses to peer up at it and talk to each other about what was going on. The general consensus seemed to be that it was some kind of advertising campaign for the newest mobile phone.

Sybella stood aside and gestured for the Imagos to come inside. No one was paying attention to them, but she thought it would only be a matter of time. They trailed into the house and clustered nervously around the closed door.

'Do you have any ideas then?' Sybella asked. 'Any clues of how we're supposed to get there? And anyway, why can't you do it yourself? If you know so much about it?'

'Only people who come from there can get themselves up there.'

'Well, that's the problem,' Sybella said, exasperated. 'I'm human. How am I supposed to get there?'

'From what I can tell, it's because you've had some intimate contact with Otherworld beings. The lion and your friends who are involved. It may have rubbed off on you, in a manner of speaking.'

Sybella looked doubtful. 'Don't you think I would have noticed?'

'Look,' Jack the Fish said, stepping forwards. 'We just know we have to get there. Our best friend, the only one who has ever helped us or believed in us or loved us or seen us as valid and special creations, might be in trouble, and we'll be buggered if we will let him deal with all that alone. He needs us, and the JanJans clearly agree because that's why they sent us to you.'

'The JanJans are very comfortable with giving directions but not so much with doing the heavy lifting, I've noticed,' Sybella said from between her teeth. 'What exactly did they say? What did they tell you to do, and what did they say about me helping?'

'Well, they talked to Frankie, mainly.'

He smiled broadly. 'Yep, that's right. The JanJans told me that all the Imagos needed to get together, to come and find you, and when we were all together, we would find the solution.'

At that moment, there was an enormous noise, like the grinding of millions of rusty, malfunctioning gears, and the house shuddered, and the sun blinked out completely.

40

Egragore stood in front of the lion, trying to keep his voice under control. It wasn't working. 'You expect us to give you special treatment after the absolute clusterfuck you might have caused? You think you can be so negligent as to release a chaos agent and just expect to come in here and play happy families?'

'I have my rights,' Leo said. 'I have every right to be here. You have no ability to monitor my movements or reprimand me.'

'You may have ruined the entire Tournament, you ridiculous, pompous overgrown house cat. If we end up with—'

'Sweetheart,' Brigid hissed through clenched teeth. 'This aggressive vibe isn't going to be helpful at this particular juncture.'

'Um,' Connall said, coming up to them with a casualness that looked utterly contrived. 'There may be a slight issue. What's he doing here? You're an absolute liability, at this point.'

Devin clutched his head and dropped down into a crouching position. 'I don't think I can deal with any more of this. I can't even look at it, it's so embarrassing.'

Brigid grabbed him by the shoulder and hauled him to his feet. 'Nope,' she snapped. 'No nervous breakdowns, no tapping out. There will be none of this. We are all going to cope, we are all going to smile, and we are all going to be the ones who are in charge, right?'

She glared at Egragore and Devin, waiting for a reply. 'Right?' she said more forcefully, and Devin and Egragore muttered assent without making eye contact.

'Right,' she said, looking first at the lion. 'You, go and sit over there and keep your head down. If things get untidy today, you're going to have to become part of the solution, so get your interfering busybody head around that. Next?' she said, her eyes swinging to Connall. 'What have you done now?'

'Well, as you know, the boys were trying to power up the food vans because people needed to be fed.' He directed this bit at Devin, who was now on his feet. 'They went into one of the cupboards off the main corridor looking for somewhere to plug in all the leads. By the way, you're just asking for an electricity fire in there. You're not supposed to piggyback double adaptors like that. It's a disaster waiting to happen.'

'Go on,' Brigid said. Out of the corner of her eye, she could see that most of the seats were full now. The crowd stretched off into the distance, and the raucous conversations and loud revelry of the past few hours had lulled into a murmur of expectancy. A screen had been erected for the competitors to sit behind if they wanted to get themselves together in privacy before the show, but others preferred to get the crowd onside, mingling, schmoozing and shaking hands. Not that the crowd would be the final decider on who the victor was, but it did help to have them on side. The energy, if nothing else, made a difference.

'So, they got the food vans up and running, which I, for one, think is a priority, and I think you'll find that everyone else agrees,' Cally said, taking over the story.

'Mum, let Connall finish.'

'Yes, so I think they must have accidentally unplugged the sun, and then it seems to have short-circuited somehow,' Connall finished.

'I beg your pardon?' said Brigid.

'It's temporarily down. But we're absolutely on to it, and normal service, as they say, should be resumed presently. Morty's looking into it.'

'The sun is down,' Egragore said pointedly.

'Correct. Temporarily.'

'Oh, for fuck's sake,' he snapped. 'The sun that keeps the Earth, you know, alive, is down, is it?'

'I mean, they're used to not having the sun for half of every twenty-four hours, aren't they?' Devin said. 'Surely it won't cause that much of a disruption. Will they even notice?'

'Night,' Brigid said. 'We're used to it being dark at night. Which we expect. And plan for. We're not used to the sun just blinking out of existence. Is that what happened? Did it just blink out of existence?'

'In a manner of speaking,' Connall said. 'Eventually. It dimmed a bit at first. Possibly fluctuated. Then it blinked out. Made a hell of a noise, from that I can tell.'

'This is not good,' Egragore said, rubbing his head. 'This is really not good. The last thing we need at the moment is panic and discontent on the planet.'

'Isn't that their usual go-to position?' the Cailleach asked.

'Not today,' Egragore snapped, 'We don't want it today. We need everyone to be calm and happy and going about their daily business, oblivious to anything that might be happening in the Other World. We can't have people panicking and needing emotional support and extra care and attention and all praying at the same time today, can we?'

'Why?' Lauren asked.

'Because everyone's up here. Everyone's personal deities or guardian angels or emotional support imaginary friend or spirit that lives in the rock in their garden that they like to stroke when they're getting stressed is up here. One of the most important parts of the Tournament is making sure that everything on Earth is peaced out and low on stress on the date. We have entire teams who have been down there making sure that happens, setting the foundations for this for years, ensuring this is a relatively easy-going time in the Earth's history, and now in one fell swoop, your bloody food vans may have knocked out the sun and half the population of the planet will be apoplectic with terror.'

'Still your fault though,' the Cailleach said.

'Are we sure they're going to panic?' Devin said. 'Are we sure they're even going to notice?'

'Yes,' the Cailleach said, 'they'll probably just think it's on purpose.'

'Yeah, they're going to notice,' Connall said.

'We've got the phones set to voicemail at the moment,' Devin said, 'but can you imagine the sheer volume of prayers that are going to be coming at me when I have to check the messages?'

The Cailleach cackled a little at the thought of it.

'Don't you laugh,' he snapped at her. 'You still get attention, you know. There are plenty of people down there who still have you as their personal deity. We've been intercepting them all to give you a bit of a break for the last few hundred years, but I can forward them all to you if you'd like. If it's all so funny. See how you like it. Trust me, it's headache inducing.'

'There's only one thing for it,' Egragore said. We need to get this Tournament going, appoint a new Ultimate Ruler, and then they can get it all sorted out, and I can take my wife and go and find a beach somewhere. You said that someone's on to fixing the power supply?'

'Morty's looking into it,' Connall said.

'But he knows nothing about anything,' Lauren said. 'He's the opposite of helpful.'

'You underestimate him, you know,' Connall replied mildly.

'In the absence of anyone who actually knows what they're doing, that will have to do,' Devin said.

'Let's get this thing started. Do we have eyes on the ground for the chaos agent?'

'We have people,' Egragore said. 'We have watchers. But you know those agents. They're bloody stealthy. I say our best option is just to get this started and hope for the best.'

"Do we have a microphone?' Brigid asked suddenly. 'Is the sound system still working? I have an idea.'

As Brigid stepped out into the arena, she smiled broadly and felt a slight spring come into her step. A spotlight flicked on above her, and there was a smattering of applause as those on the seats at the front realised that something was happening.

She raised the microphone to her lips and decided to wing it.

41

'Heeeloooooo lovely people,' Brigid's voice boomed, and the feedback screeched into the speakers, causing the audience to cover whatever they used as ears. She recovered rapidly. The main part of this game was acting as if everything was done on purpose.

'It's so good to be here,' she said, her voice projecting several light years around the stage thanks to the wonder of a state-of-the-art sound system. 'I can see some familiar faces out there.' She squinted off into the distance and waved vaguely. A few limbs waved back at her, and there were some distant cheers. A few table groups had clearly been making the most of what seemed to be a recently established open bar somewhere out on the 4th quadrant.

'You all look amazing. The last three thousand years has been good to you! You've hardly aged at all.'

More titters. That was good. They were in an excellent mood. That was going to make things easier.

'Don't tell me,' she continued. 'I know why you're all here. You want to hear some of my husband's stand-up comedy, don't you?' She waved to Egragore as the spotlight swung towards him, catching him in what looked like an impassioned discussion with Devin. He stopped, a stricken look on his face, and then smiled and waved nervously.

'And look, there's Devin, the big cheese, the head honcho. Let's give it up for Devin, the Ultimate Ruler of Everything, The Chief Executive Officer. Heeeereees God!'

The applause was louder now, the crowd really starting to warm up. She gestured to Devin to come over, to take the mike, but he waved her away and turned back to Egragore.

'Management,' she laughed, turning back to the crowd. 'The most important day in three thousand years, and they're trying to fix a blown fuse, amirite?'

She could feel the comfortable buzz surrounding her now as if she was being embraced by a warm feeling of acceptance. The crowd liked her, were happy to be here, were enjoying being part of something big.

Devin and Egragore beckoned her over.

'Oh of course,' she said expansively to the crowd who was, she was convinced, falling in love with her. 'Of course I'm needed. They just can't be without me can they? You know what they say, the right man for a job is a woman.' She flicked the microphone off.

'Right, I think the best thing we can do is just get on with it,' Egragore said. 'Given that we don't really know what we're dealing with, we can't plan for it, so best get it over with.'

'You did enough planning for it when you send him to Egypt, didn't you?' the Cailleach said, with a dangerous glint in her eyes as she appeared next to them as if out of thin air. 'That was always going to come back to bite you on the arse.'

Devin stared at her pointedly. 'What do you know about it?'

'More than you think,' she snapped. 'Much more than you think. I know that your habit of exiling people to random places when you're annoyed at with them had to come back round to you eventually. And there's a reason that damn lion is staying out of my way.'

Devin glanced at her nervously. 'You'll keep quiet about it though, won't you?'

'Doesn't really matter if I'll stay quiet, does it? You've unleashed him now. You've pissed him off, you won't make eye contact with his gift, and now you'll have to deal with the fall out.' She gestured around. 'It looks like this will be the reckoning, doesn't it? Here and now? Maybe if you'd had a conversation with him, like a rational adult, then all this could have been saved. Rather than banishing him, you could have had a talk. If you weren't so obsessed with him in the first place, you would have been able to concentrate on other things.'

'It's not my fault,' Devin protested. 'I didn't do it. And I'm not obsessed with him. I don't have strong feelings either way, I'm just conscious that we need to keep things in some sort of equilibrium to stop the entirety of bloody reality imploding. The Imagos are becoming the real issue. You know, that little thing.'

'Stop passing the buck,' the Cailleach snapped. 'You've never liked thought forms, and you decided to pass it on to someone else in the hope they would become someone else's problem.'

'Hang on,' Devin said defensively. 'I never said that I can't stand Imagos, I need them to maintain the flux. I don't understand them. They're not mine, you see.'

'You're a megalomaniac who only likes the things he has control over.'

'That's absolutely not true. And as soon as I heard about the murders, I was as appalled as you.'

'Devin,' Cally snapped. 'The truth is, if this chaos agent came back and started killing things, it was for a reason, and I can't help but think it's got something to do with you. From what I've heard, I know it's all to do with you. Just you wait.'

'Okay, okay,' Brigid said, feeling like the stakes were rising above what she was able to deal with right now. 'Mum, what do you know about the chaos agent?'

'Let's just say things have escalated. And, as it turns out, our chaos agent is a little more powerful than we realised. And also not a chaos agent.'

'You're going to need to be more specific,' said Brigid.

'Who have you annoyed, Devin?' the Cailleach asked, a glint in her eye. 'Who have you really pissed off? Who have you annoyed enough to really, really get the shits with you?'

'Probably lots of people,' Devin said nervously.

'One particular being. One particular being who you treated especially badly.'

Egragore, who was keeping one ear on the increasingly rambunctious crowd, glanced back and forth between the two of them. 'Would you please tell us what you know. Stop playing games and help us out.'

'All right, I'll just come out and say it. If you're going to have a torrid and passionate love affair just after becoming the ultimate ruler of everything, then you should probably choose someone more appropriate than your dark counterpart.'

'Wait, what?' Lauren said, confused.

The Cailleach started giggling, a wheezy old woman laugh that sounded both amusingly infectious and creepy at the same time. 'Let's put this in Earth terms. Devin is your God, yes?'

Lauren nodded. 'Not mine, specifically, because I'm a pantheist, but I know what you mean.'

'Using Earth terms then, he dated…' She laughed again and had to dab away the tears that were falling down her face. 'With every being in the Universe that he could have hooked up with, with the choice of every corporeal being, every demigod, every trans substantial and otherworldly being, he had to hook up with his dark counterpart.'

Brigid gasped and her hand slapped to her mouth. 'No? What?'

The Cailleach nodded, her body still rocking.

'You mean…' Lauren said, the reality finally dawning on her. 'Oh, my god, you can't mean that?'

Yes, the Cailleach cackled, ignoring the stricken look on Devin's face as his eyes pleaded with her to shut the hell up. 'Devin shagged what you call Satan.'

Egragore's head fell into his hands at the sound of the words being spoken. 'You didn't have to say it out loud,' he moaned.

'You've got to be fucking kidding me!' Lauren yelled. 'You hooked up with the prince of darkness? What were you thinking?'

'I think what was he thinking with is the real question,' the Cailleach said, 'and the answer is his—'

'Okay, Brigid said, attempting to get a handle on a situation she felt was rapidly escalating out of control. 'You had a messy break up with Satan three thousand years ago.'

'Two thousand years ago, give or take,' Devin said. 'We were on again off again for a while,'

'Did anyone else know about this?' Lauren asked. 'It seems like a massive conflict of interest.'

'It was a massive conflict of interest,' Egragore said, 'but when his friends tried to point it out to him, they got exiled to remote places on the planet, didn't they?'

Connall nodded emphatically.

'Nothing like a bit of demon dick to cloud your judgement. Trust me, I know,' the Cailleach said.

'Mum,' Brigid snapped. 'That's totally unnecessary. But what you're telling me is that this unleashed chaos agent, this thing that we're all scared of, is, well, Satan.'

Cally nodded. 'Beelzebub.'

'Or the Antichrist,' Demniac added.

'Father of Lies,' Egragore offered.

'This isn't bloody Family Feud,' Devin snapped. 'Stop just listing names.'

'But yes,' Egragore said. 'It's what I've been dealing with lately. Devin here was trying to keep it quiet, trying to keep him exiled at various places throughout time and space, but he realised that with the Tournament coming up, he might need some help.'

'I wasn't very good at keeping Him exiled,' Devin said apologetically. 'He kept getting lose and coming and finding me and, well, one thing would lead to another and— 'But the fact is, we didn't know he was pretending to be a chaos agent. We knew the chaos agent was a problem, but we hadn't put two and two together. That's why we've been so—'

'Escalated,' Connall offered.

'Nope,' Lauren said, swinging around and heading off into the crowd. 'Can't handle this. Can't handle what I'm being told right now. I need a drink.'

'What I don't understand,' Demniac said, 'is why this ultimate evil person didn't use their real body. I take it they have a real body.'

'Oh, yes,' Devin said, 'they have a real body. One that I find ridiculously good looking. How do you think I got into this mess? He could throw out some influence and power apparently. He's powerful in his own right.'

'Well,' Demniac said. 'I can definitely tell you that I did not have 'unleashing of a terrible evil because their reigning God couldn't keep it in his pants', on my bingo card for the day.'

From the crowd a slow clapping had sprung up. 'Why are we waiting?' was starting to echo from some of the more unruly sectors, and Brigid turned around, her finger poised to turn on the mike again. 'So, just to give me a heads up, we're waiting for some kind of physical manifestation of Satan to arrive, are we?'

'Yes,' Egragore said firmly. 'We are waiting for that.'

'And are we worried about him taking possession of one of the competitors or –'

'I think,' Egragore said, 'that what Devin is actually more worried about is him making a scene and spilling all his secrets and embarrassing him.'

'But if he has a body, then why did he possess our friend?' Brigid asked.

'That we don't know,' Devin said. 'But we have a panel working on it.'

'Right,' Brigid said, her lips pressed together into a tight line. 'So not the horrific and murderous taking over of the Universe we were worried about. That does frame things differently.'

'I mean, it's still Satan,' Egragore said quickly. 'He's still pretty shit, all things considered. It's not one of the good guys and the whole flux issue is problematic.'

'No,' Brigid said, 'that is true, but I like to know what I'm dealing with.'

'And he was still killing all the Imagos,' Connall said. 'Don't forget that bit.'

'But he was doing it to impress Devin,' Demniac said.

'Look, it was just pillow talk,' Devin said, looking flustered. 'And this job is hard. No one understands what it's like to have so much power. Only someone with –'

'Your evil equal,' Brigid said quietly. 'Only someone with nearly as much power as you understood you, right?'

'That's right,' said Devin quietly.

'Remind me to draft a really good How-To-Manual for the new one,' Egragore said to Brigid. 'That might stop this sort of thing happening again.'

Brigid rolled her eyes at him and turned around to address the crowd again. 'Let's get started,' she yelled into the microphone. 'So I want to hear you all put your hands together, or limbs together, or protrusions or at least something that can make noise, to welcome the current reigning Ultimate Ruler of

Everything, Devin!'

Devin strode out on the stage, his game face utterly on. He was smiling, gorgeous, commanding and debonair, and every inch the ultimate ruler. He waved, smiled and blew kisses into the audience as Brigid handed the microphone to him. The welcome was thunderous. Everyone loved him; he was an absolute crowd favourite, and Brigid could see why he didn't want his reputation as retiring supremo to be sullied by an awkward sexual scandal.

The spotlight lit off Brigid and onto Devin, and with relief, she stepped off out of its glare. Grabbing Egragore and Lauren by the arms, she dragged them into the privacy of the corridor.

'I think,' she hissed, 'that if this horrible thing is going to manifest in the middle of the arena and spill all of his kinks, then I don't know how that's our issue,' she said. 'Actions have consequences, and so maybe Devin just shouldn't have sex with demons if he wants to keep his pure reputation unsullied.'

'But it's not just that, is it?' Egragore said. 'If this comes out, it will cause huge, deep rifts in the whole institution of Ultimate Leader of Everything. How do we expect a new leader to be chosen every three thousand years and have people head back to their respective lives and live happily and carefree knowing everything is being safely taken care of if they're living in the constant fear that their leader is canoodling with evil forces? That the Absolute Good of the Universe is shagging the devil?'

'I wish you wouldn't say that,' Brigid said. 'It brings about some really upsetting visuals.'

'Exactly,' Egragore hissed. 'Imagine what it would do to that lot out there?'

'So we have to find this … do they even have a name? I feel that calling them Satan or Beelzebub or the like gives him a certain ominous patina he doesn't deserve. What's his actual name?' asked Lauren.

'We do like to promulgate a certain feeling of fear around them though,' Egragore explained. 'I mean, the Universe does need the myth of an evil force to keep people in check. The whole yin/yang, light/dark, good/evil paradigm. It's important for keeping things in balance.'

'Does he have an actual name?' repeated Lauren.

'Lucius.'

'Lucius. Nice. Classy. I like it. So we're keeping an eye out for Lucius and making sure they don't spill embarrassing secrets.'

'For the good of the Universe,' Egragore said.

'Of course,' Brigid agreed.

'And for retaining and maintaining the dignity and glory of the position of the Ultimate Ruler of the Universe.'

Brigid looked at him and sighed. 'You're lucky I'm already married to you,' she said. 'Because if today was our first meeting, I have to say, I wouldn't be overly enamoured.'

There was a burst of applause from the stage as the Atrearta of Quarn stepped into the spotlight. Her team, a group of lesser deities, assembled around her, ready to have their prescient powers stemmed for the duration of the match. The executive who had been given the role of placing the conductors and conduit stoppers that would stem the psychic thoughts checked that the diodes on their heads and chests were securely in place, and attached the crystal that would muffle their powers for however long it took for Ally to undoubtedly collapse in a puddle of tears and admit defeat.

'See,' Brigid said, winking at Lauren. 'That's the only time one of your crystals has been any actual use.'

Lauren hit her on the arm playfully.

Devin took the hat proffered by a young Tarmutine wearing a tasteful sequined bikini, with multi-coloured tassels hanging from each of the three cups. He drew a piece of paper from it and then passed it formally to the Atrearta of Quarn, ready for them to read their first challenge.

Lauren and Brigid turned as they heard someone approach from behind them.

'I think I've got this power thing sorted,' Morty said, holding an extension cord and a power board in his hands. 'Definitely sabotage. If my grade 9 science memory is right, I just need to connect this up to this, and the sun's power will be re-established.'

'Good job,' Connall said, smiling warmly at him. 'I knew you could do it.'

'Should I then?' Morty asked, looking expectantly at Egragore.

'Should you reconnect the sun, which is the only things that keeps the planet Earth, the actual purpose of most of our existence, alive and functioning?' Egragore said.

'Um, yes,' Morty replied uncertainly. 'Should I?'

'He's just being an arsehole,' Connall said. 'You absolutely should.'

'Okay, well, here's hoping it works. Three…two…'

There was a hubbub of voices on the stage, and the Atrearta of Quarn let out an affronted yell. Swinging around, Lauren saw her friend Roxy standing in the middle of the stage, as if she had appeared out of nowhere. She had a blank, empty, hopeless look on her face. Lauren took a step towards her, and the words 'Roxy,' fell out of her mouth before Morty called out 'one' and the entire arena was plunged into darkness.

42

Sybella peered out of the window.

'The streetlights have gone on,' she said, 'so it's not pitch black, but there isn't any sun. The sky is full of stars. Looks lovely. Wish I had a telescope.'

'We weren't told about this,' Jack the Fish said in a worried tone. 'We were just supposed to come and find you and go up to the Other World. There was nothing about the sun going out.'

'Maybe they didn't know it was going to happen,' Sybella said, flicking on the light and then going to the cupboard and pulling down some packets of chips and nuts. No one was going to fault her hostessing skills, she decided. As she rattled food into bowls and poured soft drinks, she offered the Imagos places to sit around her lounge room. Now they were all in one place, she realised that there were about forty of them, but because they varied so much in size, and because some of them were being carried in others arms, it had been hard to judge. They crammed into the room, all pressing against each other in some way.

'But the old ones told us,' Maeve said in a small voice. 'They're the old ones of the land. They know all there is to know.'

'Except this vital development,' Sybella said, peering into the back of the fridge to see if there was any hummus left.

'You don't understand,' Guntar said. 'They're the ancient ones. They've been here in Australia forever. There was never a time they were not in this place.'

'They're our friends,' said Maeve.

'That's nice,' Sybella said, sniffing the hummus and deciding to risk it. 'Because, not to be rude or anything, I thought that all those other beings hated you. I mean, people don't hate you because they just ignore you, but all the beings from the, what do you call it? The Other World? I thought they all hated you. Must be nice to have someone on your side.'

'They don't hate us as much as not understand us,' Trinity said, shrugging. 'We're only partially formed in their eyes.'

'Well, that and the fact that you are literally partially formed,' Sybella said, gesturing to one with only one eye. 'I'm sorry.' She stopped herself. 'I don't know why I'm so rude to you. Maybe it's a leftover from the possession. I'm usually nice to everyone, I swear it. I'm kind of a people pleaser.'

'We're used to it,' Frankie said without any self-pity. 'It's how people are to us. It's part of our evolution or something.'

'Still,' Sybella said. 'It's not my best self. I'll try to do better.'

A quiet came over the room. It was awkward, definitely, but also expectant. The Imagos looked to Sybella as if waiting for her to come up with some wisdom, and Sybella looked to Frankie for the same reason. She broke the silence after about a minute. 'So, here we all are then,' she said.

The resulting silence was even more awkward.

'Are you sure you haven't missed something?' Guntar said. 'We were absolutely told that you'd be able to get us there, and the JanJans aren't often wrong.'

'Aren't ever wrong.' Maeve said firmly.

'I understand that,' Sybella said. 'I really do, but you need to understand that I've got no idea what they're talking about. I managed to summon a giant spectral lion once by imagining it and drawing pictures of it. Do you think that might work?'

'We're not trying to manifest something as much as move ourselves somewhere, but I'd say that's on the general right track. Maybe using the force of our minds. Perhaps if we all imagine really, really hard then we'll just … get there?'

'Yes,' Sybella said. 'Yes, that sounds like just the thing. Like, The Law of Attraction. You know, The Secret. You must have heard of it. If you imagine something hard enough then it happens!'

'So you mean I can just imagine one of these limbs gone?' said a many legged Imago from the back of the room.

'I'm not sure if it works biologically, on actual body parts,' Sybella said apologetically. 'But maybe we could add it in?' There was no response to this, so she continued. 'Let's all imagine really, really hard that we're in the Other World.'

'Should we all have, you know, a certain idea in mind?' Jack the Fish said doubtfully.

'No idea,' Sybella replied. 'I thought you'd be able to tell that

I'm just making this up as I go along. Now concentrate.'

Baby was fidgeting, wriggling to get down, so Dirty Annie put her on the floor and she crawled happily off, dragging herself along the ground, putting anything choke-able that she could find in her mouth.

A hush fell over the room, broken only by the occasional bump and burble of Baby making her way around the room. The hush was one of deep concentration this time, rather than awkwardness, and as it deepened over the minutes, an almost meditative air grew. Two minutes passed, then three. Someone suggested that they should chant, but this was quickly shushed. After five minutes, the awkwardness had resumed in full force, and various eyes began to crack open, not just to see if anyone had been manifested upwards but mainly to see if it was time to admit defeat and call the ridiculous proceedings to a halt.

Sybella felt a pushing under her legs, and the baby's head appeared from where it had been buried under the sofa. In her chubby hand, she held a small device like a remote control, but it was not one Sybella could ever remember owning. She prised it from the child's tight, sticky fingers and wiped it pointlessly against her trousers, turning it around to examine it.

Everyone had opened their eyes by this stage, and they were looking towards Sybella expectantly. 'Does this belong to any of you?' she asked. 'It almost looks like a battery pack of some sort.'

The next two things happened almost simultaneously, although Sybella would later discover that this was purely a coincidence. At the very moment that she felt her fingers slip into a deep indentation on the box, the light of the sun flooded to room again. She just had time to think, oh look, the sun's come back again, fancy that, when her finger instinctively pressed down into the groove, and all the inhabitants of the room winked into another reality.

43

'Shit.'

'What the hell's that?'

'Whose foot is this?'

'Get off my beard.'

'Sorry! Must have been the wrong circuit,' came an apologetic voice.

'Fuck's sake, Morty. What have you done now?'

Brigid could hear people falling over each other, the scrape of seats as members of the audience threw themselves to their feet, panicking in the utter pitch blackness that the arena had been plunged into.

'How can the entire light system be controlled by one power board?' Morty yelled above the rising noise. 'I really don't think I can be blamed for this one. That's just basic incompetence.'

'Back-up generators!' Egragore yelled. 'I know we have some back-up generators. I saw them when I was looking for the welcome banner for Devin when he came back from his last holiday. They're in a cupboard somewhere.'

'Just sit down, everyone,' Devin was yelling, although his voice could barely be heard through all the noise. 'Stay sitting down, and normal service will be resumed as soon as possible.'

The Atrearta of Quarn could be heard loudly asking whether this meant they could get a new challenge as now they were totally frazzled, unfocused, and would need a moment to compose themselves.

'Roxy,' Brigid called, alarm in her voice.

The sound of new confused voices appeared right in the middle of the arena.

Dark and a lot of tripping over. That's all Lauren was aware of.

266

She kicked something, which let out a cry, and she instinctively leaned down and picked it up. It was a baby. A chubby hand reached out and patted her cheek.

She felt hot breath on her face, and she heard the Cailleach's voice in her ear. 'Don't say anything, but the Imagos are here. With your friend Sybella.'

'And Roxy,' Brigid said from nearby. 'I saw her just as the lights went out.'

Lauren could feel the baby being pulled from her arms as the Cailleach took control. 'Give her to me,' she said. 'You'll trip over in the dark.'

'What about you?'

'I have nocturnal vision. It was given to me to help with the animals.'

'Well, what's happening then, for god's sake,' Brigid hissed. 'What can you see?'

The Cailleach looked around. 'Panic and disorder mainly. Oh, hang on, your husband has an idea. I quite like him, you know. Resourceful. And sexy too. You don't notice it at first, but he does grow on you, doesn't he? Is he any good in the —'

'Mum, this is hardly the —'

Brigid heard a sharp whistle, and Egragore's voice rose above the noise. 'Bussy, here boy. Come on.'

From far in the distance, Brigid saw six blazing pinpoints of light growing larger and larger as they floated, seemingly disembodied, towards her. Within moments, the entire central arena was thrown into a shadowy relief as torches of fire hovered about ten feet above it. Egragore stepped forward and rubbed his hand along the hell-hound's dark wiry fun. 'Good boy Bussy. Good dog. Just sit for a while. Stay.' A tongue from one of the three heads snaked out of the slathering mouth and ran down his back. Knowing that his favourite velvet suit was now covered with the viscous spit of a blazing eyed, huge hell-hound seemed to make everything just that bit worse.

As the area lit up, and they realised that if they could see what lay before them, then everyone else could too, The Cailleach swung around and yelled to Demniac, 'Drop the curtain!'

'What curtain?' he yelled in response, eyes wildly casting around.

'There,' she yelled, jabbing her arthritic finger towards a sign on the wall that was clearly labelled 'Panic Curtain Drop button', which was the most useful and relevant thing Demniac had seen in recorded memory.

With a swift movement, he hit a groove in the wall, and a red curtain dropped from the upper reaches of the auditorium, plummeting from untold heights to shield the stage from the audience. The exacto-lock technology neatly partitioned this section from the entire audience, so at least they wouldn't have to worry about people demanding more slushies and finger food.

The flaming eyes of the hell-hound threw the scene before them into stark relief. It looked like a scene of the kind that Hieronymus Bosch would have painted if he'd woken up with a headache, stubbed his toe as he got out of bed, and then realised he was out of milk and would have to have black coffee for breakfast. The red glare that flickered over it all made it infinitely worse, and the bodies that lay all over the floor seemed to undulate and move, but this was only because the dog kept moving its heads, meaning that the fire leapt and cavorted around, and the pale and misshapen bodies, horribly distorted from some unknown horror, glowed in their own bleak desolation.

Recognising some of her friends in the pile, Lauren grabbed Brigid's arm. 'What's happened?' she almost sobbed.

One of the figures began to move, and Lauren and Brigid shrieked in horror.

'Oh my god,' the Cailleach, who was jiggling the baby on her hip and extending one hand to pull the nearest Imago to their feet, snapped. 'Calm the fuck down, why don't you. They're fine. They're just scared.' And sure enough, the bodies that covered the floor were just Imagos who had dropped to the ground in panic when they'd arrived to a dark room full of screaming. Now they were pulling themselves to their feet, dusting themselves off, and congratulating themselves on the fact they had made it to the Other World.

Sybella uncurled herself from the ball that her body had involuntarily flexed itself into as they were hurtled from one reality to another and grabbed her forehead. 'That wasn't a remote control, was it. My head hurts.' She had gone a disturbing green colour, visible even in the weird light that suffused the area.

'Someone get this girl some popcorn,' the Cailleach yelled, passing Baby to Dirty Annie. 'She's just been transmogrified up here without warning, and I think she's going to be sick.'

All the Imagos who were near her stepped back.

Devin snatched the gadget out of her hand and held it up. 'Where did you get this? I've been trying to keep track of these. There are masses of them missing. I thought that perhaps Connall had taken them when I exiled him.'

'Oh, that might be mine,' Lauren said. 'Or Brigid's. Where did you find it?'

'Under my sofa,' Sybella said blearily.

'Convenient,' Lauren said.

'How did you both have one?' Devin snapped. 'These are supposed to be top secret.'

'That's not what Matron said,' Lauren muttered.

Connall had thrown himself into the midst of the Imagos, hugging them, the babbling of greeting raising up around him. Morty was drawn in too and resigned himself to a barrage of kisses and hugs.

He didn't hate it.

'Roxy,' Lauren called out again. 'Roxy, where are you?'

The Cailleach placed her hand on her arm. 'Be careful,' she said in a hushed voice. 'It's not—'

'I am here,' a voice said from the shadows on the far side of the stage. 'Behold me.' The voice was strong, neither male nor female, and its timbre and nuance made everyone's skin crawl.

Not that many heard it. The Imagos were noisy once they got going.

'Behold me, I am here.' Louder now. Angry. A hush fell over the group, and people turned around to see whose voice it was.

It was Roxy, but it wasn't Roxy. Her body seemed to be taking on another form, and her skin seemed pulled tauter than it usually was, although she could have had Botox, Lauren reasoned.

Roxy's hands reached up to stroke her face as if to test the consistency of her skin, and she smiled. Then she put out one hand and stepped forward, moved unsteadily, as if just learning how to walk.

'Um, hi, Roxy,' Lauren said, and Demniac and Morty followed suit, although their voices were hesitant and uncertain. 'It's good to see you.'

'How...' Brigid frowned and bit her lip. 'How did you get here?' she asked. 'I don't mean to be rude, but ... what's your connection to the Tournament?'

Roxy's face stretched into a smile that pulled at the geography of her face painfully, and she spoke again in the strange, disembodied voice. 'My connection?' she said strongly. 'My connection? Oh, I don't know. Let's find out my connection. Oh, Devin? Devin, where are you? Would you like to come and tell these lovely people what my connection is?'

Devin, who had been bent over the power box in the corner, encouraging Connall to connect a red wire with a blue wire to see what would happen, turned around slowly, his mouth forming a hysterical grin, his eyes like a rabbit trying to make friends with oncoming headlights. 'Oh, no,' he whispered, and Roxy smiled even more broadly.

Her face changed a little, just a little, so it no longer looked like her at all. There was a slight overlay as if another figure was transmitting over the top of her. It was shorter and fatter, and the hint of red eyes and a shock of black pompadour hair could be made out with every pulse of Roxy's head.

'Hello, lovely,' the voice, which now didn't sound like Roxy's at all, said. 'Did you miss me?'

Devin stepped forward. 'Lucius,' he replied in a choked voice. 'Look, Lucius, I'm sorry. I can explain, really —'

'Oh, I think you can,' Lucius said. 'I'm sure you can. I'd love it if we could have the chance to talk privately. Maybe in one of these lovely rooms that you've so beautifully furnished. So palatial. So lush. You always knew I have a special love of the Victorian era, didn't you? So much better than —'

'Lucius,' Devin said as if in warning, but his voice cracked nervously.

'So much better than A FUCKING PYRAMID!'

Lucius' eyes flashed now, and there was the smell of sulphur in the air. A cracking sensation lifted the hair on Lauren's arms, and she glanced around. The Imagos had all shuffled to the back of the circle, instinctively knowing that they were dealing with something very, very bad, and now only Devin and Egragore stood in Lucius' direct eye-line.

'The pyramid was my idea, to be fair,' Egragore said. 'I assume your body's still there, and you were able to transmit only your soul out. Or what passes for a soul when you're, you know, the Prince of Darkness.' He used air quotes for these last three words.

'Stop trying to be bloody brave and heroic,' Lucius snapped. 'It's Devin I want to talk to. It's Devin who broke my heart and then pretended he didn't know me and then locked me in a fucking pyramid so I wouldn't bloody well embarrass him.'

'Oh, you did not,' Sybella, who had regained some of the colour in her face, said. 'That's a really shit thing to do. Even ghosting him would have been better than that.'

Devin's eyes swung around to her, whites showing. 'I don't even know who you are,' he pleaded. 'Why are you having an opinion about this?'

'Yes,' Lucius said. 'See? Even she agrees with me. Thanks for the use of your body, by the way. You were lovely and lithe and energetic. I did like being in you.'

The Imagos had now shrunk right back into the shadows of the curtain.

'Wait, you're the chaos agent?' Sybella said. 'No, I'm not on your side. You made me kill things!'

'Urgh, make up your mind. And I'm not a chaos agent. I was only moonlighting as one. For some fun. I was bored.' Lucius' eyes flicked back to Devin. 'But you. My love. My only one. I thought better of you. There's no one in all of creation I'd rather be than you. And look what you did to me. To us. We are meant to be together. I did this for you. All for you. I know they give you a headache, those Imagos. I wanted to rid you of them. I'm just trying to take some of the pressure off you, my love. No one understands. No one appreciates you. Only me.'

Devin's eyes softened, and he took a step towards him.

'I don't think so,' the Cailleach snapped, stepping lightly in between them. For a tiny wizened ancient crone, she could move surprisingly quickly, because Lauren could have sworn that she had been over on the side with Morty only seconds before.

'Nope, we won't be having any of that today.' She lifted her leathered hand and slapped Devin neatly across the face. 'Snap out of it, boy. This is your adversary that you're mucking around with. I don't care how well he kisses or how nicely he fries your bacon in the morning, this is a demon, and this is no place for him.' She swung around, her eyes now fixed, gimlet like, on the demon in front of her. 'I do not know how you even managed to get up here. I'm fairly sure that's against the rules, and someone sure cocked up dreadfully somewhere, but that's a question for another day. The point is, you are not wanted here, and you need to leave.'

A laugh began in the middle of the stage and filled the whole arena, swelling and bubbling with a maniacal fury, before petering out into tiny screaming yelps. 'Leave? Old woman, it has been a long time since you were powerful enough to tell me to leave anywhere, and your powers are now well and truly on the way out. You're more suited to looking after orphaned marsupials and...' He jerked a finger towards the Imagos that were trying to blend into the background. 'And those abhorrent fake constructs.'

'While we're here,' the Cailleach said, utterly unperturbed by the hysterical laughter that would have reduced a weaker deity to a gibbering imbecilic mess, 'Why did you kill them? You've got better things to do than possess some girl and kill Imagos, surely. Something isn't making sense here.'

'That I think I know,' Connall said, stepping into the glowing lights that continued to flicker across the ground. 'Because you found out that they're my life's mission, didn't you? Because you found out that I have, finally, after all this time, found something that I love, and that I'm good at, and you wanted to destroy it.'

'That bit certainly helped.' Lucius said. 'Destroying things you love is so fun. I could have gone and caused genocide in one of the smaller African nations, but I thought, look, I don't know how long I've got here, so why don't I fuck with Connall's life a bit just for kicks.'

'So I'm right,' Connall said.

Lucius winked at him. 'It was part of it, I admit. Not all of it, but part. It worked, didn't it? You haven't been having a good time lately.'

'Can I just,' Brigid said, raising her hand awkwardly. 'Look, I realise this is all frightfully serious, and I realise that we probably have an imminent showdown of some at sort any moment, but I'm going to absolutely kick myself if I don't ask this. Why? Why do you hate Connall so much?'

'Jealousy,' Connall said.

'Love triangle,' the Cailleach interrupted, tapping the side of her nose with one finger. 'Goes way back. Devin liked Connall, Lucius loved Devin, Devin was just putting it about, as far as I can tell.'

'The power did get to my head a bit, admittedly,' Devin said. 'And mistakes were made.'

'Connall and I have been able to function normally, though, haven't we?' Devin said to Lucius. 'I don't know why every time you're around, things have to burn down or explode or die. It's a bit of a bloody pattern.'

'You know I'm the Prince of Darkness, right?' Lucius said, putting his hands on his hips. 'It's in the job description.'

Egragore gestured to Morty. 'Can we get some joy with these lights? The hell-hound needs to go for a pee, and we've got no other illumination.'

'What do you actually want?' the Cailleach said to Lucius. 'Are you just here to embarrass Devin? Because everyone knows, now. Your love affair is old news. Did you want to compete in the Tournament? Because as far as I can tell, this whole power outage has put the kibosh on that for now.' She glanced towards Egragore, who now waved what looked like a thick A3 rule book at her.

'Just working out how to proceed,' he said

'Oh, please,' Lucius said. 'I have no intention of competing to be the Ultimate Ruler of Everything. No, my job of luring souls away from heaven and raining on weddings is much more fun. I am amassing my team again, and soon, I will be ready.'

As if on cue, there was a shimmer from the panic curtain, and Leo stood in the room. This gold fur shone to perfection and his lush mane rippled and glowed. Demniac noticed that the lion was making sure that he held his head so that his good side was in profile.

'And here we have my ultimate gift to you, your most prized possession,' Lucius said. 'The majestic and total embodiment of our great love. Remember this? My supreme gift to you? The greatest thought form ever created. This is the reveal time,' said Lucius, extending his arms. 'It's time to show everyone what we mean to each other. My tireless crusade to rid the earth of all other thought forms, anything that would dull the light of our great and glorious passion.'

'That's Leo,' said Sybella, confused. 'I thought that he was mine originally?'

Devin spluttered in a very un-god-like manner and looked as if he wanted to drop through the floor. 'If we could just dial this down a little Lucius, that would be great.' His eyes darted around nervously. 'Time and place and all, you know.'

'I got rid of the unofficial ones for you. So that this one is the greatest. I did what you should have been strong enough to do yourself.'

Demniac felt that some clarification was needed. 'Sorry, Leo, can I just get your input here. Are you evil, then?'

'No,' Leo said. 'I'm not evil. I'm not evil at all. I'm neutral, if anything. Like tofu. But given that I was created by Lucius, and he made me the absolute greatest, and the embodiment of a great and glorious love I am a tad indebted to him.'

'Anyway,' Lucius continued, 'I have been able to do no real evil down on Earth for millennia, and it's time things kicked off.'

'Wait,' Demniac said. 'You haven't had power on Earth for

millennia?'

'That's right. Good listening.'

'But what about the wars? And the nuclear bomb? And the holocaust?'

'No, that's you lot. I'm much more weather focused these days, but a good drought can cause untold misery, so I've been comforting myself with that. You're horrible, you humans. You hardly need me at all. But it is more fun for all of us when I'm around. I did want you all here though, collateral, if you like. You, Goddess Brigid, and you, Connall, and you, Cailleach, and of course you, Devin. And that lot out there. All the movers and shakers. All the big names, good and bad. Ooh, the fun we would all have. Getting the band back together. Just imagine, all of us, the gods, the demigods. With no mortals at all. We could just...' He made a flicking motion with his fingers.

Lauren couldn't tell if he was detonating a grenade, or lighting a match, or pulling a trigger, but either way, she could tell it wasn't good.

'Get rid of all of them. Clean slate. Just have us gods and immortals. Find Bacchus. Is he out there? Make him the caterer and it would go off. I mean, you did it once before, didn't you Devin. Got rid of all the people. That whole flood thing. That was hilarious.'

'That was an accident,' Devin said tightly. 'We don't talk about that.'

'But I wish we would. That's the kind of pillow talk that I like. Remember? And there's the added bonus of causing that lovely fluxy thing everyone time I kill an Imago, and a human disappears! They're disappearing at a rate of knots, have you noticed? At this rate I'll have killed two groups of annoying disgusting birds with one very enjoyable stone in no time.'

'That's a terrible metaphor,' protested Brigid. 'So clunky. Do better.'

'This is ridiculous,' Egragore said briskly. 'You have no power. You're using a human body. I could walk over there right now and put you in a headlock, and then this would all be over.'

There was a rumble as Leo moved slightly.

'Don't even think about it you mangy cat,' Egragore snapped. 'Have you met my fucking dog? He'd eat you for a snack, and you wouldn't even touch the sides.'

'Oh, you could put me in a head lock,' Lucius said in a sign song voice. 'But if you did, I'd explode this human's brain, and I don't think your friend would like that.'

The humans glanced at each other nervously.

'That's right,' he said. 'One wrong move, and I'll explode this brain.' He pointed randomly to Lauren. 'And I might start with some of those disgusting little Imagos too.'

'Lucius,' Devin said firmly. 'I feel like you need to know that I don't find genocide even vaguely attractive. Or a turn on.'

'Oh, please,' Lucius snapped. 'Have you read your Bible?'

'The Cailleach pressed her lips together. 'You've got us, haven't you? You win. Checkmate and all that. We might as well just give you what you want. What is it that you even want? Do you have an actual list of demands?'

Lucius glared at her. 'Of course I know what I want.' But his voice sounded uneasy. 'Powers and principalities.'

'Do you have a list of demands? Show me, and I'll get started,' snapped the Cailleach.

Lucius looked at her dubiously. 'I know you don't mean that. I know you're just making fun of me somehow. You're not going to make it that easy, are you?'

'You're the second most powerful force in this reality, aren't you? I mean, Devin is obviously number one, but you're next. Good evil balance, light dark. What else could there possibly be? The rest of us are nothing compared to you. We bow before you.'

Lucius glanced around the room uncertainly. 'I don't feel like you're saying this in the spirit I'd hoped for.' For the first time his face looked nervous. 'What are you doing?'

'Do it,' she said stepping towards him. Egragore and Devin glanced between themselves anxiously. 'Give us your list or kill someone. Go on.'

'Maybe we shouldn't push him,' Egragore offered. 'He's never been the most stable —'

'I think we should push him,' she snapped. 'You want power? You want a team? You admitted yourself that you haven't done anything properly, usefully evil for thousands of years. You've been putting it about in anything that will stay still for long enough, but you've done precious little else from what I can tell. So go on, cover yourself in glory. What are your demands?'

44

'You want to know,' Lucius said, his voice rising to a shriek. 'You want my demands? All right. I want to be able to do whatever I want, whenever I want, with and to, whoever I want, without constraints. I want as much power as the ultimate ruler.'

'You want to be the Ultimate Leader?' Egragore snapped.

'Oh, no, of course not. Power without actually being the ultimate ruler because I've seen how it's aged Devin, and quite frankly, there's no way I need that kind of responsibility. But I'd like the option, at least.'

'That's ridiculous,' Egragore hissed. 'That goes against the way the entirety of the Other World has been established.'

'And I also want us to have a nice meal together Devin, with five courses and paired wine and silver service. A nice proper romantic dinner. Maybe a violinist too.'

The Cailleach narrowed her eyes at him. 'Five courses? What kind of a meal has five courses? You're just making this up as you go along.'

Lucius took his eyes from Egragore and glared at her. 'A five course meal. You must have heard of that. It's very fancy. Very exclusive.'

'No,' she said. 'That isn't a real thing. What would it be, even? What would the courses consist of?'

Lucius held out his hand and counted off his fingers. 'Soup, entree, main, dessert.'

'That's four,' she said. 'I know about four. I'm not a philistine. You said five. What's the fifth course?'

Lucius frowned and counted off again in his head. 'No, there's another one,' he muttered.

'Cheese,' Demniac said helpfully

'I'd say that's more after dinner with nice dry sherry or something,' Lauren offered. 'Hardly a stand-alone course.'

'Soup, entree, main, dessert,' Lucius said, more loudly this time. 'What's the fucking fifth?'

'Oh, salad!' Devin called, and Lucius high-fived him. 'Yes! Salad, that's it. Salad, soup, entree, main course, dessert,' he declared triumphantly.

'And cheese and sherry for afters,' Lauren said. 'That would be a nice touch.'

'Oh, bloody salad,' the Cailleach scoffed. 'That's not a course. Lettuce doesn't count; it's a garnish. No, aim for a four course meal with side dishes. That would be much more romantic.'

Lucius looked thoughtful. 'No, five courses, and that's my final offer. Complete power and five courses, or I'll...' he looked around. 'I'll kill these humans.'

Devin shrugged. 'Look, I'm willing to say yes to the dinner. The paired wines has my interest piqued, and you know I love you in a suit, but it's a hard no on the power.'

Lucius gestured to Lauren, Demniac, Sybella and Morty with a flourish. 'I'm not joking, you know. I'll kill them.'

'Quite frankly,' Devin said, 'I'm all about the greatest good for the greatest number these days, and if it's them dying or you having as much power as me, then I'll get the concrete and the barrels and lend a hand if you like.'

'Oh, really?' Lucius' face fell. 'That's no fun. I want to cause trauma and anguish. It's not fun if I'm not upsetting you.'

'Sorry. I have to have high bar for trauma and anguish on this job. Can't get too fussed at the death of a few humans. No offence,' he called to them.

'Who can I mess with then?' Lucius rolled his head back and twisted his neck around a few times. 'This body is well and truly past its used by date,' he said, putting his hands on his hips and swinging them around widely. 'I can feel it literally falling apart on me. Might be time for a change.' He glanced around. 'You?' he said, frowning at Sybella. 'No, I've had you. You?' he said, looking at Demniac. 'No.' He shuddered. 'You?' He looked at Morty. 'No, not yet.' His eyes fell on the lion. He smiled widely, a grin that seemed to creep of the edges of his face, and made a gesturing motion with his fingers. 'You said you would always serve me, didn't you?'

'Serve with you,' Leo clarified. 'I said I'd serve with you.'

'Ah, but it looks like that's not going to happen, sadness of all sadnesses. So I might just pop into your body, if that's okay with you. Devin seems to not be as taken with you as I'd hoped he would be.'

'No,' Leo said, his voice tense.

'Veto,' said Lucius with a smile that now seemed to reach out beyond his actual face. 'I think it's time for me to see what it's like to be in the body of the greatest thought-form ever created. Shift over.'

There was a cracking, and the body that Lucius had been inhabiting, which had taken on his form so convincingly they had forgotten it was Roxy's, began to shudder and vibrate inhumanly. The head threw back, and all the veins in the neck stood out as a buzzing sound infused the arena. There was a cry. Later on,

Lauren would swear it came from the lion, but Sybella thought it was Roxy's voice coming from what sounded like another dimension. There was a burst of light as Lucius left Roxy's body and a bolt jutted out and hit Maeve who was sitting on the floor with the other Imagos. She slumped to the floor.

And then Roxy was standing up straighter, differently, the look on her face completely Roxy again. 'Oh my god,' she gasped. 'That was a terrible nightmare. What's happening? What's going on?

Maeve's broken body lay on the ground, her head horribly skewed. Lauren and Sybella ran towards her, but they knew before they reached her that it was useless. Sybella slid her hands under Maeve's head and cradled her, stroking her hair.

'What the fuck is wrong with you, you arsehole,' Lauren yelled. 'You didn't have to kill her.'

Suddenly there was another pulse, and a river of light became visible, crisscrossing the room. It swelled and began to run right through Roxy's body. She looked down, too full of her recent experience to be surprised, but there was another flare of light and she and the glowing river disappeared from the room.

'Whoops, sorry about that,' came the voice from Leo's body. That would be the flux or something. My bad. That one wasn't on purpose, if it makes any difference.' The golden mane rippled as he swung his head from side to side, stretching his back up and flexing his claws. They caught the light and he lifted them to his face, admiring the length and the sharpness. 'Now, this, I like. I know that this body is a construct, but I might keep if for a while. It will be fun. Don't worry, Devin. I'll put my own body back on before dinner. Can you fix that up for me, please?'

'Where has Roxy gone?' demanded Lauren.

'An alternative reality somewhere I imagine. Hopefully one with carbon-based life forms, for her sake.'

Devin coughed awkwardly. 'You know that if you hadn't

interrupted the Tournament, someone else would be in charge soon, and you and I could go and have a proper talk,' he said. 'If you had just waited, I wouldn't be god anymore, and we could … well.'

Connall had been pacing back and forth in front of the Imagos, pulling at his beard and staring fixedly at all the conversations. 'I feel like I'm being pranked,' he said looking around at the assembled crowd. 'Why are we having these conversations? Why are we countenancing negotiating with Satan? I feel like I'm at a really bad cocktail party where no one has the courage to just stand up and say they're having an awful time.'

'Are you having an awful time, Connall?' Lucius asked, his voice now the low, velvet timbre of the lion.

'Yes,' he said. 'I am. For some reason, you seem to have convinced everyone that you have some kind if special status when in actual fact, you've spent most of history being locked away places and pretending to talk to teenagers through Ouija boards. You're all hype, Lucius. You rely on tight pants and sarcastic comments and the belief that you're evil. But you and I both know that in my own form, I have dealings with the underworld. The Horned God has tricks of his own. We will find your friend,' he said to Lauren and Sybella. 'But now…'

The lion's tail had begun to flick back and forth. He fixed his eyes on Connall. 'You always were a smug prick,' he said. 'Even when we were all exactly the same, back in the day, you always thought you were better than me. It's time I really showed you how things go now.'

He crouched down, pulling his legs under him, before leaping forward into the middle of Imagos. A shriek came coming from Ariadne as the lion's teeth closed around her. One enormous paw caught Jack the Fish in the head, and he was thrown across the arena. Lucius dropped Ariadne's body onto the ground, and she remained there unmoving. He swung his head around, advancing on Connall, who had thrown himself into the midst of them. 'Where's that girl you were hanging around with, the one who was in the pub?' the lion growled. 'The human? I'll do her next. I could eat her, actually. I'm not eating any of this filth, but I don't mind eating humans. Lovely and tangy when they're scared. Are you scared, girl?'

With a look of horror on her face, Lauren stood up from where she had been crouching next to Maeve's body. 'No! she yelled. 'This isn't going to happen. Stop hurting people. The Tournament is supposed to be a fun thing! An important thing! We will have no killing here.'

Connall stepped in front of her, blocking her body with his. 'If it's me you're angry at, then fight me. Don't involve humans.'

'Both of you is fine. Two birds with one stone and all that.'

The lion pulled his haunches under himself ready to spring on Connall, when there was a cry from Egragore, who was brandishing the dossier that he'd been holding in his hands. 'Lucius, you're going to regret this. See here, in article 588 subsection 00.11 it says, no killing will be perpetrated during the Tournament.'

'Oh, calm down. They're not dead. Well, most of them. Just stunned. Or faking it.'

'All right, no violence then,' Egragore said. 'It is a judgement zone, and normal rules of cultural relativism and the free allocation of ethics and personal belief do not apply. Any disregarding of this will result in sanctions applied by the old ones if they're around at the time. If not, then just see yourself out and think about what you've done.'

'Egragore,' the lion said, his body relaxing for a minute. 'Do you think I care what rules you cobbled together in one of your committees? Do you think I'm bound by that in any way, shape, or form? You know I have no interest in the directives of you or Devin.'

In the middle of the stage, a figure began to manifest. A tallish, greyish, humanish figure that became amorphous as it progressed downwards. The appearance of the wimple left Lauren in no doubt who had arrived.

'What's going on here?' The Matron's stern voice projected across the room, freezing everyone in their tracks. 'What on earth are these shenanigans? Why has the Tournament stopped? And why are there dead Imagos on my floor?'

'Mostly not dead, stunned,' the lion snapped.

Matron ignored him. 'Lauren, why do you look like you're about to cry? And what are you wearing? I hope you haven't lost that gown I gave you. It was expensive.'

The Matron's eyes swept the room and fell on Leo, whose body quivered. 'What are you doing here, anyway?' she snapped. 'You can put a lion suit on as much as you want, but I know it's you, Lucius. You always look like a naughty private school boy who's been caught stealing ice cream from the freezer, no matter which form you're stealing at the time. I thought you were locked in a pyramid.'

'It's a long story,' Devin called.

'Cally, aren't you supposed to be able to manage all this kind of thing?' the Matron called. 'Isn't the Tournament over yet? I was hoping you'd have won and we could catch up for a drink.'

'Funny you should say that,' the old woman called. 'Things have escalated slightly. I think I've lost my touch. Care to step in for me?'

She sighed hugely and raised her eyebrows at the Cailleach. 'Really?'

Lauren, without taking her eyes off the lion, tilted her head to one side. 'Can anyone hear that noise? It sounds like drumming or chanting or something. Like, it's a long way away but getting closer. Anyone? Surely we don't need any more elements of weirdness at the moment.'

'Yes, I can hear something too,' said Brigid. 'Like a singing and wood knocking together. It feels like it's in the air all around us.'

'Lucius is having a bit of an episode,' Cally called to Matron, 'and it seems beyond Devin here to deal with it.'

'He always was a pants man,' the Matron said dismissively. 'Terrible at effective discipline. Distracted by a pretty face.'

'Do you think I'm pretty?' the lion purred.

'No. You look ridiculous. Even Devin wouldn't be attracted to you at the moment.'

'Hey, I'm right here. If you could critique my personality after this particular life and death situation is over, I'd really appreciate that.'

'I've had enough of this.' The low rumbling from the lion's chest, which had been a low background noise to the conversation, suddenly exploded into a roar, and Lucius, his legs drawn under him, leaped forward towards Lauren and Connall. At that precise moment, several things happened at once.

45

Lauren flung her arms up to cover her head, even though she knew they would do nothing against the lion's teeth. Connall's body pushed in front of hers, and she had the momentary, ungrateful thought that it was bloody stupid to have both of them eaten at once. At least he could have shoved her out of the way, or something, rather than wrap his arms around her. There was a blur as she thought she saw Leo's huge body shrink down to the size of a kitten and dart away into the auditorium. She felt a swirling sensation as if she had been caught up in a tornado, and the throbbing, drumming sounds that she had heard filled her head. She could see colours and shapes spinning past her as her body lifted up, weightless, her head falling back and a soundless shriek leaving her mouth as she grasped hold of Connall's strong body. Stars streamed past her eyes, a miasmic spectrum of colour that melded together. She could feel other people, other bodies, spinning past her as her head filled with the throbbing thrumming sounds until she felt that she couldn't possibly…

She was standing in a soft, quiet meadow. The sky overhead was inky black, the breeze warm against her face. In the distance, she could see, scattered around in the darkness, the orange glow of fires, both close and so far away that they were just pinpoints of light in the tapestry of the night. Tall trees clustered together in patches, and in the distance, there was the darkness of a mountain range against the velvet sky.

The stars are singing, she thought to herself, as the noises she had been hearing seemed to converge above her, streaming shooting stars lighting up the sky, their tails flickering like sparklers.

Next to her was Connall, and a little further away stood Devin, the Cailleach, Brigid and a short, black haired man who Lauren realised must be Lucius. Matron stood in front of them, hands on her hips.

'Well, you've done it now,' she said. 'They really didn't want to be bothered with this, but you left me no choice but to tell them. I wash my hands of the lot of you.'

'Why am I involved?' the Cailleach barked indignantly. 'I haven't done anything wrong, I don't need any—'

'Not you, obviously,' the Matron said. 'But I assumed you'd want to be here.'

The breeze, that had been warm and pleasant, almost conversationally brushing against their faces, became stronger, and the gathered group could hear words in it.

'Thanks very much,' the voices whispered, the words rolling and cascading through the air. 'We didn't have anything better to do tonight, but deal with this.'

Another voice laughed. 'Not,' it said. 'We got rid of all these responsibilities for a reason, you know.'

Lauren felt Brigid's arm snake around her waist, and she leaned into her friend's ear. 'What's going on?' she asked.

'We're in the time in between,' Brigid whispered. 'We've clearly really, really cocked things up this time.'

The voices again.

'You three, the ones known as Brigid, Connall, and Cailleach. You have been given roles and responsibilities. Why have you not been performing them?'

'We have,' Cally protested. 'We have been.'

The wind whipped them again, and the words were snatched out of their mouths. 'If you had been performing your roles, things would have not got to this stage. Devin. Your role has been to rule with wisdom and magnanimity.'

'Yes,' he started.

'And keep the evil one in his place.'

'Well…'

'No well. The balance of light and dark is firmly demarcated. There's no wriggle room. There's no margin for error. No indecision.'

Another voice. 'This whole Tournament thing was a terrible idea. I knew it would end badly. Politics as entertainment. Ridiculous. What's wrong with a good old-fashioned show of hands?'

'That's what I thought,' Lauren offered to no one in particular.

'Things are going to need to change,' the voice replied. 'They can't go on like this. It's ridiculous. All that bloody red tape. There are some very, very simple rules that we have laid down, and you lot have absolutely buggered it up.'

'I agree,' the Cailleach called. 'In my defence, I agree completely with this.'

'And you.' The wind threw itself towards Lucius, who staggered back. 'Who do you think you are coming to the Upper Realms and interfering with the Tournament? Sure, it's an imperfect system, but apparently, it's the best they've got. And then spilling blood at it. There will have to be a reckoning.'

'Oh, bullshit,' he yelled into the air. 'Nothing important got killed. No harm done.' The wind slapped against his face, and he staggered again, his dark hair falling into his face, which now held a look of fury. 'I am the evil force. I'm supposed to do this. You made me this way. You're the ones who set this up. You're the ones who decided there needs to be dark and light. You can't create me like this and then reprimand me when I do what I've been grown to do. Tell them, Devin.'

'To be Devil's advocate,' Devin said, 'literally, as a matter of fact, it's true. This is how things have been set up. You can't activate everything into motion and then hold us to account if it hasn't gone the way you wanted. I mean, you lot did decide to set it all up and step back. You could have kept tight hold of the reigns, but, you know, you wanted to hang out here in one of the chill, timeless dimensions. I can't quite help but think that it's not fair for you to wash your hands of all of this and then hold us to account.'

'Yes,' Lucius agreed. 'You're either in or out. You can't keep...'

'Gas-lighting,' Devin offered.

'Yes, that's right, thank you, gas-lighting us like this. It's really not on.'

Lauren glanced at Brigid out of the corner of her eye. Brigid shrugged her shoulder imperceptibly.

'There need to be changes,' the voices said.

Matron looked into the air and nodded. 'That's what I said.'

'And we've been watching,' the voices continued.

'See what I mean,' Lucius and Devin said together. 'You've been watching and critiquing but not helping at all. It's toxic.'

Devin nodded. 'Toxic management.'

'We should start a union,' Lucius added.

The voices ignored them.

'Quite frankly, we're not going to step up to the plate again. Those dimensions are awful; they give us a migraine. But what you're doing isn't working. So we have made a decision.'

'Oh, here we go,' Lucius said, rolling his eyes.

'Firstly, we don't need an evil supernatural force of mayhem and deviance anymore,' they said.

'But that's my particular skill set,' Lucius replied.

'Yes, we know. Your services will no longer be needed. We're letting you go.'

Lucius' mouth fell open stupidly.

'And Devin, you're an absolute liability. It's lucky your time is up, and we don't need to sack you. You two can do what you like, go where you like, but you're off the clock permanently. We've revoked your powers. But, as a thank you, we have set up a lovely five-course meal for you.'

A spotlight lit up a space about a kilometre away, a stream of light flooding over a pristine white tablecloth covering an expansive table. Coming across on the air, they could hear the lilt of a violin playing Mendelssohn.

'It's better than a watch with my name engraved on it, I guess,' Devin said, shrugging. 'Shall we?' He held out his hand, and Lucius took it, and they walked together towards the perfectly laid out dinner.

Connall, Brigid and the Cailleach glanced at each other nervously.

'And you three can stop looking so nervous. We don't want to have to go back to polytheism. That's almost as bad as the committee structure. Nothing gets decided. You can stay doing whatever it is that you do. No, we have thought about it, and discussed it.' The voices clustered around Lauren. 'We've been watching you.'

'That's deeply creepy,' she muttered.

'And we have decided that you, human, would be the best

option.'

'I beg your pardon?' she said. She felt Brigid's arm tighten around her waist.

'You are beautifully uncomplicated. And strangely moral. Far more moral than those ones who are trying to take over. You have a special ability to just roll with the punches and keep your head in the face of patent ridiculousness. And also you're … here. We don't have that many options at this late stage.'

'There are a shed load of beings in the Otherworld right now just itching to take over,' protested Connall. 'There are other options. There's literally a list of options. I've seen it.'

The voices fluttered around above their heads like irritated moths. 'We don't like those options. We don't feel they would be a good fit. We like Lauren.'

'But I don't quite want to,' Lauren said nervously, glancing about. 'Can I say no?'

'Would you like to think about it?' the voices asked.

'Sure,' Lauren said. 'I'll think about it.'

There was a pause. 'Yes, I have thought about it. No thanks.'

'Good decision,' Brigid said.

The wind swirled around their heads speaking in languages they couldn't understand, rising and falling. The voices seemed to some from the trees, the fires, the rocks, the stars. There were sounds everywhere.

Lauren glanced around. 'Yeah, I definitely don't want to be in charge of this,' she muttered.

'This is a different dimension entirely,' Brigid explained. 'It's not your jurisdiction, anyway.'

'None of this is my jurisdiction,' Lauren said, 'because I'm not doing the job.'

The voices coalesced again, speaking from the grass, the trees the rocks. 'We have reached a decision.'

'Great,' Lauren said firmly.

There was another pause.

'Are you sure you don't want to do it?'

'I don't know how I can make this clearer,' she snapped.

'Damn, we were kind of counting on this.' The voices sounded exasperated.

'I don't know what to tell you.'

'Let us know if you change your mind, though.'

Matron was staring pointedly at the Cailleach, jerking her eyes back and forth from the old woman and then up into the air.

'What?' Cally mouthed.

'Do it,' the Matron signalled.

Cally held her hands up in the universal gesture of bemusement when the voices asked for her.

'What? they asked.

'We were just wondering,' the Matron said.

'Yes?'

Finally catching on to what was being asked of her, the Cailleach spoke up. 'I was wondering if you'd like me to do it?'

'Again?' they said.

She shrugged and smiled gamely. 'I've still got it in me.'

The humming noise began again, and Lauren realised that it was the sound of them speaking to each other.

Connall sighed and raised his eyebrows at Brigid. 'And they wonder why we don't want to have anything to do with it?'

'I know right,' Brigid agreed. 'The demarcation between dimensions has become absolutely untenable. Are you sure you want to do this, Mum? It's a bit of a shit show.'

She nodded. 'I'm an ancient crone with plenty of wisdom, wild days and good sex behind me. I'm ready to rule the Other World with patience and magnanimity. Again.'

The voices swirled back.

'Okay, look. We've got somewhere to be in a minute, so if you're happy to do it, and if you promise to do your best and not involve us, we're happy with you taking over for the foreseeable future.'

She nodded firmly. 'Absolutely.'

'So be it,' the voices said.

And with that, the Cailleach became the ultimate ruler of everything.

46

As they arrived back in the auditorium, the smell of the meadow and the feel of the warm breeze still on their faces, the lights blazed into action.

Morty stepped out from the corridor. 'Fixed it!' he announced triumphantly. 'I might do a sparky apprenticeship when I'm back down on Earth. What do you think?' He directed this at Connall who smiled at him.

'Sounds good. We'll need to get the wiring at the pub worked out when the repairs are done.'

Egragore wrapped his arms around Brigid. 'Everything sorted?'

She nodded. 'They really have checked out of the whole ruling thing haven't they?'

He laughed. 'Yeah, I'd heard that.' He glanced around. 'Where's Devin?'

'Having a very long multi-course dinner,' the Cailleach said. 'With a garnish as an entire course, apparently.'

Resting her hand on Egragore's arm, she smiled at him. 'How do you feel about working for your mother-in-law?'

His eyes grew huge with terror as he glanced back and forth between Cally and Brigid, hoping for a punchline. 'Are you … it? he asked Cally.

'Yep, they've decided that the Tournament is a terrible idea, which I have to say I agree with. So they've appointed me for the time being. And Connall, my first order of business will be making them an official species.' She gestured to the Imagos, who had made themselves comfortable around the stage. We need to make them all legal and above board and then the flurries will stop, right?'

Egragore nodded. 'A simple signing off on a new statute will fix all of that.'

'Wait,' said Lauren. 'I thought that the flurries were endangering the entire fabric of space and time and were an imminent threat to the universe?'

'Yes, they are,' confirmed Egragore. 'Dreadful business.'

'But you're saying a simple stature would have stopped it?'

Egragore frowned. 'I don't think you quite understand how difficult it is to get a stature passed in a thousands of years old regime. Now Cally is in charge we can hopefully things get moving.'

Cally pulled at the panic curtain and it rose.

'Everyone's gone,' Demniac said sadly.

'Of course they have,' she said. 'It was dark, the food ran out and there was no show. Would you stick around?'

'Are you really in charge now?' Morty asked.

'Yes,' she said. 'Sanity has prevailed. There will need to be some changes around here, obviously. Do you want to help?' she asked Brigid.

'Can we just clarify whether you've removed the wheat from my hallway?'

'Emmer.'

'Can we just clarify that you've removed the emmer from my hallway?'

'Yes, ages ago.'

Brigid leaned over and kissed her husband. 'Actually, I wanted to talk to you about that. How about we head back to Melbourne for a while? My house is still there. The fish died, and there was wheat growing in the hallway, but the lights are on, and the fridge works. Maybe we could have some babies or something.'

Egragore laughed. 'Sounds good. I'll need to find a job.'

'Mum, can you find Egragore a job please? Mum?'

She glanced around and saw that Sybella was sitting holding a bracelet that had fallen from Roxy's wrist when she had been transported. The Cailleach stooped down next to them. She quietly walked over to them and rested her hand on Sybella's shoulder.

'Do you know where she has gone?' she asked.

The Cailleach nodded. 'Yes, we will find her. And maybe,' she said to Sybella, 'would you like to stay here and work with me?'

Sybella smiled at her. 'I'd love that.'

'Along with Demniac you understand,' the old woman clarified. 'He's going to be on my team too. And you lot?' she called to Connall, Morty and the Imagos. 'Are you heading back down or staying here?'

Connall glanced from her to the Imagos. 'I think we'll head back to Earth,' he said. 'We like it down there.'

'You could have had all this, you know,' the Cailleach said to Lauren with a twinkle in her eye.

Lauren laughed. 'That sounds like a bloody awful idea. I have a nice little shop that needs some redevelopment.'

'You like it now, do you?' Brigid said, raising her eyebrows.

'Yes, well, I had some other offers, but I've realised that selling crystals and incense might be more my scene.'

'Now I think of it,' the Cailleach said, 'if you want me to come down and take some classes, let me know. I think I'd be very good at that. I've got years of advice stored up. Eons. The wisdom of the crone or some such. You could put up flyers.'

'Yes,' Lauren said doubtfully. 'Although don't you think you might be a bit busy?'

The Cailleach waved her hand dismissively. 'I'll put some systems in place, and the joint will take care of itself. It'll be a doddle, I promise. Just you wait and see. Clockwork.'

'All right,' Lauren said, nodding he head. 'I'll defer to your expert judgement. Maybe you and Brigid could teach some courses together? Maiden, Mother, Crone or something? People love that sort of thing.'

Brigid laughed and put her arms around her best friend. 'As long as no one expects me to massage any ones yoni, I'm all yours.'

'I can guarantee that yonis are off limits,' Lauren said. 'Massaged or otherwise. I have no intention of running that kind of establishment at this stage of my life. I have some great new ideas, some channelling that I'm wanting to try, and if I head back to that beach, the JanJans might help me out with sourcing some really good mystic sea glass. And anyway,' she finished, grinning at Brigid, 'I always have another job offer up my sleeve if things don't pan out here. You never know where life is going to take you, after all.'